# SHADOW WINGS

## THE DARKEST DRAE: BOOK TWO

RAYE WAGNER & KELLY ST. CLARE

1

"*What* the hay?" Dyter yelled a moment after walking into The Raven's Hollow.

My heart skipped a beat at his bellowing voice, and I couldn't help a slight stumble as I stepped to the bar, the ale sloshing over the rims of the mugs I held. The crowded tavern smelled of brewed yeast and sweaty men, not much different than my previous stomping grounds at Dyter's old tavern, The Crane's Nest. Dyter had brought me here after my night of mourning in the barren Harvest Zone Seven. His sister, Dyrell, owned a tavern in Harvest Zone Eight. Most of the survivors from Zone Seven had been staying here since our Zone was burned to a crisp.

"What do you think you're doing?" Dyter called, pushing his way to the front of the bar. Despite missing half his arm—the reason he'd been able to return alive from the emperor's war—the old man could hold his own in a crowded room.

I swallowed, mentally preparing myself for what I knew was coming.

Dyter continued his assault until he was standing across from me. "You're supposed to be resting, Ryn, recouping after what the king did, not serving ale."

The jovial mood in the bar had been nonstop for the last three days as the people of Verald celebrated the upcoming coronation of their beloved Cal and the downfall of the tyrant, Irdelron. They deserved a festive reprieve after thirty years of hardship and hunger. We all did. Not that I was going to get it because *some* people had unrelenting standards.

Schooling my features, I acted like his comment about what I'd been through didn't bother me. *Pretended.* I was getting better and better at denial. I forced my face into the blank expression I'd been practicing—one good thing I'd learned from a certain jerk with wings I refused to think about. I reached toward my stiff hair, dyed a dull mousy brown, but stopped myself and turned to grab more mugs from the shelf behind me.

I played like my mom hadn't stabbed herself with a Phaetyn blade.

Acted like Arnik still had a head.

Almost tricked myself into believing Tyr and Ty really existed and weren't fake extensions of the Drae I *pretended* didn't exist.

Staying busy at The Raven's Hollow *was* resting. The tavern was bustling, business was booming, and the constant activity kept me from thinking, from *remembering* my harsh, depressing reality.

"I have customers, Dyter," I said, pouring ale into four mugs. I slid them down the line and nodded at the young man ordering stew for himself and a friend. The two had been daily visitors at The Hollow since my arrival. Both had received summons from the Emperor and would be going to serve in the war next year. Even though we'd killed Irdelron, Verald was just one of the three kingdoms in the realm, and Emperor Draedyn ruled over them all. Which meant we were still at war with some overseas land most of us had never seen.

"You need to give this up tomorrow, Rynnie. You have too much responsibility to be hiding here," he chided. Then, quieter, Dyter said, "Your mum didn't raise a coward."

"I need to give my employer two weeks' notice and wrap up my financials."

"You don't have any of those things."

I crossed my arms and said defensively, "I do, too."

Dyter lifted a brow. "I've explained the situation to Dyrell, and you have a pile of carrots, Rynnie. That's not the same thing as financials."

"It's a big pile," I mumbled. I had plans for that pile. My simmering anger spiked at the look in his eyes, pity and understanding, but I refused to let him goad me into a reaction. I stalked to the kitchen and ladled up two large bowls of stew for the boys. The potage was thick with legumes and vegetables, much heartier than it had been three days ago. I wondered if these people knew I'd cried on the vegetables to make them grow . . . I'd keep that to myself. People got a bit funny about body fluids.

My Phaetyn powers were doing some good, but I didn't feel any better for it. When I was busy here, it allowed me to forget my current heartache and the terrors I'd been exposed to. Otherwise, I just sat in my room above the tavern, or in the garden, and cried. Why couldn't Dyter understand that?

I stepped out of the kitchen, and Dyter launched his next verbal assault. "You promised you'd help, and serving drinks isn't going to help with what comes next."

*Right*. What came next consisted of becoming a Drae on my eighteenth birthday, *tomorrow*, and then taking on the emperor. It sounded like my idea of a *super* good time. "I serve stew for a reasonable price, not just drinks," I quipped. "Never underestimate what a hot stew can do." I paused. "That would be a great slogan. *Never underestimate what a hot stew can do.* Maybe I'll open up my own tavern."

I took the bowls out to the young men and nodded at the three men sidling up to the bar. They were brawny brutes who must've been from one of the wealthier families in Eight. We didn't see people from the Money Coil this far out from the castle. That's for sure. Even Arnik hadn't been as big as these three. Brothers by the looks of it, they all had the same chestnut hair and high cheekbones. Filling a tankard for each, I asked, "What'll you have?"

Dyter snorted, but I ignored him. We didn't have much variety:

Ale, bread, brak, and stew, same as the other taverns in Verald. But Dyrell must have better recipes than her brother because The Raven's Hollow was busier than The Crane's Nest ever was.

"Mutton, if you have it."

I quirked a brow, certain he must be joking. The strapping young man stared at me like I'd lost my acorns, which seemed unwarranted. *Just go with it, Ryn.* "I'm sorry. We're all out of that. It's a bit pricey, so we don't get much. Maybe tomorrow." *Maybe never.* "I've got lentil stew."

He wrinkled his nose, and his brother nudged him and jerked his head at me.

"Lentil stew would be fine," the biggest of the three said in a voice much deeper than his brother.

Unease skittered down my spine at their obvious foreignness. Everyone knew the menus at taverns like Dyter's and Dyrell's.

The one who'd asked for mutton muttered under his breath, loud enough for my increasingly sensitive ears to pick up, "Why can't we at least have fish? I hate peasants."

I glanced at the darkest corner of the tavern, an area previously used for storage. The morning after my arrival, the jerk with wings, aka Broody-Britches, cleared out the boxes and set up a small table and chair there, telling me he wasn't leaving until I was Drae and could protect myself. For the first time, I wished I hadn't stacked up the boxes around his table to block him from view. I didn't like him watching me, but I did feel safe when he was there. Not that I'd admit that to anyone. One more day, and I'd be invincible, and Lord Nightmare would finally leave me in peace. Maybe then, my heart would forget.

I glanced back at the trio. They were just three ginormous rich people looking for a meal. My fear was irrational, left over from what I'd been through. I turned for the kitchen, and my heart skipped a beat as the man called out above the noise of the tavern, "I heard the king found a Phaetyn. Is Irdelron keeping her at the palace?"

Silence descended, and I pretended I hadn't heard, scurrying into the kitchen as various responses flooded the room.

"Irdelron ain't doing nothing. He's dead."

"Agatha from Harvest Zone Nine said the potatoes there are huge."

I smiled. Yeah, those were my potatoes, al'right.

Perhaps without meaning to, the three strangers had declared their foreignness to the crowd. There were plenty of people in Verald still talking about the wonder of finding a Phaetyn. A tiny percentage of the population from the Penny Wheel slums might not know Irdelron was dead, but the rich Money Coil and well-to-do Inbetween knew for sure; the conversations in the markets were flooded with talk of the king's death.

I was grateful Dyter told me to dye my hair again. Grateful he'd found an herbalist who could concoct an ointment to make my eyes look more blue than violet. Grateful he'd told king-to-be, Caltevyn, I wasn't coming back to the castle.

I *wasn't* grateful Lord Black Wings was really the one telling Dyter to pass on all this advice and having the ointment made. But I could deny the Drae was involved if I only had to talk with Dyter. If I had to deal with *him* directly, no way. I had standards.

My hands shook as I reached for the ladle, and the talk in the tavern swelled. I willed them to be strong and still, but when I upset the first bowl of soup and sent it tumbling to the polished wood floor, I closed my eyes and had to lean against the benchtop for support. If I couldn't convince myself I was fine, who else would believe me?

"They're Druman," Tyrrik said from behind me.

I'd recognize his voice anywhere, *had* recognized it in many places: the pits of a dungeon, the delirium of heat stroke, in his secret Drae lair.

"From the emperor. Several of his mules left the castle in Verald to report when Irdelron first discovered you were Phaetyn. These ones are here to gather more information for Emperor Draedyn. That's how he operates; first he sends out his minion Druman to test the strength of his enemy, and then he uses someone else to crush them, like ordering Irdelron to deal with my kin."

I remained with my back to him, afraid if I turned around, I wouldn't be able to conceal the fear his words instilled in me. I wasn't going back into a dungeon cell. Ever. I'd rather die. I wouldn't be a slave to anyone ever again. I wasn't strong enough to go through that twice. Once had put me here, thinking up marketing slogans and happy to serve ale. Twice would be the end of me.

"He doesn't know the rest—about . . . your other side, but he will sense your existence once you come into your Drae powers. Emperor Draedyn is the alpha of our kind."

The alpha Drae. Apparently they had alphas. *Mistress Moons.* Every morning, I wanted to fool myself this nightmare life would end with the sunbreak. But it hadn't. And I still only had one good source for information. I let my standards slip because I wanted to understand more than I wanted my pride. "Will he know I'm Drae and Phaetyn?"

Tyrrik sighed. "I don't know. Maybe not right away, but he's not an idiot."

*Great.* I ground my teeth. Because one twisted ruler wasn't enough. I wondered if Gemond and Azule's rulers were as bad as Irdelron had been. Probably. "Will he come for me?"

"I've never known the emperor to get personally involved. He sends humans to fight in his war and uses his kings and Druman to do everything else. But you are a female Drae. He will go to great lengths to secure you, *any* length. And he might come anyway . . . if he is not satisfied with the reports of Caltevyn."

"Might?"

"Might," Tyrrik replied.

But he'd *definitely* come to Verald to check out the new female Drae in town by the sounds of it. I sighed and faced Lord Black-Wing-Broody-Britches-Nightmare-Man. Putting my hand on my hip, I asked, "What exactly can an alpha Drae do?"

Tyrrik licked his lips, his eyes widening a fraction. His gaze radiated an intensity I was all too familiar with, and he stepped toward me.

I scowled in response. He shouldn't be *that* surprised I was talking to him. Who else was I going to ask?

He froze, and his face went blank. In a flat tone, he said, "The alpha can sense other Drae, their whereabouts. Once we are sworn to him, he can bend us to his will."

"Hey," a man yelled from the tavern room. "Where's the wench?"

My fear shifted to anger in a split second. Wench was one of my least favorite terms. Anger steadied my body, and I ladled the stew into the bowls on the counter, grabbed a handful of the chunky soup that had fallen on the floor and added a bit into each bowl, and dropped them on a tray.

The inky-eyed Drae stood only a couple feet away, studying me with his impassive mask on. His sculpted features were carved in stone, his lean muscled frame still as the night. His skin was the color of Meemaw's burnt sugar, and he was larger than any man in the tavern, probably because he wasn't just a man but also a dragon with huge black wings and fangs. As I stared, scales erupted on his chest, the ebony gems flecked with vibrant blue, peeking from the V in his aketon. He continued to study me, his gaze dropping to my lips *again* before returning to my eyes.

"What?" I snapped. "Do you want me to get you a bowl of soup too?"

He shifted so he was out of my way and didn't answer. *Of course not.* He didn't lower himself to explanations. Not even when he pretended to be three different people. I felt his gaze on me as I brushed past, all the way out the door.

Seemed like everyone was pretending these days.

*I* set the bowls in front of the Druman, too angry at the Drae I'd just left to be afraid. The three of them were looking over at the two young men, my regulars, with an intensity that bordered on creepy. Pushing my lips into a smile as insincere as it was uncomfortable, I asked the Druman, "Was there anything else you needed?"

Dyter was still at the bar, pouring a refill for one of my customers. His features twisted with concern, the scar he'd gotten while fighting in the war blanching, as he watched the three men. Dyter was king-to-be Caltevyn's right-hand man and knew a great deal more than he let on. He'd probably recognized these guys as soon as they entered and had been worrying ever since. As if that ever helped anyone.

The mumbler said something about meat, but the other two shook their heads. None of them reached for the bowls I'd given them, let alone glanced my way.

Like a festering wound I couldn't leave alone, I asked, "Do you want to pay in coin, or do you have something to trade?"

I saw Dyter's expression tighten in warning out of the corner of my eye.

The biggest Druman dropped several coins on the counter, way too many for the stew, and scanned the room, not even bothering to glance my way.

"I need ale," a gray-haired man barked, taking a seat next to them. "And make it quick, wench."

"Manners don't cost a thing, old man, but your ale will be twice the price if you call me that again." I dropped the tray on the bar and turned to get the rude codger his mug.

One of the Druman moved closer to the man, and I listened, trying to pick out the conversation.

"What do you mean?" the Druman asked in a low voice.

"Oh, you missed the revolution," the old guy chortled. "Caltevyn is the ruler now. Our Phaetyn comes out at night to heal our land. That way the Drae can protect her."

One of the other men grimaced and added, "He also killed hundreds of the rebels and torched our Harvest Zone. A mixed bag, that one."

*Drak.* How did he know all that? I wasn't sure even Dyter knew I still went out to heal the land. I glanced at him, and the glower he wore let me know this was news to him. That didn't explain how the old man knew.

"Does the king still keep the Phaetyn? We'd very much like to meet her. Emperor Draedyn is most anxious to have her visit."

The old man chuckled. His gaze flitted my way, and his face seemed to blur a moment. I blinked, but when I looked again, his weathered features were back in place.

"Caltevyn would love to keep her, but she refuses to stay there," the old man said.

"Where does she stay? It's hardly safe to let his only Phaetyn wander," said the brawniest of the three. The two other Druman were also focused on the strange man.

"Lord Tyrrik won't let her out of his sight, so she's plenty safe. Although why a Drae would be interested in a Phaetyn is anyone's guess." The man raised his eyebrows at me. "Were you going to bring me that drink, Ryn?"

My heart stopped.

9

How did he know my name? I'm sure there was an explanation for it; perhaps he'd overheard Dyter. I filled another mug and set it down in front of the old bloke, my anxiety climbing as he assessed the beverage but didn't pick it up.

"Isn't that what you wanted?" I breathed. He'd yelled at me through the kitchen for it only a minute before. "Why are you even—"

"Ryn," Dyter warned.

I snapped my mouth shut with a click of my back teeth.

Several things happened at once. The three Druman stood and drew weapons, wicked curved swords with blades the color of blood. The noise in the tavern switched off as though a tap had been turned, and the silent and frantic crowd scrambled back to give the men space.

Lord Tyrrik appeared next to me. I tilted my head up and, as expected, his eyes were all midnight black, and ebony scales had appeared on his forearms and neck. As I watched, his fangs slid down.

The old man disappeared, the air shimmering for a few seconds before a man with silver hair and pointy ears sat in his place. A *stunning* man. He drew out a short blade the color of his hair and balanced it on the tip of his forefinger, eyes sliding to the standing Druman.

"Are you boys looking for a fight?" the stunning man asked in a lilting voice.

Tyrrik swore long and hard in Drae. The shadows gathered around him, heeding his call, and the strange flickering blue color in his onyx scales flashed for all to see. He stepped behind me, wrapping his arm around my waist and pulling me to him, a menacing sound rumbling in his chest.

I stiffened and tensed to shove away from him, but he grabbed my bare wrist and spoke in my mind. *Not now. I need to get you out of here. You can be angry at me later.*

The darkness continued to coil around us, wrapping us in its silky embrace. Tyrrik pulled me closer. This was the first time I'd let him touch me since we'd left the castle, and something in my chest felt funny with the contact. Probably indigestion.

*Come with me now.* Tyrrik moved us out of the tavern room in a blur that left my head spinning. I gasped and opened my eyes to find we were in the back alley, and Tyrrik's skin was rippling with black scales.

"No, Tyrrik," I screamed. I knew what would happen if he turned into a dragon. My heart ripped and bled, the pressure mounting in my chest. "Please," I begged. "Don't shift here!"

The air around Tyrrik shimmered, and I covered my head, ducking as an inferno of heat erupted. The heat grew, sweeping upward, billowing and coiling until all I knew was the consuming warmth of the Drae.

My pounding heart settled as the sensation dimmed, and I uncovered my head.

Then blinked.

"Holy pancakes," I murmured. I was standing between two huge, onyx-scaled Drae legs. "Holy pancakes," I repeated, edging out. "Please don't squish me. The community will be devastated."

The Drae was oddly still. As I crept past Tyrrik's armored chest and came alongside his giant fanged head, I saw why.

"The tavern," I mouthed. The back half of Dyrell's tavern was demolished, Tyrrik's Drae butt now sitting where the kitchen used to be. It was the second tavern he'd demolished, and even though I hadn't owned either of them, both The Crane's Nest and The Raven's Hollow had been safe-havens in my life.

"You ruined my tavern!" I grabbed at Tyrrik, and he lowered his head. Holding either side of his Drae face, I narrowed my eyes at his slightly sheepish expression. "You are so paying for that," I snarled, staring into his inky eyes. "In coin, not carrots." I released his head and sank to my knees. "Everything . . . I've worked for. In ruins."

Tyrrik nudged me with his snout. *It's only been three days.*

He breathed out warm air, and I shivered as it hit my back. Glancing back to shoot another insult his way, my breath caught as bright blue rippled through his scales in a wave.

11

"Why do they do that?" I whispered, getting to my feet. I laid my hand on his scales, and as I did, the blue flickered in its depths. Warm tingles ran up my arm, and the skin where my scales had started to appear pulsed. "What is that?"

But shouting and screaming broke my trance before he could answer.

"My patrons." I burst into a run down the alley, leaping over the rubble of Tyrrik's transformation. I got to the end, and a whining crack had me whipping back around.

Tyrrik was squeezing through the alley after me, demolishing the rest of The Raven's Hollow and the wall of the store next to the tavern as he did so. Lifting his head, he huffed at me.

"I don't believe this," I muttered.

I was not waiting for him and his stupid Drae butt to squeeze from between the two buildings. I sprinted to the front and rounded the corner, skidding to a stop.

The crowd was outside and staring at the tavern in shock. Hopefully all of them got out. People from the nearby businesses poured into the dirt streets, and I scanned the increasing mass of humanity for the one person who mattered most. I heaved a sigh of relief when I saw him.

Dyter caught sight of me and hurried to my side.

"Ryn," he said, gathering me up. "What happened?"

I resisted the slight discomfort at Dyter touching me. I avoided touching most people now, but I refused to let what had happened affect things with my only remaining family. I jerked my head at Tyrrik as he escaped from the alley. "He accidentally shifted. Though, after one hundred and nine years, I'm not sure how that happens. *I* certainly don't have accidents anymore."

Tyrrik hadn't done this on purpose, had he? After spending months in his company, only to discover he'd deceived me the entire time, I really couldn't be sure. He was manipulative to the extreme.

The Drae stomped into the road, clearing a space in the crowd before the pile of wood, iron, and bricks that had been The Raven's

Hollow and the inn next door. There was a heartbeat of shocked silence, and then the screaming started anew. Really, it was amazing how quickly the crowd cleared after that.

The illusion I'd built of returning to my normalcy ran away with the patrons. I wanted to cry, scream, and run away, too. I wanted to scream and never stop screaming, but I shoved the emotion away, refusing to let it take hold of me. Standing next to Dyter, I stared after the crowd of humans fleeing. "I didn't know Seryt could run that fast."

Hearing a scratching sound, I turned to see Dyter rubbing his chin. "He's in front of all the young'uns," he said. "Impressive."

Within seconds, the space was empty and the only 'people' remaining were the three Druman, the stunning man with silver hair, and the three of us.

Tyrrik stood over me, still in his Drae form, and puffed out a small jet of flame. The molten heat landed just in front of the three Druman before angling up.

A cloud of smoke appeared. I coughed, waving my hand to clear the air, and my jaw dropped.

"Where'd they go?" I went to stand where the three large men had been.

"Look down, Rynnie," Dyter said drily.

I glanced down and saw I stood in the middle of three piles of ash. I swallowed and, with my voice shaking, said, "You could've warned me." Not so long ago, it hadn't been Druman being burned to white ash; it had been two hundred rebels who had come to save me.

I swallowed again and stepped out of the Druman remains, avoiding Tyrrik's gaze.

Dyter was eyeing the stunning man with pointy ears. I turned to study him and found I couldn't really blame Dyter's blatant interest; I wanted to keep looking, too. The stranger wore hugging brown breeches and a loose forest-green tunic ornamented with golden buttons down the front. The curved top of his chest muscles peeked through the open neck of the tunic, and I cataloged the sight. A leather belt with two sheathed daggers hung around his hips. Another loop of leather was slung across his torso, holding three more daggers. I should have been scared of the newcomer, but I couldn't figure out how to connect with my emotions after I'd just banished most of them. I was curious, so maybe that was something.

A growl filled Tyrrik's chest as I continued to look my fill.

Rather than being put off by the ginormous Drae at my back— when had *I* stopped being afraid of that, by the way—the stranger pulled his dagger again, stepped forward, and balanced it on the pad of his finger.

I watched the action, certain if I could learn that one trick, I wouldn't need to actually learn to fight with a dagger. It'd be a great bluff.

The air shimmered, warmth flowing over me as Tyrrik shifted back.

I refused to look at the Drae even though his presence assured my safety from the strangers in the tavern. Instead, I folded my arms and asked Pointy Ears, "Who're you?"

The man sheathed his dagger and extended his hand. "I am named Kamoi."

Something about the man called to me, and without conscious thought, despite the fact that physical touch with anyone but Dyter had given me a sensation of bugs under my skin for the last three days, I clasped his hand. I gasped as I stared into his eyes for the first time. *Violet.* The area where our hands touched flared, and a smoldering heat swept through me.

"You're Phaetyn?" I whispered, continuing to hold his hand though I knew the hand shake had officially gone on too long.

"The rumors are true," he said as he bowed over my hand. "My lady, I am glad to find you, another Phaetyn."

Unease crawled over me with his words where his touch hadn't bothered me. I couldn't help where my mind went. I formed the words with a thick tongue. "We're the only two left?"

A teasing light entered his eyes. "No, my Lady. I am merely one of our kind. I am the Prince of the Phaetyn."

# 3

"*I* . . ." I inhaled sharply. "I thought I was the only Phaetyn left."

Tyrrik spoke from behind me. "The only one in Verald."

"You knew?" Dropping Kamoi's hand, I threw the accusation at Tyrrik. There were other Phaetyn, and he'd kept that from me? I wondered what else he knew that I didn't, and a seriously long list of questions ticked through my mind. "How did you fail to mention that?"

"I'm fairly certain, I told you to go to Zivost when I tried to help you escape the dungeons." He tilted his head at me, and continued in a dry voice, "And somehow, the Phaetyn didn't come up again in the last three days when you were pretending I didn't exist."

I cleared my throat, refusing to dignify that with an answer.

The stunning Prince of the Phaetyn peered past me, and I felt the heat at my back increase as Tyrrik neared. The Drae stood just behind me, and I shot a look at Dyter who wiped the smirk off his face in a flash.

"The emperor would have felt his three Druman dying just now," the prince said. "You've just alerted him that things here may not be as calm as they were."

Tyrrik nodded. "Better that than having them carry back reports of what they saw here, or what they would certainly discover here in Verald. Even worse would be if they followed us on our journey."

"I thought you couldn't kill Drae," Dyter said, joining the small semi-circle outside his sister's ruined tavern.

The old coot hadn't said a single thing about The Raven's Hollow being ruined. Dyrell wasn't even my sister, and *I* was pissed.

Tyrrik broke off his stare down with Kamoi and faced Dyter. Replying to the implied question, he said, "I cannot kill *Drae*. Or my blood. They were neither Drae nor my blood."

Druman were half human, half Drae. The emperor had a horde of them, and Tyrrik had been forced to create a large number here in Verald for King Irdelron, the only way to keep him safe from the emperor's Druman force in our land.

The Drae's comment about travel caught up with me. "Wait, wait. What journey? I haven't signed up for a journey." I surveyed the mess before me and in a voice trembling with emotion, said, "I will rebuild."

The Phaetyn prince burst into laughter—if the sound of a quartet of singing birds, burnt-sugar candy, and fresh-cut grass could be called that. I smiled despite myself.

"You're funny, my Lady," he said. "I wasn't happy to be sent here at first, but now I'm glad my mother assigned this quest to me."

"We were coming to Zivost Forest anyway," Tyrrik snapped, pulling me away.

I tilted my head up at the broody Drae. *What's got your aketon in a bunch?*

Too late, I realized we were touching. The Drae's lips quivered, but he made no reply.

Kamoi sighed. "I am glad to hear it, Lord Drae. I was sent to see if the rumors of a Phaetyn here were true. My mother wishes to assess her powers and teach her of the Phaetyn ways."

I scratched my forearm through my long sleeves. I'd taken to wearing them when lapis lazuli scales began erupting all over my skin. Whenever I got emotional, which felt like all the time now, bits of my skin would change to scales. "There's probably something you should know —"

"We need to speak with the king." Dyter overrode me. "Before she can leave Verald."

I frowned at him. What was his deal? Pointy Ears was clearly my kin. I felt it. He wanted to help me. Seemed impolite to not inform him I'd transform into a monster tomorrow. Maybe that would affect whatever training I needed.

Tyrrik covered the resulting awkwardness. "I agree. An audience with Caltevyn would be best."

I closed my eyes, anger trickling into my body, and I dug in my heels. "*I said*, I'm not going anywhere. I'm not going to be a part of this fight! It's not mine. I'm done with it."

Dyter crossed to me and took my hand. "Rynnie, no one is asking you to be ready to fight tomorrow. If you still don't want to fight when the time comes, that's your choice. But wake up, my girl. There are other reasons to go to Zivost Forest. And if not to help yourself, consider the people of Verald. They may not be safe during your"—he shifted his eyes to the prince and cautiously finished —"transition when a certain person is alerted to your existence." He pursed his lips before continuing. "*I* will be going to Zivost Forest, just so you know. There is much to discuss with the Phaetyn now that things have changed here."

*Drak*, he knew just where to stab. Dyter was the only person I had left from my previous life. He'd first helped Mum and me when we arrived in Verald, and he'd always been my mentor, and in recent times, my boss. He was the only father I'd ever known. I needed him. I did want to learn how to be a proper Phaetyn, and I didn't want to hurt the people here . . .

I opened my eyes, heaving a bone-weary exhale. "I'll *think* about it. But the answer will probably be no."

Despite my words, I'd already decided I'd be going. Judging by the gleam in Dyter's eyes, he knew it, too.

Ignoring the other two man-creatures, I stomped in the direction of the ruined tavern to find a corner to spend the night. "I'm done now. I need some rest. You can all leave."

"Be at the castle at first light," Tyrrik said, I assumed, to Kamoi. The Drae knew better than to talk to me in that voice.

I heard someone leave and glanced up to see both Dyter and the Phaetyn prince were gone. I paused, one foot on a pile of broken bricks. My birthday was tomorrow, and there was something I needed to know and only one person I could ask. I knew he wouldn't leave me, he'd already said as much, so without turning around, I called out to Lord Tyrrik, "Is it going to happen tonight?"

I heard him inhale long and hard. *Because that's not creepy at all.*

"Not tonight," his silky voice carried to me. "Tomorrow, Ryn . . . when darkness falls."

---

I WAS JUST GOING for the company, I decided. I didn't want to spend my birthday alone. In a bout of morbidness, I'd elected to walk into the center of Verald to the King's Castle through my old zone. And, potential birthday company aside, I wasn't about to let Dyter leave the kingdom without me. Who knew what kind of trouble he could, and probably would, get in with Tyrrik there?

Harvest Zone Seven was still mostly a wedge-shaped hunk of ash from when Tyrrik burned it to the ground, with the exception of my Tyr flowers. Now he'd also demolished The Raven's Hollow, I had nowhere else to go. The people of the Inbetween and Money Coil were yet to come back and rebuild Zone Seven. Who knew if they ever would? And I doubted any more of Dyter's relatives would want to take me in, knowing I was cursed to be shadowed by a destructive Drae.

I trudged through the mostly barren Harvest Zone that had been my life only a few months ago. The Zone still had no buildings, but there was life now.

Harvest Zone Seven was filled with fields of blue flowers, the shape of the metal one my mother took me to during my childhood. In the moonlight, my vibrant blooms glowed. Thinking about them, I wondered if maybe it hadn't been that hard for the Phaetyn prince and emperor to find me. The pressure of my emotions built behind my eyes as I moved between the thick stalks of blossoms, but I shoved the feelings back, instead concentrating on the soft petals as I trailed my fingers over them. Those blooms I touched flared with light, standing to attention as I passed.

They were *Tyrs* as I'd named them. Tears to everyone else who didn't know about the man I'd fallen in love with while captive. A gentle, kind, caring soul who I'd believed I could've spent the rest of my life with. If he'd been real.

I sighed, walking across the Market Circuit, the ring road that went through all twelve Harvest Zones. I entered into the quota fields on the other side of that, trudging through a field of pumpkins. Not one to miss an opportunity, I spat on my hands and touched the pumpkins as I passed, willing them to be huge tomorrow.

I was reasonably certain the land in Verald would survive while I was away, but a bit of extra pumpkin soup never hurt. I made a mental note to ask the king how he was going to keep his subjects fed. Everyone had just been taking what they wanted thus far, but with the king now coronated, he'd soon have to establish order.

As I began my climb up the mountain pass to the castle, I pulled down my sleeves to cover the blue scales. The iridescent gem-like additions to my body hadn't disappeared since I awoke, and they weren't the only noticeable difference. My mind must've been playing tricks because my teeth seemed awfully sharp, and my sense of smell was *quite* a lot better. *Happy birthday to me.*

I chuckled nervously, feeling dizzy. Those things probably meant nothing. My being Drae still wasn't certain. My gaze fell to my arms, the scales beneath my shirt calling my bluff.

Reaching the castle gates, I halted and sat on a mound of grass directly outside them. I crossed my legs in my ankle-length, practical, brown skirt, smoothing my deep-blue aketon over the top.

Assuming I'd need to wait here for a while, I sank my hands into the ground and sent my Phaetyn mojo out.

"They've been waiting for you in the castle."

I didn't shriek. I'd smelled him coming. Why did he smell so good? Like leather, pine needles, and smoke. I gritted my teeth. "I'm not going into the castle." Never again. I'd made a vow, and I would keep it, even if it killed me. "You, of all people, should know. If you want me involved in the talk, you'll need to bring it out here."

Lord Tyrrik snorted. Always dressed from head to toe in tight-fitting, liquid black, the Drae looked rumpled this morning. Being a creature of the night, I doubted he appreciated the early start, and it showed in his dark disheveled hair and the slow blink of his eyes. "Would you like me to ask the king to come outside to talk to you?"

I arched a brow. "That's what I said."

His lips curved into a smile as he dipped his head. "As you wish, *Khosana*. And . . . happy birthday."

"Yeah, yeah." I waved him away. He'd remembered my birthday? Not that forgetting was easy when said birthday ended with me growing wings and alerting the emperor to my existence. What did it mean that he'd remembered? I shook my head. It *meant* I should return to sending out mojo into the ground. I took my own stellar advice, humming in a deep voice to see if that helped clear my mind of his presence.

"Ryn," Dyter said tightly a few minutes later. He strode out of the castle gates toward me, the king trailing in his wake, with Tyrrik and the Phaetyn Prince not far behind.

Dyter used that tone of voice with me whenever I burned the stew, and I knew he deplored my poor manners to the new sovereign of the kingdom. But Dyter had only a fleeting glance of the horror my life had been inside the castle, so I didn't hold his irrational feelings against him. Beaming up at him, I said, "Good morning!"

The irritation on his face softened, but he came and whispered to me, "What you did was disrespectful."

What Cal's father and his crony-Druman, Jotun, did to me was *way* more disrespectful. I believed Irdelron's son, Caltevyn, would be just what this kingdom needed. Regardless, I wasn't about to re-enter the place that still haunted my nightmares. The palace was the setting for some of the worst experiences of my life; I'd meant it when I said I'd never go back inside.

"My lady," the prince greeted me, bowing low. As he straightened, his eyes widened.

"Hey, Kamoi." I smiled at him, dusting off my skirt as I stood.

He stared at the ground around me, his mouth agape.

I glanced downward. Nothing had changed to my eyes, but I could feel that the ground was a lot happier than before, almost like I'd felt after eating Mum's lavender honey-cakes. Could he feel it too? Or what did he see?

Caltevyn, the king, reached for my hand, and I jerked it back. Dyter gasped and the others silenced, but Caltevyn merely surveyed me for a few seconds before dropping his hand and saying, "I understand you would prefer to conduct the discussion outdoors. I should've thought of it myself, dear Ryn. I'm sorry."

"Right," I said, uncomfortable with his courtesy. I made some semblance of a curtsey to make up for snatching my hand away and scanned the others. "So?"

The king smiled. "So, I'm told all of you must make a journey to Zivost. Once the emperor knows my father is dead, and there is a stray Phaetyn about, his curiosity will be piqued."

"It'll be more than piqued when he feels her existence tonight," Tyrrik said darkly.

My mouth dried. "Why? He can feel your existence, and he isn't chasing you down."

He cast me a look. "You are a female Drae."

I grimaced at what he left unspoken. "Cool. Great . . . Awesome. That's . . . that's awesome."

My legs folded as I returned to my spot on the ground.

"You are also Drae?" the prince said, aghast. "How is that possible?"

Tyrrik opened his mouth but darted a look at me and pressed his lips together, not answering.

The prince's face firmed. "That is . . . unprecedented, but we must leave immediately. She'll be safest with my people."

The king turned to Dyter. "You must go with them, my friend, as my voice."

Dyter bowed low. "I know it is best, but I don't like leaving you now. Be careful, Caltevyn. You're still vulnerable to attack."

Caltevyn smiled, but his kind blue eyes hardened. "I have Lord Tyrrik's Druman. I am not without protection, and through them, Tyrrik will be able to tell if any are slaughtered. The Zivost Forest is only five days on horseback from here"—his gaze slid to the Drae —"*less* as the Drae flies, I imagine."

The king turned to the Phaetyn prince. "Kamoi, the time is soon coming when our kingdoms must unite. I believe it will be the only way to defeat the great evil."

"The emperor?" The Phaetyn pursed his lips.

"It is our plan to unite the three kingdoms and the Phaetyn against him. To rid Draeconia of his vile presence once and for all. We have a Drae on our side, and," he continued, dipping his head at me, "I hope we soon have two. Your people are equally powerful in their own right. I hope you will discuss this with your liege and your people."

The Phaetyn prince crossed his arms and shifted his weight from foot to foot. He caught me watching and assembled his features, his Adam's apple bobbing. "I will take your proposal to my mother, King Caltevyn."

"It is all I can ask," the king replied. He clapped Dyter on the shoulder. "Lord Dyter is my chief advisor and truly my right-hand man. He will act in my stead and answer any questions you may have."

The prince's eyes shifted to Dyter, then to me again, then finally to Lord Tyrrik where they rested, but the Phaetyn did not speak again.

4

*D*yter stepped forward on the grassy knoll, bowing to the king again. "We will take our leave, your majesty. I've horses and provisions readied for an immediate departure."

"What about my provisions though?" I asked, my eyes narrowing. "You can't have mine ready because you didn't know if I'd come or not."

With a sardonic laugh, Dyter jerked his thumb at Kamoi, and they went back through the castle gates. Tyrrik lingered just far enough away to give the appearance of privacy. The king remained, and I shifted, searching for a topic. Before I could come up with something, he spoke.

"I don't blame you, you know?" he said with a kind smile. "For not wanting to enter the castle."

I shrugged, feeling an obligation to explain. "It's not you. I just . . ."

The sandy-haired king reached out to rest a hand on my shoulder but caught himself and withdrew the caring gesture. He tipped his head down to meet my eyes. "I know, Ryn. My father was awful; believe me, I know. You don't need to explain."

I reckon he probably did know. My disposition toward the king softened. "So . . . how's it going?"

He chuckled. "Fairly well, all things considered."

I thought of the pumpkins on my walk up to the castle. "I've been meaning to ask how you'll keep everyone fed."

He gave me a sad smile. "Thanks to you and what you learned about Phaetyn blood, I don't believe we will need to worry about that. My father had vials of blood that Prince Kamoi has given permission for us to use to renew the land. It will likely last several decades. We'll have plenty of food to fill the emperor's quota, send the expected supply to the other two kingdoms, and have ample amounts to feed our own. My plan is to establish a ticket system people can use as a means to exchange for food from our royal market stands."

"Like using coin."

"Yes, but worthless for anything other than picking up food rations each week. The system will be based on need, not wealth or status."

I smiled. "I like that idea."

Dyter and the others approached with our steeds. I eyed the beasts nervously. Tyrrik separated from the others, leading two of the horses. As he approached, he passed me the strap of leather attached to my horse. It was like a looped leash.

The others mounted, and the king spoke to us, stepping to one side. "I wish you Drae's speed on your journey, my friends. When the time comes to fight, I shall be beside you, an army at my back."

After a mumbled goodbye, the others looked at me, still holding the strap attached to my horse. I tugged the leash but scooted away as the animal came toward me.

A low sigh alerted me to Tyrrik's approach. I glanced up to see him stalking toward me.

How was it that the horses didn't want to run away when he looked like that? He could eat them in one gulp in his Drae form. But my horse just stayed next to me, waiting.

"You don't know how to ride," he stated.

I blustered and stuttered, hating to admit that I was once again the weakest link.

Tyrrik raised a brow, and I deflated, saying, "No."

"Sorry, Rynnie. I forgot," Dyter said, tucking a case into his saddlebag with a nod to the king.

My *friend* wasn't even looking at me and didn't seem the least bit sorry, so I scowled his way.

"I've just got to sit on the thing?" I asked, assessing the horse. They didn't look all that big until I was standing next to one. But how hard could it be?

The Drae paused. "There is a little more to it than that. Perhaps you best ride with me for a few hours."

The polite façade we'd kept up so far disintegrated in an instant. The idea of having Tyrrik's arms around me left me nauseated and chilled. "I'd rather ride with the emperor."

His painful inhale was the only indication my words had achieved their purpose. I couldn't afford to let my guard down around him. I wouldn't let him lull me back into his twisted web.

A heavy moment passed before Tyrrik averted his inky eyes. With a clenched jaw, he stepped closer, though. His hands were at my waist, burning through my aketon and skirt for a scant beat before I found myself atop the horse. He withdrew contact as soon as I was situated.

I adjusted to sit astride the mount, hiking my long skirt up to the knee. The Drae's eyes fell to the now bared skin of my calf, and heat filled my cheeks.

Without meeting his gaze, I asked, "Now what?"

He closed his eyes, clicked his tongue, and the horse moved forward.

I gathered the reins and held on for dear life, the feel of the horse's shoulders rolling beneath me utterly foreign. But I didn't fall off, so as I reached the others, I offered a cheeky smile and called, "You better get trotting ahead of me. I don't know how to stop this thing."

Dyter grinned and clicked his tongue. "Don't worry, my girl. We have four days to teach you on the way."

Lord Tyrrik rode beside me, and I forced myself to ignore him. I let my gaze wander as we rode away from the castle. Over the Quota Fields which now displayed vibrant-green growth, then the bustling Market Circuit, then the prosperous Money Coil. As we exited the Inbetween, I marveled at the growth of the plants of Verald.

When we reached the Penny Wheel, Tyrrik drew near.

"By nightfall, we'll be out of Verald and in the mountains of Gemond."

I'd never been out of Verald before. In my memory, anyway. Then again, I'd never experienced a lot of things before three months ago. Most of which I'd never asked for.

"But this far into the outskirts of Gemond, King Zakai has little control over the nomads who roam there. You should not wander by yourself. Especially not tonight."

*Tonight.* Another change I'd never asked for would be added to my list. Rolling my eyes, I replied, "Wonderful. I can't wait."

"Happy eighteenth birthday," Dyter said, pulling his horse up next to mine. "I had plans to make you a muffin."

"What happened?"

He shrugged. "The only kitchen was in The Raven's Hollow, and that was destroyed in untimely fashion."

I smiled. "Well, I thank you for the thought of planning to make me a muffin."

"How're you doing, anyway?" he asked then jerked a thumb at my horse. "You're a natural rider."

I raised my eyebrows at his blatant lie. My legs ached from sitting astride the animal for so long, and I was sure the steed was just as tired of me as I was of it. An hour ago, Tyrrik had informed me I didn't need to clench my legs so tight, that I'd stay on top even without clinging for dear life. I'd tried to relax, really I had, but I found myself, time and again, squeezing my legs to make sure I didn't slide off. After hours of riding, every single muscle in my body was taut, and my emotions were just as knotted. "I'm freaking amazing," I drawled. "Never better, in fact."

We hadn't stopped for lunch, just once for a bush restroom stop.

Whatever fluids I'd consumed hadn't been enough. What I really wanted was some of that nectar Tyrrik used to give me. But he hadn't offered me any in the last four days. Unsurprising when I'd made it clear I wanted nothing to do with him. Which also meant I couldn't ask him for nectar either.

"For it being your first time on a horse, you really are doing well," Dyter amended. "I'm sorry this is tough and so soon after . . . well, *everything*."

His kindness undid me. My eyes welled with tears, and I stared up at the blue sky until I could blink them away.

"Come now, Lord Dyter," Prince Kamoi said, drawing near. "Don't upset our beautiful companion."

He smiled at me, and I couldn't help returning the gesture. Something about the Phaetyn prince infused me with warmth. I liked to think it was the qualities of his personality, but I suspected a fair portion of the warmth was due to more superficial traits.

"Tell me, my Ryn, what was your childhood like? Tell me your favorite foods, your favorite colors, your favorite everything. I want to know all about you."

Tyrrik growled. "Maybe she doesn't want to tell you."

The prince waved away Tyrrik's protestation. "Ridiculous. We are practically kin. Not related, you understand, but joined by something you wouldn't understand, Lord Drae." The Phaetyn winked at me. "We'll make a game of it. I'll tell you something, then you tell me. One for one."

I nodded. "Keep it light though, please?" I darted a glance at Tyrrik and averted my gaze as soon as our eyes locked. Blushing, I added, "There are some things I'm not ready . . ."

The prince rested his hand on my leg, and his warmth infused with me. "Of course not, Ryn. I would never want to make you uncomfortable." He removed his hand and with a deep breath, said, "Now, where to begin? My favorite color is green. What's yours?"

"Blue," I said. "The color of the night sky right after the sun dips below the horizon."

"Beautiful," he said, his violet eyes bright. "My favorite food is morel mushroom bisque."

*What the hay was that?* I tilted my head and thought. I'd had lots of different foods while staying in Irrik's, I mean *Tyrrik's*, rooms, and so much of it was delicious. "I like honey-cakes, or burnt sugar. Oh, and this fruity. . ." *Nectar*. Ducking my head, I said, "My mum's honey-cakes are my favorite."

Kamoi studied me before continuing. "I was born in the Zivost forest, in the very heart of our land. My father was married to the queen of our people, Luna Nuloa. When she died without children, my father inherited her throne, and after a decade of mourning, he bonded with my mother. I am the oldest child, but I have a younger sister, Kamini. Now, will you tell me of your family?"

I listened to his tale of Phaetyn royalty and took pains to remember it then shrugged. "My mum and I lived in Harvest Zone Seven. She was my only family."

He furrowed his brow. "And your father?"

Lord Tyrrik growled again, and I rolled my eyes though I felt a similar irritation rise within me. "I never knew him."

Prince Kamoi pursed his lips. "I'm sorry. I hope you have not suffered for it."

"Dyter was the only father I needed," I said, clenching my teeth. The anger spiked, and a distant part of me wondered why I was getting so mad. I was being irrational, but I couldn't help but think the Phaetyn prince was a dolt. I also couldn't help feeling suddenly and unaccountably furious about that. I looked at him out of the corner of my eye and noticed his fair skin was flushed, immediately feeling bad for my rudeness.

"I beg your pardon, my lady. I didn't know. Of course, Lord Dyter has proven to be most intelligent in the short time of our acquaintance."

This light game wasn't light anymore. While he was happy to chatter about his mum and dad, I didn't need the reminders of what I'd lost.

"And anyone can see that he is kind and clearly cares about—"

"Stop apologizing, and move on," Tyrrik said as he approached.

I wasn't going to admit it, but Tyrrik had impeccable timing. I took the moment he offered to try and get a handle on the swift anger which had risen unchecked inside me.

The fair Phaetyn straightened, but before he could continue his apology, Dyter interjected.

"Prince Kamoi, I was wondering if you would spare a few minutes for me. I have several questions about Zivost and your customs. Would you mind?"

The prince bowed to me and then rode toward Dyter. I glared at Tyrrik. "I was going to handle it."

He quirked a brow. "I could see. But we need Prince Kamoi alive to get into Zivost. And then you will need someone to train you there. Neither of those things would happen if you killed him."

"I was not going to kill him," I ground out. Hit him, possibly, but that wouldn't kill him. I needed to get a grip.

"Of course not," Tyrrik replied. He studied me and then continued in a subdued tone, "It is not a weakness to call a halt. A little time off your mount would allow your powers to heal you."

I shook my head. I was tired of being the weak one. Tired of being broken. Tired of it all. "I'm fine. We need to keep going to get us to Zivost as fast as possible."

Tyrrik glanced over at Dyter and the Phaetyn and muttered, "This is ridiculous."

The Drae glanced at our horses with a grimace and then long-ingly at the sky.

It didn't take a genius to interpret his look, and I would never want to admit Tyrrik could help, but really . . . Why ride a horse when Tyrrik could just fly us wherever we needed to go? I caught another shared look between the three of them and narrowed my eyes.

"What are you hiding?" I asked softly when they shared yet another quick look. A fist-sized rock landed in my gut. Tyrrik was keeping something from me, *again*, just like in the castle. They all were.

Tyrrik glanced up, expression smoothing into blank lines, *manipulative lines,* and my simmering anger exploded into a full-boil. "Don't you dare!"

I reached to Tyrrik, grabbing a fistful of his black aketon, and pulled him to me. "Don't you dare keep secrets from me again. Don't you dare!"

5

One moment I was upright in my saddle, and the next, I was tangled in my stirrups, pulling Tyrrik from his horse. I landed on the hard rocky ground, and Tyrrik somehow landed on his feet like some kind of cat. *Stupid Drae.* I screamed at him from the ground as the horse dragged my sorry butt along the uneven path, stopping only to munch on a patch of grass. I kicked, trying to pull my foot from the stirrup.

"Stupid horse," I shouted. "Stupid Drae. Stupid world!"

"My lady," the prince cried, bounding from his horse in a graceful arc to help me.

Suddenly, my horse was still. I crossed my arms, staring at the sky as Tyrrik extracted my foot, and didn't say a word.

"Oh, dear lady," Kamoi said.

"My name is Ryn," I sighed. "Stop it with the lady this, lady that, please."

I tore my gaze away from the prince to look at Tyrrik and got a glimpse of his backside. It would've been a more pleasant view if his aketon wasn't so long.

I froze at the errant thought and furiously scrubbed my mind clean of the sentiment. *Bad Ryn!* I heaved a sigh and sat. "I'm fine. Just give me a minute."

Tyrrik turned and extended his hand to me. His bare hand.

I reached out, hesitating inches from his palm. Would he shut me out, or would I get some cryptic message when our skin touched? Part of me wanted to yell at him. But if he, Dyter, and the Phaetyn prince were all in on a secret, it wasn't just Tyrrik I was pissed at.

I grabbed Tyrrik's hand, but he blocked me from his mind as he pulled me to my feet. *You better not be keeping secrets from me,* I blasted at him.

*What if it's not what you think?* he immediately replied.

"I don't care," I snapped. I turned to Dyter and Kamoi. "I'm done with secrets. If you want me to get behind this quest, or whatever you want to call it, you'd better start telling me what the hay is going on. You want me to train, you want me to save the land, you want me to help you fight the emperor, but you tell me nothing? I'm walking away *right now* unless you tell me everything. I'm one hundred percent, I-will-never-speak-to-you-again serious."

I stomped over to the Phaetyn prince. "If you know something about my powers, you should be telling me, not keeping it secret."

I turned to Dyter. "I've trusted you my entire life. I never once betrayed you while Jotun tortured me. Not once. The least you could do is prepare me for any more surprises. And don't yell at me when I need a minute to decompress. If I want to serve ale, let me serve ale for a day."

I turned to Tyrrik, but my words dried up in my parched mouth. I hated him for lying to me. I hated myself because although I hated him, I felt safest when he was near. My head was messed up, and though the abuse I'd suffered wasn't all his fault, so much of my distrust of the world was.

"If you ever want me to trust you, *ever,* you need to stop hiding things from me. Stop omitting details. Stop passively letting me come to the wrong conclusion. If you want my trust, you need to stop doing what you're doing." I pointed at Dyter and the prince. "If the three of you know something I don't, you better start showing some modicum of confidence in me and some respect for what I've been through, or I'm leaving right now, and I'm not coming back."

Tyrrik's eyes darkened until they were all black. His skin rippled but soon stilled. His gaze went over my head to Dyter. "You'd better ride as fast as you can. We'll spend two days in the caves and then come find you."

The Phaetyn prince asked, "Do you think that's wise? She's still part Phaetyn. I can see it even now on the cusp of her change."

Dyter sighed, and I turned to see him rubbing his bald head, his shoulders sagging. When he looked up, he offered me an apologetic smile. "I'm sorry, Rynnie. I only wanted to spare you a little longer. I hope you'll forgive me."

It felt like he'd scooped my heart out. "Spare me what?"

Dyter pointed to Tyrrik. "I'll let him tell you."

My head spun as Dyter and Kamoi rearranged the packs and said their goodbyes to Tyrrik and me, but I didn't really hear them. After they were gone, I turned to Tyrrik. "What is it then?"

He shook his head. "Not here."

I glared at him. Again. "What do you mean not here? That's not how this works. Did you hear a single word I said?"

"Yes, I heard." He was suddenly before me.

"I'm not leaving this spot until you tell me."

Tyrrik blurred and brought his lips close enough to brush my ear as he whispered, "If we don't get to the caves before you change, you will have more to worry about than what secrets I might have. We can talk while we ride."

His warm breath sent shivers down my spine, and a current of energy pulsated between us. I swallowed, pushing down the desire to turn toward him. Instead, I batted him away. "Why did you have to whisper that in my ear?"

His gaze dipped to my lips. "No secret on that, Ryn. I wanted to be close to you."

"That's . . . not allowed," I finished lamely. "And I'm not falling for it. Tell me now, Tyrrik, or go away. I can't be bothered with your tricks anymore."

"You're sure you wish to know?"

I closed my eyes, waiting. I was pretty sure at this point nothing he could say would surprise me.

"I would've waited until you had the privacy of a cave, but I suppose you'll know soon enough anyway." Warmth touched my body as the Drae stepped closer. "You are the Emperor's daughter."

I snorted and waited.

"I'm telling the truth."

I opened my eyes and stared at him. "Wash your mouth out."

"What?" Tyrrik asked, concern in his eyes. Probably for my mental state because that sure was under pressure at the moment.

I choked out the words. "You're not serious?"

"I never joke when it comes to you."

*Or joke in general.* "I don't understand . . . How? You said the emperor didn't have a mate, and that Drae can only . . . procreate with their mate." I pulled up short as I recalled something else the Drae said not many days before about the 'emperor's experiments.'

Tyrrik nodded, but his attention was fixed on the sky. "I will answer your questions. All of them. But you must listen to me. When you transform the first time, you are vulnerable. We need to get to the caves so we are hidden."

*Sure. Right. I'll just put aside that startling bit of news and go about my merry way to the caves so I can turn into a Drae.* Surprisingly, I did just that, turning toward my horse. "Do I have to get back on my horse?"

I was not looking forward to riding that animal again. What I wanted to do was ask Tyrrik to change into his Drae form and fly us to wherever we were going.

"No," he said, mounting his own horse. "But I won't risk changing unless I have to. I'm sure Emperor Draedyn has sent more Druman, and he might be patrolling this area himself for all I know. For now, we ride."

"I thought you said I didn't have to get on the horse." I put my hands on my hips in protest.

"No, *Khosana*. I said you don't have to get on *your* horse." He held out his hand. "We need to be quick, and you're tired."

I shook my head. Being near him messed with me, and my head and my heart didn't need any more strain. "I'll ride my own horse. You just want to touch me."

His features softened, but he shook his head. "We don't have time to go at your pace. If we make it, it'll be just in time. Your energy is all over the place, and I don't want to risk a talon to the eye if I don't have to. The sun has already started its descent, so you'll be feeling night's call soon, if you're not already."

Tyrrik was right; I could feel something deep inside me sending tentative tendrils out. Something huge slowly unfurling from within, raising its head in anticipation.

I didn't want to transform here. I accepted the Drae's hand, and he pulled me up in front of him.

"And I always want to touch you," he whispered in my ear.

With a click of his tongue, we were off. If not for Tyrrik's iron-hold around my waist, I would've toppled from the horse.

"How far until the cave?" I asked, clinging to the front of the saddle.

"Several hours," he answered.

I barraged him with questions for the first hour, and he patiently gave me my answers, most of which I wanted to forget as soon as I'd heard them. Because the emperor was my father, he would be able to sense me every time I shifted into my Drae form. He might even be able to read my mind like Tyrrik could when we touched. And after Tyrrik's little fire in Verald, resulting in three less Druman, the emperor would likely send out more of his mules.

I wasn't sure how long had gone by when the night's call Tyrrik had described began to override everything else. My muscles spasmed, contracting and stretching with flashing bolts of agony. My body seized and shook, and I gritted my teeth to keep from crying out. My body alternated between searing pain and extreme fatigue, the cycle shortening as the night approached. I shuddered and gasped, "Am I going to give birth?"

Tyrrik's response was to tighten his arm around my waist, tuck my head in the hollow of his neck, and urge the horse faster. Before the pain began, I'd done my best to make sure our skin did not touch. I'd kept my sleeves pulled up over my hands. I'd sat straight in the saddle, determined not to lean on him, but I was far beyond that now. King Irdelron himself might've sat behind me, and I'd still be a whimpering sack of potatoes.

Another wave hit me. I bit down on my lip to stop from screaming but couldn't help arching in the saddle, going taut with the throbbing pain.

We veered off the path toward the base of a mountain range.

"Not long now, *moje láska*."

I hung onto his voice like a lifeline. As the sun dipped lower and lower in the sky, the tendrils of night reached out for me, singing to me, inviting me toward them. I'd longed for the touch of darkness for months, but now it was an endless chasm of blackness that wanted to trap me inside, just like the dungeon. I'd never get out. "Tyrrik." My voice was thick and heavy. "The night wants me. It won't let me go."

"No, *Khosana*. You belong to the night, and the night belongs to you."

"Scales!" I hissed, as they appeared on my hands. A sharp stinging sensation crawled over my skin, like needles were scratching me raw. I cried out, clutching the sides of my neck as the pain crept upward. More of the lapis lazuli pieces appeared, and I whimpered. What if they never went away?

Tyrrik whispered encouragement in my ear, the words of a language I was only beginning to understand.

My muscles cramped more and more. A dull pressure in my chest expanded until it felt as though the Jotun of my nightmares was sitting on my heart. Sharp, stabbing pains rippled over my body, and as the sun kissed the horizon, my hold broke. I screamed, the sound piercing the twilight, terror-filled and yearning at the same time.

Tyrrik pressed his lips to my neck, to my *scaled neck,* speaking in my mind. *The first time is the hardest. You are strong, Ryn, plenty strong. Just hold on.*

He drove the horse to go faster, faster, faster.

My vision blurred, bright blue-and-green colors shattered and splintered amidst the darkness swirling around us. My body seized, and the pressure built inside me. I tipped my head back against Tyrrik's shoulder and screamed through my raw throat as the pressure exploded. Pain overwhelmed me, and the darkness coiled and wound unabated around my body. Blue tendrils unfurled, expanding as the ache deep within my bones flared.

Tyrrik's shouted cursing was the only sound surrounding me as he pulled me from where I sat. But I never hit the ground. Instead, I floated high above, staring up at the silky night with unblinking eyes.

Night had fallen.

# 6

*I* groaned. Every single part of me ached, and I wondered why my Phaetyn powers hadn't healed me. Rolling onto my back, I hissed in pain and tried to heave myself back on my side. Large warm hands helped me turn, and I forced my eyelids apart. A distant part of me couldn't believe I'd managed to drift off—though it was more likely I'd passed out from exhaustion at some point during the night.

Tyrrik scooped his arm under my shoulders and lifted me upright until I was sitting. My head swam, and I clutched the neck of his aketon to steady myself. "Dizzy."

He held still until I nodded then reached behind me to grab something. The sweet smell of nectar floated to me as the Drae held a goblet to my lips.

"Thanks," I rasped. I took a long draught, and the nectar soothed the ragged edges of pain from the inside of my throat. But as soon as Tyrrik withdrew the chalice, I stammered, "M-more."

He obliged, filling the shiny stemware and giving it back to me. I took another long drink, although this one was more to avoid talking about what happened last night. That Tyrrik saw me as a screaming, blubbering, contorting mess deeply embarrassed me. I was inordinately grateful that he *had* been here. He'd said I'd need help, and as I thought of the hourly baths he'd given me in the pool of nectar and the words of encouragement through the night, I no longer doubted this fact.

His dark hair was disheveled, and his cheeks and chin dusted with a day's worth of growth. Darkness clung to him, like wisps of spider's webs, his black aketon was rumpled, and he offered a wan smile.

"You look as bad as I feel," I said, breaking the silence. The black threads seemed to be emanating from within him, and when I blinked, they faded. Even my eyes were exhausted.

He huffed, a mannerism that would look less odd in his Drae form. "It is not easy to watch someone go through that," he said. "I have never cared for another Drae during their transformation before."

"You did a stellar job," I mumbled. My pitiful gratitude was lost as the buzz of languid fatigue spread through me, and I closed my eyes and leaned into him. I could probably sleep for a week.

"Your transformation seemed worse than I remembered."

"Because I'm part Phaetyn, do you think?" I asked, my eyes opening a crack before floating closed. "It was pretty horrible." And didn't compare to the torture sessions with Jotun; this pain had a reward at the end—it wasn't meaningless pain meant to break me but pain resulting from something I hoped would make me stronger. A thrill of excitement vibrated through my chest and out to my extremities. I could feel the new strength in my fingers, in my body, even as weary as I was. Aside from that, I seemed pretty much the same as I'd been, though this was coupled by a knowledge that my skin would be impenetrable to weapons, even those dipped in Phaetyn blood—or so I assumed. I blinked my eyes open again, and testing my sense of smell, I inhaled deeply . .

.

And stiffened.

My mouth watered, and I slapped a hand over my lips before any of my saliva spilled out. My cheeks heated, and I dropped my gaze and yelped when I saw thread-like energy in vibrant blue and green coming from my core. I blinked again, and the wisps of color disappeared, but the captivating scent did not.

"What is it?" Tyrrik rumbled beside me, his breath washing over me.

*What is it?* I swallowed. Tyrrik smelled freaking incredible is what. I took another deep breath and let the scent wash over me. Like pine needles and smoke and leather. Slap me with a pancake and call me a potato! I could exist on that smell alone. I loved it so much I could roll around in it, lick it up like syrup, I could . . . I blinked through the sudden fog of desire surrounding me. "N-nothing?"

"Ryn," Tyrrik said through clenched teeth, backing away from me. "You need to rein it in." His nostrils flared.

Horror flooded me, and I hastened to make sure we weren't touching, but it appeared as though the Drae was merely smelling . . . me. Playing dumb, I asked, "Rein what in?"

My feigned ignorance disappeared when I turned to face Tyrrik, and I gasped in awe. For well over a week, he'd been flashing a vibrant blue color underneath the onyx black of his scales, but I now saw it as though for the first time through my new and improved Drae eyes. The wispy strands of darkness around him had threads of blue, and his scales pulsated with lapis lazuli. My gaze zoomed in and focused on the sight, and I crawled closer to him on all fours. Kneeling in front of him, I reached out in a daze. I brushed my fingertips across his exposed collarbone, touching his scales.

"They're beautiful," I breathed.

He puffed out his chest, and his shuddering lessened.

Why was he puffing up like that? I inhaled again and—what would my mother say—*swayed* on the spot. My heart pounded, and my breaths became shallow as I leaned toward him. The desire to close the distance was a magnetic force, and I remembered how his kisses tasted like nectar. "Tyrrik," I whispered. I shook my head, trying to clear the fog. "What is going on?"

"You need to switch off the . . . signal you're sending," Tyrrik said, his own shallow breaths an almost desperate panting.

"What signal?" I asked shrilly, my fear spiking. "I don't know what signal I'm sending!"

He stood abruptly. "It's a signal to male Drae. Your scent."

"Y-you mean—" My lips parted in awe as I stammered, "Like a . . ." *Mating call?* "Oh."

"Yes, oh," he ground out. In a blur which my new eyes easily tracked, he exited the cave.

Perhaps, it would be best if I didn't sniff people anymore. Or, at least, not male Drae. Which meant I shouldn't smell Tyrrik anymore. I pursed my lips as I contemplated not smelling that scent. In truth, I wasn't sure I didn't want to smell him. That stuff was better than honey-cakes.

"Ryn!"

I blew out a long exhale and looked up into the darkness of the cave, which welcomed me as though I was an old friend, and I set my mind to platonic observations. Like how I could see everything though it was pitch black in here. The cave was beautiful, and I wondered if Tyrrik's lair back in Verald was this pretty inside. The walls here were sleek granite, and a glistening pool bubbled languorously in a stream through the middle of the chamber.

Several body-sized indents had been made into the side of one wall, and I wondered if Tyrrik and other Drae used the hard resting places to sleep when they were here. A pleasant humming rumble came out of my mouth as I smiled and gazed around the cave. The dark cavern could use a comfortable touch here and there. Not so much flowers or pictures but maybe some gold treasure and gems and a blanket or two in case I got cold. I frowned. Actually, I was really warm. Last time I'd been in Tyrrik's cave, I'd been freezing, hadn't I? Or was that the heat stroke? What if I could breathe fire now? Perspiration broke out on my brow. Was that why my voice was so hoarse? I was not ready for fire to come out of my throat.

"You can't breathe fire," Tyrrik called in.

"Are you kidding? Why not?" I clambered to my feet and paused halfway to the entrance when it occurred to me I hadn't spoken my fire-breathing thoughts aloud. "No," I said, straightening. "No way. Please tell me your answer was a coincidence."

"It was a coincidence," he said, standing in the mouth of the cave. Sunlight streamed in around him, putting his strong, towering frame in silhouette. I eyed the bright light in distaste. That would hurt my eyes, I was certain, so I stayed back in the darkness.

*What's thirteen plus three?* I asked silently, seeing another wisp of blue in the darkness.

*Sixteen,* he answered.

"We don't need to be touching to hear each other now?" I asked, my shoulders slumping. Had he heard all the sniffing stuff, too? How humiliating. Telepathy wouldn't be awkward. Not one bit. "Is that a Drae kin thing?"

He shrugged. "I'm not ecstatic about it either."

A foreign joy seeped through to me, tinged with fear. The emotion didn't reflect my current mood, and I studied the feeling skeptically until I put it together, and my mouth dropped open. "But you are. You—you want it. The telepathic stuff. You like it." I studied the hints of fear he was putting out. "At least, mostly."

He scratched the back of his head, and I wished his expression was visible.

I changed the subject. "So, I'm strong, and I can smell," I said. "That's all I get?"

"For now. Smell is the sense most crucial for survival, so it is present from the beginning. You possess the ability to use your other senses in this form, too, but using them will require practice."

"My senses were all over the place before the transformation." I frowned.

"You were partially transformed and scared. Your senses in this form will be most accessible when you feel threatened." He waved at me, beckoning for me to join him outside. "We need to begin your training. We'll need to leave here the morning after next, and you need to know, at least, the basics. The rest will come in time or as you get older."

Training? No way. That sounded like work, and my body was

still tuckered. I yawned, and my jaw cracked. I curled up on my side and, with a shooing gesture, said, "Maybe once night falls. I feel like a nap."

"I was going to teach you to fly," Tyrrik beckoned.

"Tonight," I repeated lazily, partially asleep already.

A high-pitched clink echoed through the cave from the entrance. I opened my eyes, sliding my gaze back to Tyrrik. My mouth dried as I saw what he held aloft. Playing it cool, I asked, "What's that?"

"A gold trinket."

Desire shot through me, and I propped myself up, licking my lips. "What kind of trinket?"

"It's an antique pill box that once belonged to an esteemed baroness." He tossed the pill box in his hand. "Want it?"

The gold beckoned me. It was just what this cave needed. A bit of sparkling wealth. Actually, I needed it. I got to my feet and murmured, "Yes."

"Come for your flying lesson, and it's yours." His silky voice wrapped around me, pulling me to him with a warm undercurrent to it.

I narrowed my eyes and studied him. Tyrrik's face was smooth, his impassive mask on, and I couldn't help my suspicion. His offer *seemed* fair. I walked toward the gold and said, "Flying lesson, and it's mine; no tricks."

At least, I *meant* to walk, but I went faster. A lot faster.

I shrieked as I blurred toward Tyrrik, my arms flailing. He caught me around the waist as I crashed into him, the air whooshing out of me as my silver hair fanned around us.

"Sorry," I managed, brushing back my locks. Was all of the brown gone? My Drae transformation must have burned the dye out of my hair.

He snorted and slowly withdrew his arm. "Nothing I can't handle." He brushed the rest of my hair over my shoulder. "I like it better silver."

*Right.* We'd better not go through *that* again. I straightened, pulling on my rumpled aketon. "Show me the shiny."

"Not until after the lesson," he said with a sardonic smile. "First things first: You'll need to shift."

I glanced around the clear area outside the cave. "Is there enough room?"

Tyrrik nodded. "Female Drae aren't as big as males."

"Why not?"

"Because they play different roles. They have different strengths and weaknesses."

"Like what?"

"The females are the calming balance to the male's volatile nature," Tyrrik said.

*Lame.* "But I'm stronger and faster, and I have claws, wings, and fangs, right?"

His eyes softened. "Yes, just not to the same degree as a male. Except speed, that is."

"Then what cool powers do I get?"

The Drae cleared his throat. "Enough questions, Ryn." He lowered his voice and stepped closer. "Shift."

Apprehension filled me, and my heart fluttered against my chest. What if I couldn't do it? I opened my mouth to ask, but the question evaporated as Tyrrik ran his finger over my right shoulder blade.

"Shift," he said in a deep voice.

Something primal took over, led by the unrelenting power in the baritone of his Drae voice. Dark energy caressed me, and I cried, "Tyrrik."

Except the cry came out as a roar. A shimmering blue light exploded around me. Brilliant-blue scales erupted up my arms and neck, down my legs, and over my face. My fingernails became black hooked talons. My face lengthened, a thick bi-curved plate growing over the front of my chest. The blue energy pulsed from within, and I swelled in size, snorting in alarm as Tyrrik shrunk on the ground beneath me. Gigantic wings burst from my shoulder blades, the blue leathery skin stretching between the hollow bones still strong enough to keep this form in the air. Pain pinched at my lower back as I curved over to rest on all fours.

The pressure there continued until a horned tail curled around to rest by my side. Razor-sharp fangs slid down over my powerful jaws, and I arched my Drae spine. I felt invincible and couldn't help the deep satisfaction in my chest rumbling out in a deep purr.

The shimmering energy surrounding me settled and faded. The thoughts of my normal mind, my Phaetyn mind, settled into a corner, and the foreign, instinctual thoughts of the creature I'd become filled my head.

I was Drae. My race was as old as time.

Tyrrik approached with care, hands turned up in a gesture I recognized as deferential. I surveyed him down the length of my snout and decided to let the man touch me, but the decision was calculated. He was a Drae and far more powerful than me. The closer he came, the more I could feel his prowess and strength. Yes, this wasn't one to anger. If anything, he'd be an excellent mate to provide strong young. My human mind broke out of its tiny corner. *Whoa. Mate? Where did that come from?* Me and my Drae form needed to get some things settled.

He rested his hand on my foreclaw. *You are perfect, Khosana.*

*You just called me princess.* That's what Khosana meant? He'd been calling me princess this entire time? *Do I speak Drae now?*

*In this form, yes.*

My chest puffed out. I was Drae, and my *form* was perfect. My scales were unflawed lapis lazuli, my fangs were daggers; my tail was a battering ram. But I would not let his pretty words cheat me from the gold. A small part of my mind said I was being weird, the Phaetyn side again; I'd never really cared about wealth. But I really needed a golden trinket. *We had a deal, Lord Tyrrik. Teach me to fly, then give me my treasure.*

Though the urge to stretch my wings swelled from deep within, I worried. What if I did it wrong?

"We can only practice in this clearing," he said, pursing his lips in a frown of apology.

I sniffed in disdain.

Tyrrik rounded behind me, and I tensed, instinctively knowing that was my weakest point of defense.

"Shh, Ryn," he said soothingly. "You know I would never hurt you. I'm just going to show you what it feels like first."

He took my right wing, and I followed his lead, stretching it out. I arched with pleasure as the breeze danced over my wing, the air causing it to lift.

"You were made to fly, and it will come to you naturally, in the same way you do not consciously inhale after exhaling," the Drae said. He held onto the end of my wing, slowly lifting and pulling it down. "Can you feel how the air catches underneath when I do this?"

*I can*, I answered.

"Now pull them down together, both at the same time. Your wings will reflexively lift after a down stroke."

He stepped around me, eying the drop off the edge of the clearing, then glanced out at the semi-circle of trees about ninety feet back from the edge. "There is not as much room here as I would like, but you'll get the idea. When it's safe, I promise, we'll go for a real flight."

*I'm ready*. I strode to the edge of the drop, my steps resounding with my body weight; I was about half the size of Tyrrik's Drae form by my estimations. I stretched my neck over to survey the drop. It was about one hundred and fifty feet down.

Tyrrik continued muttering advice beside me. "Tuck your legs into your body. Flatten to speed up, and raise your head and tail to slow."

I rolled my eyes and dropped over the side. His startled yell echoed behind me.

Stretching my wings wide, joy filled me as the current caught and held me, the air billowing beneath my wings. My fall was gently slowed until I was floating. I banked to the right around the semi-circle clearing then pulled my wings tight and stretched them wide, pushing down against the currents. I lifted and lifted until I was in line with the tree tops. The temptation to continue upward and soar into the unknown was nearly overwhelming. I wanted to see how fast I could fly, if I was faster than the other Drae I'd seen streaking through the sky, and if I could go on endlessly—it sure felt like it.

I circled around the clearing another three times, taking the opportunity to flatten myself for speed and arch my neck and tail upward to slow down. I reveled in the knowledge that I was a fearsome beast, powerful and strong, and in flight, I was graceful, even elegant. Flying was a dance, and I was a master.

I did one last lap then decided I was done. The sunlight was irksome, and I really did want my nap. Extending my legs, I landed at the top of the clearing, tucking my wings in as my feet made contact.

Tyrrik's eyes shone as he practically ran toward me. His smile, a rare thing to behold, was as wide as I'd ever seen it.

I furrowed my brow, concentrating on my body. The air shimmered with blue energy as I shrunk back into my human form, or rather my Phaetyn form. The air cleared, and I glanced down to make sure my clothes were in place before extending my open palm to Tyrrik.

He placed the golden pill box in my hand without a word.

"You know," I mused. "I thought this Drae business would be harder."

The Drae cleared his throat before speaking. "We are predators. We need to be able to protect ourselves once we transform. Your powers should come naturally—"

"Should?" I asked, raising my eyebrows.

"I'm unsure how your Phaetyn blood will affect some elements of your transition," he admitted.

I nodded, gaze fixed on the golden box. So shiny. This was my greatest treasure. I'd put it in a great spot. The thought halted me. No, it had to go in a secret spot, somewhere no one would find it. My eyes slid to Tyrrik. Would he try to steal it back? I'd need to be careful. *No one* stole my hoard. Even knowing I was being irrational, I couldn't talk myself out of my obsession with treasure. "I'm going inside now."

"Okay," Tyrrik answered.

His tone was odd, and I peered back at him as he drew another object from deep within his aketon. The golden pill box was nothing in comparison to the huge ruby he held.

My chest rose and fell as I fixated on it. "Where'd you get that?"

"Doesn't matter, does it?" he said. "Although, I'll give it to you if you stay for another lesson."

The ruby was a real treasure. I'd put it in the secret spot, too. I'd take extra, *extra* care no one found it.

"Just one more lesson?" I asked. My feet were already walking back toward him.

"Just one more," he agreed with a smile.

"One more time," Tyrrik said, rubbing his chin. "Then we'll stop."

I rolled my eyes. One more attempt would only make me feel like a bigger failure. A Drae-loser. Totally incompetent.

He'd had me shift from my human form to my Drae form and back at least a dozen times, or rather, *attempt* to shift. I could easily go from Drae to Phaetyn, but the Phaetyn to Drae had been impossible on my own. If Tyrrik touched me? Boom. No problem at all. And now I was seeing webs of black and blue color again. "I'm tired. Let's just try again later."

"Come on, Ryn." He patted his aketon and pulled out the ruby. "One more time, and it's yours."

I looked at the gem with mixed feelings. When Tyrrik first showed it to me, I practically salivated, but now the stone represented what I couldn't do on my own. Disgusted with myself, I waved my hand in dismissal. "Keep it," I said, turning back toward the cave. "I don't want it anymore."

My words weren't exactly a lie, but they weren't the full truth, either. I did want the sparkling gem, but we'd set the terms for winning the ruby already, and I had yet to master the current lesson.

So much for it coming naturally.

*Khosana*, he called. *Don't quit.*

*I'm not quitting forever.* I threw the thought back without looking his way. *You said it wasn't a weakness to call a halt. I'm tired. I'm not progressing. Let me sleep. I'll try again in the morning.* It had been a challenging day after an even more challenging night.

He sighed, and I shrugged it off. Why did he care so much? It wasn't like it was *his* fault I couldn't shift on my own.

The darkness swallowed me whole as I trudged into the cave. My eyes adjusted with a blink, and I scanned for a good place for my golden trinket. I pulled it from my pocket and studied the shiny treasure with a smile I knew was pretty crazy.

I strode through the main chamber, past the pool of nectar, and stopped. I glanced around the space but couldn't find the goblet Tyrrik used last night. He probably hid it, not that I blamed him. If I remembered correctly, it was gold and encrusted with gems, the perfect chalice for nectar. A perfect addition to, what would be, a glorious hoard.

I knelt, feeling the weariness in my body. I dipped my hand into the cool liquid, thinking of how he'd held me in the pool of nectar during my transformation. If I was this tired, Tyrrik must be tired, too. He couldn't have rested that much in the last two days, and he had expended a lot of energy on my behalf. If I knew how, I'd do something nice for him. Bringing my hand to my mouth, I slurped the sweet goodness eagerly and choked in surprise, sputtering as my taste buds identified water instead of nectar. I was certain I drank several cups full of nectar from the pool last night, and Tyrrik brought me some earlier today. There wasn't another pool, was there?

I stood and glanced around the chamber, but there was no other pool in sight. Perplexed, I called out for my only source of information. "Tyrrik?"

I turned back toward the front of the cave as he stepped into the darkness. My gaze went to the stemmed goblet in his hand. The *bejeweled golden* goblet, the cup of my dreams. If I got him to hand it over, I wondered if he'd let me keep it. Or maybe I could steal it while he slept. Would he notice? My covetous thoughts made me stop. *What the hay is wrong with me?* I'd never been envious of people's wealth before. I'd never been a thief either.

*But he kind of owes me.*

"Do you need a drink?" he asked, his voice rumbling through the darkness.

"Do you have any nectar?" I asked. "Somehow the pool turned to water. I swear it was nectar before." Not that I minded water, but I'd much rather have nectar.

If I hadn't been watching Tyrrik, I would've missed his eyes widening as he inhaled.

"Has it never done that to you before? Did I mess something up?" *Drak.* "Was it my Phaetyn powers?"

That would be just my luck. I was bad at shifting, and now I'd messed with the nectar in the cave.

Tyrrik shook his head, another dubious non-answer. He went to the pool, dipped the cup in, and then took a sip. After swallowing, he asked, "Did you put your hand in there?"

*How would that matter?* Last night we'd both been lying in it. Or was he implying he was the magic behind the cave nectar, and I'd messed it up by putting my hand in the water? "Yes," I said, drawing the single syllable out. "Because you had the only cup . . ."

He took another drink, tilting it up until it was almost gone.

"Hey," I complained, "I want some. Why are you drinking it all?"

He finished his gluttonous chugging of the fluid and said nothing as he dipped the cup back into the pool and brought it to me.

I took a sip and narrowed my eyes at the lingering sweetness on my tongue. "It was water before," I insisted before draining the goblet. I held the beautiful treasure, but my gaze went to the pool. "If I go over there and dip this in, am I going to ruin it again?"

Tyrrik studied me with pursed lips.

We were back to that again. "You know, I'm pretty much over the whole let's-keep-secrets-from-Ryn thing. In fact, I think I was

51

really clear yesterday." Was that only yesterday? "About how I felt. We had a good day today, as far as trust goes, up until now—"

Tyrrik took the goblet from my hand and threaded his fingers through mine. With a gentle tug, he led me to the pool. "It has to do with our kind. How our males and females balance each other's powers. I can't make *výživa,* what you call nectar, for myself; no Drae can. This pool is water until one of us makes nectar for the other."

"You've been making it for me this whole time?" I waited for his nod. "How do you do it?"

A teasing gleam entered his eyes as he waved a finger in the air. "I will it, knowing it will help you heal and replenish your energy. It's just a matter of wanting that."

"For another Drae," I ventured slowly.

He paused before giving a quick jerk of his head.

"So we're dependent on each other for nectar?" I asked. My thoughts, however, weren't on how I could never make nectar for myself. All I could think was Tyrrik wouldn't have had *any* since his enslavement to Irdelron. I also wasn't sure I wanted to make it for him. It seemed . . . personal. Too personal.

A slow smile spread across the Drae's face, his dark eyes lighting. "We're interdependent."

He let go of my hand and knelt at the edge of the pool. He dipped the cup into the water, took a sip, and then handed it to me. "More?" *It's an honor to serve you nectar.*

My eyes widened at the errant thought, and I hurried to school my features, certain I hadn't been meant to hear it. I took the goblet, and blinked at the deep sincerity I felt from him as our skin touched. I gulped the nectar to cover the moment, and the sweet drink soothed my throat and nerves, then my aching muscles.

I drank every last drop, even licking the rim.

With a totally straight face, Tyrrik said, "I guess this means you like my nectar."

I blanched. "You did not just say that."

Tyrrik cracked a joke? Was the world ending? I thought back to my fake dungeon buddy, Ty, and his funny quips when we were in the dungeon. I supposed Ty was Tyrrik, so . . . It took a few moments for my head to wrap around my altered perspective of the Drae—all the funny quips really came from Tyrrik. If I hadn't known Ty, fake as he'd been, I would've never known Tyrrik had a sense of humor.

He stepped forward until he was in my personal space and wrapped his hands over the jeweled chalice in my grip. "Oh, come on," he said. "I could've said much worse than that."

My heart pounded, running a race I would never win. "Here," I said, thrusting the cup into his hands. "I'm good now."

I fled into the depths of the cave, Tyrrik's throaty chuckle chasing me. If I were to turn around, I'd see him, but some part of me, a rather large part, was terrified of meeting his eyes and standing too close. Why did I feel so unsure? Was it a Drae power thing? I'd never been unsure around him. At the start, I was so scared I could've peed my skirt, but unsure? Never. His place in relation to mine had always been clear and easy to navigate.

I wandered through several caverns, searching for a secure place for my treasure. Plus, I wanted a comfortable place to sleep. I meandered for a while, not in any hurry to get back, looking for somewhere safe. Every room I entered felt off, and eventually, my Drae instincts led me back to the cavern with the pool in it.

Tyrrik was lying in one of the indentations in the wall. His eyes were closed, and his chest rose and fell in a rhythmic pattern.

Disappointment and relief pulsed through me, but I told myself it was probably for the best—though what I meant by that I didn't want to dissect. I paced around the cavern, letting my thoughts unravel the last few days. It wasn't Tyrrik's fault my emotions were all over the place or that I was irritable. For being so bodily tired, sleep was the last thing on my mind.

"You still don't trust me," he whispered across the darkness.

"Hmm, what?" I responded, deflecting. There were three more indentations in the wall, all three near Tyrrik, which made me all kinds of nervous, but to not go over there would prove his point. I mentally kicked myself, wishing there was a way to block my emotions so he couldn't read me.

"There is," he said after a pause. "I'll teach you tomorrow if you'd like."

"Will I be able to do it?" I asked, my shoulders sagging. "Or is it going to be like shifting? Because that would kinda defeat the purpose, right? If you had to help me block you." My weak chuckle trailed off almost instantly. It hadn't been my best joke.

He shifted, rolling to his side to face me. "What would it take for you to trust me again?"

I grimaced. That question didn't leave much avoidance wriggle room. "For real?"

Lying in a dug out hole was more appealing than facing Tyrrik, so I crossed the room, feeling his gaze on me. *Creeper.* I didn't throw the insult with the same vehemence I had weeks ago. I guess the nectar and his help had softened me. That discovery unnerved me to no small degree. I climbed into the space farthest from him, a whole arm span. At least I could look at the ceiling of my cubby and know his eyes weren't on me.

"Will you please tell me?" he asked.

I closed my eyes and thought of Tyrrik and our interactions to date. There were many of them if I included the conversations with Ty and Tyr—which I guessed I had to as much as I didn't want to. Tyrrik must have felt so alone for so long with his only consistent company the twisted Irdelron or a few dozen Druman children Tyrrik had been forced to spawn. The blood oath had caused him excruciating pain, both physical and emotional, for one hundred years, and he'd no hope of escape. Until he found me. If I were in his situation, I might have been a little desperate to be free too. No matter the cost to others.

"The cost to others was all I thought about," he corrected, his voice aching with a depth of pain that made my heart hurt.

Relieved, but distrusting, I pressed him. "Why did you lie? The entire time. You lied, played with my emotions, and now, somehow, I feel guilty because I don't trust you and you want me to. But how can I? How do I know you're not just playing"—*with my heart* —"some game again? Or that you have an ulterior motive like last time?"

He sucked in a breath. "You think it was *all* a lie? You believe that?"

I remembered Tyr's gentle caress . . . the sweetness of his kiss. I thought of the tears he'd shed while wiping away my blood after Jotun beat me. I recalled the jokes and hope Ty gave me, his companionship. However, through Ty, Tyrrik had betrayed my plans, *our plans,* for the rebels to free us, the plans he'd helped me make, to Irdelron. Tyrrik had killed Arnik and all of those rebels. The Drae had put so many people in danger . . . even me, so he could break his blood oath.

"So we could be free," he said. "All of us. Is what I did really any different than what Caltevyn or Dyter did?"

"You hurt me," I said with difficulty. "A lot." So much I wondered if I would ever be able to trust anyone again.

I'd always thought I'd be able to tell if someone was lying to my face. I'd seen other people in love before, matches where one partner lied or cheated, and wondered how someone could be blind to their partner's duplicity. I never thought I'd be one of those blind fools. I never thought I'd love someone with those qualities.

"I did lie. And I hated it. If I could've come up with any other way to break the oath, I would've."

His words rang with honesty . . . but then, they'd done that before too. "So you say," I mumbled, rolling toward the wall. "It's been less than a week, and I don't know if I have it in me to forgive that kind of thing. Just don't deceive me anymore."

8

$\mathcal{A}$ loud roar startled me awake. I sat up, smacking my head on the granite above. Before I could swear loud enough to bring the cave crashing down, a hand covered my mouth.

*Be silent,* Tyrrik said in my mind. *He's out there.*

*Who?*

*Your father.*

My father. Emperor Draedyn. *Pops.* Pretty much the worst being in the entire realm. As a Drae he was all but invincible, like Tyrrik, but much older. More powerful, too, remembering Tyrrik's comment about the emperor being alpha. As emperor, he had the entire populace at his disposal. His war of expansion had cost the realm countless lives. *Are you sure he's my father? How would you even know that?*

*Your mother told me. Before she died.*

*I can't believe that I'm related to someone who kills so easily . . . or who experimented with Phaetyn and Drae.*

*He's desperate enough to win the war that he'll try anything to create a stronger army.*

I took Tyrrik's hand off my mouth; there was no need for him to force me to be quiet. Before I could release it, he turned his palm to mine and held tight.

The Drae outside roared again, and the darkness of night was suddenly alive with flame, the orange blast stretching a few feet inside our cave.

My heart leaped into my throat, but irritation overrode my fear when Tyrrik squeezed my hand. I lifted our joined hands, shaking them a little. *Why are you holding my hand?*

*It's better than you screaming.*

*I was not going to scream.* If I did scream, it would be at him.

*Are you sure? Because you were the one who took my hand.*

I glared at him and withdrew my hand, but he re-captured it, tugging me off the bed. I followed him deeper into the caves as Emperor Draedyn lit up the sky again with a deafening roar of flame.

*He's calling to you.*

*Really?* That took creeper to a whole new level. Like I was a hypnotized donkey or something.

*Can't you feel his call?* Tyrrik stopped our hurried escape to study me. His gaze traveled over my face, relief appearing briefly when I shook my head.

*If he can feel us, why doesn't he come in and join us?* I didn't understand what was keeping us safe. The caverns were narrow, but certainly if the emperor shifted back to his human form, he'd be able to chase us.

*He can only feel your general location and doesn't know about these caves. They were discovered by the Drae long after Draedyn left the clan. Our alpha decided we needed new secrets when Draedyn ascended the throne; the old caves were abandoned, and the new ones were a guarded secret for a generation.*

A generation? *How old is he?*

*He has been the emperor since before my grandfather was born, but that's all I remember.*

So, at least a few hundred years old. My stomach churned. Why wasn't anyone Ryn-age? Or even under one hundred?

Tyrrik led me down another corridor.

*Where are we going?* If I thought about how my sicko father was a

57

million years old, I was going to throw up. I needed Tyrrik to talk to me about something else. Anything else.

*The caves will take us halfway to Zivost. We'll have to fly the rest of the way in the morning and hope Dyter and the Phaetyn are there.*

The sneer in his voice when he spoke of Kamoi was unmistakable.

Personally, I felt quite bad about how I'd spoken to the prince when I last saw him. I'd need to explain that the transformation got the better of my temper back there. Hopefully he'd still let me get within staring distance.

*Why do you hate Kamoi?* I asked.

*I don't hate Kamoi. I hate the way he looks at you.*

I heard the trickling of water and threw a quip back. *Why? You think I'd like his nectar better?*

Tyrrik stopped so suddenly I crashed into him. In one fluid movement, he turned, caught me in his arms, and pulled me to his chest.

*Whoa. Easy there, Drae-man.* I tried to pull away, but he only loosened his hold fractionally. His heart pounded against mine, and for a brief moment, his want was all I could fathom. Then a veil dropped over his side of our telepathic bond.

*Would you?* he asked me.

Even in my mind, his voice trembled. I knew my answer was important to him. The retort was on the tip of my tongue, to ask if he was really getting worked up about his nectar being better than Kamoi's—which as far as I knew, Kamoi couldn't even make as a Phaetyn—but hadn't I just thought about how personal making nectar was last night? *I don't know. Kamoi can't make nectar, can he?*

I knew immediately my answer hadn't been what he was looking for. Removing his grip from my arms, Tyrrik spun without a word and picked up the pace through the caves.

This time leaving my hand dangling at my side.

"Ryn," a man's voice rumbled in my ear. Still caught in my dream, I flailed, and my fist shot up. I came to, listening to Tyrrik's muffled cursing from where I clipped him.

"You hit me," he grumbled, stating the obvious.

I blinked the last bit of sleep, and my dream, away. "Sorry, you woke me at a bad moment."

He dropped his hand from where he rubbed his jaw. "Oh? A good dream?'

"What?" I frowned. "No. A bad one." The emperor had been chasing us through the caves, and we couldn't find the end. I yawned loudly, stretching my arms high above my head as I sat, and scowled at Tyrrik when I saw him watching.

The Drae was as fresh as a daisy—if that daisy was dressed in a rumpled black aketon.

After walking through the cave system for most of the night, we'd stopped to sleep close to the back exit. My eyes were scratchy and my shoulder muscles tight. My Phaetyn powers didn't seem to be healing my Drae side, and I wanted to drink a gallon of nectar and sleep for a week.

"You'll be able to sleep when we get to Zivost, *Khosana*." He touched his jaw again, his gaze thoughtful. "At least for a bit."

I pouted; he was plotting more for me. I was so tired I couldn't muster the energy to be ashamed of a little lip-droppage. "How much longer? I mean until we get there."

I wasn't ready to hear how little rest I'd be granted.

His gaze dropped to my lips, and his reply came out strangled. "One day."

A whole day. That sounded like ages.

Tyrrik reached into his aketon pocket, drew out a small burlap sack, and then tossed it to me.

Smelling the brak, I tore into the bag as soon as I'd caught it. I stuffed a handful of broken pieces into my mouth then paused and looked in the bag. Empty. I chewed and spoke around my food. "Um, did you want any?"

Tyrrik snorted. "If I do?"

I chewed again, pushing the food to the side of my mouth. "I'm not sure, honestly. I was hoping you'd say no."

He grinned, teeth flashing white in the dim cave light. From his belt, Tyrrik unhooked a waterskin and held it out to me. "Have some nectar before we get started."

I accepted the drink but groaned. Still speaking with my mouth full, I whined, "We'll be traveling in daylight?" *Why?*

"Because that's when the emperor is least likely to be in the skies. He patrolled all night, remember?"

We'd seen his flames in the sky from this side of the caves too. Tyrrik had pointed it out when I'd stumbled toward the entrance last night. *Right. That goes to show you just how tired I really am.* I chewed a few more times and swallowed then pushed out my bottom lip again as I double checked the bag for more brak. Maybe there was more in the saddlebags. "What about our horses?"

*The horses will meet us in Zivost. They left as soon as we got to the cave.*

They did? I shook the bag upside down and threw it away when nothing came out. I sipped at the nectar, knowing I'd have to share with Tyrrik.

*Don't backwash.*

His thought hit me, and I choked. If a little of the nectar happened to go back into the waterskin, it served him right. *Har-har. You're such a jester.*

I sighed, handing him back our only form of sustenance.

*I know you're tired and hungry. This isn't how I would've planned your transformation time. But, soon, you will get both sleep and food. I promise.*

I got to my feet. "Let's get this show on the road then."

If there wasn't a steak the size of a horse waiting for me when we reached the forest, I was going to find one. Even if it meant my fangs made an appearance. I stomped forward.

As the dot of light at the exit grew larger, Tyrrik reached out to touch my elbow. I nodded at his cautionary look and lightened my steps. And my breathing. *Mistress Moons*, did I really breathe that loud?

"What can you hear, Ryn?" Tyrrik murmured in my ear.

Now that I was breathing like one person instead of one hundred? I focused on the sounds rising before us.

*Squirrels barking? There's a larger animal out there. And . . . a stream.* We could refill the waterskin if we needed. *Tumbling rocks.* A gust of wind blew into the cave. *There are birds playing in the air. But no Drae.* My amazement echoed in my mind as I conveyed it all to the silent Drae by my side.

"Your senses are good," he purred. "Very good."

My chest swelled. *I have a golden trinket, too.*

"It's a beautiful trinket. You will take good care of it."

"Thank you," I said gravely. "I will." The weirdness of the conversation didn't elude me, but, somehow, it was important that Tyrrik knew I could take care of precious things.

"When you are able to shift back and forth, you will have your ruby. When you can *partial* shift . . ." He stepped out of the cave, and I flung an arm up to block some of the light as I hurried after him.

"What were you going to say?"

He glanced back from a boulder several feet away. "What?"

I dropped my arm as my eyes adjusted and jumped from massive boulder to massive boulder after him. "You were going to say something after the partial shifting bit. I thought you might be offering something else. Maybe more treasure."

He grinned.

9

*T*yrrik bent his legs and executed a massive jump from the boulder we stood on to the next. The rocky foothills had disappeared, and we were climbing through the stony pass of the Gemond mountains. Large crevasses were scattered through the range, and I eyed the sixty foot gap, my human mind getting in the way of what my body was now capable of.

*Do you expect a priceless heirloom for everything?*

*You set a precedent is all I'm saying.*

I glared at the gap and decided a run up would be best. I stepped back to the outer limits of the boulder I stood upon and took the crossing at a run, launching off the boulder with a muffled squeal. The air whipped my hair back as I flew across the gap. I was moving faster than I ever had, but I knew, inherently, I didn't need to worry. My senses were so much stronger now that everything seemed to move in slow motion when I focused. When I landed next to Tyrrik, I knew the best spots to place my feet. My abdominals and thighs were tensed to counter the forward motion, and my bodyweight was poised on the balls of my feet.

A smile tugged at the corner of his lips. "How about when you are able to partial shift, I'll give you a choice from my hoard?"

He had a hoard? Why did he have a hoard?

He jumped forward again, and we continued leaping boulder to boulder down the hill.

My mind boggled at the possibilities of treasure. He had to have a decent collection. "Is it a Drae thing to collect?"

"No. Not all Drae do it. Male Drae collect items during their life, but not for themselves."

I wasn't really collecting shiny stuff for myself either, now that I thought about it—more because the objects deserved to be protected.

He landed on the rocky ground below, and I thudded next to him, not half as graceful, though I thought I was doing pretty well for being skill-less Ryn from Harvest Zone Seven. They didn't cover boulder-bounding in turnip toddlers.

We walked on in silence for a bit. If walking could be applied to what we were doing. If I glanced to my side, I couldn't ignore the fact that the sparse trees and patches of grass were literally blurring by. Yes . . . walking was certainly a loose term.

*You said we'd fly.*

*I want to put some distance and a hill between us and the caves before we shift and go airborne.*

*But it's faster.*

*Yes, but the emperor doesn't know about that cave system, and I'd like to keep it that way. Also, we're more vulnerable in the air and easier to spot. But it will mean one day of flying, instead of four days running, so I believe we must risk it.*

The trees continued to blur by until Tyrrik slowed his steps, and we began picking over boulders again. He was leading me around the base of another hill.

"You know what you said about teaching me to shield my thoughts from other Drae?" I paused as he stiffened. "Could you teach me?"

Tyrrik remained still, his back to me, and when he spoke, his voice was icy. "If you wish it."

My thoughts hadn't been my own for a long time. Irdelron had seen through my lies, and he'd filled my mind with pain and horrors. Tyr had been able to hear me though it hadn't bothered me before I knew he was Tyrrik. I didn't want to rely on others to give me privacy. I needed to have power over who I let in and who I didn't. And though I was used to Tyrrik speaking in my head now, I wasn't sure I wanted him in there. At least, not all the time. And definitely not at his whim.

Tyrrik had already shown his jealousy of Kamoi, and we were headed to his kingdom. There were so many risks. This journey to the Zivost forest was apparently a risk, and I imagined a friendship with the Drae before me would be a risk too. Not to mention my evil Drae father. I needed to be prepared. Even if it hurt Tyrrik's feelings, I needed this. I took a deep breath and said, "I do."

His shoulders didn't relax, and he stayed rooted to the rock he stood on.

I bounded onto another boulder. "Look, I just want to be in control of my mind."

"Against me," Tyrrik said shortly, heaving a sigh.

I puffed out a breath and turned to face him. "Against everyone, okay? I want to know I have control of my innermost thoughts, and no one will know them unless I will it."

He jumped, moving from stone to stone ahead of me.

I hurried to catch up. "Surely you of all people understand?"

He stopped, and I pulled just short of barging into him. He glanced at me over his shoulder, black eyes searching my face. "If I do this, will you trust me?"

I clenched my jaw, keeping the scream of frustration inside. He was always manipulating me. "How about, for once, you give something with no strings attached?"

Darkness flooded his eyes, but I stayed where I was, staring up at him defiantly. He spun and continued over the boulders at a faster pace.

Another no-answer, but I wasn't about to retract my words.

We reached the apex of the bend and began around the other side. Hopefully we'd take to the air soon. I was eager to stretch my wings again and maybe score that ruby.

"Think of our telepathy as flow of energy," Tyrrik said when I landed next to him.

I ground to a halt, watching him continue. "What?"

He inhaled through his nose, his face fixed in the mask I knew too well. "You wanted to learn how to block me."

*Everyone*, I immediately corrected.

"Do you want to learn or not?" he asked, jaw clenched.

Sheesh, someone wasn't used to not getting his way. I couldn't understand his tone. He was offering to teach me but also didn't want to, and there was another element I couldn't identify.

"Yes, Tyrrik. I would love to learn," I said demurely. I peeked through my lashes as he threw me a suspicious look through his narrowed obsidian eyes. When he turned back around, I poked out my tongue.

"When you communicate with me, you send a bolt of energy through our Drae connection. If you send a lot of energy, if your emotion is high, not only do I hear you, I also get a sense of the sentiment behind the words. If you put a lot of energy in and focus, you'd be able to send a visual too." He faced me, his features soft and open. "Maybe even a smell and touch."

"Whoa." Those threads actually did mean something. Staring up at him, I scooted closer as I asked, "Really?"

He grinned, a wide carefree smile, and the boyishness it lent his face stunned me. I stumbled on the uneven ground, and my heart flipped.

"You okay?" he asked, frowning as he closed the distance to help.

I regained my step and ignored his hand but couldn't stop the blush from creeping up my neck. I forced a laugh and quipped, "Pretty sure I'm a Drae and a Phaetyn."

"So, if you send out energy to communicate, you simply draw it in, in order to—"

"Become a fortress of silence," I finished in awe.

"Sure," he said drily. "Something like that. Want to give it a try?" When I grimaced, he added, "Perhaps try to identify how it feels to communicate telepathically first."

*Testing, testing, teeeeeessssstiiinnng.*

Tyrrik winced, and I smirked, but now that he'd pointed it out, I could see the thinnest of tendrils weaving between us when we spoke. I'd seen them intermittently ever since I shifted. I focused on the thin threads of energy; their essence was black and blue, a silky connection linking the two of us. I worked on pulling the blue threads in, but the notion of drawing anything in with my mind was counterintuitive. Even with my Phaetyn powers, I tended to push, and pushing was what I wanted to do here as well, not pull. I suddenly wondered if I would be able to see my Phaetyn power now too. Wow. I could fly, sense crazy far, and now feel and even *see* my energy. I tried to grab the wispy form, but couldn't make sense of it. I had to put it in normal terms. Letting my mind wander, I thought of my mother towing water in from the well. Lowering the bucket and hauling it back up, the rope winding around the wooden reel.

Taking a deep breath, I did the same with my energy, imagining it was the full bucket of water and I was at the top of the well, pulling it up to me. Gathering that energy, my energy, closer and closer.

"That's it," Tyrrik whispered.

He was right in front of me; I could feel his presence, but I ignored him as I continued drawing the energy in like winding up the rope in the well to get the bucket of water at the end. As our contact disappeared, I shivered at the loss. It was uncomfortable, unsettling. But I kept drawing the energy in until it was within my body. "Now what?"

"Now, you practice holding it there," he bit out. "See if you can hold it until we take flight."

I took a firm grasp on the energy and opened my eyes. When my hold didn't break, I began to walk after Tyrrik again. "That will keep my thoughts private?"

"Your thoughts, yes. I will teach you to block others from invading your mind once you have the hang of pulling your energy in."

He was right. A light sweat broke on my forehead as I held my energy tight. The idea of keeping others' thoughts out sounded fantastic.

"You did well."

I smiled, feeling his pride through the link he sent, though the tendril of Tyrrik's thought made me battle to keep hold of my own energy. After a moment, I had control again and cleared my throat. "Thanks."

Over the next thirty minutes of travel, the boulders we hopped over flattened into a clearing. Tyrrik scanned the area as I focused on keeping the thread of energy inside. He jerked his head to a raised shelf and grunted in satisfaction as we crossed to it to find a small drop on the other side.

"Think you can manage that?" he asked.

It was a quarter of the drop of yesterday, but I couldn't manage a witty retort. Instead, I nodded agreeably. "I should be okay with that."

"You can release your energy now. We'll need to shift."

I'd been wanting to for more than twenty minutes now. With a heartfelt groan, I let the thread fly free. My energy shot straight to the other Drae, and I shivered in bliss as we reconnected. My gaze went to his face which lit with a fierce joy as our energies brushed against each other.

That . . . seemed unusual. Unease skirted down my spine at what that could mean. He better not tell me I was his other half or something stupid like that. "Umm, so all Drae can do energy thread stuff, right?"

His face smoothed. "No."

I felt him pull his energy back, and I narrowed my eyes. "No, what?"

He schooled his features. "Not all Drae can do 'energy thread stuff.'"

"But Drae other than us can, right?" I wasn't sure I could handle that kind of special right now.

"Yes, Ryn. We've already established we're not the only two Drae that can do energy mojo."

I grinned. "You said mojo. I knew I was rubbing off on you."

He rolled his eyes, and the air around him shimmered.

*Drak*, he'd known I was procrastinating. I could feel him gathering his power into himself.

"Think of the ruby, Ryn," Tyrrik said. "I know you really want the shiny gem. You just need to . . . poof. It's as simple as that."

A moment later, a chuffing sound came from the Drae now standing over me. I tilted my head back and stared at his onyx scales.

With a booming leap, Tyrrik dove off the drop. With powerful draws of his wings, he rose into the air, just above the tree line, and began to circle.

My stomach churned. What if I couldn't do it? I pushed some tendrils of my silver hair back.

*Stop procrastinating.*

I glared at the huge Drae and mentally ventured through the streams of energy between us until I was at his Drae form. I reached to feel his power; it was dark and mysterious and endless. I allowed my energy to dip into his, surprised at what I felt. It wasn't cold—which is how I often saw Tyrrik—rather, his power was warm and comforting, like the dark nights in Verald with the hot air rolling in from the southern deserts.

This was what I felt when he helped me shift.

I stayed here wrapped in his power for a time, trying to use the feel of his energy and the sight of his Drae form to shift, unsuccessfully. I thought of the countless times he'd helped me shift in the clearing. He'd always touched my shoulder blades.

"Why do you touch the ridge of my shoulder blade?" I asked, already pulling his energy toward me. He was letting me. I could feel his acquiescence, and there was an indulgent edge to it; like I had wobbly legs, and he was nudging me up a steep hill.

*The wings are extremely sensitive. It is the easiest place to get a reaction.*

Something clenched within me, and I remembered how it felt when he touched my wings yesterday. He'd been gentle, but every nerve ending had stood at attention with his hands on them. I drew his energy close, slowly, nervously, coaxing it to curve around my shoulder until it hovered over my shoulder blade. Then, deciding if this didn't work I'd have a tantrum, I let the energy connect.

Shimmering light burst around me. I catapulted into my larger form, scales erupting in the fastest shift I'd had yet. My neck extended high, and even in my Drae body, my breath came hard and fast from the huge jolt of energy.

*Well done.*

I panted in a crouch. *That was intense.*

*I imagine so . . . you used my energy.*

For a fraction of a second, I felt his triumph, and then he closed me off from his emotions.

*Next time, use your own power.*

Embarrassing. *I could've done that with my own?*

*Yes.* He seemed to consider his next words and then continued. *Though it might've taken longer to get the hang of it. You should be fine now that you've experienced it once.*

I pushed onto all fours and flexed my talons. He was right. Now that I'd done it myself, I knew I could replicate the release of my Drae. *Is it the same for all of us? How we shift?*

*No. Everyone sees energy in a different way. You are visual.*

I dove off the drop and beat my wings hard to lift to his looping level. The sun had moved, cursed thing. I'd spent at least an hour figuring out how to shift. My stomach grumbled, reminding me it still wanted steak. In Drae form, it sounded like an earthquake.

Tyrrik flashed his fangs beside me in what must've been a Drae smile.

*Shut up, I'm starving.*

In response, he took us higher.

As I circled upward, I noticed patches of vibrant green in the distance. *What's that back there?* Could I really see all the way to Verald?

Tyrrik glanced toward Verald. *That's where Phaetyn powers have healed the land. Some might be yours, but those patches of green are how Draedyn knows there are still Phaetyn.*

I ground my teeth together.

Without saying anything, Tyrrik picked up the pace.

We skimmed over the treetops, and I let my mind wander, seeing that Tyrrik scanned the ground and sky around us. Confident he was alert to any Druman underwing, I indulged playing with the air currents as I ran over the events of the last couple days.

I was now Drae. And, somehow, I didn't feel completely out of my depth. My reptilian gaze slid to Tyrrik, and I acknowledged this was because of him; he'd made this easier. He didn't owe me anything beyond what guilt might force him into doing. Tyrrik chose to help me, and considering everything, he'd been nice about it too. He'd also helped me in Irdelron's castle, though in a completely botched way. Is that why Tyrrik had helped me today? No way.

Somewhere along the way, a new dynamic had snuck up on us, or maybe I was just slow to recognize the evolution. At some point in the cave, things became *different*, and the new undercurrents from Tyrrik made me uneasy. Those emotions were what I'd felt with Tyr. I didn't want to be feeling them again, especially not when I was undecided whether I even wanted a friendship with Tyrrik. How was it that after two days in his company, the friendship thing seemed a given? I hadn't consciously decided to give it. What if I didn't want to?

I needed to rein things back and put them in perspective again. I didn't want to be lured into feeling one way or another; manipulation was unhealthy and wrong. If I was going to feel anything for *anyone*, it would be reasoned out, and it would be my choice. I owed that to myself and to Tyrrik and to whoever else I came across.

*Nearly there. Maybe another hour or so.*

His voice broke me from my reverie. There was an inquiring edge to his thought, and I wondered how many hours I'd been lost in my head. Judging by how far the sun had lowered in the sky and the streaks of red and violet reflecting off the clouds, several hours.

I inhaled and gave him a tight nod. Knowing it wasn't going to get easier, I focused on my energy. Then, bit by bit, I drew the thread of my energy between us back into myself.

He flinched but gave no other reaction, but then, slowly, I felt him drawing his energy in too.

## 10

*T*he craggy peaks of the Gemond Mountains jutted into the blue sky as we continued our flight to Zivost Forest. The highest points, capped in snow, extended to where the air was thin and unbreathable—even for Drae. The dark rock was interspersed with the sparsest of growth, most of which were gray and sickly cedars. Abandoned homesteads dotted the larger ravines with snaking trails winding between them. The houses were lean-tos, piles of rocks with dried foliage draped to limit exposure to the elements, and looked abandoned.

Without the telepathic connection with Tyrrik, the silence in my head was thunderous and somehow empty. My thoughts rattled, continually turning to him between thoughts of what would happen once we arrived in Zivost. Huffing through my snout, I reminded myself I didn't trust him and turned my attention to the ground.

We passed over another deserted town of scraggly shelters, though this time I smelled smoke. Gray billows of acrid smog puffed into the blue sky, creating a dirty haze above the settlement. I circled lower and flattened my body as my sharp eyes detected movement in the rocky valley below.

The jutting cliffs made spying hard. I tucked my wings in closer to my scaly body and cut through the air current holding me aloft. A descent of a few feet was all I needed, just enough to see better through the smoke. I'd never ventured out of Verald, though the Gemond Kingdom had often been featured in Mother's stories. I knew little of the people, beyond their mining reputation, but after hearing the words 'alliance' from Caltevyn's and Dyter's lips, I assumed an attempt to rally Gemond to their cause was imminent. If they planned to recruit these people, and I was being dragged along for the ride, I needed to learn as much as possible.

In my heart, I hadn't mustered the strength to throw myself into a rebellion against Emperor Draedyn. I *was* resigned to being hauled through the civil war, regardless, because of who I was and my friends' roles in it. I didn't want to just *go through the motions,* as I was doing, and felt no small measure of guilt about my lack of dedication, but I didn't feel capable of more. Deep down, I wondered if this realm was even worth all the pain I'd been through, let alone the pain I expected was ahead if I entered into this fight.

I steadied myself at the lower altitude, feeling Tyrrik close by my left wing.

Concentrating on the diminutive forms, several seconds of my attention remained fixed before I could accept what I was seeing. Even in my Drae form, my stomach tightened at the sight. I'd believed Verald owned a monopoly on suffering and hardship. The people below appeared barely human. Their hunched and emaciated bodies were twisted and gnarled. Their long stringy hair, all gray, giving them the look of an ancient community of women. Their clothes hung tattered and ill-fitting off their wasted frames.

I would expect more women present than men, given the Emperor's War, but something about the community sent shivers running to the tips of my wings. Were there *no* men?

Tyrrik shifted beside me as a man, distinguishable by his white beard, hobbled from a dilapidated structure in the center of the settlement. The guy was ancient. A woman rushed up to him, and another chased after her, waving her arms.

*Ryn,* Tyrrik called. He dipped down, circling back until he was alongside me.

His voice felt like warm embers, and a strange sense of longing welled from deep within. Irritated, I shoved the emotion away.

*Come on; we're really close now. See the golden energy by those rocks?* I didn't answer, and his tone dropped and was laced with warning when he added, *You don't want to see that.*

*How would you know?* I shot back, gliding off to the side so I could orbit back around the encampment. The golden energy he referenced radiated into the sky, but this was my first glimpse at the neighboring kingdom's people. This wouldn't take more than a few minutes at most. *Have you been in Gemond before?*

*Trust me, you don't want to see what happens next.*

Therein lay our problem. If I could have rolled my Drae eyes at him, I would have because he asked the impossible. Trust was earned, not demanded, and even when earned, trust could be broken rapidly. As he should know.

I kept my gaze on the pocket-sized ancient humans and their pocket-sized problems. One of the women had caught the man by his tattered shirt hem. The man turned and pushed the woman to the ground. The second woman stopped her chase as the man towered over the first. A moment later, a dozen other women came running, and then another dozen shuffled from the tumbledown shelters. They coalesced on the fallen woman with sticks and rocks and even their own bodies, beating her. The second woman hesitated for only a second before joining in.

*Why are they beating her?* My insides chilled as I watched, transfixed by the horror of the scene below. These were Gemondians? I was certain at any minute, the women would stop, that they would come to their senses or someone would control them, but there didn't appear to *be* anyone else. Mother's stories never mentioned Gemond's violent culture. Had their society crumpled under the stress of starvation? Or had their ruler, like our previous king, put his needs above his people's?

Tyrrik's hesitancy leaked through our connection, and I snapped my fangs together. *Why are they beating her?*

*Because she tried to monopolize him. He is their only man.*

*You're kidding, right? He's the only dude, so he gets all the ladies? For real?*

*I don't make their rules, Ryn.*

The horror I felt wasn't Tyrrik's fault, but I couldn't dam the emotion when the tendrils of the woman's screams echoed in my ears. I whipped my tail, a growl swelling in my chest. *They're going to punish her because she wanted to . . . ?*

Tyrrik remained silent, waiting for me to finish my question.

*They're doing that because she wanted to sleep with him?*

*When it wasn't her turn,* he corrected. *Yes.*

*So they'll torture her. All of them on one person.*

He sighed. *Yes. Are you happy now that you know?*

*Would you prefer I bury my head in the sand?* I asked sarcastically. *Why would we seek alliance with these people? People* seemed too generous of a term. This community was filled with the worst kind of animals.

Tyrrik picked up his pace, and I cast a suspicious glance at him and then circled down. My gaze shifted back on the people below as I scanned the settlement anew. Most of the women were dispersing. No, just backing away. Two of them held the unconscious female by the feet and were dragging her across the stony ground toward a ring of large, smooth rocks with a fire pit in the middle.

From the shadowed entrance came yet another woman, though this one had layers of beaded necklaces covering her bare chest. She looked as bad as the rest of the emaciated females, but the way she carried herself indicated rank.

The unconscious woman was dropped inside the ring of rocks, and the leader held her hands high, addressing her horde in a clipped language I couldn't understand. My nostrils twitched at the thin scent of the women's sweat and adrenaline; their overpowering smell was evident from where I soared.

*Let's go, Ryn.* Panic laced Tyrrik's words, snapping me from my transfixed stupor. Then he added, *Please.* He began to circle me, his dark Drae eyes wide, and in their depths, I could not only see, but *feel,* his alarm. His wings beat the air. His tail thrashed in warning.

If he thought I was leaving now, he had another thing coming. Gemondians weren't cute mining dwarfs as I'd thought; they were terrifying. If the people were like this, what was the king like?

*Tell me what's happening.* I batted him with my tail, but he dodged and continued in his tight circles, inching us away from the colony of Gemondians. *Tell me what they're going to do.* I could guess they weren't dragging her to an infirmary. *Are they going to kill her?*

*Please, Princess. I'll tell you everything, but please . . .*

*Because your track record is so great.* The community disappeared behind a ridge of dark rock, and the ravine and its inhabitants disappeared from view as we approached the gold dome. Through the Phaetyn energy, there were trees, but vision wasn't the only heightened sense I now possessed.

I inhaled, grimacing at the taint of smoke. So many scents, but one smell overpowered the rest. The scent of searing meat tickled my nostrils, and I gagged. *Holy-freakin'-Drae.* My stomach roiled as understanding punched me. They were *eating* her.

My mind blanked, my concentration evaporated, and my energy snapped as coherent thought fled my mind.

*Tyrrik,* I called through our connection as spots filled my vision. Something was happening. I couldn't feel my energy. My wings weren't working.

I tumbled from the sky, roaring in panic.

The wind battered my limp limbs, and my roar became a bellow of pain. My heart stopped, skipping as I looked at my hands. My Phaetyn hands.

"Tyrrik," I screamed, my voice disappearing into the rushing air.

A splitting roar filled the air. I plummeted toward the rocks below, sensing Tyrrik's energy blasting toward me as he dove alongside and then catapulted below me.

I shrieked as my body slammed into solid stone. My vision spotted black again, and the pulse of agony made my head spin. The breath whooshed from my lungs, and I retched. A fraction of a second later, I blinked in the darkness. Another fraction later, I understood. I was in Tyrrik's claws. I hadn't hit stone . . . he'd caught me. I sagged into the flesh of his palm just as he crashed into the ground. He'd been too close to the ground to stop his trajectory. *Holy pancakes.*

He screeched beneath me, fire shooting from his Drae mouth into the sky, wings caught between his body and the rocks. One second, I was in his black scaly palm, and the next, I was lying on top of Lord Tyrrik. He gasped, and I scurried off, my mind blank with shock.

"I'm s-sorry," I said, teeth chattering as I backed away from Tyrrik's prostrate form. "I'm so, so . . ."

No. No, no, no. I blinked, trying to clear my tunneled vision. I stared at Tyrrik; my chest hollowed out, and a buzzing filled my ears, numbing my lips and rooting me to the spot. I sucked in a breath, but the air disappeared, and I couldn't catch my breath.

We'd landed a few hundred meters from a lush forest, with golden filaments of energy shrouding the woods, except between us and the trees sat a thick barrier of jutting, stone spikes. Tyrrik lay impaled on a spike on the very edge of the barrier.

I rushed to his side and dropped to my knees as I stared at the jagged piece of rock protruding from above his right breast. I swallowed the sob working its way up my throat and hovered, my hands trembling above the injury. "What have I done?"

Tyrrik gasped again, the wet sucking sound enough to shake me from my stupor.

"Bloody, bloody . . . Tyrrik, what do I do? What . . . ?" My mind refused to catch up. How had this happened? Rocks shouldn't be . . . they shouldn't go through a Drae's chest like that. We were invincible. "Do I pull it out? Do I pull you off?"

His eyes were glassy and unfocused as he continued to gasp with ragged soggy breaths. *Stars above.* He was drowning in his own blood. The thought of him dying like this, dying at all, threatened to tip me over the edge.

"I'm so sorry, Tyrrik." I ran my hand over his face, brushing his lips with my fingertips. I circled so I stood at his head and scooped my hands under the back of his shoulders.

The shard of stone was not even two feet tall. I could do this. *I can't believe I'm about to do this.*

I took a deep breath, and with another whispered apology, I heaved with all my strength. The sickening sound of blood and tearing flesh was all I could hear, and I whimpered.

The blood in his mouth gargled as he wailed. The muscles in his neck tightened, his eyes flooded black, and a moment later, his body went limp. His eyes rolled back in his head, showing only white.

My heart clenched, and I dug my fingers into him as my palms grew slick with sweat. Tears streamed unchecked from my eyes, dripping onto Tyrrik's pale face.

I shuffled to the side and lowered him to the ground. Scooting to his side, I chanted, "Please don't die; please don't die."

Blood, the color of onyx, gushed from his wound, staining the rocky ground.

*I* rested my hands on his scarred chest, and focusing on my fingertips, I called forth the warmth of my Phaetyn power. I closed my eyes, startled when I recognized the green glow near the blue energy of my Drae. I'd seen this vibrant color when I'd gone through the Drae transformation. I gathered the familiar force and directed the power through my hands and into Tyrrik's body, wishing desperately for the blood to congeal and clot. I hiccupped and let my tears fall into his wound, willing his bronze skin to knit together and be whole once more and for the gaping hole in his chest to be gone. I poured my strength into the wound, willing it to heal.

I opened my eyes.

The wound had barely changed.

Tyrrik's head lolled to the side as his wet breathing became shallow, and my small understanding of anatomy told me that his lung had to have been punctured.

How could I heal that? What did his lungs look like on the inside? I had no idea.

"Don't you dare die, Tyrrik. I'm the only one who gets to kill you." The jumble of my emotions for the Drae was irrelevant. I had to save him.

The jagged gash continued to ooze, my Phaetyn-wishing doing nothing.

The memory of our conversation in his room came back to me, followed by our moment in the prison when I'd kissed him. I leaned over him. His eyes were closed, the pallor of his skin a frightening shade of gray. His shallow breath only faint gasps as he clung to life. As I drew closer, the rest of the world fell away.

I brushed his dark hair from his cool brow, streaking his blood across his forehead. My tears dripped on his whiskered cheeks, his pale lips. His dying breath still smelled like the nectar he gave me. I closed my eyes and rested my forehead to his, the temperature of his skin warming beneath me. I let his breath, his skin, his *presence* fill me. And then, I pressed my lips to his.

His lips held the chill of morning air, and despite being soft, they were unmoving beneath mine.

I thought of the times he'd come to me as Tyr to give me food. To dress my wounds. To cover me in blankets. I breathed in through my nose and exhaled into his mouth, pushing my need for him into his lungs. I thought of the lapis-blue color dancing in his scales, the color that matched my own Drae. I thought of the secret gratified emotion as a wisp of power and breathed it into him.

I broke the kiss to let him exhale, but then covered his lips again.

Irdelron had beaten him with a whip dipped in Phaetyn blood when he didn't kill me in the fields. My kiss, my will, had healed him then. I would do it again.

I pushed my healing energy into him, and as I did, my mind's eye noticed a strange presence within him. I searched deeper, flinging out my Phaetyn senses like nets. There were golden droplets through Tyrrik's body. There was light where there should only be dark. The gold was poisoning him, and I knew only one thing could poison a Drae—the spikes were coated with Phaetyn blood—Tyrrik was dying.

I systematically moved through his body, using my Phaetyn ability to sear away the gold drops. I worked, losing track of all time, until I eventually came to his heart. My lips quivered where they were pressed to his. His heart was *covered* in a golden film as though the droplets had converged there and grown into the organ like roots. I thought of my heart pumping blood through my body, the loud pounding in my chest, the roaring in my ears. I thought of my power in him and willed the healing force I barely understood to fill him, to replace what he'd lost all over the slick ground beneath us. I pushed the green energy into him, surrounded the film around his heart with the vibrant intensity, and squeezed the Phaetyn power as if it were the shell of a nut. The golden roots fractured and fizzled, loosening their grip as they broke into pieces.

With a gasp, I broke the kiss, my head spinning. Tyrrik's head lolled to one side again.

Blinking to clear my vision, I listened to his thin heartbeat and willed it to match mine. He exhaled again, this time more breath than the last, and I could feel his heart beating against my palm.

Whatever Phaetyn reserves were within me, they were seriously depleted. I was scraping at the barrel, but I knew if one drop of the gold barrier stayed, Tyrrik was dead.

Steadying myself, I gently brought his head back to the center and sealed our lips again. Envisioning the blue flame deep within my core, I stoked the power of my Phaetyn energy and pushed, no gushed, this force into Tyrrik, bathing him inside and out with my healing force. Tyrrik was Drae, dark and warm like night; his heart had to reflect this. A sharp pain stabbed at my temples, but I doubled my efforts as I saw the golden beads dissolving and even held fast when Tyrrik arched off the ground. I burned away everything, every single piece of poisonous gold, until everything was dark and warm once more.

I slumped against Tyrrik. The sun beat down on us, and the cool mountain air had warmed at some point. I'd faded out, exhausted by the expenditure of energy. I huddled against Tyrrik, tears slipping down my cheeks into his clothing. How had that happened so fast? One moment we'd been flying, and the next, Tyrrik was nearly dead. I should have listened to him and not looked. I hadn't known that seeing what those women did would snap me out of my Drae form. Had Tyrrik realized? Why didn't he just tell me the risk?

The wound was still there but much smaller and no longer a hole all the way through him. The lesion still oozed blood but at a much slower pace.

I could barely keep my eyes open, and the thought of willing *anything* seemed insurmountable. But he wasn't even conscious, and he was still bleeding. My mind raced for another option. I discarded trying more tears on the wound because there was something stronger . . . King Irdelron drank Phaetyn blood from his golden vial.

I picked up a stone, breaking the brittle shard so one side had a sharp edge. I sliced the rock through the meat of my palm and stared as blue-tinged blood dripped out. I pushed the gash to his chest, mixing our blood. His confidence that I couldn't hurt him better be right. I waited, staring at the wound, hoping for a miracle. Was he getting better? The wound seemed smaller. I looked at my palm and swore. My palm had healed; Tyrrik had not.

I cut my palm deeper this time, squeezing the blood into his wound. My heart pounded in my ears as my blood oozed, and I dripped it into the deep erosion. I wiped at his blood with the bottom edge of my aketon, trying to see if anything was helping. I sobbed as the width and depth of the lesion waned. The tissue fused, the terrible, punctured injury melding together.

I swallowed the lump at the back of my throat. Tyrrik was still out of it, and he'd lost so much blood. How much blood could a Drae lose and still live?

I didn't stop until Tyrrik's skin had knit together into a pale line. I sagged against him, head pounding, vision blurry. Wavering, I lay my head on his chest, concentrating, and hiccupped again when I heard his heartbeat. The rate was steady but slow. His respirations weren't wet anymore, and although they were slow, his breaths were deeper.

My lips trembled, and I heaved a sigh. Not dead. I closed my eyes and whispered, "Please be okay."

The sky was dark and the air crisp when I awoke. Our twin moons provided the only light, hugging high in the blackness. My body was stiff and achy, and my disorientation disappeared as soon as Tyrrik shifted beside me.

He groaned, and I sat bolt upright.

"*Drak*," I mumbled, shaking off the lingering fogginess. I ran my hands over his now perfectly smooth chest, assuring myself his wound hadn't opened again. "Tyrrik," I said in a tight voice. "You're al'right?"

He chuckled wearily, a low throaty sound of warm embers. "Just weak. Are you okay, Khosana?"

A tear slipped from my eye, emotions breaking away from my control. "You're worried about me? I nearly killed you."

His eyes found mine, slightly unfocused. "You've been Drae less than three days; the fault was mine. I should've been clearer. You saved my life."

I sniffed, nodding my head, my chest heaving. "I thought you were dying."

Smiling, he tugged on my hand, and I let him pull me down. Resting my head on his chest, shoulders still shaking, I listened to the steady thumping of his heart as I absorbed what he'd said. "What happened to the rocks here? Why are they covered in Phaetyn blood?"

"Maybe it's how the Phaetyn protect their forest." Tyrrik ran his hand over my hair, trailing his fingers down my back.

Welcome to Zivost forest.

Tyrrik's touch was a major breach in our boundaries, but I was too tired to care. In fact, if I was honest, I craved reassurance right now. "You really would've died?"

His face was painted with gore, but when he smiled, my heart lifted.

"I was dying, Ryn. You saved me."

I harrumphed and patted his chest through his torn and bloody aketon. With a deep breath, I sat up and said, "I figured I owed you."

"How are you feeling?" Tyrrik asked, sitting and wincing with the movement.

I grimaced, watching him. I hadn't almost died, so I had no idea why he was asking me. "Al'right. How are you?"

He smiled sardonically. "About how you'd expect. I'll not be much help today I'm afraid." Tyrrik shifted on the shale, the rocks rubbing against each other, and winced again. "I need to stand up; my ass is numb."

I held my hand up to stop him from saying anything else. "I did not need to know that." I stood, stretching more, and my muscles loosened. "I'm guessing I'm not getting steak today." I pointed at the woods on the other side of the rock wall. "How do we get into the forest?"

Tyrrik watched me with hooded eyes. "I'm not sure. Will you help me up?"

His words were a punch to my gut, and I spun to face him. "You can't stand?"

One glance at his stained and torn tunic, his still pale skin underneath, and his trembling hands told me he really wasn't healed. "Didn't I heal you?" I thought of our kiss and brought my fingers to my lips. Blushing, I wondered if he knew how I'd healed him. "Did it not work?"

He tilted his head and raised his eyebrows. "No, you did more than I could've imagined possible." He frowned. "Truly."

I helped him stand and, less than a minute later, helped him sit back down because he was too weak to maintain standing.

Tyrrik scrubbed at his face and dropped his head in his hands.

"What do you need?" I asked. Guilt churned in my gut, making me nauseated, and the hollowness in my chest was an ache I deserved. I'd almost killed him.

"Nothing," he answered. "I'm just exhausted. I-I . . . It's going to take me a little time to heal." He grimaced. "A long time, judging by how I feel. I've never been injured this badly."

I shook my head. "We can't stay here for a long time. We need to meet Dyter and . . ." What was his name? "The Phaetyn guy."

Tyrrik quirked an eyebrow, drawing a reluctant smile out of me.

"What can I do to help you heal?" My feelings for Tyrrik were a tangled mess, and seeing as I'd only admitted there *was* a tangled mess, I wasn't yet sure I wanted to sort those feelings out. My chest clenched as I recalled the rock splicing through his right shoulder.

He sighed. "Kissing me might help."

My heart thumped in my chest, and I blinked. "Are you serious?"

The prospect excited me more than it should, though witnessing Tyrrik nearly die had brought more dread than I'd expected too. I scowled as a smirk lifted the corner of his full mouth.

He reached into his pocket and drew out the ruby, extending the gem toward me as he said, "You shifted."

"I also lost control." I felt guilty, but I also really wanted the pretty gem. I accepted it with a smile, and tucked the ruby next to the gold trinket in my tunic. A deal was a deal.

"You earned it." He groaned and lay flat on the rocky ground.

The first moment I got, I was going to inspect my shiny objects side by side, but for now . . . "Tyrrik, seriously, what do you need? I want to help."

He said with a sigh, "I need to eat and sleep. I'm whole; you healed me. But I need to regain stamina."

85

"What if I get some water? Will you teach me how to make nectar? Would that help?"

He blinked, and his nervousness coursed through our bond. "Yes. That would help. But I don't have a waterskin."

I grinned and held up the empty one he'd given me before we took off. "Good thing I have mine. Just point me in the direction of water and Ryn the . . ." I wasn't useless any more. I was . . . "*Fearless shall provide.*"

"Ryn the Fearless has forgotten about her new Drae senses," he drawled, tapping his nose.

*Oh, yeah.* I tilted my head back, feeling the ripple of my silver hair down my back, closed my eyes, and sniffed. No good. My attention was too divided. I let the chirping and chittering of the small animals in the surrounding area fade and forced myself to tune out Tyrrik's quickened breathing too. *Water, water, water.*

I sniffed again and pulled in a long inhale. Now that my other senses were muted, I focused on the scents assailing me. Tyrrik's pine needle, smoke, and steel aroma overwhelmed everything else.

*Hot potatoes,* he smelled so good. I opened my eyes and glared at him, clambering to my feet. "I can't smell anything with you near."

He lifted his head and peeled his eyelids back for a brief moment. With a small smile, he asked, "Why are you still sniffing then?"

I caught myself mid-inhale. *Because you smell amazing.* There was no way I was going to tell him that. Oh wait, maybe I just did. *Drak.* "Umm," I mumbled, trying to cover my thoughts. "Allergies."

He snorted as he shifted on the shale, obviously not believing my lie.

As he closed his eyes, Tyrrik murmured, "Right."

I didn't bother responding. I turned my attention to the ground and wobbled off down the row of sharp pikes. As I got farther away from the deadly rocks, I noticed the spikes extended all around the forest in a wide, sharp band, creating a deadly barrier.

"I don't think they want visitors," I mumbled to myself. Clearly, the Phaetyn weren't the welcoming type Kamoi portrayed them to be. Still, with someone like Emperor Draedyn around, I couldn't blame them.

About a hundred paces away from the Drae, I closed my eyes. Pushing away the constant barrage of information from my skin, ears, and eyes, I inhaled again. Sorting through the smells away from Tyrrik proved much easier, and the crisp, clear scent of water sang to me.

"There's water just over that way," I shouted back to him, pointing away from the wall of death.

He called in a dry voice that barely reached me, despite my super sensitive hearing, "I know."

I wrinkled my nose but said nothing. *Sure,* he'd known, and *I* was an egg with five yolks. I'd ignore his haughty attitude and lack of gratitude. Being Ryn the Fearless also meant being the bigger person. I could give the win to others on occasion—I could be gracious. I took another deep breath as I trudged over the rocks like a lumbering mule. Life as a hero wasn't all it was cracked up to be, but I could roll.

Setting out in the opposite direction to the forest and its morbid welcoming mat, I walked, swinging the empty skin, and my weary muscles slowly released their tension and woke up. As I continued picking through the rocks, my stiffness disappeared, and my usual energy emerged. I recovered enough that I stopped walking like I was riding a horse, too, so everything was on the up and up. I glanced back at Tyrrik. He was still lying right where I'd left him, looking pretty much dead.

"Good, good." I gave myself an inane pep talk, not believing a word of it.

I rounded a mound of large boulders, and the pointy rocks and lush forest were lost from view. My ears twitched at the faint trickle of water ahead. I sniffed, and my mouth watered. Oh yeah, there was water ahead, and for some reason it smelled *really* good.

I climbed up the side of the hill a short way, and a few boulder mounds later, about a quarter of the way up, I crouched by a thin stream squeezing out from between two bulky rocks. My eyes followed the filter of water where it continued down the slope, branching and twisting toward the wall of death. I squinted, focusing on where the water ran down, disappearing into the spiked rocks, in the direction of the forest.

I filled the waterskin and guzzled the contents before re-filling it. The water wouldn't sate my hunger for long, but it was all I had for now.

After taking care of my other business—that a woman didn't want to do in close range of a man with heightened senses—I made my way back to Tyrrik.

The morning rays lit the sky, even though the sun still hid among the Gemond mountains. More light painted the horror of yesterday, vividly displaying the dried evidence all around the Drae.

"Hey," I said, approaching him with forced cheeriness. "I found water."

He didn't reply, but his chest rose and fell in steady rhythm, my only reassurance he wasn't dead. I sighed as I sat down next to him and mumbled, "Guess I'm making nectar on my own."

I uncorked the waterskin and stuck my forefinger in the hole, wiggling the digit around and thinking of nectar and Tyrrik being better as I hummed. Removing my finger, I sniffed at the contents. Still water, *delicious* water . . . Did its mouth-watering scent have something to do with the forest?

This nectar thing wasn't as clear cut as I'd thought. I cracked my neck while I contemplated how I might get the water to change. Clearing my throat, I chanted, "Water, water, in the skin, turn to nectar and I'll . . ." I paused, thinking hard for a suitable rhyming word. "Grin, win, thin . . . din?"

"What are you doing?" Tyrrik asked.

I yelped and threw the skin in the air. The liquid, *still* water, spilled over the rocks. Face burning, I scurried to pick the waterskin up, taking my time re-corking it before turning back toward the Drae.

"Umm . . . making nectar?" I squeaked.

The silence behind me was suspicious. Had he fallen asleep again?

I glanced over my shoulder to find Tyrrik wide awake, his expression smooth like when we were in the Quota Fields. Except his lip twitched and his eyes were watering.

"Are you okay?" I asked, crossing to him. Was he going delirious? Was that even possible?

"Fine," he wheezed, and his hand twitched.

He didn't sound fine, more like he'd lose consciousness any moment. I waggled the waterskin over him. "Any pointers on making Drae juice? You said that would help."

Tyrrik shut his eyes, shifting on the flat rock. "Yes. Put your finger in—"

"Tried that."

Several moments passed before he continued. "And think of how much you want to help me. Remember you just need to will it."

"I did," I growled and then scrunched my nose at my own hypocrisy. Sure, I'd saved Tyrrik's life. And yeah, in the moment, with blood everywhere and his sputtering breathing, I'd been frantic to save him. But most of the time, I didn't want his help; I wasn't even sure I wanted to be near him, yet part of me felt like I may need him. This Drae business was serious, what with turning into a Drae and making nectar. And, the sparkly object obsession . . . I absently patted my pocket to make sure I still had my trinkets. So, to sit under the sun now, when the danger was past, and to not only say I wanted to, but truly feel a *sincere* desire to . . . help Tyrrik? He'd callously broken my heart, and I wasn't sure I could ever forgive him.

Did I want to help him?

With a sigh, I uncorked the flagon and dipped my pinky inside. *I want to help Tyrrik; I want to help Tyrrik.* I sniffed the flagon and sighed again.

"Maybe you could try another poem?" Tyrrik murmured, his eyes still closed.

"You *did* hear," I said, aghast. How mortifying.

89

He didn't answer.

I scowled because there was no way he'd been sleep-talking just now. I was beginning to understand that the Lord Drae possessed a wicked sense of humor, one which reminded me of . . . my dungeon buddy, Ty.

My heart gave a sharp pang. His humor reminded me of Ty because Ty's humor had come from Tyrrik. Admitting that the characteristics of Ty and Tyr were real parts of the Drae scraped at a barely-healed wound. After just a few days in the Drae's company, the gaping wound *had* begun to heal. I sat dumbfounded with my finger in the flagon as my heart told my head what it hadn't yet acknowledged. I knew why he did those things; I mean, I knew *why* on a surface level. If I had been in his shoes, how far would I have gone to break the blood oath with Irdelron? But I wanted to know why the Drae manipulated me in the way he had. Why get me to fall in love with Tyr when Ty would've sufficed?

Until I had an actual explanation and apology from him, there would always be something between us. But did that mean I wanted him hurt? I took a deep breath and let my heart answer. No. Not anymore.

"That's it," Tyrrik croaked.

I frowned at the waterskin. "Really?"

"It will just smell like water to you, but I can smell the difference, just as you can smell the *výživa* I make for you."

"Nectar!" I announced, bounding to my feet, taking his word for it. If all it took was me wanting to heal him, I'd probably created the most potent nectar ever. "I have glorious nectar for you. Ryn the Fearless has provided for the incredibly weak, once again!"

Tyrrik dragged an eyelid open. His skin was sallow, and the coloring under his eyes appeared bruised. He really didn't look great. I'm sure blood loss did that to a person . . . or a Drae. I should get some of the nectar into him pronto.

I cupped the back of his head and lifted, holding the waterskin to his lips and tipping a small amount in. The muscles in his neck worked as he swallowed. I repeated the process, tipping in as much as he could handle, and then lowered his head.

He rested his hand on mine as I made to re-cork the skin.

"Thank you for making me *výživa*," he whispered. "It is a great gift."

I swallowed, staring at his forehead as I answered, "Don't mention it. I hope it helps you heal."

I met his eyes, and my breath caught at the blazing darkness there.

"Nothing has ever tasted so sweet," he said in a rough voice.

His smoky scent surrounded me. My heart skipped a beat, and my mouth dried. I might want him healed, but I wasn't going to let him hurt me again. I wriggled my hand out of his grip as my cheeks warmed. "Okay, right. Swell. *Great.*"

I searched for somewhere else to look and bit my lip, but my gaze returned to Tyrrik like a stupid magpie to a stupid glinting object. I rationalized my reaction by telling myself I was just checking to see if he was still awake, but his eyes were dark pools of secrets, and I couldn't stop the desire to know their depths. Shouting caught my attention, and I reeled away from Tyrrik's hypnotizing eyes and shot to my feet.

"People are here," I said, enormously relieved at the timely interruption until I realized *people* were here. I whirled toward the voices and squeaked, "People are here."

"Get behind me." Tyrrik slurred from the ground.

"Uh-huh." There's no way he had enough strength to protect anyone, not even himself.

I narrowed my gaze across the pointy rocks to a band of five hooded figures on the other side. Five against one . . . and a quarter, *maybe* a quarter. Not ideal. Should I change into my Drae form? I straightened, and relief washed through me when the group pushed off their hoods. "Dyter."

"Ryn!" he yelled.

Just seeing him made me feel better. My gaze shifted, and I met

Kamoi's intense gaze as he removed his hood. He stood beside Dyter, silver hair lit from the sun, glowing like a halo. He waved.

"It's friends," I said over my shoulder to Tyrrik, still studying the rest of the party. I didn't recognize the other Phaetyn with the rest of our traveling party, but my heart leaped as I took in their violet eyes and silver hair across the lethal rocks between us. I lifted a hand and waved back at Kamoi. His mouth moved, and I tried to focus my hearing to catch what he said, but Tyrrik was right; I'd clearly need to practice engaging my senses more.

However, I didn't have long to wonder what he'd said. With a grand wave of his arm, a three-meter section of the rocks in front of Kamoi sunk into the soil as easily as a cat's retracting claws.

13

The party began to cross, and I was mesmerized by the four Phaetyn. They didn't walk; they *glided*. Dressed in shining aketons with braided leather belts hanging low on their hips, two carried bows, and another a spear. Kamoi's hands were empty, and where the other Phaetyn glided, he appeared to be floating. Dyter lumbered toward us with thudding steps that made me smile.

"You found us," I said, stating the obvious as I threw my arms around him.

Dyter patted me on the back and said gruffly, "We expected you a day ago. We were waiting farther east, but the scouts here rode to Kamoi when they saw two Drae plummeting from the sky."

"That was us," I said with a nod.

He rolled his eyes. "I gathered. We rode through the night to reach you here. What happened?"

I wasn't sure what to say to that, so I redirected the conversation. "Thank the moons you got here so fast. We wouldn't have been able to move until Tyrrik healed." I glanced at the Drae. "Oh, he's lost consciousness again." My heart flipped. *Again.* I was diseased; that had to be the reason.

I turned to check him, but Prince Kamoi caught my hand and pulled me back. "What happened?"

His skin was warm on mine, and a pleasant current passed between us. I flashed him a small smile, which faded as I came back to my senses. I withdrew my hand and gave the group a quick recount, noticing the other Phaetyn's deference to Kamoi.

Kamoi spotted my divided attention and swept an arm toward the other Phaetyn. As I looked closer, I could distinguish there were two females and a male. All three were beautiful, but the men were masculine and muscular with broad shoulders, and the female had definite feminine curves. "Tamah, Makoa, and Akani are part of the guard on the southern side of the forest." He faced the other Phaetyn, drawing me forward. "This is Ryn," he announced. "She is one of us."

The violet eyes of the tallest female Phaetyn widened. "Where have you been? How is such a thing possible?"

Kamoi looked down at me, his eyes searching my face, shaking his head slightly. "I plan to discuss this with our elders, but her existence is surely a miracle."

A weary groan sounded behind us, and I extracted myself from the prince's intense attention and crouched by Tyrrik's side. "He needs rest and food. He's been in and out of it this morning."

Kamoi frowned and walked to the pointed rock tip with the Drae's black blood still staining the rocks around us. "He landed on this?"

*Mistress Moons.* That rock tip was ghastly. The last several hours flashed through my mind, and my stomach turned. I rested my hand on Tyrrik's chest, assuring myself he was alive. "Yes. It took everything I had to heal him."

Kamoi froze, and the other Phaetyn turned toward me with their mouths agape. After a beat of silence, Kamoi asked, "You healed the Drae of a Phaetyn wound?" When I nodded, he asked, "How?"

I cleared my throat, tucking my silver hair behind my ear. I wasn't admitting I'd kissed the Drae. "Oh, bit of this, bit of that."

Dyter quirked his brow, and I knew he'd try to pry the information from me later. *Too bad, old man.* I took one of Tyrrik's arms and bent my knees before pulling him up so he was draped over my shoulders. I grinned at the look on my old mentor's face. "I'm stronger now."

"Clearly," he said after a pause. "I can't wait until we can catch up."

I wasn't sure if he was saying he had something to tell me or he just wanted me to tell him, so I shrugged, adjusting Tyrrik's weight.

Kamoi neared, his handsome face marred by an apologetic frown. "I'm afraid the Drae will not be able to enter the forest. Zivost is protected against our natural enemy."

Dyter's face turned stony, and he said, "You never made mention of that before."

"The Drae knew it," the prince replied with a shrug. "There is nothing of light within him, so he'll not be able to pass through the barrier. You and Ryn will only be able to cross because you possess something of life within you. Though I'd still like to test Ryn before she enters the forest. I don't know what problems her Drae nature may create."

Tyrrik groaned again, his head dangling over my left shoulder, and I just stood dumbstruck. He'd known Drae couldn't enter the forest? That he'd have to stay outside when we got here? Why did he bring me?

"We can't leave him while he's injured," Dyter said, interrupting my thoughts. "We'll have to stay out here until he's able to protect himself."

"I won't leave him out here," I said. "The emperor has been patrolling the skies."

Kamoi's brow wrinkled. "I see. Then I propose this. Dyter, if you and two of my guards wish to remain here with Tyrrik, Akani and I can escort Ryn into the heart of Zivost. Your party can join us in a few days."

Dyter began to nod, but I interrupted. "Nope. I'll be staying with Tyrrik until he's healed. He needs another Drae here to help make this nectar stuff." I shook my head at their inquiring glances. "I can't leave him. Either Dyter, Tyrrik, and I all come in, or we all stay out."

There was no way I'd enter that forest without Dyter *and* Tyrrik around. As much as Kamoi was hotness incarnate, Mum would've skinned me alive to hear I'd gone off with some boy alone.

After a few more attempts to convince me, the prince sighed. "I'm warning you, an attempt to take him in will likely hurt him further, but if you insist."

We crossed through the thick rocky barrier that had nearly killed Tyrrik, and I wondered how easily the rock pikes could slide back up through the soil to impale us. I was fairly certain I wouldn't be hurt, but I'd already witnessed the damage the pikes could do to Tyrrik. I never wanted to see anything like that ever again.

Once we crossed the barrier and neared the forest, Dyter helped me lower Tyrrik to the ground.

Kamoi pointed to the closest tree. "Rest your hand here."

"Will it hurt?" I asked. I'd become well enough acquainted with pain to want to know if more was coming.

He deliberated. "You'll know as soon as you touch it."

*Awesome.* I edged to the tree and steadied myself. I could do this. If it hurt, I'd just break contact. I was in control. I'd be fine-a-roo. Swallowing my fear, I slapped a hand on the tree.

Nothing happened to begin with, but after a moment, a delicious cooling sensation swept up my arm to the crown of my head and down to where my booted feet were planted on the ground. I shivered, eyeing the Phaetyn's bare feet. No wonder they didn't wear shoes when the forest felt like this, like the trees were *alive.* A welcoming joy radiated through me, and I grinned at Dyter as I dropped my hand to my side.

Dyter gave me a one-sided grimace, the odd look that meant someone was short a few acorns.

I wrinkled my nose in response and tipped my head toward the tree. Obviously, he didn't feel the emotion. The happiness of the forest tickled my skin, whispering secrets into my ear. Just from one touch. I wanted to sit down and hug the tree and let it share its wisdom with me.

Dyter cleared his throat, tilting his head at Tyrrik.

"Al'right, now for Tyrrik," I said, still in a bit of a daze.

Dyter helped me maneuver the Drae, not that I wasn't strong enough, but bodies were awkward to carry. Even with his missing arm, Dyter helped pull Tyrrik so his body was flopped over my shoulder.

Kamoi gestured to the tree in invitation, teeth gleaming in a smile that reminded me the Phaetyn and Drae were not friends.

Dyter followed as I lugged the Drae to the edge of the forest. With a deep breath but no other ceremony, I took him inside the tree line.

Nothing happened, and gasps rose behind us.

"It works?" I asked with a smile as I grasped our triumph. I wondered if the trees would help him feel better too. "Let's try the tree."

I turned and then let Tyrrik slide to the ground. As soon as I stepped away, he contorted violently, frothing at the mouth as he seized.

I fell to my knees and made to roll him out of the trees, but as soon as my hands touched Tyrrik, his agonized movements halted. *What the hay?*

"Your touch is enough to grant him entry," Kamoi said in awe.

When I looked up at the Phaetyn, I could see in the furrow on his brow . . . he wasn't happy about that revelation. Seeing as Drae were Phaetyn's natural enemies, I couldn't blame him.

I stared at my hand on Tyrrik's chest. "How does that work?"

The prince stared down at my hand, too, eyes flickering. "I imagine it has something to do with your Phaetyn lineage."

Had Kamoi suspected I could do this? Confusion tangled my mind and thoughts. Was there more he wasn't telling me, or had my time in the prison made me suspect everyone of deceit?

Dyter crouched, the ropey scar on his cheek pulling as he squinted at Tyrrik. "He can enter the forest, Rynnie, but it's not practical for you to have your hand on him the entire time. We might be here for several weeks."

"Several weeks, at least," Kamoi quickly agreed. His violet gaze settled on me and then drifted to my mouth.

I couldn't make sense of the Phaetyn prince, so I turned to the only person I knew I could trust. "I can't leave him out here, Dyter. He saved my life; I can't leave him until I know he's better."

One of the Phaetyn coughed, and I looked up in time to catch Kamoi making a sharp gesture in her direction.

"What is it?" I asked, gaze narrowing as my frustration mounted.

The female Phaetyn bowed her head to Kamoi and made no answer.

I was done. The last two days had exhausted my quota of turd shoveling. I didn't care how much we needed the Phaetyn later; right now Tyrrik needed me. And, though the Drae was a twat, like full on turd-twat, I wasn't abandoning him. I was sick of repeating myself, sick of deciphering hidden meanings, and sick of trying to guess who I could trust.

I scooped under Tyrrik's arms and pulled him out of the woods. Once he was safe, I stood and, with my hands on my hips, squared off with the Phaetyn. "Is there something I should know, Kamoi? Because even my Phaetyn side is sick of games."

His violet eyes flared, and his jaw clenched before he broke off the contact. "If you can get the Drae to our city, *Kanahele o keola*, he'll be okay."

"Wh—?" I stumbled over the Phaetyn city name before dismissing it in favor of Phaetynville. But I needed to understand what this power was, and how it was affecting Tyrrik. I wasn't getting him in there just to have him froth up again. "Why will he be okay in . . . your city? What's so special there?"

Kamoi's expression closed down, his lips pursed, and his nostrils flared.

Dyter touched my elbow, saying in a low voice that everyone could still hear, "I don't believe Prince Kamoi wishes the workings of Zivost Forest to be known to an outsider."

Dyter pointed at himself and tilted his head to Tyrrik. Dyter pushed to his feet, his single hand on his knee. He crossed over to the Phaetyn and said, "Prince Kamoi, I believe Lord Tyrrik will prove a great ally in the months to come."

Dyter was being way more diplomatic than I would be, but his words reminded me of the other reason for our visit here. Alliances were important, immensely so, if my friends were going to be successful against Emperor Draedyn. I took a deep breath and waited for Kamoi to say something.

"If he causes any trouble, no matter how minor, he will be escorted out of the forest and left." Kamoi frowned first at Dyter and then at me, though the prince didn't meet my eyes. "We'll leave him, no matter how strong he is."

The silence that fell between us was rife with tension. My heart pounded, and my instinct was to give the Phaetyn another piece of my mind. But I watched Dyter nod and followed suit.

The prince entered the forest before us while Dyter and I trailed after with Tyrrik in tow.

The trunks of the trees in Zivost Forest were thick, brown, and spaced several paces apart, with smaller trees between them. There were a few species I recognized—ash, elm, and cedar—and others I'd never seen before. Some with white bark and others more grayish-green. Sunlight streamed through the luscious canopy in glittering beams, creating a spattering of spots over the rooted, leaf-littered ground.

Less than fifty meters into the vibrant trees was a small clearing, and four pristine white horses stood, pawing at the ground. Kamoi approached them and spoke in a hushed voice.

"Is he al'right?" Dyter asked me, pointing at Tyrrik.

I glanced at the Drae and grimaced. "I'm not sure. Lay him down; let's give him more nectar before we head off."

I woke up Tyrrik, relieved to see his eyes flutter open. I kept my hands on his chest as Dyter trickled more sweet fluid into the Drae's mouth.

"What's happening?" Tyrrik slurred.

"We're safe," I replied, watching him swallow the nectar and feeling the steady thump of his heart under my hand. "We're in the forest now." His heartbeat calmed my nerves, and I matched my breathing to the rise and fall of his chest.

Tyrrik managed to drag his eyelids open once to look at me before he lost the battle again.

"His strength is depleted," Kamoi said as he approached. "This occasionally happens to my people, too. He will require much rest." He touched my shoulder and offered a small smile. "But he'll be okay."

My shoulders relaxed, but I wasn't quite ready to forgive the prince. Still, my mum raised me right, so I gave the Phaetyn a tight smile. "Thank you."

The Phaetyn stood over me silently until Dyter corked the waterskin.

Kamoi said, "I'm sorry I snapped at you, Ryn. I lost my temper, and it was wrong of me to take it out on you. The Phaetyn and Drae have bad blood between them. If you tell me Lord Tyrrik is trustworthy, I believe you. I didn't mean to slight him."

I looked up and met his direct gaze and the sincerity shining in his violet eyes.

"And definitely not you," the prince added with a small smile.

14

*H*arder than tipping nectar into the Drae's mouth was getting him onto a horse without losing contact. I stood and helped lift Tyrrik upright and then climbed onto the horse while holding his hand. Then I leaned down, straightening as Kamoi and Dyter lifted the Drae and draped him in front of me and over the steed. I felt the warmth of his body where he overlapped on the tops of my knees.

"Tamah, Makoa, please resume your posts here," Kamoi ordered. "Akani will escort us in and return tomorrow morning."

The two Phaetyn dipped their heads and strode out toward the edges of the forest, facing the deadly wall and the brutal landscape just outside.

My horse trotted after the others with Dyter plodding behind on his horse.

"Dyter," I called back. "What do you know of the Gemond King?" Now that the danger to Tyrrik had passed, and we were heading toward safety, my mind wandered back to what had caused all of this trouble in the first place.

"Can't say I speak to many Gemondians, but those I do make no complaint against him. Their kingdom is a hungry kingdom, as

Verald was. Those of their people who joined the rebellion were those wishing to overthrow the emperor."

There he went again with the talk of overthrowing the emperor. I'd seen hundreds of rebels die in a single jet of Drae flame. How could Dyter even talk about another attempt so soon? I had just transformed, and Tyrrik—being nearly one hundred and ten years of age—possessed much more control and power. How much control and power did the emperor possess? If power increased with age, he would be tough to beat.

"I saw something before we fell," I said, running my thumb over Tyrrik's back. "There was a tribe of elderly Gemondian women fighting over a male, and the others . . . *ate* one of the women when she tried to take the man for herself." Bile rose in my throat just thinking about it. "How could that happen? How could a king allow that kind of atrocity? Does he know that happens, and he does nothing? And, if he doesn't know . . . how could he not know? They are his people, Dyter."

Dyter took a deep breath, forehead wrinkling. He pursed his lips while he contemplated and then said, "We do not know much of Gemond, Ryn. We do not know the circumstances."

I blinked several times as his words sunk in. I set my jaw, and with a shake of my head, I said, "I know what I saw."

I thought of the people of Verald, and I couldn't conceive of any reason they would debase themselves to cannibalism. But the women in the Gemondian camp didn't seem to share my view. I couldn't make sense of their madness.

The smaller trees disappeared as the canopy grew thicker from the foliage of the larger trees. Our horses wound between the enormous trunks in single file. I assumed the Phaetyn knew where we were going because the spots of sunlight beaming through the canopy disappeared, and only filtered light trickled through. It was impossible to use the sun's position as a guide, and that would only help if I knew which direction we were supposed to be going.

I checked Tyrrik and shifted my legs as much as his weight

allowed. The restlessness of my mind made no sense. "Tell me of Gemond, Dyter. Please."

I couldn't shake my repulsion over what I'd seen, and to me, the Gemond King and the emperor were pretty much on equal footing in terms of horrors induced on the helpless. Dyter couldn't ask one villain to join his team against another.

"You know their kingdom is nestled deep in the Gemond Mountains at the northern tip of the realm?"

I nodded as his voice carried forward to me.

"They're miners. They excavate everything from minerals, various rock, and precious gems. But, like we in Verald, the hunting of the Phaetyn resulted in the slow death of their kingdom. Their land is stripped just like Verald. Their population has also suffered loss—there are more women than men."

I nodded. I understood all of that. We might grow some plants on our own, but the way Dyter spoke of Gemond, it didn't seem that much different than Verald.

"Their society does have some distinct differences."

"You mean besides eating each other?" I muttered.

Dyter continued as if I hadn't spoken. "Gemond is a polygamous society. Rather than have large numbers of single and widowed women, they adopted polygamy. It's been that way for years . . . as long as I can remember."

That was nothing like Verald. The idea of sharing—I sucked in a deep breath and realized I was gripping Tyrrik's aketon. I forced myself to relax my hold as I thought of the rationale of that type of society. Was that worse than what I'd seen growing up? With the ratios of men to women, maybe not.

"But you're referencing their eating habits, I assume."

*Eating habits?* "That's putting cannibalism mildly."

"As I understand it," he said, ignoring my quip, "In a bid to keep his people fed and his kingdom viable, King Zuli decreed women over the age of fifty and men over the age of seventy would have to leave the kingdom proper. Only those who can reproduce are kept fed by the kingdom; the rest are escorted into the depths of the

Gemond Mountains to live out their remaining days as best they can."

My mouth dropped open. "That's *horrible*. He throws out the old people? How could he do such a thing? How can their families bear it?"

"I don't know, Rynnie," Dyter said softly. "King Zuli was the first king to institute the practice, and he left when he turned seventy, just like the others. His son, Zakai, is the king now."

Obviously the king of Gemond was a monster, and his son was equally insane. Just as ours had been, a power-hungry tyrant who cared for no one.

As I sat simmering in anger, Kamoi called back to us, "Another two hours, and we shall reach the heart of Zivost and our people."

*Our people.* The two words pulled me from my darkening thoughts. I was going to meet my people and learn Phaetyn ways. Maybe Kamoi could teach me how to make things grow without my spit or blood. That would be handy when I went back to Verald . . . or maybe while I was here by Gemond. "Will you teach me how to do the plant stuff?" I called ahead. "Like how can I make things grow, and how do we replenish the land? Oh, and can you explain the healing mojo, how that works?"

The two Phaetyn winced though the prince turned to me. With his features settled into a weary expression, he replied, "Yes, Ryn. Power like yours could do much good if properly honed. We will teach you all we can."

*All we can.* "Can't you teach me everything?"

Kamoi shifted in his saddle, facing back to the front, but not before I caught sight of his frown.

"Can't you?" I pressed.

His voice was tight as his words floated back to me. "I'm afraid only time will tell us that."

---

THE AIR in the middle of the Zivost forest smelled of mint, pine, and citrus; the scent calming and clean. The clearing looked like a cross-section of the Market Circuit back in Verald—stalls of produce were interspersed with artisan crafts: ceramic bowls, tapestries, woven baskets, and bolts of fabrics in natural hues.

The Phaetyn varied in size and shape, but none appeared sickly or wan. Their pale skin practically glowed, and their glistening silver hair hung straight and lustrous; most of the men wore their hair pulled back at the napes of their necks while the women wore their locks loose.

As we passed, the murmur of their voices followed. Despite the melodic sound, there was a clipped edge to their whispered conversations. Many violet eyes widened as Kamoi escorted us toward a large tree in the center of the clearing in Zivost, or Phaetynville—as I'd dubbed it.

"What are they saying?" I asked Dyter. As if he would know.

He rolled his eyes at me, and I responded with a one-shouldered shrug. I couldn't help my instinct to ask him. Until recently, I'd always assumed Dyter knew everything in the realm. In reality, he probably still knew way more than me.

I shifted Tyrrik's body again. Despite his leanness, the Drae was heavy and his weight was putting my legs to sleep.

I met the gaze of a female Phaetyn around my age, but she broke off our shared stare and walked away. I tried the same thing with another Phaetyn, and another, yet as soon as I caught someone's eye, they averted their gaze.

"Do I have something on my face, Dyter?" I asked.

Stupid question. I was a mess. My aketon was torn and bloody, both with Tyrrik's black blood and my blue. I had an unconscious Drae draped across me, who was *also* a bloody mess, not to mention he was their sworn enemy. Could they tell what he was just by looking at him? To me, he'd never looked 'of this world,' too handsome, too world-weary, too fond of black clothing. But could they tell?

"Kamoi spoke with the elders as we neared," Dyter told me in a whisper.

"How?"

"Through the trees." The old man shrugged. I had to admire his ability to adapt. The girl he'd known from early childhood was both a Phaetyn and a Drae, and we were walking through a forest of sentient trees, and Dyter looked as calm as if he was serving stew and ale on a Thursday night.

"It's likely word has spread about what you are. I'm sure they are just as curious about you as you are about them," he added.

I was a mess and a novelty. Excellent. Great. *Best news ever.* And why was he whispering if they already knew? Alarm bells rang in my head, and my skin crawled as the Phaetyn's eyes continued to avert upon landing on me, like I'd stepped in horse turd and no one wanted to tell me. "But we're safe here, right?"

As if in response, a high-pitched whistle buzzed in my right ear, and I instinctively leaned forward, covering Tyrrik with my body.

A sharp pinch in my side made me gasp. Warmth spread from the area, and with it came a jolt of energy that made my heart race. *What the hay?*

I reached around my torso, and my hand brushed a feathered shaft . . . stuck in my body. *In my body.* Which would've been Tyrrik's body if I hadn't covered him. *Mistress moons!* That made me furious. Did they not know how much effort it took to save him?

I yanked the dart out and stared at the three inch needle. I could feel my skin knit back together. My simmering anger turned to rage in a heartbeat, and scales exploded up the sides of my neck. I had *not* gone through all that trouble to save Tyrrik only to have him killed here.

"Kamoi," I said. Except a harsh growl came out instead, resounding through the clearing.

Someone screamed, and more erupted. Several Phaetyn darted out of the clearing and into the trees.

The gorgeous Phaetyn prince turned in his saddle, and I threw the dart at him. "You bloody well better not be intentionally betraying me, or I'll personally make sure the Phaetyn are extinct."

I breathed hard, trying not to Drae-out completely. That would be a bad thing, especially for Tyrrik.

Kamoi's eyes widened, and his skin paled. *"Leoleo, laina i luga,"* he barked. *"Taofi ia saogalemu, aemaise le fafine."*

A dozen male Phaetyn appeared, each with a spear in one hand and an expansive shield in the other. These men looked nothing like the civilians in the marketplace, obvious by their muscular bodies, their matching purple aketons, and the way they carried themselves. They wore fierce expressions, and their corded arms were sleeved in winding and intricate tattoos. They surrounded our party in a protective circle.

Kamoi faced me, his violet eyes glowing. "I'm so sorry, *Kealani.*"

15

The Phaetyn prince dropped back to ride beside me. After an uncomfortable moment, he continued his apology, "I hadn't anticipated bringing Lord Tyrrik with us, so I had no time to prepare my people."

I glared at him. "I wouldn't think you'd have to prepare your people. He's riding with us, so he should be safe. And what about your talking trees?"

"Of course. You're right. I had notified our elders, however the forest is large and our people spread throughout it. Not everyone would have been alerted, and Drae are our natural enemy."

Tyrrik wasn't their enemy any more than I was. My gaze caught Dyter's, and I read the caution in his eyes, so I bit my tongue, instead of yelling anymore at the Phaetyn prince, and skimmed over the now gathering crowd, searching for any lurking threats.

The gathered Phaetyn crowd contained a mixture of wide eyes and gaping mouths as well as others who just plain ol' glared at me, their jaws set into rigid lines as they took in my blue scales and what felt like my reptilian eyes. So much for them being a peaceful race. My body was reacting to the threat they posed.

I remained hunched over Tyrrik as I scanned the area.

That central tree didn't seem to be getting any closer, and the serenity I'd felt when I first stepped into the forest was ebbing away. Taking a closer look, I noticed the crowd had divided into two distinct groups on either side of our escort. Those to my right didn't seem angry at me, but rather at the rest of the Phaetyn. Those to my left were all young men and women, and judging by the glares aimed my way, they didn't like me and Tyrrik one bit. I wasn't so sure Kamoi's twelve guards would hold them all off if they charged. I would go full Drae if they didn't watch out.

"How much farther until we're safe?"

"Not much farther," Kamoi said with a frown. "Ryn, you are safe here."

"Mm-hmm," I replied, making sure to be just as helpful as he'd been.

The guards halted and faced outward, banging their spears and shields together with a loud clatter. I turned to look back, and a wave of energy rippled over me from the direction of the tree. I gasped, staggering with a deep and sudden sense of yearning.

I forgot about the guards, the faction of young Phaetyn, and almost Tyrrik as I slid from the horse to the ground. I released my hold on the Drae, watching for any signs of agony, but Tyrrik's limp body remained draped over our horse. We'd moved into the central safe zone, apparently.

Giving into the new yearning with a sigh that I felt soul-deep, I moved toward the ginormous gnarled elm reaching into the sky, its branches extending out as wide as the limbs extended above us. The rough bark was warm beneath my palm, and I ran my fingertips over the trunk in a soft caress, my heart shuddering.

A sense of home washed over me. A deep feeling of belonging, a tenderness that reminded me of my mother, the love she'd had for me, deep enough that she would sacrifice her life, and this brought tears to my eyes. I dropped to my knees.

The feeling didn't stop but expanded, and images flashed behind my closed eyelids. *A beautiful Phaetyn woman, laughing as she ran through the forest, her lover chasing after. The two of them kissing in an obvious binding celebration. A crowd of Phaetyn cheering as she spoke to them.* This was their queen with her mate? The images shifted, and shadows fell over the forest. *Blind panic was etched on the faces of Phaetyn, young and old. The numbers of Phaetyn dwindled, and the queen addressed her people, resignation on her face. The queen kissed her mate, she and a few of her attendants leaving the forest. As she left, the queen pulled the rocks up into jagged teeth, the jaws surrounding Zivost in a protective barrier none could penetrate.*

At one with the trees, I longed to reach out for her and was crippled by my loneliness when she didn't return. The images receded, fading into shadows of gray before dissolving into a canvas of solid black. A whisper of curiosity brushed my mind, but when an image of Irdelron standing over me surfaced, I broke contact with the elm with a gasp.

I closed my eyes, the bright light blinding me with stabbing pain in comparison to my time spent within the tree's memories. Sitting, I pushed my palms into my eyes and put my head between my knees.

"What did you see?" Kamoi asked in a hushed voice. "Did the tree show you anything?"

I processed what I'd seen, opening my eyes and blinking so they'd adjust. "What happened to her? The previous queen?"

Kamoi's lavender eyes darkened. "Luna Nuloa?"

I nodded. Her name fit her, like a sliver of moonbeam, delicate but strong.

"She—"

"Highness," a guard yelled.

A crowd of Phaetyn marched toward us. *Drak.*

"I thought you said we'd be safe here, Kamoi."

Prince Kamoi puffed his chest and extended his hand. "I did say that, *Kealani*, and I meant it. This is sacred ground."

I let him pull me up, but as soon as I was standing, he released my hand and went to the guards.

Their murmuring was an indistinguishable chorus, but the low undercurrents betrayed their angst. Three of the guards waved their arms at me, and I ran to where Dyter stood by my horse and Tyrrik.

"This is not good," Dyter said, stating the obvious. "I had no idea I was agreeing to take you into the middle of a war."

I wrinkled my nose as I thought about it. "Is that what this is? Wait a minute. Can the Phaetyn harm each other? Is that even possible?"

Dyter shrugged, but beads of sweat glistened on top of his bald head. "I always thought the Drae were invincible and the Phaetyn extinct. I know hardly anything about them, except what I've learned from you and Kamoi on the journey here."

I'd stopped listening, realizing I knew the answer, thanks to Ty, aka Tyr, aka Tyrrik. Phaetyn and Drae canceled each other which meant the Phaetyn needed Drae blood to kill one another.

I rested my hand on Tyrrik to assure myself he was still alive but pushed down my worry about his state as I eyed the crowd again. What the hay were they so angry about to begin with?

A second group of guards marched toward us by the sacred tree clearing, and the crowd of angry Phaetyn slowly dispersed.

Kamoi returned to us, shaking his head. "I'm sorry for the interruption, *Kaelani—*"

I held my hand out to stop him. "Don't apologize. And don't call me Kaelani. My name is Ryn. Just Ryn. I don't have any pet names, except Rynnie, and only Dyter calls me that. You don't control the people, do you? Is that your father's job?"

Dyter cleared his throat, and I had a feeling I'd stepped in horse poop again.

"His mother's job," Dyter said. "His mother is the queen. The Phaetyn are a matriarchal society."

*Yikes.* I winced. "Sorry," I said with a grimace. "I've never been very good at politics." *Or cared.*

Kamoi took my hand, and my heart started thumping despite all my bluster. Being that good looking wasn't fair. His skin was really, really smooth. He led me back past the tree, and I stumbled to a halt. There was a path. A *golden* path. Like beautiful shiny gold that made me want to walk down it . . . and possibly dig up the sparkly bricks and put them in safe keeping. *Drak.* There was something wrong with my head when it came to shiny objects of late.

"My mother and father are expecting us. They live just over this way," he said, indicating another, *not shiny*, path. "I'm sure they'll have food and beds ready."

"Wait," I said belatedly.

I turned to see Dyter leading the horse with Tyrrik on it. I was about to walk off with sexy-schmexy Prince Phaetyn without my unconscious . . . friend . . . my acquaintance? *Gah.* I couldn't leave Tyrrik.

I met Dyter halfway and put my hand back on Tyrrik as I asked, "How long is he going to sleep like this?"

Dyter lifted a shoulder. *Right.* Dyter doesn't know everything.

I guess it'd be better to ask Kamoi my questions—at least the Phaetyn ones. "Do the Phaetyn all have the same powers? Can everyone do everything?"

Kamoi tucked a strand of silver hair behind his ear—could ears be hot—and came back to walk beside me. "No."

"No . . ." Was that a no, I'm distracted? Or a no, I'm not telling you anything?

We started down the dirt path, but the road was narrow, and Dyter and the horse were forced to drop behind.

"So, do you have similar powers?" I pressed. "Phaetyn are all healers, right?"

"Yes," Kamoi said, his eyes shifting to the left. His gaze returned to me, and he continued, "Phaetyn are all healers, but some have an affinity for animals, some for plants, some for the earth, and some, well, really only one—for people. The queen holds the most power, having the responsibility to protect our lands—"

*Smoking bonfires.* "Your mom is the most powerful Phaetyn?"

Kamoi chewed his lower lip as if contemplating his response. Or perhaps he was embarrassed by his mother's superpowers.

"Honestly, I think that's amazing." I rushed to assuage his discomfort. "Does that mean you have superpowers like her?"

He chuckled, a low throaty sound, as he shook his head. Giving me a pointed look, he said, "My only superpower seems to be an inordinate amount of good luck."

My mind blanked as our narrow path opened, and we stepped into a clearing.

The verdant grass sparkled like green emeralds. A beautiful ash tree, larger even than the elm that had just flashed images at me, sat directly in front of a pristine mansion made of rose quartz. With four spires, the house had a distinct castle feel although on a much smaller scale. And, while I was distracted by the gleaming structure for a moment, my attention snapped back to the tree.

Similar to the elm back in the sacred clearing, this tree was wide and tall. But the elm's leaves had been green and its bark, although rough, thick and brown. *This* ash tree's foliage looked as though the plant had been infested with disease. The leaves of the tree were yellowed and their curled tips brittle and cracked. While the trunk was thick as well as the branches near it, the tree's extremities were bare and broken. Twigs littered the ground beneath it. Where the elm had awed me, the sight of this tree broke my heart.

"Come, *Kealani*," Kamoi said, his face twisting into concern.

Kamoi took a step forward on the path leading to the house, but I left him there and went to the ash tree, drawn once more. There was no wave of emotion calling me, except the unsettled feeling in the pit of my stomach left from receiving snatches of the previous queen's life only moments before. I was tired of non-answers, hints, avoidance, and most of all manipulation. The trees wanted me to know something. I felt a duty to them.

I was tired of missing out. Of making my decisions based on the information others fed me. The trees held memories, and in my heart, I knew they spoke truth. To know that, when truth seemed so hard to come by these days, made me eager to oblige them.

Placing my hands on the grayish bark, I closed my eyes and waited. The trees didn't take long to answer my call.

*A stunning woman with wavy silver hair appeared, laughing and smiling, the joy in her eyes breathtaking. Next to her was a man, a Phaetyn, the same Phaetyn who was mated to the previous queen. He had slanting brows, high cheekbones, and full lips.*

Was this Kamoi's father? There was a strong resemblance to the prince. Kamoi's story of his parents and his childhood came back to me, and I knew I'd guessed correctly. Was this stunning woman his mother?

The image dissolved, and another took its place. *The beautiful lady now wept, and the Phaetyn man pulled her into his arms. Another vision took hold, and this time, the same woman sat on a throne, rocking a tiny infant in her arms. The image faded, and then the woman knelt on the floor, alone in a dark room, holding a drawing of the previous queen, Queen Luna, while she wept. Her anguish was echoed by the tree, and my heart ached for her sorrow.*

"Can you see her? How she used to be?" Kamoi asked in a rough whisper.

His warm hands covered mine, and I opened my eyes to see his violet eyes glistening with unshed tears.

"Did you see my mother?" He choked on the last word, his Adam's apple bobbing. Kamoi gritted his teeth and closed his eyes, breathing hard.

I took the opportunity to study him. This close, I noticed his lower lip was fuller than his upper, and the definition of his chest muscles peeked out from the dip in his aketon. His fists were clenched, accentuating his corded arms; his chest was broader, and instead of being lean like Tyrrik, the Phaetyn prince was much more muscular and thick, like a tree trunk.

There was something about Kamoi: his kindness, his patience, and the fact that he made me feel like I belonged with just a small touch, which spoke to me on some level. My blood knew his blood.

I reached forward and rested my palm on his cheek. He gasped and pulled me to him, wrapping me in a warm embrace. He smelled like spring, like fresh rain and herbs with an undertone of smoky pine.

His hands gripped my back, pushing into my skin. Energy pulsed between us, and I could feel his eagerness for my touch. But a memory of the torture room slammed into my mind, the feeling of being confined and trapped and out of control. Something deep inside screamed.

I pulled back from the Phaetyn prince, stepping out of his reach.

"I'm sorry. I'm so sorry," I said, face heating. *Jotun's face, slamming doors, rows of scalpels.*

I squeezed the memories away, locking them deep inside. I choked out, "I-I I did see your mother; she's beautiful. She's sick, isn't she?"

"Let's go meet her. You can see for yourself." He held out his hand in invitation.

I looked at Kamoi's hand, willing the shivering remnants of my panicked moment away, telling myself I was being ridiculous. He'd been nothing but nice to me, and I'd never had that response with his previous touches. But then, what we'd just shared was more than a simple hand hold. I was absolutely certain whatever just happened, the panic was dregs of darkness from inside of me, left over from the castle. I looked at Dyter watching our exchange with a furrowed brow.

There with him was Tyrrik, still unconscious and draped over the horse like a sack of potatoes. As I looked at the Drae, my heart tripped, skipping a few beats. Swift anger followed the light sensation. *Mistress moons.* There was something so not right in my head. Tyrrik had lied to me from day one; I wasn't okay with feeling anything for him. I *wouldn't* feel anything for him.

Kamoi stood waiting, his hand still extended, although as he turned to follow my gaze, his hand sunk back toward his side. Before he could completely withdraw it, I resolutely reached forward and grabbed his hand and stepped closer. The way Kamoi treated me was normal. The way Tyrrik had treated me was anything but.

Kamoi's eyes lit, and he offered a tentative smile.

Dyter glared at me from behind the prince. Whatever. Dyter could be mad. He hadn't been in prison with Irrik, Ty, and Tyr. The old man had no room to judge.

But the rolling of my stomach didn't quite agree with the rationale in my head because, despite everything, my mind was churning out on repeat that my stupid heart knew what my heart knew.

And after only a couple of steps, I withdrew my hand from Kamoi's.

## 16

$\mathcal{A}$s we approached the rose quartz house, the filtered light it refracted cast rainbows into the meadow. The building was not created exclusively of stone. The double doors were made of wood that had been polished until it *shone* like the stone, but the wood was pale gray.

We got closer, and the door was flung open, and a young Phaetyn girl of no more than eight ran out to meet us, screaming in Phaetyn language. The only word I understood was Kamoi's name. Judging by her wide smile and bounding enthusiasm, she was ecstatic to see her brother.

I slowed my steps and watched as the girl crashed into her brother, wrapping her arms around his narrow waist.

"*Uso ua ou misea, Kamoi, fea na e iai.*"

"Kamini, you must speak in the language of man. We have guests, and we would not want to exclude them."

The girl dropped her arms, and her cheeks tinged pink all the way to the tips of her pointed ears. "You don't have to be a Drae about it, Kamoi." She sniffed. "Next thing I know, you'll be acting like Father—"

Kamoi put his hand over his sister's mouth and shook his head.

"Part of growing up is knowing what to say, when to say it, and how to say it, little Kami."

Regardless of the rudeness of the little girl, I couldn't help feeling sorry for her. She'd been raised to believe what she was saying, and even three months ago, I might have agreed with her about the Drae.

The girl batted her brother's hand away then sniffed and offered me a tentative smile.

Wow, this girl could change emotions like the weather.

"Are you one of the lost Phaetyn?" she asked me.

"Kami, please stop talking," Kamoi said with a shake of his head. "Just go tell our parents I'm home and I've brought a Phaetyn from Verald as well as Lord Irrik and Lord Dyter. Lord Dyter is King Caltevyn's ambassador."

Kamoi rattled the information off quickly, but I noted his sister's flinch when he said Lord Irrik. Obviously, the Drae was known here, and I felt a flash of irritation at the prince for not giving Tyrrik a clean slate by using his real name. Kamoi clearly meant this as an insult.

Kamini dropped a perfunctory curtsy and darted away.

This crawling sense of unease that skittered over my skin and burrowed deep into the pit of my stomach should not be so familiar after so short a time.

"Is your mother up for visitors, Kamoi?" Dyter asked. "Is she still the one making decisions here in Zivost?"

Kamoi chuckled after a pause, but the tension in the air was only reinforced by the forced laugh. "Of course. Queen Alani makes all of our decisions in regard to our country and our people. Just like the king does in Verald."

Without further small talk, Kamoi led us through the open double doors and into the foyer of the stone house.

Dyter and I exchanged a quick look.

I might've narrowly missed my calling as Soap Queen of Verald, but that didn't make me an idiot. I'd seen the same hungry looks on the young men in Verald as those on the younger Phaetyn rioting at the tree. Whatever was happening here, either the queen wasn't making the choices, or she was making the wrong ones. Happy subjects didn't have that look on their faces.

Trees didn't decay when properly tended to.

Dyter was right. We'd walked into a civil war.

---

KAMOI LED us through the rose quartz home, Dyter and me staggering after while holding up Tyrrik. I swiveled my head without shame to take in the sparkling walls. There was no decoration in the hallways, and I could understand why they'd left the area so sparse with the way the walls glowed as though we'd stepped into another realm. I *did* wonder if I could maybe chip some of the quartz off and add it to my stash, just one tiny piece. Would anyone even notice?

"We'll put Lord Tyrrik in here for now. He'll be more comfortable," Kamoi said, entering a small chamber.

The room had two beds facing the outside wall and a small table between them. A pitcher and bowl sat atop the table, and there was still space for any personal things. The outside wall was a bank of opaque windows, letting in soft filtered light. The room was otherwise bare, but an adjacent door opposite the entrance made me think of the washroom in Tyrrik's tower. What I wouldn't give for a bath . . .

"He'll be safe while we—"

"Uh-huh," I said, hunching over as Dyter and I deposited Tyrrik on the closest bed. I straightened and fixed Kamoi with a hard stare. "How safe will he be, considering we were attacked *and* required two sets of guards to get here?"

Kamoi's violet eyes narrowed, and he raised his voice and called out, "*Malaleo.*"

A guard appeared.

"You and two others are to guard Lord Tyrrik," Kamoi said with a glance at the Drae. "He is a guest in this house. It's your responsibility to ensure he does not meet with any harm, or the royal family will take it as a personal insult."

He quirked a brow at me, and I rolled my hand in a gesture, indicating for him to continue. There was no way I was going to come back and find he'd been injured. I didn't quite understand how people twisted words and made loopholes, but I knew words and orders could be easily manipulated and misunderstood by now.

Kamoi sighed and added, "If we return and find a single scratch on him, your lives are forfeit."

The guard shifted uneasily, his gaze darting from Kamoi to me then back.

*Threaten their families*, I mouthed, once the guard's attention was back on the prince.

Kamoi glared at me.

*Like I care.* I smiled back, putting my hand on my hip.

"And your families will also die," he said. "Understood?"

The pale-faced guard nodded and exited the chamber.

I turned to see Dyter pulling off Tyrrik's boots. I raced over to help. Grabbing a pillow, I lifted the Drae's head to push it underneath.

"Will he be okay, Dyter?" I asked in a low voice. "Shouldn't he be awake by now?"

"He came as near to death as is possible for a Drae," the prince answered. "His healing will be slow, but he will heal."

"Don't sound so happy about it," I muttered.

The Phaetyn shrugged, saying, "There will be time to care for the Drae afterward. I will see that everything you need is brought here, but my mother, the queen, awaits us."

I stole one last look at Tyrrik's relaxed face, my gut churning at the thought of leaving him vulnerable. My options were limited, and I *hated* that. Dyter jerked his head to the door, and I nodded, following Kamoi out.

"Your wives and children," I hissed at the, now, three guards outside. I watched their eyes widen, and I hurried after the prince.

We wound down two more halls before the Phaetyn prince

stopped. I bumped into him, putting both of my hands on his back to steady myself. *Yep, about as muscular as I expected.* I stepped back, rubbing the tip of my nose as he turned around to look at me. I did my best to ignore his small smile, acting as if I'd meant to paw at him like that.

The smile faded as he took hold of the handle and, with a deep breath, pushed the door open.

Dyter and I shared a glance, and he entered; there was something more going on, only I wasn't sure what. I inched into the room after him, and the scent of stagnant air and illness slapped my senses. Someone needed to open a window and air the place out and maybe offer to bathe the queen.

Queen Alani lay in the middle of a four poster bed made of polished ash. Her sallow skin was almost as blanched of color as the bedding. Deep purple-blue circles marred the area under her eyes, and her silver hair held no luster. Her thin body was hidden in the folds of the hemp blankets, and she didn't even stir as we came to stand around her large bed.

Movement in the corner drew my gaze. A handsome man stood there, staring at Dyter and me, gripping a spear though Kamoi's presence seemed to be holding the man back from advancing. The strange Phaetyn acted like we'd surprised them by entering the room, yet I distinctly remembered the prince telling his sister to go and alert the king and queen of our approach.

"Kamoi," the queen whispered, her dry and raspy voice sounding like rubbing paper.

Everyone turned to the bed, but I angled my body to keep the unknown man in sight.

"Mother," Kamoi bent and kissed her waxen cheek. "I have some people I would like you to meet."

"If this isn't a good time . . ." I said, eying the door. The queen looked ready to kick it; she was practically decaying in her bed. The Phaetyn outside already hated me. I didn't even want to contemplate what they'd do if their leader died with me in the room.

"It's as good a time as any," the queen said. "Help me sit."

Kamoi helped prop her against the headboard, stuffing pillows behind her.

"Are you ill, Queen Alani?" Dyter asked, bowing low.

"After a fashion, yes," she said, eyeing first Dyter then me. Her pale lavender eyes were flat and watery.

Great. Another one of those cryptic people.

"Mother," Kamoi said, nodding at the other man. "I traveled to Verald and discovered the rumors to be true. There was indeed another Phaetyn there." He gestured to me, and I waved. "This is Ryn. She is Drae and Phaetyn."

The Queen gasped, "*Faatasi uma? Leaga le malaia.*"

I frowned at Dyter. "That didn't sound complimentary."

"Life and death," the man behind us said. "How is such a thing possible?"

Why were they acting so surprised? Kamoi tree-talked ahead and told them all this. I held up a hand, which was all I could think of to be polite. No one said anything, so I jumped in and asked the man, "Are you Kamoi's father?"

"I apologize, Ryn," Kamoi said. "Yes, this is my father, Kaelan."

"Nice to meet you." I dipped my head and bobbed a little then did the same to the queen because she was their leader.

The three Phaetyn observed me, and the silence stretched and became awkward. I shifted my gaze between the three royals, waiting for one of them to speak. Maybe I should've asked Dyter for etiquette lessons instead of the history of Gemond.

Kamoi broke the weird staring contest. "The Ash Tree showed Ryn visions, Mother. She was also able to grant Lord Irrik access through our barrier by resting a hand upon him."

"*Tyrrik,*" I corrected with an edge to my tone. "His name is Tyrrik."

Queen Alani's gaze snapped from Kamoi to me, her eyes now bright and focused. She studied me, her expression hardening. "Indeed?" she asked, returning her attention to Kamoi.

"Indeed," he repeated with a nod.

The queen shifted in the bed, asking, "What did the tree show you, child?"

Clearly they didn't care about Tyrrik's name. Or mine. I smiled at her, pushing my lips up in a meaningless motion as I replied, "I'm not a child."

Dyter cleared his throat, but I ignored his unsubtle hint to mind my manners.

"You are surely not older than two decades—" she said, her fists gripping the bedcovers.

"Eighteen."

Her violet eyes flashed at my interruption, and she raised her chin. "Eighteen, you say? Then I was right: just a child. Here, we are considered children until seventy. My son has only recently entered adulthood at one hundred and fifty years."

Kamoi was one hundred and fifty? He'd aged really well.

"I am only half Phaetyn," I replied. "So, I repeat. I'm not a child."

"That is what every child would say," the queen said with a condescending smile.

I opened my mouth and Dyter took my hand, squeezing it gently.

"Good," the queen said, observing my simmering silence. "Now, what did you see when you touched my ash tree?"

*Right.* She expected me to divulge my secrets after being that rude? "There is a river two miles west of here," I replied, cocking a hip out. "That's what the tree showed me."

We held each other's gaze, and I ignored the squeeze from Dyter, another hint for me to pull my head in.

She sunk into her pillows and closed her eyes. "I have upset you," she said, stating the obvious. "Let me begin then by telling you why I am so weak. Perhaps then you will trust me with what you saw."

I didn't answer, a creeping sensation filling me. I was beginning to realize entering this place might have been a terrible idea. I may have an enemy in a place I'd never expected to have one.

"Phaetyn used to roam throughout the Draconian realm," she began. "It is only in the last century we were forced to confine ourselves in the heart of our familial forest where we are strongest. When the Veraldian King and Emperor sought to destroy us, my sister, then the Queen of Phaetyn, erected an unbreakable protection around our home which fed off her ancestral power."

"Queen Luna," I said. "She left this place."

The temperature in the room dropped.

"She did," Kaelan, Kamoi's father, said, stepping closer. "In answer to the emperor's summons, and she took her ancestral power with her, leaving us vulnerable. The emperor forced her, as he had with other Phaetyn, to use her powers in experiments on Drae women he'd impregnated. Drae cannot reproduce unless it is with their mate, but the emperor wanted more Drae, and none of the women he'd forced himself upon would carry to term. He drained Luna's power over the years in an attempt to keep the pregnancies viable, without success. He killed many of our kind in this way. Years later, we heard rumors Luna had died—drained of her power completely."

My lips numbed as I guessed the rest. "She healed my mother?"

The queen shrugged. "I would assume so, given your nature."

Dyter neared, but I shot him a look to let him know I was okay. I'd put some of the pieces together myself since learning the Emperor was my father. My mother had run from him to hide in Verald; it didn't take a genius to piece together she hadn't liked him. But, since learning I was Drae and Phaetyn, I'd wondered how such a thing had happened with two Drae for parents. If what the queen said was correct, I was only Phaetyn because of Luna's power.

The emperor hadn't wanted a child with both sets of powers, just another Drae. If I'd been there, if he'd known what he was doing, he would've gotten way more than he bargained for. I blinked several times, processing. Remembering what the elm tree showed me earlier, I realized some of their story wasn't quite true. They'd made it sound like Luna chose to leave the forest for selfish reasons, but that's not what the tree had told me.

"Why did you encourage Queen Luna to leave the forest?" I asked.

*T*he queen didn't look well to begin with, but her color worsened, and she sagged against the headboard of her massive bed, her head lolling to the side. She took several deep breaths with her eyes closed as if she were trying to garner more strength.

This time, Dyter dug his nails in hard, and I inhaled sharply at the pinching pain before noticing all three Phaetyn had stilled.

Queen Alani's breathing stuttered. "You have no idea how that memory tortures me, child."

*Not a child.*

"We thought Luna could reason with the Emperor. The land was already showing signs of dying. My sister hoped to show Emperor Draedyn we were indispensable and use this as a bargaining chip."

That's not how the trees remembered the conversation going down, but I had enough wits about me now to interpret Dyter's unsubtle warnings. We'd wandered into something deeper here, and my skin was crawling.

"That must have been hard for you," I said with a smile.

The queen's gaze landed on me, and I held my breath until she nodded and glanced away.

"It has been. I am now Queen of the Phaetyn, but our ancestral power is passed from mother to eldest daughter. I never possessed this power, and I never will. It takes everything I have to keep up the barrier against our enemies."

Dyter spoke, "This is why you're sick?"

Kamoi gripped his mother's hand. "She gives everything so our people can survive here, yet the barrier is slowly crumbling without the ancestral power to reinforce it."

"That is terrible." I was speaking in earnest this time. If the barrier broke, the emperor and his Druman would descend on the Phaetyn in a flash.

Dyter peered at me with an intense expression I couldn't interpret. He lifted his head, the expression gone, and addressed the queen. "Your Majesty, there is no better time for your people to unite with those of Verald against the Emperor's rule."

The king and queen broke into quiet laughter.

"Us? Fight the Emperor?" Kaelan said, shooting a mocking grin at a frowning Kamoi before facing me. "Why would we do that?"

I frowned at him. "Why wouldn't you?"

"Let me ask another way," he said. "Why would we help those who hunted us? When did anyone in this realm ever help us? They just used our powers and killed our children."

"You would judge the entire realm based on the actions of two men?" Dyter asked.

Kamoi placed a hand on his father's chest, stopping him from rounding on Dyter. I tensed, ready to kick some Phaetyn butt into the nearest talking tree.

"Don't you?" Queen Alani asked. She looked at me. "Don't you judge the realm by a few men? Don't *you* wonder if the realm is worth saving?"

I glanced at Kamoi to confirm my suspicions. He gave me a sheepish look in return. The queen was aware of my time spent in the dungeons, judging by her comment. Her question dug close to something that had troubled me immensely ever since the night King Irdelron was killed. I *had* wondered the same thing—whether the realm was worth my time—whether the battle was mine to begin with . . . Whether I should find a small corner to escape to and leave the work to someone else. Why did I have to sacrifice my life for a cause? I'd never wanted to, never asked for this power. I'd lost so much, my own mother and friends, and to lose more wasn't fair. Why did some people have to lose everything and some people nothing? Until now, I'd been determined that someone else could do the losing this time. Her words shamed me, and I swallowed. "You're right, Queen Alani. I've asked myself the same question."

Light flared in her eyes, and she leaned forward eagerly and asked, "And?"

I tilted my chin. "And I know what the right choice should be."

"Nothing is more deceiving than the word *should*." The queen smiled and closed her eyes, reclining into her pillows. "Even though you know what *should* be, you cannot give me a reason why this is the right thing to do."

No, I couldn't. I wouldn't lie like everyone else. I refused to mislead her or anyone knowingly. I had that power.

"And yet, your barrier, your main defense against the emperor, is crumbling. *That* seems like a good reason to be proactive. At least to me," Dyter said, scratching his chin.

"I grow weary," the queen mumbled. "Please excuse me."

Kamoi and Kaelan hurried to lay her flat, piling blankets upon her.

Her sickness seemed to rear its head at the most convenient times, in my humble opinion.

Dyter bowed. "We will leave you to rest, Queen Alani, and rest from our journey as well. Thank you for this audience. May your health return, and I hope to speak with you again soon."

I didn't bother curtseying or even inclining my head. If she could be conveniently ill, I could conveniently forget my manners. I stalked out of the chamber after Dyter without a word to anyone. To be gracious would be a lie, and I was *over* the lies.

"Wait," my mentor cautioned me.

Blue scales erupted on my forearms, and my face burned. A

pulsing need to transform and burn my way to the truth seized me. I was holding myself together, barely.

Dyter shoved me into the room where Tyrrik lay and muttered a hasty dismissal to the three guards.

I sat on the bed next to Tyrrik, glancing at him to check if he was still breathing. His chest rose and fell, and I rested my hand where the spike had torn through his aketon.

"What—" I started, but I cut off as Dyter held a finger to his lips. We listened in silence as three sets of footsteps receded.

Dyter popped his head out of the door and, after he'd closed it again, asked, "Hear anyone?"

With the threat in the air, my mood was heightened; focusing my hearing wasn't hard right now. I turned my head side to side. There were no sounds of life in this hall. I stretched my senses farther, but something, maybe the rose quartz, had to be dampening my Drae-hearing. I couldn't hear the queen's breathing two halls away, though I knew I should be able to.

I shook my head at him and crossed to pick up a wash cloth, dipping the spongy material in a basin of cool water. I wrung the cloth, returned to sit by Tyrrik, and began to wash his face.

"I *really* don't like that woman," I said quietly.

"I'd be worried if you did," Dyter said.

He sighed, sitting heavily on the other bed. "I'd thought they would be more willing to help, judging by Kamoi's eagerness to get us here."

I dabbed at the black-and-blue blood spots caked on Tyrrik's skin and studied his smooth face. Heavy despair settled over me, pulling my heartstrings with hopelessness. "They seem to hate us here. I don't get it. Why was Kamoi so friendly to us?"

"You have no idea?"

Pausing in my ministrations, I lifted my head to study Dyter. He raised his eyebrows, and I asked, "What? You know why?"

Shaking his head, he leaned over to pull off his boots. When he sat back up, he gave me an exasperated look. "Rynnie, you need to start thinking of yourself as a power of this realm and not a farm girl."

I snorted. "I was never much of a farm girl, anyway."

"Fine," he chuckled. "A soap girl."

"Now *soap* I can help you with."

We shared a brief grin.

Dyter drew closer, standing behind me, and together we leaned over Tyrrik's face.

"You were able to bring Tyrrik inside the barrier when Kamoi was adamant a Drae couldn't enter. And those moments you had with the trees earlier . . . you should've seen Kamoi's face. The queen sent her son out of this place to find you, and I have a feeling these people don't leave the forest lightly. Rynnie, what if you possess the ancestral powers needed to strengthen their barrier?" he asked in a low voice. "It would explain a lot."

I dropped the wet cloth, hitting Tyrrik in the face, and quickly picked it up. "*Drak*."

Dyter was right. Sending a prince to go locate a stray Phaetyn was going overboard. Had something happened when Luna poured her powers into my mother so I could live? My jaw dropped and a long moment passed before I stuttered, "I-I think you may be right."

"*Drak*," Dyter repeated. "And, unless I'm misunderstanding their hierarchy, the fact that you have ancestral powers poses a threat to the current queen's rule. Possibly a serious threat."

I dropped the wet cloth on the Drae's face again, and this time, Dyter picked the washcloth up and rinsed the blood off in the basin. He handed the cloth back to me and pointed at Tyrrik's blood-smeared arms.

"I'm not here to be their queen," I said, my chest tightening just at the thought. That queen better not die, even if I wasn't in her room at the time. I wasn't the queen type. I wiped down Tyrrik's arms and then went to the basin to rinse the cloth again. The blood settled to the bottom of the large bowl, leaving the water crystal clear. Heaving a sigh, I returned to the bed, but Dyter had taken my place. He held out his hand for the washrag and then said, "*I know* that. But, judging by the division of Phaetyn here, I'm not sure everyone else does."

My legs turned to jelly, and I collapsed on the wooden floor with a thud. Resting my forehead on the bed frame, I mumbled, "I'm not the reason there's a civil war out there, right? You think their problems started when we got here?"

When I looked up, Dyter was washing Tyrrik's other arm.

"I'm pretty sure our arrival didn't start anything, but your presence is definitely flaring tempers."

"I never would have come here if I'd known," I said.

"I doubt Kamoi would've brought you here if he'd known either."

I craned my neck to study Dyter, watching the way the ropey scar on his face pulled when he pursed his lips and cleaned the Drae. "He didn't know? I guess that makes sense."

"I don't believe he knew all the details of Queen Luna's time in the emperor's power, not enough to guess why you were Phaetyn and Drae as his parents immediately did. I was watching him as Alani spoke of that time . . . But he had to have guessed you had the ancestral power when you were able to get Tyrrik through the barrier. He made a point of mentioning that to his mother. That's my guess, anyway."

"Holy pancakes," I groaned. "I can't believe we're in this mess."

Dyter handed me the cloth, jerking his head at Tyrrik "I'm not doing his feet."

I shrugged. "Neither am I. He's unconscious; he can't smell them."

"I can, and they stink." Dyter pointed at Tyrrik's feet.

I glared at the old man and snatched the cloth, rinsing it once more. "You realize this Drae stole my dignity and hurt my feelings . . . *really bad*. I shouldn't have to wash his feet; it's demeaning. Sometimes I think you forget I'm no longer a farm girl."

"Didn't he wash your feet a few times in the dungeons? I don't see why you wouldn't return the favor."

I stiffened but didn't reply, avoiding Dyter's gaze as I rinsed the cloth extra, extra well.

"Sorry, my girl, that slipped out. You know I didn't mean to be cruel."

Tears stung my eyes, and too many emotions to name squeezed at my heart. "No, I know," I said hoarsely. "And you're right, really. Tyr did; *he* did many times. He just . . . *He* also lied."

"Aye, he did at that." Dyter's gaze rested on the unconscious Drae. "Do you ever wonder what it would be like to be a slave for one hundred years?"

A tear fell, and I dashed it away. I was exhausted and over-whelmed, making me extra weepy, not to mention I had just learned a number of mind-boggling things about myself. "No."

"I would think," Dyter spoke as he took the cloth from me and began washing Tyrrik's feet, "That I would hardly know myself after that. I would think remembering what my parents taught me at nine years old would be near impossible. I'd do whatever I could to be free, but I'm not sure I'd know how to be free either."

I rinsed out the cloth for him and continued to listen as I watched Dyter wash the other foot.

"Rynnie, he should have only had thought for himself when he discovered you were Drae. But it sounds like his thoughts were mostly for you."

"But, why, Dyter?" I whispered. "Why would he do that?"

"You can't guess?"

I avoided his piercing gaze, changing the subject. "We've dragged him into the heart of enemy territory. We've got to leave."

Dyter finished and stood with a weary moan. "What you said, in the queen's chamber, about not knowing whether this realm was worth saving—"

"I *said* it was the right thing to do," I snapped, defending myself.

"Aye, but knowing what is right and doing what is right are vastly different. You don't know whether you want to go up against the emperor, and I can respect that even if I can't understand it after what you've gone through. However," he said, holding up his only hand to stop my interruption, "I told my king I'd do my best to form an alliance with the Phaetyn, and I mean to do just that. In the meantime, *you* have an opportunity to learn about your Phaetyn powers. I know this situation is uncomfortable, and if you didn't hold a trump card, I wouldn't suggest staying, but I feel we need to . . . for a little longer." He dropped his hand and with his snarling smile said, "What do you think, ex-farm girl?"

What did I think? There was a deep calling inside me to be in the forest here. I was not beholden to these people, but my connection to Queen Luna, whether because I seemed to possess her power or because she'd helped to give me life, was undeniable. More than learning about my powers—or forming an alliance with these people—was the feeling that the trees had more to tell me, that they were desperate for my help.

And then there was the more tangible concern of Tyrrik.

"We can stay until Tyrrik is better and then go," I said, keeping my other agenda to myself. "You're right. I may never get another chance to learn about the Phaetyn and my powers." I'd rather give up pancakes for the rest of my life than come back at the rate things were going.

"We're agreed then," Dyter said.

"Yes, yes." I waved a hand in the air. "But what's our trump card?"

"*Your* trump card, my girl. This old man hasn't got any cards at all."

I rolled my eyes. "What's *my* trump card then?"

He stretched out on the second bed in the room. Closing his eyes, he said, "If you have ancestral powers, you can put the barrier up."

"So?" I glanced between the two beds, wondering where I factored in the sleeping situation.

Dyter cracked an eye open and then closed it again, grinning at the ceiling. "*So*, I'm guessing if you can put it up . . . you can also take it down."

18

*W*arm heat cocooned me, and I snuggled closer to the source. My Phaetyn mojo must've kicked in overnight because my muscles were relaxed and my mind clear. I had a dream about being chased by Druman shortly after falling asleep, which nearly made me physically sick, but after my heart settled again, the rest of the night I'd slept *amazing*. I felt kind of great, considering yesterday involved slashing my hand open and dripping blood into a Drae's open wound. Tyrrik's arm fell to my side, and I snuggled closer.

Wait a minute.

My drowsiness disappeared in a flash, and my eyes popped open. *Drak.*

Maybe my mind wasn't so clear.

I looked across at the other bed, but it was empty. Dyter had folded his blanket and fluffed the pillow before leaving. I'd gone to sleep on the floor; that was a definite. I'd taken Tyrrik's blanket, folded it up for a pillow, and fallen asleep on the *ground*.

Not in bed with Tyrrik.

*Holy potato-stuffed pancakes.*

The Drae mumbled in his sleep, his mouth against the nape of my neck, and his arms circled my waist, pulling me against him. My heart thumped and then began a race as if to pound out of my chest. Clearly my conscious and subconscious mind were not on the same page.

I lay tense, and the queen's words from yesterday echoed in my mind. Did I truly think the world wasn't worth saving because of a few people?

I'd always believed the workings of the world and its people were black and white, yet black and white were merely far ends of a spectrum. Between them resided a bajillion shades of gray.

Everything was gray. Choice, people, beliefs.

My thoughts turned to the Drae behind me. Tyrrik was . . . I hated thinking about what Tyrrik was. Was my avoidance of exploring that a refusal to acknowledge the truth? That there may be grays involved in what he'd done. Was it fear? Of admitting his choice had been an impossible one and fear of how that admission would change my life? Was that why I didn't want to help fight the emperor and why I'd gone to sleep on the floor last night? Was I too scared, too ruined, too broken to do anything but deny where my life was headed?

I pulled Tyrrik's arm up and scooted to the edge of the bed, gently placing his arm back at his side. He mumbled again, his forehead creasing into a furrow that smoothed as soon as I tentatively reached out and touched it.

*Yeah.* This was next level stuff. The guy stopped frowning when I touched him. *Don't panic; it's probably nothing.* A cold sweat broke out on my forehead. Whatever *this* was would have to wait.

I went to the washroom and allowed myself a muffled squeal of delight when I saw the large tub filled with water. Nearby was a smaller basin of water, and by that sat a pile of unbleached folded material. I shook out the top piece to find a baggy forest-green tunic made of soft wool. The garment wasn't nearly as nice as the silvery threads the Phaetyn wore, but it was clean.

I stripped out of my torn and bloody clothing, a little disturbed I'd slept in all that essence of Tyrrik, and slipped into the tub.

Once dressed, I rifled through my drawstring bag back in the bedroom and found the waterskin. It was completely flat, and when I opened the cork, not a drop of nectar remained.

I returned to the restroom and emptied part of the basin of crystal clear water into the flagon, and then I stuck my index finger into the fluid. My thoughts turned to Tyrrik again, to how I wanted him whole. I wanted him healed so I could pester him with questions about the Phaetyn, and why Queen Alani knew about the emperor's experiments, and how the heck we could get out of here without escalating the tension. Mostly, I wanted Tyrrik healed so he wasn't vulnerable. I wouldn't be able to stay with him all the time, and I didn't trust the Phaetyn when things here were so volatile. Tyrrik was always so decisive, and he knew more about the Phaetyn than Dyter and I combined.

With each thought regarding Tyrrik's healing came a deeper understanding; while I might still question Tyrrik's motives for many things, clearly I relied on him in some ways.

I returned to the bedroom and sat on the edge of the bed where the Drae still slept. My insides churned, despite his smooth expression and even breathing. He appeared *almost* peaceful right now. His face was unlined with the tension it normally carried. Gone was the haunted look in his eyes, the self-deprecating smile, and his occasional furrow of worry. His chest rose and fell with even breaths. The pallor of his skin had waned during the night. Was that because I'd slept next to him?

I debated leaving him to continue sleeping, but the previous empty waterskin in my hand was enough of a reminder that he'd had nothing of sustenance since our arrival at the heart of Zivost. I rested my hand on his chest, shaking him gently at first, and then not so gently when that didn't work.

He caught my hand with his, but as soon as he opened his eyes, his fierce expression melted into a look of drowsy peace.

"You need some nectar," I said in a voice still rough from sleep.

He rose to his elbows and allowed me to tip the flagon to his lips. He drank and drank and drank, and as he continued to guzzle, my eyes widened, even though I accommodated his thirst by tipping the waterskin up.

Once he'd drained the contents, he reclined and muttered, "Thank you."

His gratitude clenched my heart, and I cleared my throat, pushing back the emotions lodged there. With a nonchalant shrug, I said, "No problem."

Apparently gratitude from others wasn't so easy to take either. Belatedly, I realized I was still touching his chest, and I blushed as a small smile tugged at the corners of his lips.

"How long have we been here?"

"A day," I said. "And one night."

"A whole day and night?" He frowned.

"Yes, is that not normal?"

He blinked, his eyelids heavy. "Never been this injured. Unsure."

I nodded. "Tyrrik, the Phaetyn have . . . problems." I thought of how I could sum up what I had learned thus far, but before I could say anything else, Tyrrik squeezed my hand.

"Be careful, Khosana," he whispered. "Remember what you learned in Irdelron's castle. Everyone has an agenda."

His words slapped me, and I pulled my hand back. "Okay."

The grip of his hand loosened as sleep claimed him.

I returned to the washroom and filled the waterskin again. After making nectar and leaving it next to Lord Tyrrik, I took note of my weary body and decided finding sustenance would be wise.

I exited the room, meeting the hardened gazes of the two soldiers in the hall with a glare of my own. "Listen, I don't really care what Kamoi said to you. I don't care if his threats are meaningful to you or not. I'm telling you, if anything happens to the man in there, you will *wish* Kamoi had gotten to you first. Because you, and everyone you ever *thought* you might have the possibility of caring about, will be destroyed. I'm Drae, and I will chew on your family and spit them out."

The two Phaetyn blanched, and the one on the right swallowed repeatedly, his Adam's apple bobbing in his neck.

"Are we clear?" I asked.

Both guards nodded, but that wasn't enough. I didn't want them to simply humor me; they needed to know to cross me on this was a life and death decision. My heightened emotions, worry over Tyrrik's state as well as the obvious hostility we'd walked into, allowed my Drae to peek out. My eyes shifted Drae, and scales climbed up my neck and down my exposed arms. In a voice more Drae than human, I growled, "Are we clear?"

The female Phaetyn inclined her head.

They straightened and chorused, "Yes, Your Majesty."

*What the hay?*

I heard the tread of footsteps and glanced down the hall, spotting Kamoi's friendly smile and glowing eyes as he neared.

"Ryn, come," he said, waving me toward him. "Have you eaten?" When I shook my head, he passed me a plate containing slices of yellow fruit. "Here, it's mango, a sweet fruit." He watched as I bit into a slice and then asked, "Will you allow me the pleasure of showing you Zivost?"

*Perfect.* I actually did want to explore and get a better sense of what I'd dropped into. I swallowed my mouthful and said, "Yes." Picking up another slice of the yellow fruit, I added, "This is delicious."

"I'm glad you think so."

I grabbed the remaining slices off the plate and handed it to one of the guards.

Kamoi led me out of the quartz house. There were more guards outside the house than when we arrived yesterday. Several were constructing a railing around the queen's ash tree while more set up long tables around it.

"They are getting ready for a welcome party," he said in his lilting voice.

I smiled because I knew it was expected, but I wasn't sure I wanted a party. I wasn't sure I didn't either. Not that it mattered what I wanted. As soon as we stepped off the elevated porch, I halted as every thought but one fled my mind. "Just a sec." I bent over to pull off my soft boots with my free hand. As my bare feet touched the ground, I sighed. "I knew this would be amazing. It's almost like the energy radiates from the soil?"

Kamoi smiled. "It actually does."

He closed the small gap between us and took my free hand in his. I shivered at the contact. The Phaetyn mojo we had going on was pretty strong; deniable but strong. Before I could withdraw my hand, he tucked it into the crook of his arm and, with a slight tug, indicated we go.

*Al'righty then.*

I let him lead me through the forest, chewing on the fruit slices. Kamoi explained how the different affinities to plants and animals manifested during childhood and how some developed more powers as they aged. He spoke of the lineage of royalty and the expanded powers those Phaetyn were blessed with. He told me of the peace they had enjoyed for centuries until the Drae and Kings began murdering his people for their healing blood.

"I can't imagine how that felt," I said softly. "For the people you'd fed for eons to turn on you."

His face darkened, and he stared into the trees for a long moment before giving me a small smile. "Our lives are not all bad, you know. Did you know that each Phaetyn has a tree? The soul of the tree and the soul of the Phaetyn are one."

"So do I have a tree?" Would I be able to see some things of my life? Would I be able to see my mother as clearly as I had Queen Luna or Queen Alani?

"I don't know, *Kealani*," he said and then amended with a blush, "Ryn. I meant Ryn."

I was grateful he at least made an effort to respect my wishes. There was something about seeing a handsome man blush that had my stomach flipping.

"We know you have significant power. But I'm afraid your power may not be enough to win the Phaetyn's loyalty."

I blinked as his words registered. Was I trying to win the Phaetyn's loyalty? I mean, the more the merrier as far as fighting the emperor was concerned. Their healing power would certainly come in useful. Regardless of fighting a war, they should've been helping the other kingdoms with growing food so people could eat. Tyrrik's warning bounced around in my head, planting seeds of distrust. The prince had his own agenda. Tyrrik was right; everyone did. What was Kamoi's? There was one way to find out. "Hey, can I see your tree?"

The prince tripped, stumbling forward, and I released his arm.

Two guards stepped out from behind the trees, and the closest cleared her throat.

"Your highness," she said, violet eyes hardening when she met my gaze. She broke the contact and glided up to Kamoi. "Your mother has requested you return, immediately. The rebels have overrun the Circle of the Sacred Tree, and she needs you to lead the armies."

The first elm tree I'd touched? My initial impression of the convenience of the guard's interruption made me wince. Had that been a cover so Kamoi didn't have to show me his tree? My chest sunk with shame at the thought. I shouldn't be judging Kamoi so harshly. Maybe asking to see someone's tree was a big Phaetyn no-no. How would I be if my people were at war? The Phaetyn rebellion wasn't a convenience for anyone, and he was bound to be a little tense.

"Do you want me to come, too?" I asked. At the very least, I could go Drae and protect those who needed it.

Kamoi smiled at me and scooped my hand in his. Holding my hand gently, he raised it to his mouth and brushed his lips over the top. "You are filled with honor, Ryn. It's one of your many gifts. There might come a time when your presence will help immensely, but for now, I'll attend the queen and see what I can do to dissolve the tension." He nodded at the male guard just inside the tree line. "Harlan, you will accompany Ryn wherever she goes. Do not let any harm come to her."

I wanted to roll my eyes, but Kamoi was only being protective. I guess I'd let him.

RAYE WAGNER & KELLY ST. CLARE

Kamoi and the female Phaetyn left. Harlan and I stared at each other.

"I'll be fine. If you want to go back to the Pink House, that's totally okay with me." Maybe he'd take the hint and leave me alone.

"I appreciate your kindness, Highness," he said, the hardness of his features a direct contradiction to his words. "But, my loyalty lies with Kamoi. He has asked me to guard you. Unless someone else from the royal family tells me otherwise, I'll be with you until you return to the Rose Castle."

*Flip my pancakes.* Pink House, Rose Castle. Obviously my politicking skills needed work. And what did he mean that he was going to guard me? Was he protecting me from others or others from me?

I decided to ignore Harlan and stepped off the path into the trees. I scanned the trunks in front of me, chose the thickest one, and placed my hands upon it. Closing my eyes, I pushed away my thoughts of Kamoi, Tyrrik, and the Phaetyn conflict and asked the tree to share its memories with me.

"What the Drae are you doing?" a young girl asked.

I pulled my hands back from the trunk and turned around. Phew, just Kamini, Kamoi's younger sister.

The young girl was dressed in hemp fibers similar to what I wore, only hers fit as if they were made for her. Her tunic was more of a short dress with a ruffled hem at her knees. Her silver hair was plaited, and she'd pulled the long braid over her shoulder and played with the unbound ends.

"It's Kamini, right?" I asked, extending my hand in greeting.

The young girl looked at my hand, and her gaze chilled as she met mine. "Why are you here?"

*hoa.* The Phaetyn princess was direct. I hadn't gotten that vibe from her yesterday with her one million emotions per minute.

How to explain to the young girl what was happening in the world outside of the Zivost forest? That it made me sick to know there were so many Phaetyn here who could change so many lives in the realm. There was no way I was going to explain about Gemond and their cannibalistic ways. I thought of Verald and its recent coup. Not at all appropriate for a seven-year-old. I wasn't going to get into how power-crazy my father was . . . a recount of how he'd tortured the girl's aunt to try and make a super race wasn't exactly a conversation starter.

"I want to learn about being Phaetyn," I said, finally.

"But you're not Phaetyn," she retorted, putting her hands on her hips. The young girl flicked her braid. "You're going to try and take away our kingdom, aren't you?"

If she'd hit me, I would've been less surprised. "No way. I don't want this kingdom. I don't want any kingdom. I really came here to learn about the Phaetyn and get some understanding of my powers."

The girl dropped her hands to her side and narrowed her eyes. Several seconds passed, and I let her study me uninterrupted.

Finally, she said, "Did you know I can tell if someone is lying? Did Kamoi tell you?"

Good thing I told the truth. I shook my head.

Kamini waved at Harlan. "You can go."

Harlan puffed out his chest and said, "Kamoi has commanded—"

"How dare you?" Her violet eyes blazed with anger. "You know I'm a royal just the same as him. Regardless of what my mother might say about my age, I am plenty old to issue commands."

*Right.* I couldn't let Kamini's small stature and youthful appearance confuse me. She wasn't seven or eight. I was probably talking to a thirty year old. That creeped me out. They should wear badges or something.

Harlan inclined his head and stalked off, disappearing among the trees.

"How do you know he'll really leave?" I asked. I leaned to the side to see if my Drae vision would allow me to see how far the Phaetyn had gone. My vision didn't change. My sense of smell seemed instinctual, but everything else required control or a healthy dose of fear, anger, or some other heightened emotion to help me in this form. *Drak.*

"Oh, he won't leave. Harlan is only loyal to Kamoi. He humors me because Kamoi told him to, but there's no way Kamoi is going to let you out of his sight." Her violet eyes studied me, and she waved me forward. "Come on; you wanted to find out how the trees work? I'll show you."

I followed Kamini deeper into the woods, and my hearing confirmed what she'd said. Harlan followed, his movements obvious in the underbrush where twigs and leaves had fallen.

"Did you know about our war before you came?" she asked, turning to look at me after she delivered her question.

"No." I probably wouldn't have come if I did. One civil war was enough—at least, for me. Actually, one civil war had been too much.

As soon as I answered, she turned around and pushed forward again.

"I thought the Phaetyn only had healing powers," I said.

"That's true for most Phaetyn," she said, an answer that wasn't really an answer.

Kamini stopped in front of a small spruce tree. "Do you see how the needles on this tree's branches glow? Do you see how the trunk of the tree almost pulsates with energy? If you touch here"—she put her hand on the tips of the needles in front of her face—"you will see the tree's most recent memories or the messages that float through the air like gossip."

That was . . . awesome. I rested my palm on the prickly spines of the blue spruce. Fleeting images of a Phaetyn crossed the canvas behind my eyes. The images were pale, almost faded, and only pieces of the picture were clear; almost like a puzzle with only half the pieces.

"If you place your hands on the branches, you will see further back. The thicker the branch and the closer to the trunk, the older the memories will be. The trunk holds the truth of the person's life as well as those events that shaped it."

I reached forward, placing my palms on the branches, letting the needles scratch at my skin with their blurry and distinct visions. Keeping my eyes closed, I let the truth from the tree sink into my mind. *A toddler, no more than three, giggled as he ran through the woods, an adult Phaetyn male chasing after him. Their features declared them relatives, most especially the wide smiles that stretched across their faces as they burst into a meadow. A flash of black rolled over the pair, and a moment later a black Drae landed in the clearing, the air around it shimmering.*

I pulled my hands away before Tyrrik materialized in his human form.

Kamini's eyes gleamed as she studied me. "The trees know who's important to you, who you have connections to, and what you should see. You could sit here all day and sift through their memories, but usually what they show you when you first touch them will be their answers, or the truths pertinent to you."

"Can all Phaetyn read the trees?"

"All Phaetyn have their own tree, usually near where they were born. The trees can share . . . we'll call them memories, right?" When I nodded, she continued, "But most Phaetyn can only see from their tree." Kamini tossed her braid back over her shoulder. She took a deep breath and squared her shoulders looking more like an adult than child. *So creepy.* "But you're asking the wrong question. What you want to know is whether you can see all truths, not just those pertaining to you. Only the queen with the ancestral power can see the truth of all past and current events from any tree."

I wondered if she was supposed to disclose that. Did she already know I had Queen Luna's power? Or was Kamini guessing? She was the first to actually teach me anything, so even not knowing her motivation, I asked, "Can you teach me about the ancestral power?"

She shook her head. "I taught you all I know. My mother said she'll teach me more when I am older." She paused and then blurted, "Are you going to bind yourself to Kamoi? Is that true . . . ?"

"W-what?" I stammered, completely taken off guard by the shift in subject.

"Is it true you'll become his mate?"

I sucked in my breath. "What the . . . Absolutely not!"

I blushed as I remembered we were speaking of her brother. I rushed to mitigate my appalling manners. "I mean Kamoi is the full harvest, for sure . . . Uh, I mean he's nice, and I'm sure every girl in Phaetynville probably wants to mate with him or bind with him. And sure, maybe he's as amazing with everything else as he is good looking, but . . . Anyway, no." Shaking my head, I added, "A solid no. I'm not going to bind myself to Kamoi."

The young Phaetyn girl's face drained of color, and her eyes widened. "You're not in love with him?"

My face burned like it was on fire, and I shook my head. "I don't know him. To bind myself to him would be completely shallow." *And he's prettier than me.*

Without another word, Kamini ran away from me, disappearing into the woods.

"Well . . . okay. Bye." I stood there and attempted to process my bizarre morning thus far. I felt like a fool, especially after being so adamant with Dyter that I wasn't an idiot. And then here I was, a *total idiot*. Kamoi was telling people we were going to, like, dance the maypole together? Shouldn't he have asked me first? If Kamini *was* seven, I might've excused her comment, but the girl was thirty. My humiliation turned to anger as I grasped Kamoi's plan. I was not going to bind myself to him to solve their political and societal woes. I couldn't fault him for wanting an easy answer, but I didn't like feeling like a tool.

My musing was interrupted by the rustling of branches. The surprise combined with the spike in fear, as well as my simmering anger, caused my Drae to burst forth. Scales again erupted above my heart and down my arms. My hands shifted so that my fingers became talons. I turned toward the noise to see three Phaetyn emerging from the brush. They stopped as soon as they saw me. The youngest, who appeared to be twelve, which probably meant he was fifty, gasped.

"We mean you no harm," the eldest man said, dropping his spear and raising his arms in surrender. "We only want the opportunity to speak with you."

"Really?" Everyone I'd met in Phaetynville seemed to have an agenda involving me. "If it involves binding with Kamoi, the answer is no." My aggravation spiked, and I narrowed my eyes, noticing the colors sharpen as they shifted, and the rest of my retort was lost in a low growl.

The other Phaetyn dropped their weapons and held up their hands. "We pledge our oath on Luna's elm that we mean you no harm," the man said, and the boy and big Phaetyn nodded. A slow smile spread across his face as he studied me. "Even if we did, I doubt we could. Please, we just want to talk."

I closed my eyes and took slow deep breaths, allowing my Drae to settle and recede. When I opened my eyes, the three Phaetyn surrounded me, but the boy and husky Phaetyn held their weapons at the ready facing outward toward the forest—protecting me.

"Please, come with us. Soon, Harlan will return."

I followed the three Phaetyn deeper into the forest until we came to a small clearing with several lean-tos, much like the ones found in Gemond. If the Phaetyn were about to eat me, I'd be really, *really* mad. We stopped outside one of the make-shift shelters, and one by one, we ducked inside. The eldest indicated a chair and invited me to sit around a small table.

"May we offer you some food?" the youngest asked.

I'd followed them into a dark place in the depths of a forest. I wasn't quite stupid enough to eat their food. "No, thank you."

The Phaetyn shrugged and popped a red berry from a bowl into his mouth.

The eldest one didn't waste time beginning. "Our people are at a crossroads as I'm sure you've seen."

Even a fool could see the civil unrest in their community. "Crossroads is putting it lightly."

The oldest Phaetyn inclined his head. "Yes, you're right." He took a deep breath and asked, "Will you indulge me in a little history? I think this is the best way to describe our conflict."

"Please," I said. "I'd love to understand what's going on."

The youngest Phaetyn snickered, and the beefy one nudged him.

"Queen Luna partnered with Kaelan when she was very young, perhaps a hundred annum. They seemed happy for a time, but Luna didn't produce an heir after several decades, and there were murmurings that Kaelan was not worthy to be her partner.

Our Luna was a soft ruler, not lazy or indifferent, but perhaps a little overly generous and kind. She enjoyed healing the land, saying it gave us purpose. Even when the rumors of Phaetyn being captured by the emperor came, she encouraged us to leave the sanctuary of Zivost and heal the land. She led this charge by example.

When Queen Luna left, she gave the responsibility of rule to her sister, Alani. Even though Luna was partnered with Kaelan, she left sometimes for weeks or months to do what she called the Phaetyn's work. Perhaps this is what drove Alani and Kaelan together. Perhaps, it was the other way around."

*Holy Drae babies* . . . or rather Phaetyn babies. This was the inside scoop. Alani and Kaelan got together while he was still *with* Luna?

What a turd. But how much merit did the gossip have? What people saw and interpreted was not always truth, a lesson I'd learned in Irdelron's castle. Still, Kaelan was a jerk, so I was inclined to believe it.

I nodded, not wanting to interrupt the story, letting the Phaetyn know I was listening.

"Alani acted as regent often, and the Phaetyn accepted their ruler's choice. In truth, we thought nothing of it. Luna still set the rules, although there were very few, and on the rare occasion there was a dispute amongst our kind, she still passed judgment. But Luna's trips out of Zivost increased in frequency and then in length. One day, she left and several annum passed without Queen Luna's return. Almost two decades ago, her tree stopped growing."

An odd sense of trepidation settled deep in my chest. I looked at the three Phaetyn and couldn't help but feel like they were looking at me with eager anticipation in their eyes. "What do you think happened?"

The older Phaetyn furrowed his brow, and the air in the room grew heavy. "Initially, the Phaetyn thought her dead, but The Sacred Tree, Queen Luna's elm, did not wither and die like it should've had the queen's power been extinguished. Even if Luna is gone, her power did not die with her. The rumor is she infused you or your mother with her magic, passing the ancestral force to you."

"Do you think that's true?" I hedged, not wanting to reveal anything.

The older Phaetyn shrugged. "It seems like it. You can talk to the trees, right?"

I shook my head in disbelief; news sure traveled fast. Maybe I could get some more answers from them. "So, why don't the Phaetyn heal the land anymore? What happened with that?"

"Queen Luna erected the borders around Zivost when the Phaetyn started disappearing over a century ago. The border that cloaks the skies is the one that keeps us safe from the Drae, and the stone one around the forest protects us from humans. However, Luna dropped the physical wall regularly for the Phaetyn to visit other lands. Remember, she felt it our purpose to regenerate and renew the earth. Less than a decade after Luna's disappearance, Queen Alani decreed the outside world unsafe for all the Phaetyn. She pointed to those captured and killed as reason for her decision. She insisted that if the wall had been up, her dear sister would've been safe. The majority of the Phaetyn supported Queen Alani's decision for isolation, if for no other reason than their love for Luna."

As I listened to the Phaetyn explain their history, I wanted to ring Kamoi's neck. His grossly abbreviated history was rife with missing bits.

"The intent of our rebellion is not to protest Alani's right to be queen. Luna gave her that right, and it was hers to give. But it is our calling and purpose to heal the land. Word has reached us of the need of the kingdoms in the Draecon Empire. We just want the choice to leave Zivost."

"It's not like there aren't a few Phaetyn out there anyway. Or there were when Alani raised the wall. The emperor probably got them all by now," the biggest Phaetyn said in a rumbling low voice.

"We want to leave, and she won't let us," the youngest of the three said.

"But if you leave, you might die," I argued. "Isn't she just trying to keep you safe?"

"Some want to leave to heal the land; some just don't want to be trapped. Others want to look for their loved ones even if only to bring closure to their disappearance. They can lower and raise the wall, but they rarely let anyone leave. *Very* rarely." The eldest Phaetyn gave me a sad smile. "Have you ever felt trapped?"

The question made me nauseated, and I nodded.

"Is it true you saw visions of Queen Luna?" the eldest Phaetyn asked.

I shifted on the hard seat and stared into the empty bowl, contemplating my answer. The biggest problems I'd experienced in my life were because of other's lies. I took a deep breath and raised my head to meet the three Phaetyn's gazes. I didn't want to be a liar. "Yes," I said. "I did."

"Then you must come back to The Sacred Elm tree and ask it to show you the truth about Queen Luna. Alani said it was her sister's last wish to keep the Phaetyn safe. If that were truly her wish, we would all comply. She was our true queen. She held the ancestral powers."

"But if Queen Alani is lying," the stocky Phaetyn said in a deep voice, "then we would ask that you drop the rock barrier so those of us who want to leave are free to be one with the world again. If you can see the truth from the trees, you have the ancestral power, and it is your right to do it."

"You can't move it like Kamoi?"

He shook his head. "Only the royals have that power."

I wanted to tell them not to be stupid or rash, but I didn't know what life was like here or how it was affecting the Phaetyn. I also didn't want to drop the wall and leave them exposed, but the safety they were told they had here, just like the high tower I'd once been in, was only an illusion. Alani's grip on the barrier would inevitably fail.

Knowing the Phaetyn in Zivost were divided, I wasn't about to agree to just anything. But they weren't asking me to do anything more than tell them the truth, and I was more than willing to do that. Everyone deserved the truth.

"If you want to take me to the tree, we'll have to do something to disguise me. Let's face it," I said, holding up my hemp sack tunic. "I stick out like a sore thumb."

# 20

*W*hen we got to the Sacred Circle and no one stopped us, I mentally patted myself on the back. I could blend in with my new silver robes. I could be a Phaetyn *spy*. Wait. That *was* what I was doing. For some reason, I heard Tyrrik's suffering sigh in my head at that moment, and my lips twitched.

The royal guard surrounded the Sacred Circle. The Phaetyn warriors, dressed in their purple aketons, created a barrier to the tree.

The smallest Phaetyn grabbed my hand and said, "Do they know you have Queen Luna's power?"

I nodded, and the young Phaetyn cringed. A sinking feeling settled in the pit of my stomach. Why did I always have to blurt everything out? I was so going to get better at keeping secrets, starting right now.

"If we go around through the trees, you can climb over," he said, pointing to where the branches of the large elm tree entwined in the forest canopy above.

My Drae vision told me that those branches were not very thick, and my climbing skills weren't nearly as good as my nectar-making skills—which weren't very good. As Ryn the Fearless, I felt obligated to do something. As Queen Luna's surrogate, I felt honored to serve the Phaetyn, but I was done being an idiot.

"The trees can talk to each other, right?" I asked, repeating what Kamini said. "What about if I ask the trees to tell me?"

The three Phaetyn exchanged glances, and the youngest one blushed. "Of course, that will work if you have ancestral power."

Al'right. Although, why did we have to come all the way here if they knew that? They just finished telling me I had the power, and now they were questioning it? "Then let's go find out the truth."

"We haven't had someone among us with ancestral powers for so long," the stocky Phaetyn said apologetically, leading us back into the forest. "Most of us don't know how the power works, or what all can be done with it. Did one of the royals tell you that?"

"Um." Was I not supposed to know? "Someone must've said something." I shrugged, relieved when they let it drop. Plus, I didn't have to fight my way through the Phaetyn guards or climb any trees. *Good, good.* I stopped in the middle of the trees and found a large oak that reminded me of the trees at the edge of Zivost. I placed my hands on its rough trunk, closed my eyes, and asked the tree to tell me what it knew about Luna.

*The beautiful Phaetyn queen appeared in an accelerated blur of memories. She lowered and raised the wall multiple times as she left and returned. Sometimes, she had guards with her, and other times, she was alone. The images flashed faster and faster before one stilled with jarring suddenness. The Phaetyn Queen left, lowering the jagged rocks, but this time as she crossed the path, a man waited for her. She returned, and the images faded.*

*The scene sped up, and the next time Queen Luna left, her belly was swollen with child. She wore a hood, and two guards flanked her. She glanced furtively behind her, her eyes welling with tears. The images blurred, showing the queen holding a child. She was outside of the wall. She kissed the baby and gave it back to the man, and she kissed him before returning to Zivost.*

*When she returned to the tree line, Alani stepped out of the forest, her face contorted in rage as she faced her sister. Angry words flew between the two, and when they stood in the tense aftermath, both of their expressions were pained.*

*A new image of Queen Luna materialized as she left again, this time as a hooded figure, alone, stooped as she tried to avoid prying eyes.*

*Alani was hiding in the forest, this time with Queen Luna's mate, Kaelan. When Luna embraced the man on the other side of the wall, his hood tipped back. His ears were rounded. He was human.*

I gasped. Queen Luna had a baby with a human.

*Another image materialized. Luna embraced her sister at the edge of the rock barrier. Tears streamed down the queen's face, but though Alani embraced her sister, her eyes were as hard as agates. Luna stooped to pick up a small valise, and the walls lowered. Queen Luna and her two guards crossed to the broken rock. As the wall rose, and the queen's human lover rushed out to embrace her, dozens of Druman swarmed around the group. Swords glinted in the moonlight, and the Druman slaughtered the queen's guards and her human lover, all while they held her, forcing her to watch.*

*And all the while, Alani and Kaelan observed from the shadows of Zivost, their eyes gleaming.*

*A shadow flew overhead and descended to the blood-splattered rocks. An emerald Drae landed, and the air around him shimmered as he shifted.*

I wrenched my arms to my sides, clasping my hands to my chest as I curled over, keening for the queen of the Phaetyn. I fell to my knees and sobbed for the twisted and sick betrayal I'd witnessed in the images. The previous queen had a child; I'd seen it. Luna had loved a human. If Alani so badly wanted to strengthen the barrier, why hadn't she sent out search parties to find this child? Unless . . . Alani didn't *know* about the child? Unless none of them knew.

Alani and Kaelan had just stood there and watched while Luna was taken.

My stomach turned, and a black hollowness spread through my chest.

"What did you see?"

I'd been crying for several minutes and had completely forgotten the presence of the others. I stood, my fists clenched at my sides, and looked each of the Phaetyn in the eye. My very life was a gift from Queen Luna, and I owed her a debt. Even though I didn't want to be involved, I was, and I couldn't turn my back on the very reason I had life. There was no question Queen Luna would help her people if she were here. The story of her life was a clear example of her belief in self-governance. Still, I needed to think of the implications before I divulged what I'd seen. This situation was out of control.

I dropped my eyes. "I saw Tyrrik falling from the sky again," I said, woodenly. "It was terrible."

---

I STORMED the circle of guards surrounding the elm tree. I was certain they were there to keep me out, no one else. Queen Alani hadn't wanted me to discover the truth.

*Holy Drae-batter pancakes.* She'd watched her sister be taken by the Emperor's Druman and done nothing. I didn't even want to think about how Alani had ended up with Kaelan. Because he'd been with Luna first. For all I knew, Alani had arranged to have Luna taken. The thought chilled me to my core.

I'd *never* expected the Queen of Phaetyn to be as evil as Irdelron. Was every sovereign in the entire realm like this? As far as I was concerned, they should be deposed, preferably followed by a public execution. Or Tyrrik could behead them. I'd even offer to help at this point because . . . really?

I reached the tree, filled with righteous indignation, and charged the guard with the most decorations on his purple uniform. I glared at him. "Where is Kamoi?"

"Prince Kamoi is presently detained elsewhere."

"You don't say," I observed, rolling my eyes.

The guard blinked at my heavy sarcasm, which only irritated me further.

"It's in Kamoi's interest to speak with me, immediately." My teeth extended, my Drae fangs emerging, and while it should've made me appear more frightening, their presence made my face contort while I spoke. "It's a matter of security."

The guard's lips trembled, and he raised his hand to cover his mouth.

If he laughed, I would pull his shiny hair out.

The Phaetyn regained control and, this time seeming genuine, said, "Prince Kamoi is on the southern side of the forest with the rest of our army, trying to quell unrest. He really is busy."

I deflated, feeling my teeth recede. "*Drak.*"

I had a few words to say to that freakin' prince. Starting with the binding-thing and ending with how his mother was a grade-A pile of horse manure.

"Please inform him I would like to see him when he's back," I muttered.

"As you say." The guard bowed.

I dipped my head. At least that guy was nice enough. Maybe they should promote him for not being a pointy-eared jerk. "Thank you."

He looked startled by my gratitude, and a real smile lifted his lips.

They should totally give him a medal or something. With a sigh, I walked away, unaccountably weary. I ignored the side-long looks from the violet-eyed Phaetyn as I passed. The Phaetyn seemed unsure of whether I was an intruder or not. These silver robes were like magic.

Emboldened by my disguise, I followed the rush of water through the trees to my right, I adjusted my course and, a few minutes later, sank to my knees beside a bubbling brook. There were many Phaetyn around, some collecting water, some just talking, and others hurrying by to get other jobs done, maybe even to go join the fight happening somewhere in the forest. No one said anything to me, and I stared at the crystal water.

I didn't want to get involved in all this Phaetyn drama. I felt a debt because of my connection to the trees and Luna, but this wasn't my battle. Yet several Phaetyn were trying to force my hand, each in their different ways; Kamoi with plans to pitch the fork and do the Maypole dance with me, and his mother . . . Well, I wasn't sure what her game was yet, aside from trying to bar me from finding out anything else, and the Phaetyn today asking me to look at the tree's memories.

I wondered if Kamini knew her mother was a turd. No, she was way worse than that.

My presence here with the scheming and calculated interest felt too similar to a game I'd been forced to play before. This place just didn't have a torture room. Or, at least, not that I could see. Somehow, that fact wasn't making my palms any less clammy.

I cupped my hands in the water and brought the clear liquid to my mouth. My nose twitched as I recognized the same sweet smell of the water I'd collected outside the forest. I drained the fluid in my hands, and some of my tension eased. "It's sweet, too."

I dipped my hands again and drank my fill.

"It tastes sweet to you?" a male Phaetyn asked.

I glanced up to see him kneeling next to me. "Yes," I said, drying my hands on my silver garments. "I've never tasted water like this, well, except for the stuff just outside this forest."

The Phaetyn smiled and made a lifting gesture with his hand. A sphere of water lifted from the brook and hovered in the air. "There is life in water, as there is in the ground, the air, and in the animals," the man said. He appeared middle-aged which probably meant he was hundreds of years old. "And Zivost is life itself. The water here is at its purest, and the rivers and streams that flow through this place carry life to those outside the forest. In times gone by, all waterways tasted like this. I'm greatly saddened to hear that is no longer true."

*Oh, boy.* If only he knew the whole of it.

Someone scoffed behind me. I turned and saw a narrow-faced woman sneering at the man. "Do not speak to this atrocity, Fabir. She's not one of us; she should not know our ways."

The man ignored her, speaking again to me. "Tell me, child, what are your Phaetyn powers?"

I shifted, uncomfortably aware of the attention we were garnering. "Well, I can grow potatoes and stuff."

"Ah, a plant affinity."

I shrugged. "I guess. I made a flower once."

He paused, the creases around his eyes deepening. "What do you mean?"

"I made a flower, a blue blossom that glowed." My heart squeezed at the thought of it, of *Tyr*. But then, Tyr was in the rose house right now . . . wasn't he? The essence of him.

There were gasps.

"I see," the man said.

I glanced at him in question and saw he was looking at the ground where a single Tyr-flower had bloomed.

"That's it," I said. My chest filled as I leaned closer to the flower and stroked it gently with my finger. The luminescent flower bent toward me, even when I straightened.

The man was blinking back tears. "Thank you, child. That is a beautiful thing to see."

"How dare you!" the narrow-faced woman seethed. "You enter our forest and try to usurp our rightful queen?"

A younger Phaetyn, one of the ones I'd spoken to earlier, snapped at her. "Ertha, she has ancestral powers. She converses with the trees."

A hush rippled through the gathering crowd.

I slowly got to my feet. Maybe I could slip away before things got too tense.

"Dark does not belong with light," another male Phaetyn shouted.

"No," the man beside me said, standing. "That's exactly where it belongs. Where there is dark, light must always exist. Drae and Phaetyn have always balanced each other as is our responsibility." He gazed out over the crowd, and then his attention landed back on me. "This young woman is that same balance, just as one."

"You've always been a fool," Ertha shouted.

"Look," I said, raising my hands to stop the shouting. "I'm not here to take your queen's job." *Though I think you'd be interested to know a few things about her.* "I came here with Kamoi, thinking your people could help me understand my Phaetyn side. That's it. Whatever trouble you've got going on here has nothing to do with me."

The young Phaetyn from earlier crossed his arms. "You saw something at the trees earlier."

I began striding through the crowd. I would not get involved, not yet. I wanted a clear path. I wanted an exit plan. I wanted to know those I loved would still be safe when this was over. I was not going to put anyone else in danger ever again.

"What did you see?" he pressed.

The tension in the air overwhelmed my frayed nerves, and the pressure to do something consumed me. Scales erupted up my arms, and my eyes blazed. I whirled on the young Phaetyn, and the watching crowd reared back.

"You do not want to know the horrible things I saw." My growl was menacing and filled the surrounding space. They didn't know how this would end, but tensions would escalate, and people, Phaetyn, would get hurt. I took a deep breath, staring at the young man. He blinked but refused to look away. With a shake of my head, I broke the locked gaze, and then pushing through the last few rows, I strode back in the direction of the Pink House.

"See," the woman Ertha called. "An atrocity."

The urge to shift was nearly overwhelming, and I rushed through the hallways of the queen's quartz house, feet tripping in my haste to get to the privacy of our quarters. I all but fell into our room and slammed the door shut behind me, my heart jumping against my ribs, trying to escape.

Dyter jumped.

"Sorry," I said through my Drae teeth, dropping my head into my hands.

"Are you okay?" he asked.

I sighed and paced the room, my blue scales climbing up my neck. The breathing wasn't working. I paced a moment longer, but when my talons began to push from between my fingers, I sat down by Tyrrik and pushed the back of my hand on his bare chest and tried to match my breathing to his.

Dyter must've washed him again, this time more thoroughly. Tyrrik wore new trousers, tied at his waist. Something about them bothered me, and figuring out just what took a moment. The trousers weren't black; they were green. *Ha!* I'd never seen Tyrrik in anything but black clothing.

"Looks like your day was about as good as mine," Dyter said. The contents of his pack were strewn everywhere. He held up the leather case and wrapped it in an aketon before shoving it back in the bag. He continued re-packing.

I didn't want to talk about my day yet. This room wasn't big enough for a Drae transformation. "The queen doesn't want to form an alliance?"

Dyter sighed. "No, they most definitely don't. I can't think of any other angle to push from either. I pulled out all the stops today. The queen wasn't interested, and then she fell into weariness again."

I rolled my eyes. "Yes, her weariness is *awfully* convenient."

Dyter tugged on his ear, a gentle reminder of potential listeners, and I closed my eyes. I was still in touch with my Drae senses, and after only a moment, I was able to block out Dyter and Tyrrik's breathing and focus outside the doorway.

"We're clear," I said.

I watched the old man pack his bag again and tuck the worn bag under the foot of his bed.

He looked at me expectantly.

I'd regained enough control, so I filled him in on my day.

Dyter sat completely still after my recount. He scratched at his stubble with his single hand. "Right."

I nodded, waiting for his insight.

"There's a child, you say?"

"Yes, I have no idea where he or she is or if the child is still alive. But there was a child." I frowned, recalling the tree's yearning during the flashback. "The forest wants the child back more than anything, which I guess means the child has ancestral powers. Do you think that means the trees know the child's alive somewhere?"

Dyter shrugged. "My mind hasn't really gotten past the fact trees can talk in the first place. But if the child has ancestral powers, the child is a she, right?"

I nodded.

Someone knocked at the door, and we both started. This time our exchanged glance was wide-eyed. Had we been overheard?

I crossed to the door and swung it open. Kamoi stood in the hall, looking pristine. And beautiful.

"Hello—"

"I thought you were controlling your people in the southern part of the forest," I said.

His brows rose at my interruption. "I was. The problems there are now resolved."

*And not a speck of dirt on you.*

"Are you okay, Ryn?" he asked, and I realized I was staring.

I didn't know what to make of the prince. His heart seemed to be in the right place as far as I could tell. He was being pressured by his mother, whom he loved as a son should. I felt like Kamoi was someone Dyter could convince to join the fight against the emperor but not while the prince's allegiance was tied so strongly to his mother. If we could get Kamoi, we, I mean Dyter and the other rebels, would have more Phaetyn to help when the rebellion fought the emperor.

"We need to talk," I said, crossing my arms.

He nodded to where Tyrrik was visible on the bed. "The Drae still slumbers."

"He does." The twinge of worry I'd been carrying for the last two days flared, and I remember Tyrrik's frown when he'd heard how long he'd been sleeping. "He should be recovered by now. Is there something wrong? Something else we should be doing?"

Kamoi studied Tyrrik. "Not that I know of, Ryn. You're doing all you can. Perhaps he was closer to death than you thought."

I frowned. He *had* been near death, but still, he'd been speaking the morning after the injury, and again this morning. Phaetyn poisoning or not, I'd definitely seared all of the poison out. Something didn't feel right, but maybe Tyrrik had woken up while I was out and then gone back to sleep. "You're absolutely sure?"

"Of course." He paused, pursing his lips. "I told you a similar thing happens to Phaetyn when we burn ourselves out. You must've felt it when you cured him?"

The utter exhaustion? Yes, I had. I glanced back at Tyrrik, his face still relaxed in his stupor, chest rising and falling. "I really hope it's not long until he wakes."

"You wanted to talk with me? Tabor, my guard at the Sacred Circle, said you'd requested my attention."

My eyes narrowed as I remembered exactly why I needed to speak with him. "Yes," I said, teeth clenched. I called to Dyter, "I'll be back soon."

I closed the door to the room, but before I could launch into my tirade, Kamoi reached out and wrapped a tendril of my hair around his finger.

"Am I in trouble, Ryn?" he asked, smiling. His gaze dropped to my lips, and his violet eyes burned.

I slapped his hand away, refusing to give in to his Phaetyn hotness. "Why do people think we're going to bind?"

His smile dropped, and pink crept up his jaw.

"Yes, I heard about that," I continued, warming up. "Don't spread rumors about me. There is no *us*. And the fact you did that, without declaring your intentions to me to begin with, makes me furious. You have no idea how mortifying it is to have people ask me questions about us. I was embarrassed when I heard."

He'd become progressively smaller during my rant, and his cheeks burned under my blazing glare.

He placed a hand over his heart. "You have my sincerest apology, Ryn. You are entirely, *profoundly* correct; I should have declared my intentions. My only defense is you are both beautiful and powerful, and I found myself at a loss as to how to broach this with you. Especially being in our current situation."

Heat entered my cheeks at his compliment, though I wasn't sure I wholly believed him. "You should have kept it to yourself until we'd spoken."

His violet eyes gleamed, and he stepped closer to me, invading my space. In a husky voice, he asked, "Does this mean you'd consider a binding with me?"

I stared at him. Whoa, I'd never talked with a man about this stuff before. The fake thing with Tyr had been explosive, born of a desperate situation. There was never any courting, nor any gradual descent. We'd fallen suddenly and all at once. I knew the asking usually went first in these things. I mean, give me some credit; Mum had told me a tale or two growing up. Had I been in a situation where a gorgeous guy with pointy ears wanted to court me? Nope. But, I was smart enough to know that entertaining said situation was a bad idea.

Did I know how to reject someone nicely, or *at all*? No, but I could try.

"No," I blurted.

He pulled back, hurt flickering across his face. "What?"

My jaw dropped. *Mistress moons*, did I just say that out loud? "Uh, what I mean is this situation that you spoke of is, uh, dousing my, uh, fire." I squeezed my eyes shut. "I don't want to think of bindings and stuff right now."

I didn't expect his quiet chuckle or for Kamoi to take my hand. "Ryn, you're blushing."

I sniffed. "You're not supposed to call me out on that. It's manner rule number one."

"I apologize again then, but I find the color enticing. You are young; I forget, and maybe you've not had a man come to you as I am now."

I gave him a shy smile, my cheeks still burning. "I haven't, but that doesn't change my answer, Kamoi." He'd put himself out there, so he deserved an honest answer. "Recently, I fell in love and was hurt. I'm not past that yet."

His violet eyes softened. He raised my hand and kissed the back of it. "Then I will be content to wait until your heart is healed. Though you should know, Phaetyn are rather good at healing."

He winked, and I blushed *again* as I slid my hand free.

"O-okay?" I said, feeling a pleasing coolness where he'd kissed my hand.

Kamoi bowed. "There is to be an evening meal tonight," he said, speaking as if our conversation had never occurred. "My mother believes a gathering of the Phaetyn will help to calm frayed tempers."

Relating this civil war to frayed tempers was like calling a Drae a kitten.

"I hope you and Dyter will join us at the royal table," he said after a brief pause.

I'd just rejected the guy, so I practically tripped over myself as I answered, "Yes. Of course."

He leaned toward me and asked, "Will you sit beside me?"

"Kamoi . . ." My heart pounded in my chest.

He smiled. "Just as friends."

I'm not sure his people would interpret the seating plan that way. "I'd appreciate if you cleared up the rumors of our binding first," I said. "As long as it's clear to everyone we're no more than friends, I'll sit beside you."

"Ouch," he said. "You know how to wound a man."

I reached behind my back to open the door and backed into the room as a grin bubbled up. "Lucky you're a good healer then."

I winked and closed the door in his face.

---

I STARED at the flower crown and the other . . . thing.

"Does that top lace up?" Dyter asked, peering over my shoulder. "And where are the sleeves."

I used the tip of my finger to pick up one of the drooping sleeves. "There."

The 'lace up top' was a silver corset with green vines embroidered into it.

Dyter's face was turning purple, and he shook his head violently. "Completely indecent. Not happening. I'll be having a word with Kamoi. I heard some of your conversation. I'll be darned if there's any Phaetyn binding going on."

"Dyter, can we never speak about binding, ever?" I asked, staring at the bottom half of the dress. Alternating lengths of wispy green and silver material fell in a curtain from the lower end of the silver corset. I'd never seen anything like it in Verald.

He spluttered. "I don't want to speak about it either, but the males are closing in, just like your mother and I always knew they would with you being so pretty. We'd hoped your independence and bad sense of humor would scare them off until you were ready to choose a partner. I thought she'd give you the talk about binding, but I guess I better step up since she's in the stars now."

My face softened, and I turned around, hugging Dyter. "I love you, Dyter. And I'm so happy you're here." I let go of him and turned back to the dress. "I also don't need a sex talk."

"Al'right then," he mumbled, the purple shade fading into red.

I picked up the dress and strode off into the bathroom. I'd gone to peek out the front doors already. I wouldn't be the only person in a dress like this.

"Al'right then," Dyter repeated.

I grinned and closed the door, pressing my ear to the wood.

"Al'right then." He mumbled something about Phaetyn and rushing things under his breath.

I sniggered. Setting the dress down, I quickly washed using the smaller basin of water. My silver hair was nearly to the small of my back now, its growth having accelerated since my Drae transformation and even more since being in Zivost. I hoped the strands didn't grow too much longer, or I'd be cutting my hair every week to avoid sitting on it.

Mother had always done my hair up nice when we went to a celebration, rare as they'd been in Verald. The memories of her touch rose, and I swallowed the lump forming in my throat.

I'd just leave my hair down. I'd have the flower crown anyway. Which the people outside were *also* wearing. I could imagine the outrage on the Phaetyn's faces if I was the only one to show up in a crown.

Picking up the dress, I loosened the laces and stepped into the corset. I shimmied the garment over my hips and then struggled with the laces over my chest, pulling them as tight as possible for fear the dress would slide off my frame. By the time the corset was on, the bottom of the corset was snug around my hips, and the double-curve top firmly covered my breasts. Mother totally wouldn't have let me out in this. The innumerable wisps of green and silver material making up the skirt extended to just below my knee. I wiggled my toes, guessing this was one place where I didn't need to wear shoes.

After arranging my silver hair over my shoulders to hide some skin, mostly so Dyter wouldn't have a heart attack, I re-entered the bedroom.

Dyter cast a quick glance at me and did a double-take. "Ryn," he said, a smile growing over his face. "You look pretty." He frowned, glancing at the door. "*Very* pretty."

I tried to keep my own smile back, but a bit of it peeped out. "Thank you." I crossed to Tyrrik and sat by his side. Running my hand down his arm, I asked, "Did you get more nectar down him?"

"Yes, he drinks it easily. His body obviously knows what he needs."

I lay a hand over his forehead. "I really feel like he should have woken up by now. This isn't right. Something just doesn't seem right."

"Kamoi seems certain it's normal."

"Yes. He said as much to me as well." Was I wanting this so much I wasn't being reasonable? How long should it take a Drae to heal?

Dyter cocked his head to the side. "Do you trust him?"

Trust Kamoi? "I feel his heart is in the right place . . ."

Dyter shook his head. "That's a no."

I shrugged my bare shoulder. "I could, I think, in time. I'm not sure I'll trust anyone new in a hurry now. And maybe never again."

Dyter smoothed the front of his borrowed silver aketon; it had vine decorations which matched mine. "That's never a nice lesson, my girl, and most are double your age when they're forced to learn it."

My eyes traced the angular planes of Tyrrik's face. I missed him. That shouldn't be possible, but it was. I traced my finger over the Drae's healed wound and wondered if it still hurt. "Dyter?"

"Yes, Rynnie."

"Do you know, sometimes Tyrrik's scales have a bit of blue in them? The same blue color as my scales?"

"No, I didn't." He cleared his throat before continuing, "What do you think it means?"

I lifted my hand and ran it through the Drae's hair. My breath hitched and came out a smidgen short. "I'm not sure."

"You'll have to ask him when he wakes."

If that ever happened. I sighed, mulling over Dyter's words. "I reckon I probably should."

Dyter covered the Drae with a blanket, forcing me to pull my hand back so he could tuck in the edges. "Al'right, we'll threaten the guards again on the way out. He'll be just fine. Let's go eat and maybe learn a few more things."

"I'm sick of learning today." I stood and picked up my flower crown, knowing I would be stepping into more games the moment I left the room.

With a heavy breath, I jammed the stupid crown on my head.

*D*yter opened the door for me and proceeded to threaten the four guards in the hallway until I interrupted him. The Phaetyn looked familiar, but I dismissed it. They all wore those purple aketons, and with their long silver hair, a lot of them looked alike.

Dyter stopped menacing the soldiers and held his arm out, but when I just peered at him, he took my hand, like Kamoi had, and tucked it into the crook of his elbow.

I half turned to him, arching a brow.

"You're a lady now," Dyter said, red creeping up his neck. "You need to be treated as such."

I laughed and snorted. "Right."

He chuckled, and we walked through the quartz hallways to the front entrance. I'd already seen the rows of cushions and low tables out in the clearing by the queen's dying ash tree, but Dyter hadn't.

The old man whistled low. "How many are coming to this party?"

"I don't even know how many Phaetyn there are." There were at least two dozen long tables, the height of my knees, surrounding the tree. Shiny silver cushions lined either side of each of the low tables.

My best guess was there was seating for forty or fifty at each of the tables.

"Four thousand," he said.

I peered at him and decided not to inquire how he would know that. He was an ambassador; I shouldn't be surprised he would know his job. After all, he was Dyter. Instead, I did the math of tables and cushions in my head. "I would say at least a quarter of them then by the looks."

Kamoi crossed the clearing, weaving in and out of tables toward us.

His gaze dipped to my chest, and I pushed my hair forward. Lacing the corset tight was great for keeping it on but did have other consequences.

The prince's eyes widened as he took me in. I may not have any binding designs on him, but his response was gratifying.

"Kamoi," Dyter bit out.

I knew that voice, and a glance at my mentor confirmed what I'd thought. Dyter's jaw was clenched, and he was glaring at the Phaetyn prince.

Kamoi missed the look or ignored it—his eyes never left me. He held his arm out to me with a warm look of appreciation glowing in his violet eyes.

A few Phaetyn stopped to watch, their conversations drying up as they focused on us.

I nodded at Kamoi, wary of what his attention might cause. "Good evening, Kamoi. I'll walk with Dyter. But would you show us where we'll be sitting? I don't know how you have the tables organized."

His gaze traveled down my dress, his lips parting as he pulled in a deep breath. He met my eyes and flashed a rakish grin. "Ryn, you're absolutely ravishing. You strike me speechless." He clasped his hands to his chest and winked at me. "You will not sit on a cushion. You'll sit with the royal family at the table."

I followed his pointing finger to a table just under the tree. I scrunched my nose as I noticed the fence surrounding the large ash, the distance enough to make touching the tree impossible.

"You are not agreeable with this?" he asked, his brow furrowing.

"The cushions look like more fun," I explained. "I sit at a table all the time."

Kamoi hesitated. "Well, if you would prefer . . ."

Dyter led me around the prince, squeezing my hand in a now familiar warning. "No, Prince Kamoi. We would not want to alter your plans. We're happy to sit at your table."

I kept my mouth shut.

Kamoi fell into step beside me. "Of course."

Phaetyn were already taking their places, apparently sitting at random at the low tables. They were the calmest I'd yet seen them. Perhaps Queen Alani was wise to have a gathering to unify them.

Kamoi led me to a seat, and as soon as I sat, I was glad I wasn't on a cushion. This corset was definitely too tight.

"You are radiant tonight." Kamoi leaned in and brushed my hair back off my shoulder. His breath hitched, and he swallowed hard.

"We're here as friends," I reminded him, waving him away as I would a fly.

His eyes dipped, and a slow smile pulled at one side of his lips.

"Friends," I said in a sharper tone.

Grinning, he held his hand over his heart and chuckled. "I must apologize once more. I find it hard to remember my promises when you look the way you do."

I mumbled, "That's at least the third apology today."

"I suppose I should apologize for that, too," he teased.

I rolled my eyes and turned my attention to the Phaetyn as food was laid out before us. Everyone was dressed in the same fashion as Dyter and me in varying states of grandeur and colors. Some corsets and vests were embroidered as mine, and some plain. The flower crowns were all made of the same pale-green flowers, interspersed with tiny white buds.

I snickered as Dyter's stomach rumbled, and the Phaetyn sitting on cushions in front of the royal table looked at him. "Bit hungry?"

"Just a little," he grumbled. "All I've had today is fruit."

My mouth watered at the layout of food. Freshly baked rolls gave off a delicious aroma, steam still rising from them in wavering tendrils; the bright colors of salad vegetables drew my eye next, and then the arrangement of cut fruit. And . . .

"What's that?" I asked Kamoi, pointing at a fountain with brown liquid.

"Excuse me," he said to his father sitting on the other side, and then Kamoi turned to give me his attention.

*Oops.*

"Yes, Ryn?" he asked, smiling as if I hadn't been totally rude. I pointed again, and he said, "Liquid chocolate."

I frowned at the unfamiliar word. Even in Tyrrik's tower, I wasn't sure I'd ever heard mention of it. "What's chocolate?"

Kamoi grinned. "Really?" When I nodded, he added, "I can't believe you haven't had chocolate."

"I guess starving people don't get access to it," I replied, feeling a little defensive. I'd kind of meant it as a joke, but as his smile faded, I wondered. Just like the abundance on King Irdelron's table, this display of food had me on edge. Verald was doing a lot better with the Phaetyn blood Caltevyn was spreading throughout the Quota Fields, but still, if the Phaetyn just made three or four trips a year out there, everything could be so different . . . for Verald and Gemond. The blood Caltevyn had would only last so long, and while I would do all I could to keep people fed, I was only one Phaetyn.

"I'd love to try it," I said, trying to cover the moment, and Kamoi recovered his smile.

He stood and rounded the table to load fruit onto a small plate. He then poured some of the liquid chocolate into a crystal bowl and placed both before me.

He selected a strawberry and dipped it in the chocolate then popped it in his mouth.

The stuff was a rich brown. Honestly, the thick liquid chocolate looked the same color as the dirt in Verald, like the mud pies Arnik and I had made as children. I took a cautious sniff, surprised when I detected sweetness.

I picked up a blueberry and dabbed the tiniest bit of brown on it. Smiling at Dyter, I popped the fruit in my mouth. My eyes widened as the chocolate coated my tongue. "Holy pancakes."

"Good, isn't it?" Kamoi asked.

I nodded frantically, pushing the fruit at Dyter. He picked a piece of apple and dipped it before taking a bite of the fruit.

He chewed and swallowed. "It's al'right, bit sweet."

Miserable old coot. I went for a strawberry next.

"I'm pleased the chocolate meets with your approval," Kamoi said when I was on my third strawberry.

Did it ever. After my connection with the trees, and seeing the man levitate water today, this was a solid third tick in the Phaetyn's favor.

The Phaetyn hushed, and I glanced around to see the cause. My gaze fell on a litter being carried out of the Pink House. No confusion as to who that was. I pursed my lips and practiced my impassive face.

Slowly, Queen Alani was carried to the royal table, and her mate —Luna's ex-mate, King Kaelan—got up to lift her and deposit her in a grand wooden chair. Unlike the floral crowns every other female wore, Alani's crown was made of silver, gold, and glittering emeralds and diamonds.

So that was how she reminded everyone who she was. My disdain for the queen deepened, and the sweetness of the chocolate soured in my mouth. I might want a crown like that, but it would be for me to treasure, not to show off.

The queen arranged her embroidered robes around her, and the talking resumed as she fell into conversation with her mate.

After what I'd seen today, how Alani and Kaelan had watched as Luna's lover was slaughtered and she was carted off by the emperor, I could barely stomach being this close to them. I thought of my conversation with Dyter about the Drae and tried to suppress my hasty judgment. Perhaps, there hadn't been anything they could've done then.

But the trees didn't think so. Just as they thought Luna's child was still out there. After talking with both Kamini and the Phaetyn rebels—and listening to my own gut—I was certain the trees only told truth. Yet, if they'd told truth, I was sitting at a table with two people who'd let their rightful ruler—one of them her sister and one of them her ex-mate—be taken hostage. Even if they couldn't stop Draedyn, they hadn't told the truth to the other Phaetyn. Not the whole truth.

*That*, I knew, could tear this place apart. However, the words from my lips would do no good. Half of these people hated me. They thought I'd come to take over, that a *Drae monster* had come to claim the queendom. The other half either didn't like this queen or didn't like being confined in Zivost, apart from the world.

I *might* gain the support of some of them if I disclosed Luna's past. The trees wanted their people to know the truth. But if two thousand Phaetyn fought two thousand Phaetyn, they would eventually heal. There could be no victor without using Drae blood. The destruction would go on and on.

The Phaetyn were fighting over whether they had to stay in the forest or not, which, really, did not even register as important compared to cannibalism, starvation, or say . . . the forced conscription of men fighting in the emperor's war of greed. *That* made me furious, that the Phaetyn were squabbling over such a petty thing when the answer was so simple. Why couldn't each Phaetyn make their own decision?

The answer was obvious, and shame sunk deep in my chest. I'd been ignoring the people's right to choose just as hard as the Phaetyn royals. Just not for as long.

The crowd hushed again, and I turned to see Alani standing with her hand raised in the air.

"My people," she said. "Tonight, I've come to you. I wanted to see your faces, your smiles and laughter, to partake in your joy. You, each of you, are why I struggle, day in and day out, to keep the barrier up, to keep us safe."

Oh brother. More than half of the gathered Phaetyn erupted into applause, but several Phaetyn remained mute, their faces stony.

"I would like to welcome our temporary guests, Ryn and Dyter. They have also brought with them Lord Irrik"—she held her hand out when several of the Phaetyn gasped and then raised her voice as she continued—"Fear not. He lies in deep slumber, and I've been assured he poses no threat."

I narrowed my eyes as I processed what she'd said. If I had faith in the queen, I might believe she'd meant our assurances regarding Tyrrik. But, the knowledge I had was that she'd leave her own sister to their enemy. Unease congealed deep in my gut.

"Please, sit with your neighbors," she continued. "Sit with your friends, your family, and your kin. Eat, dance, and uphold the values of our race."

Kamoi scraped back his chair and held his hand out to me. Without thinking, I followed his lead, placing my hand in his as I stood. Wait. Why were we the only two up? What was happening?

Music started playing.

"We're dancing?" I asked as he led me around the table.

I glanced back at Dyter, who was scowling after us.

"Yes, would you like to?" the Prince asked.

"Do you always ask later than you should?" I asked through my fake smile.

He turned, expression sheepish.

As he opened his mouth to speak, I held up a finger. "Your apologies are beginning to lose meaning."

Kamoi nodded, a grave expression on his stunning face. "I will do better. I'm not used to asking, but I see it is important to you. I'll do better."

"That's a very princely thing to say."

He led me into a cleared area just past the tables. The band, a duet, consisted of a Phaetyn with a wind instrument that looked like three wooden flutes stacked on top of each other, and another with a harp that was twice his height.

Kamoi spun me in a circle, forcing my attention from the band to my feet.

There wasn't anyone else dancing yet. I dropped his hand and put distance between us, but he simply eyed the space and stepped toward me.

"That's not how we dance in Verald," I lied. I couldn't tell if Kamoi was aware of how this looked. Maybe this was a normal occurrence for him, what with being the prince and all. But I didn't want to strengthen any of the rumors about us binding. I waved my hips and stomped in a circle.

"This is how you should dance." I held my elbows in and slid to the side and then shook my hands as though flicking off water.

Dyter better not be laughing over there, or I was busted.

"This . . . is how you dance in Verald?"

I kept my expression smooth. "What? You don't like it?" I bent in half to touch my toes and then waved my arms at either side, flicking my hair back. I closed my eyes and swayed. "Feel the music, Kamoi."

"Feel the music," he repeated uncertainly.

I opened my eyes and saw he was replicating my arm movements. Laughter burst out of me, and I doubled over as I gasped for air.

"You were jesting!" he accused.

I glanced over at Dyter to see he was slapping the table, heartily ignoring the queen and her mate who had turned to glare at him.

Kamoi joined in my laughter. "Thank the realm; I thought you were serious."

I waved a hand in the air, walking back to the royal table.

"You no longer wish to dance?" he asked, following me.

I gestured at the corset. "Can no longer breathe."

It was partially my fault that he looked where I'd gestured, I supposed.

"Yes," he gulped. "I see that."

I blushed and then yelped as Kamoi lunged at me, jerking me out of the way as a flying fruit skewer soared past my cheek.

His face hardened, and he pushed me behind him, shouting, "Who threw that?"

23

The prince drew his sword and held the hilt in two hands, head turning as he scanned the now-milling Phaetyn at the party. His voice was low and menacing as he asked again, *"Who threw that?"*

*Who cares?* It was a bit of fruit on a little metal skewer. No harm done. I stepped to the side of Kamoi, trying to put distance between us for appearances. Tensions were high; I didn't want to cause any further problems with the Phaetyn.

Kaelan was storming toward us, and I alerted Kamoi with a fleeting touch on his arm.

"How dare you make a mockery of us," Kaelan snapped, his eyes flashing more indigo than violet. He marched past the next table, stooped to pick up another fruit stick. "You are a disgrace—"

"Father—"

*Was he for real?* "Hey," I said, bringing my hands up as he threw the fruit skewer. My block worked, and the fruit fell to the ground. *Yay for Drae-reflexes.* "I meant no offense. We were just dancing."

Kaelan drew his sword, his face twisted and his lips white with fury. I was more than familiar with this look now after my visits with the trees. Odd how hatred looked the same on Druman, Kings, and Phaetyn.

Kamoi stepped in front of me as his father advanced. In a whisper that was heard throughout the clearing and with a dazed expression, he repeated, "Father."

Kaelen halted his thunderous approach, but his eyes were mere slits as he looked at me. "Move son, or I will move you myself."

The prince didn't budge. "No, this isn't right. She's not to blame for what's happening here."

"Very well," Kaelen said. Holding his blade in the air, breathing hard, he said, "Round them up!"

The royal guards in purple and silver aketons stepped from behind the trees with swords and spears at the ready. Some of the seated Phaetyn screamed, and they began to scramble from their tables, turning the gathering into a chaotic stampede.

The royal guards in the clearing drew their weapons.

Dyter yelled from the other side of the struggling Phaetyn, "Rynnie!"

My heart froze along with the rest of my body.

There was an odd moment when the air seemed to still as though all of Zivost, trees and Phaetyn alike, held their breath, and then Kaelan yelled, "Now."

Guards descended on the Phaetyn. Weapons clashed in a blur. Kamoi threw his sword in front of his face, both hands gripping the hilt to parry his father's strike.

With no weapon, I was very aware I had no chance against fighters of this caliber, but I didn't feel truly in danger; I couldn't really be killed by their blades. Did that mean I wanted to cope with a few punches or a cut or two? No. Not at all.

I did the only thing I could think of . . . I dropped to my hands and knees and crawled away through the melee. I aimed for where I remembered the royal table to be, hoping Dyter would still be there.

Above me, the ring of metal overwhelmed everything but the cacophony of men shouting and women screaming. Phaetyn were running, their sprinting legs visible from my crawling position under the table. Why were they fighting? They were Phaetyn. They were going to heal from their wounds and end up being pissed with each other forever.

The end of this table was close, and the legs of the royal table sat ahead. I froze, seeing that only the queen still sat there, surrounded by guards. Dyter had gone.

I looked around and caught sight of the ash tree between the legs of the fighting Phaetyn. The area around the tree was clear. Maybe I'd be able to see Dyter from there.

I shifted direction, crawling between the tables, wincing as a Phaetyn stepped on my hands. I continued my dash until I reached the table closest to the ash tree. Checking for royal guards, I crawled under the railing of the newly constructed barrier and sprinted around to the back of the tree. Breathing hard, placing my hands on the trunk, I peered out from behind the ash.

Flashes of colors sparked behind my eyes, fading into blobs of muted shades before solidifying. *Kaelan and Alani huddled outside the Pink House in the dark. The twin moons were at opposite stages, one a sliver just beginning to fill out, the other emptying its remaining light into its sister to reach a crescent phase.*

*A hooded figure approached through the trees, carrying a squirming wrapped bundle. Kaelan pursed his lips, and Alani nudged him with her elbow before plastering a smile on her face.*

*Luna's hood fell back, and the Phaetyn queen beamed as she drew close, running the last few steps. The sisters embraced and Luna chatted excitedly, passing over the squirming bundle, completely missing the unveiled glare from her former mate.*

Why was Kaelan glaring when he was clearly in love with Alani and not with Luna? Did he begrudge her for ending things? Surely when he and Alani had Kamoi together, Kaelan couldn't have expected anything else. Maybe the loss of his status as king bothered him.

*Another image emerged. Luna and Alani sitting outside the Pink House while a baby lay on a blanket, playing with a ball of water. A baby in a pink tunic.*

*Mistress Moons.* A sense of dread filled me as the image faded.

Because somewhere in my mind, I knew what that meant. Luna had given Alani and Kaelan her child. The images flittered in and out.

*Kamini as a toddler running to the Pink House, silver hair streaming behind her. The smile she wore stretched across her face, and she held a bouquet of the pale-green flowers. Kamoi and his parents sat on the porch; a much younger Kamoi glanced back and forth between his parents. Kaelan was frowning and Alani crying. Kamini extended the bouquet toward Alani, and Kaelan pushed her away. Kamoi jumped up and snapped something at his father, wrapping Kamini in a hug as he guided her off the porch.*

I pulled back from the tree, chest heaving. Kamini was Luna's *daughter?* Which would mean Kamini should have ancestral powers too . . . I lowered my hand and stared out at the clearing where the Phaetyn fought—

A body fell to the ground in the archway, startling me back to the present. The Phaetyn on the ground was one of the rebels I'd seen earlier today, the stocky one who barely spoke during the conversation in the lean-to. I blinked as his chest jerked in time to the gurgles of his labored inhales. I watched as his eyes grew glassy and as his chest stilled. He looked dead.

But, he couldn't be dead because *that* was impossible.

A small trickle of green oozed from his mouth. I peered down his body, and my gaze halted on the knife protruding from his side. The silvery fabric of his aketon was torn, and the skin around the wound was visible through the tear. His pale skin had lost its luster, probably typical for death, but that wasn't what made my heart stop.

The skin surrounding the knife wound wasn't the same color as everywhere else. The Phaetyn's blood was silvery iridescent and oozed from the wound, but even that didn't hide the dark streaks of black. *Black.*

I swallowed, and my mind whirled. There was only one thing I could think of that would cause that. But it was impossible because that meant this fight was a *real* fight where Phaetyn were *dying.* And there was only one way to kill Phaetyn.

179

My heart pounded to life as rage filled me. I sucked in a deep breath and stood. I'd better be wrong. I'd bloody better be wrong.

I ducked under the railing and shoved a royal Phaetyn guard out of my way, my arms moving in a blur. I charged toward the quartz house. Scales covered my chest and my arms, my talons shifted out, and my vision sharpened as my eyes changed. I was barely holding it together; only the hope that I was wrong kept me from going full Drae.

Phaetyn stepped in my path, but I flung them aside like flies. A sting pricked my back. I whirled and grabbed at the offending guard, my talons shredding his tunic and slicing into his skin. He bellowed in pain as his skin darkened around the wound, and I roared.

I stepped over his writhing body.

I screamed in rage, and several Phaetyn scampered out of my path as I broke into a run.

The fighting idiots blurred, and I charged up the steps and through the door of the Pink House. I sprinted down the hall, fear squeezing my chest. What if I was too late?

One of the guards stood outside the room, shouting when he saw me. With one swipe, I sent him crashing down the hall. The door was ajar, and I pushed through.

*No, no, no!*

I burst into the room, and horror struck me dumb.

Tyrrik lay on the bed, unconscious, only his lap covered by the blanket Dyter had spread over him before we left.

Five guards surrounded Tyrrik. One guard sat at the head of the bed, pouring crystal clear liquid into Tyrrik's mouth. Two guards sat on either side of the bed. One sliced deeply into Tyrrik's thigh and then spat in the open wound. Spitting . . . their Phaetyn juice would poison him, keeping his wound from healing. The other Phaetyn ran a blade through a still oozing wound on the other leg. Judging by the rows of gashes on his legs and arms, they'd been at it for a while. Black blood oozed from many of the wounds, and as my gaze traveled up to Tyrrik's chest, I saw the basins under his arms, collecting blood from the gashes on the inside of his elbows. Two more guards sat on Dyter's bed, dipping weapons in Tyrrik's blood.

Red-streaked darkness filled my chest; pounding with my heart, it filled my being. My shoulders lifted, my mouth contorting, fangs descending as I screamed a heart-ripping roar of rage and pain. Blue scales covered my frame, my talons lengthened, my eyes formed slits, but somehow, *somehow* as my wings began to stab out through my back, I paused.

If I shifted full Drae, I'd bring the entire Pink House down, and while that would kill the guards, it might also kill Tyrrik.

The guards scrambled upright, brandishing their blood-coated blades at me.

One of the guards lunged forward as another threw a knife. The blade bounced off my blue scales and clattered to the floor as the other guards moved to within striking distance. I snarled, lost to my instincts, and crouched like the predator I was to meet their attack.

I grabbed the outstretched blade of the guard and pulled him close, driving my talons deep into his stomach. He shrieked, and I jerked my hand upward, slicing through his abdominal organs until I hit bone. He opened his mouth, silvery blood gushing out, and I flung him away so his blood wouldn't further injure my Drae. The Phaetyn's body crashed against the wall, and he slid to the ground in a heap.

The other guards had halted their advance while they watched my fight with their companion, and now the remaining four Phaetyn converged and advanced as a single unit. *Like it matters.* I would destroy every one of them. They were *prey.* I was powerful.

They threw weapons at me, and I batted several of them from the air before catching one of the guards peering over my shoulder toward the door. Were they just stalling until help arrived? My anger boiled, and I bent my knees, catapulting myself toward them. I charged, slashing at the Phaetyn with my talons, roaring. I saw nothing but the monsters that hurt *my* Tyrrik, for surely he was mine. Wetness splattered me, and I continued to shred until there was nothing but pieces of what had once been life.

I stood afterward in the middle of the blood-splattered room.

My gaze landed on Tyrrik. My ears fixed on his labored breathing. I only smelled his blood. I knelt at his side and picked a blade up from the floor. I sliced through the pads of my fingers, pushing my blood over his wounds to help them heal.

I heard footsteps in the hall and whirled to face the next threat, but Dyter's scent preceded him, and though my talons didn't retract, I'd already knelt beside Tyrrik again before he stepped through the door.

"What the hay . . ." Dyter gasped, skidding to a halt. "Holy fecking Drae," he panted, closing the door behind him.

His eyes were as wide as saucers, and his mouth hung open as he struggled to catch his breath. "What—" He pointed at the gore splattering the walls and severed parts littering the floor and then turned to the side and threw up.

I felt like I should apologize to him, but I wasn't the least bit sorry. Not at all.

"Watch the door," I growled through my fangs. "They poisoned Tyrrik."

"We need to leave now," Dyter said, wiping his chin.

I listened to Tyrrik's straining heartbeat. "There will be no later for Tyrrik unless I heal him now. They were spitting on the knife to keep the wounds open and drain him. There are droplets of Phaetyn poison inside him again."

"As quick as you can then, Rynnie," Dyter said, as he bent to pick up one of the weapons littering the floor.

I closed my eyes and took a deep breath, placing my hands on Tyrrik's chest. His smoky leather-and-steel scent washed over me.

I leaned over the Drae and pressed my lips to his. His soft lips were unmoving, so I pushed my tongue to pry them slightly apart as I brought my hands to either side of his face. He tasted like nectar. I breathed into him. I imagined the darkness of my lord Tyrrik's Drae, and I shoved as much of my Phaetyn power into him, in a blast, as I could. The energy filled his body, causing him to arch off the bed.

"Ryn, hurry," Dyter yelled.

I stood as something crashed outside in the hallway, hoping I'd given Tyrrik enough help to stave off death. There wasn't time to check.

"I'm ready," I said, glancing around the room for our things, but whatever things we'd once had were now . . . ruined. "Grab whatever you can—"

"You're blinded," Kaelan bellowed outside. "The monstrosity must die."

My temper flared, and I knew when I saw the Phaetyn king, I wouldn't be able to keep it together. Not as a Phaetyn. "Did you hear that?" I snapped, but Dyter shook his head. I must have my Drae senses on high alert. "You need to get out of here now. You and Tyrrik."

Dyter grabbed something from under his bed, scooped a couple of things up from the floor, and slung his pack over his shoulder. "I'm going to need your help. I can't carry the Drae alone."

I snorted, walked back around Tyrrik's bed, and swept everything off the sole table. I picked it up and heaved it across the room. The thick piece of furniture crashed into the window, shattering the glass on impact and sailing out into the clearing outside.

I gestured at the gaping hole, and Dyter shook his head.

"I guess we're not trying to be stealthy about our exit?"

A menacing rumble filled my chest as I listened to Kamoi and Kaelan's fighting in the hall. "I'm not done here yet. They tried to kill Tyrrik, and they've been bleeding him so they could kill the rebel Phaetyn with poisoned blades."

I broke away the shards of glass on the bottom of the frame with a slice of my talons. "Get out now."

Dyter didn't argue, clambering over the sill to the outside porch.

I covered Tyrrik with a blanket and picked him up, my heart breaking at his limpness. I passed him to Dyter, who grunted.

"I can't carry him, Rynnie. Pass me another blanket from the bed."

I yanked the top blanket off and tossed it through the window, spinning back as Kaelan burst into the room.

"You," he shouted. His eyes were wild, his fair skin mottled with rage. "Look what you've done."

Behind the Phaetyn king stood his mate, Alani, her eyes burning with hatred. Behind them over a dozen soldiers in purple aketons held spears and swords at the ready.

"Get him out of here," I growled at Dyter, my anger boiling back to the surface. I stepped in front of the Phaetyn king to block Dyter and Tyrrik from view. "What I've done? You betrayed—"

"You were never welcome here," Alani screamed. "You shouldn't even exist. You're an abomination."

The heavy dragging sound continued out on the porch, and I hoped Dyter would get them off before—

"Kill her!" Alani screeched.

And, at the same time, her mate bellowed, "Kill them all!"

My vision changed, the colors becoming sharper. I rolled my neck as my body began to expand; a ripple ran through me as my scales grew to accommodate my Drae. I roared, letting instinct take over, and the room exploded as I shifted into Drae.

Pieces of quartz and wood blasted out, exploding high into the forest as I burst through the ceiling into the night, the darkness, my friend.

The air reeked of blood and death and betrayal.

I stretched my neck as I cleared the shards of glittering quartz and broken wood off my massive body. I stomped on the ground as I bellowed in rage. I swung my neck wide, crashing the side of my head through the walls of the queen's house, roaring in fury.

Kaelen threw a piece of rubble off himself and then scrambled to uncover his mate. He choked at her pulverized form. Black webs had snaked through her broken body, and her open wounds were easy victims to Tyrrik's blood dripping from the rubble with the basins flung and overturned.

Kaelen struggled to his feet, and above, the golden filaments of ancestral power protecting the Phaetyn from the emperor, dissolved into the darkness.

"You killed my mate!" His face filled with horror as he tipped his head to the sky. "You've brought down the barrier—"

I whipped my tail, lashing it across his torso. He was thrown across his dead queen, landing with a cry of pain. Using my talons, I swept at the rubble and the dipped weapons mixed in, launching them at the Phaetyn King.

A knife sliced the back of his raised hand. He stared in horror as black darkened his skin, oozing outward from the wound. His gaze lifted to mine, and I lowered myself to his level and licked my fangs. I would not be a victim to the schemes of the Phaetyn, and I would not allow them to steal from me, manipulate me, or hurt me again. I would protect my friends.

Once Kaelan was dead, I roared again, announcing throughout the entirety of Zivost I was Drae. The remaining Phaetyn had gathered when I burst out of the ceiling of the quartz house, but now, they fled. I watched them go, and then, using my tail, I laid the entire Pink House to waste. If I could breathe fire, I would've burned it to ash.

I turned and spotted Dyter at the edge of the trees behind me, eyes wide as he stood over Tyrrik's unconscious body. He'd managed to drag him a fair way on the blanket. I lumbered toward them, pausing to remind any Phaetyn within the sound of my voice I was done playing games.

*Shh, Khosana.*

I yelped in surprise, an odd rumbling in my throat. *Tyrrik?* My heart pounded, and his voice shattered through my Drae form. Only a few seconds later, I stood on top of the rubble in my Phaetyn form.

"Tyrrik," I screamed, running toward the trees.

Dyter moved out of the way, but when I got to Tyrrik, he was still unconscious. I thought of our mental barrier, but I'd not had any wall up when I changed, and I didn't have one up now. He'd spoken; I was sure of it. I ran my hand over his chest as I whispered, "Please Tyrrik, don't leave me."

---

"COME ON, DYTER," I said, hefting Tyrrik upright. "We need to leave before the rest of Phaetynville decides to come visit."

I pulled the Drae over my shoulder, hunching as I strode into the trees. I didn't care how or what direction, I was leaving this place *right now*. I tried to shift back to my Drae, but my emotions made it impossible to focus.

"Ryn."

I looked up to see Kamini staring out from between the trunks.

"You must leave now," she said.

I tensed, but Kamini was someone the trees had shown me many times. They didn't see her as a danger to the Phaetyn which meant she wasn't a danger to me . . . right? "And I suppose you're going to help us?"

She tilted her head. "Yes."

I shook my head once before I remembered my visions from the ash tree.

"Ryn!"

I spun to see Kamoi emerging from the rubble.

"If you wish to leave, it must be now," Kamini said urgently, her eyes flickering to Kamoi.

I looked at Kamini, but the Phaetyn girl shook her head. I didn't know if that meant she didn't trust Kamoi or if she didn't want him to overhear this conversation.

I deliberated. I really didn't want to linger here or want to trust anyone else, not even with the tree's assurances, but Dyter and I could wander for hours lost in this place. "Fine," I said. "Let's go."

We backed into the trees, Kamini leading the way.

We walked for what felt like an eternity to my weary body. As the branches of trees brushed my skin, I caught glimpses of Phaetyn running, hiding in clusters, royal guards giving chase. Dyter walked alongside me, silent as a mute.

I cleared my throat, shifting Tyrrik on my shoulders, and asked, "Can we stop for a minute? Are we far enough away from . . . wherever that it's safe for us to take a break?"

Kamini turned, the fear on her adult-child face smoothing to an impassive expression.

*Creepy.*

"If we stop now, we might not make it to the border in time."

"In time?" I demanded. I wanted to scream. "How about if I shift again and carry us all to the border?"

"Then we *definitely* won't make it in time. If they see your Drae form, we'll have too many visitors for you to tree-talk," she said. "How long did it take you to get to the center of Zivost when they brought you in?"

"About four hours," I said. The idea of carrying Tyrrik for another four hours made me want to curl up in a ball.

"We've been walking for twenty minutes," Kamini said. "We'll be to the border in another five minutes."

*Wait . . . What?* I tried to catch up with the Phaetyn's plan. Get to the border and tree-talk. Right.

"They do it to confuse visitors."

I was confused *now*. "You get visitors?" I asked, glancing at Dyter, who looked just as baffled as me.

"Not often, but leading newcomers a longer route to our city is protocol," Kamini said.

Seriously, having a conversation with an eight-year-old that sounded like she was thirty was so creepy.

"Why are you helping us?" I asked, helplessly. "I just killed the queen and king."

Her gaze slid to me. "I should be thanking you for killing the queen; that certainly helps our cause."

This time when I shifted Tyrrik it wasn't really because he needed it. "You're a rebel?"

She dipped her head. "Correct. Now, this is of utmost importance. I must know what the ash tree told you."

Since entering the Zivost, the only things to tell me the absolute truth had been the trees. And the trees trusted Kamini. She was Luna's daughter. That meant something. I glanced to Dyter, who didn't give me any sign of what to do . . . so I trusted my gut.

In a halting voice which grew stronger, I told the story of her mother leaving her with her aunt. I finished the story by asking, "Did you already know?"

She shook her head. "I suspected Alani wasn't my mother. I knew Kaelan wasn't my father."

"Wouldn't the trees tell you?" I asked. If the trees tell Phaetyn what they've seen, wouldn't she be able to see it, too.

She shook her head again, a slow smile spreading across her face. "I don't have a tree here, and I don't have the ancestral power, so I can't talk with all the trees as you can."

I tripped over an exposed tree root. "But your mother was Luna Nuloa."

"So you say. That's why I want you to talk with the trees at the border."

"To confirm she was your mother?" I was missing something. Granted, I was physically and mentally exhausted. Actually, I think I'd passed exhausted on the spectrum and was rapidly approaching delirious.

But if Luna Nuloa *was* Kamini's mother, wouldn't that make Kamini the new queen? Shouldn't she also have ancestral powers being born before me? The eldest daughter inherited them after all. I only had ancestral power because Luna had poured hers into me so my mother wouldn't miscarry. Surely if Kamini had ancestral powers, that would be common knowledge.

"Do you dream?" she asked, changing the subject.

I stumbled again and growled. "I've been too tired lately to dream."

But that wasn't completely true because last night here in Zivost,

I dreamed the emperor's Druman were chasing me. I was not going to share my nightmares with her.

"I dream all the time," she said. "I dream about a Phaetyn girl. She lives outside our walls. She does what the Phaetyn are meant to do; she's a land healer." She paused and then added, "I believe it is my destiny to become her."

"Is that what drove you to join the rebellion?" Dyter asked.

Kamini laughed, but the sound reverberated with bitterness. "That vision is what drove me to *create* the rebellion."

*Holy Pancakes! Kamini* was the leader of the rebellion? I shared a shocked look with Dyter.

She halted. "We're here. You can set him down," she said. "I need you to touch the tree. It should be easier now. Phaetyn powers get easier every time you use them."

I slid Tyrrik from my shoulders to the ground, circling my arms to loosen the stiff muscles. "First tell me what you're looking for?"

"The truth," she said, grabbing my empty hands and pressing them to the trunk of a large elm.

Colors burst behind my eyes, and then murky shadows formed. *Luna Nuloa and her guards stood beside the elm, the queen holding her daughter wrapped in a silvery blanket. Luna lowered the rock wall, and as she tilted her head to see to the other side of the barrier, the moonlight exposed her devastated face. She murmured to one of the guards, but her words were lost in the silence of the images. She pointed back toward Zivost and then to the outside. The wall retracted, and the three of them began to cross.*

*As Luna left Zivost for the other side, her mortal lover emerged. He smiled, his eyes lit with love, and in his arms, he held a small child.*

I withdrew my hands, realizing the moment I did that Kamini no longer held them to the tree. I grinned and opened my eyes, my heart pounding with excitement in anticipation of telling her what I'd seen. Luna and her human lover had another, *older* child together. At least, that's what I'd understood from the visions. That would explain why Kamini didn't possess the ancestral powers for her generation. Was her older sibling female and still out there somewhere, an unknown solution to the Phaetyn's troubles? My mind moved frantically, putting the pieces together. Luna had mated with Kaelan long ago but over time saw that he and Alani were in love. She'd eventually broken their binding and then fell in love with a human and had two children with him, giving the youngest to Alani and Kaelan, perhaps to babysit, or maybe Luna didn't trust them with the eldest daughter. The emperor had then slaughtered Luna's human lover and captured her. Alani became queen after this, and Kaelan king once more, while Luna was pouring her ancestral powers into my mother's womb, into *me*.

All of the pieces finally fit together. I opened my mouth to tell Kamini when a rustling in the forest made me freeze.

"Ryn? Dyter?" Kamoi called, just before stepping out of the trees with several guards.

Relief washed over Kamoi's features as his gaze flitted over Kamini and then met mine. "I've been so worried."

"I'm glad you're okay," I said. He'd taken on his *father* for me. I couldn't imagine how that was going to haunt him in time.

Kamini's gaze shifted from her brother to me, and she pursed her lips.

Kamoi crossed the dirt patch leading up to the large elm and scooped me into his arms. "Curse the night, what happened?" He breathed into my hair, the thudding of his heart tangible where our chests touched. He continued to hold me close as he said, "One minute my father is throwing fruit at you, and then chaos ensues. How did you get away?"

I drew back, tapping him on the chest at the same time. He set me down, a sad smile resting on his lips.

*Drak.* How was I supposed to tell him I'd killed his parents? "Uh, I . . . uh,"

He shook his head, jaw clenched. "I know what happened in the clearing. I watched it."

"I'm sorry," I said, and in my mind I added, *your parents died.* Because I wasn't sorry I'd killed them. Not sorry at all.

The guards continued to hover inside the tree line, their attention focused on the prince and Kamini.

Kamoi shook his head again. "I'm not. I mean . . ." He swallowed before continuing, "I'm sorry they're dead, but they were terrible leaders for our people as I'm sure you saw. That might be wrong of me to say—"

His eyes grew dark and hard for an instant before he glanced up at me with a softened gaze, and my heart squeezed at the conflict that must be rampant inside him. "What will happen to the Phaetyn now?" I asked. "The golden barrier is down."

Kamoi's gaze went from me to Dyter and then back to me. "You are the only Phaetyn with ancestral powers." Kamoi glanced at Kamini before turning back to me. "Will you lead our people, Ryn?"

25

*I* closed my eyes to control the overwhelming urge to burst out into bitter laughter. Would I rule these people who had made me feel uneasy and unwelcome from day one? Would I help the people who had drained an unconscious Drae of blood just to properly kill each other? "No," I said. "There are so many reasons, but the short answer is no."

"Please," Kamoi said, reaching for my hands. He entwined his fingers with mine and held them to his chest. "Please come back. We can figure this out; together we can rebuild a better Zivost."

I extracted my hands. "I can't, Kamoi. I'm not Phaetyn, not really. I can't ignore the problems of this world to solve your people's problems. I need to leave. I need to help Tyrrik get better, and we need to go to Gemond to talk with their king. We have a war to wage."

Dyter glanced at me, and I nodded at him. I'd made my choice. I was part of this world whether I liked it or not. I couldn't stand by while the emperor drove this realm and its people into the ground.

Kamoi nodded. "I understand. You are needed elsewhere now, but when you are done, I hope you'll come back."

I shook my head, repeating, "I'm not Phaetyn."

He smiled, his gaze taking me in. "You are Phaetyn in every way

193

that matters. You've captured my heart. Just promise me you'll come back and we can try."

*I'd captured his heart? When?* I took a deep breath and told him the truth. "I'm sorry, Kamoi. If I promised you anything, it would be a lie. There is no we, and there won't be a we. My heart is Drae; it beats as a Drae. To tell you anything else would be misleading."

The Phaetyn prince studied my face. "I understand. You can't reason with the heart. But there may come a time when you feel differently. I'll not lose hope. Not yet."

"So you'll let us go?" I asked.

Kamoi frowned. "Of course I'll let you go. I was trying to find you to help make sure you got out safely."

"I'm sorry," I said, bowing my head. I didn't know who to trust anymore. I was relying on the judgment of freakin' trees.

"Don't apologize," he said. "I'm surprised you'll even talk with me after I brought you here. If anyone should be apologizing, it should be me."

"You defended me in the end, Kamoi." I smiled at him, a tightness clamping my heart at the thought of what he'd lost tonight. "Thank you for saving my life."

"Thank you, Highness," Dyter said. "Perhaps you could convey my message to whomever rises to power?"

The Phaetyn prince turned to Kamini who stood quietly watching the scene. "If we're lucky, the Phaetyn will recognize Kamini as our queen." He put his hand on his sister. "She's the highest-ranking female below Ryn."

I looked back and forth between the two of them and met Kamini's gaze. "Your mother was Luna, not Alani." I glanced at Kamoi, and even though I knew the answer, I asked, "You know she's Luna's daughter?"

"Yes," he said simply. "But she doesn't have ancestral powers." He faced his cousin and said, "I didn't realize you knew, Kami."

"I've known for a long time. It's not hard to piece together when your supposed parents hate the sight of you. Kaelan tended to divulge too much when his ire was raised." Tears gathered in Kamini's eyes.

"I'm sorry I didn't tell you, Kami, but I didn't want you to have to shoulder a weight you were never meant to carry." Kamoi hung his head.

She bit her lip while he spoke and then said, "That wasn't your decision to make."

He winced, and I felt a zing of pride for the Phaetyn girl.

"You're right," he said, bowing his head. "I apologize." He dropped to a knee before the young Kamini and said, "I will pledge my allegiance to you, Kami, and serve however you deem best. I only want what is best for our people."

I flicked a glance at Dyter and hesitated, thinking back to what the tree had shown me. I may not see Kamoi or Kamini for a long time, or ever again. Where I was going, I couldn't be sure I'd even survive. This information shouldn't go with me to the grave. Despite the terror I'd experienced in this forest, I *knew* there was good in Phaetynville worth saving. The Phaetyn deserved to have a queen with ancestral powers if she was still alive. "What if there was another child? What if Luna had a child before Kamini? Another daughter?"

Dyter looked at me as if I'd lost my mind, but Kamoi and Kamini only raised their brows in an expression that proved they were related. It also reinforced the fact they'd both made the same connection long ago.

Kamini's eyes widened with excitement. "Did the trees show you an elder child?" When I nodded, her eyes lit. "Are you sure?" she asked, before whispering to herself, "I have a sister."

Kamoi glanced at his adopted sister and then smiled widely at me. "Where is she?"

His excitement relieved me. I'd worried he might resent Kamini being replaced. "I don't know. The trees don't know." The eldest daughter's location was the crux of the problem. With an aerial view, it probably wouldn't be difficult to find her. She was a land healer in a realm drained of life. "But we can find her."

Kamoi stood and brushed my cheek with his fingers. "Yes, we can." He turned to Kamini. "If you want me to search for her, you know I will—"

Kamini held up her hand. "First we need to secure Zivost. If Ryn hasn't found her by then, we'll reassess. I want her here as much as anyone . . . trust me. But I want there to be a Zivost sanctuary, too."

I nodded at the wisdom the childlike rebel had shared. If we never found the other Phaetyn, Kamini would still make a great ruler.

"Which is why," Kamini continued, "I'd like to ask you to put up the barrier again."

"The gold one?" I asked, shaking my head. "I don't know how to do that."

Kamini shrugged. "You have ancestral powers."

"And yet I still don't know how," I replied, arching a brow.

Kamoi took his sister's hand. "All we ask is that you try. We can control the rock barrier around the forest, that offers some protection, but the other barrier protects us from the sky, from Drae. If you can put it back up, Kamini can do her best to keep the barrier there, as my mother did before her."

Were they kidding? I grimaced and, shaking my head, asked, "You want to be bed-ridden your whole life, Kamini?"

A ghost of a smile crossed her lips. "Once my older sister is found, I won't need to be."

*No pressure, Ryn.* I sighed heavily. "Al'right, I'll give it a go, but I'm warning you that it probably won't work."

I walked back to the tree I'd been touching and rested my hands on its rough bark. Closing my eyes, I waited for the usual assault of images, but the only vision the trees provided was of the gold hovering above their tops. "Yes," I muttered. "But how?"

*Queen Luna stood at the outskirts of the forest, her palms on a tree. A golden hue spread upward, coating the Zivost with a shimmering glow.*

"Great, that's super helpful. Thanks," I spoke to the tree. Looks like I was on my own.

I squeezed my eyes, reaching for my Phaetyn power. The vibrant energy answered my call and rushed to my fingertips where I directed the flow into the forest, willing the energy to reach high, to embrace the trees and people within its midst, to keep all enemies outside, and to shine gold like the barrier before it. I poured everything into my hands and then cracked an eye open.

"Have you done it yet?" Dyter asked.

I scowled at him. There was no iridescent golden cover over Zivost. From what I could tell, nothing had happened. "No. It didn't work." I turned to Kamini. "I'm sorry."

She swallowed. "You tried. That's all we asked for."

A guard a few feet away yelped and tumbled back as the ground exploded beneath him. We stared at the giant tree root which had appeared above ground.

"How much energy did you put into the tree?" Kamoi whispered.

I turned and blinked at the trunk which was expanding before our eyes, the tree's limbs shooting into the sky. "Umm. A bit?"

Kamini grinned. "I wonder how big it will get."

I gazed uneasily at the tree, hoping it didn't destroy the whole forest.

We watched for a full minute before it became apparent the tree wasn't going to stop growing.

Stepping farther from the monstrous tree, Kamoi studied me a moment before speaking. "Ryn, I heard what you said, but I hope you'll come back one day."

Kamini's gaze shifted from me and Kamoi to Dyter. "Send word when you go to battle. I'll do what I can to aid you. I can't promise all of our kind will help; I don't know how the next weeks will go, but some of my kind are with you."

Dyter grinned, his ropey scar twisting his face to appear maniacal in the moonlight.

"Our time is up," Kamoi announced as the clang of metal sounded above the thundering growth of the tree behind us. He nodded to the guards behind him. "I'll have my men lead those of the Phaetyn still loyal to my mother and father off. Good luck, Ryn."

He bent over me, and I realized he was going to kiss me a

moment too late. His lips touched mine, and I immediately pulled back.

A flash of hurt crossed his face.

He literally had no right to be hurt. I'd been completely upfront. Forcing a smile I definitely didn't feel, I reminded him, "Friends."

He recovered quickly, and with a wink, he said. "Now I remember."

*Yeah, sure.*

Kamini waved me to her and wrapped her arms around me for a hug. "Be true to who you are. I hope our paths cross again soon."

"Thanks," I murmured a moment after she pulled away. "Thanks for everything."

"I'll see you at home," Kamoi said to Kamini with a wink.

The two Phaetyn royals turned their backs to us and marched into the forest, Kamoi leading his guards toward the noise and Kamini going in the opposite direction. They disappeared into the darkness.

---

DYTER and I blew out a breath at the same time. We peered down at Lord Tyrrik, and I sighed, saying, "I hope you appreciate this when you wake up."

Dyter chuckled beside me. "I'm sure he will. Come on now, let's get him to safety."

"Then sleep."

"Then sleep," he agreed. "I'm too old for this crap."

"You got your alliance though. In the end." I grabbed Tyrrik's arm and hoisted him over my shoulders.

We crossed where the barrier had been, and as soon as we were off the path, the rocks thrust out of the ground and climbed into the sky.

Our conversation dwindled as we continued into the mountains, and I spotted a copse of scraggly trees in the distance, silver in the moonlight.

"Should we head over there?" I asked, pointing at the trees.

Dyter looked at the trees and then pointed at a rocky overhang farther to our left. "Let's go there. That way if it rains, or a Drae flies overhead . . ."

Crossing to the overhang didn't take long; thank the moons for small mercies. I laid Tyrrik down on a dark rock under the overhang and groaned as my muscles were unburdened. We'd passed near a stream five minutes back. "I need to get some water to make him nectar."

Dyter grimaced. "I'll get water. You'd better deal with Tyrrik, Ryn. He started wheezing when we entered the mountains."

I leaned over Tyrrik and listened. "I don't hear any wheezing."

Dyter tossed me the waterskin. "Al'right. Your ears are better than mine any day. Just don't be mad if you come back and he's dead."

Dead? *Mistress moons*. I was *not* okay with that. Not after dragging him everywhere for the last few days. At least, that's what I told myself.

I propped Dyter's cloak under Tyrrik's head and ran my fingers through the limp strands of his hair. His breathing did seem shallow, but his skin had better color than in Zivost. Or was that just the way the moons were reflecting off his skin?

I tossed Dyter the waterskin and waited until I heard him climbing down the rocks.

"You better not die on me," I muttered. I traced Tyrrik's mouth and sealed my lips to his. I gasped as pure heat flooded through my body, breaking the connection. "You're not supposed to be enjoying this, Ryn," I scolded myself. I closed the distance again, this time blocking out the feel of his mouth against mine.

Tyrrik's darkness was like a cloudy night sky when the moons and stars were hidden and the warmth of the day was trapped beneath the haze of moisture. But spotting the black canvas were several droplets of pale gold, nothing like before, but still there, where it shouldn't be. Now that I knew what I was looking for, it was easy to pick off the Phaetyn poison from within the Drae and even easier to burn it out.

I let myself sink into the darkness and saw deep within the Drae's core a spark of blue dancing in the pitch. The lapis-colored flame reminded me of the blue that would pulse in Tyrrik's scales sometimes. I pushed my energy into the flame, making it burn brighter, and together we obliterated every last speck of gold.

I broke the connection and took a deep breath, pulling my energy into my lungs. I listened for Dyter, and when I didn't hear him, I leaned over the Drae and pressed my lips to his again. I exhaled, passing more of my vibrant blue energy to the Drae, and his pale flame surged briefly.

I grinned in triumph as I felt him shift on the ground, but I was careful not to break our connection.

One of his hands slid up my arm, and I squeaked in surprised. But Tyrrik's touch was like fire, and as he cupped the back of my neck, his fingers threading into my hair, I melted into him. His other arm encircled my waist, tugging me down. I relaxed my body so my torso was flush with his, resting my hands on his smooth, warm chest.

His tongue brushed against mine, and tingles burst and skittered across my skin and through my chest. Desire rose, but Tyrrik shuddered, his body heaved, and I pulled back just in time to watch him roll to the side and throw up.

*Ugh.* I grimaced.

He coughed and sputtered, bringing up more clear fluid that smelled sour and rank. I remembered the crystal fluid the guards had been pouring into his mouth. What was that? I should've asked Kamoi before we left.

My anger flared at the Phaetyn once again, and I rested my hand on Tyrrik's cheek. "Shh."

His eyes fluttered open, and he mumbled incoherently before passing out again.

"That was so not how I thought kissing you would go," I muttered. I ripped off one of the wispy panels from my skirt and dried Tyrrik's mouth. "I finally contemplate forgiving you, and you throw up. That's not allowed. You owe me a real kiss."

I tensed at the sound of rocks scattering behind me.

"About time," Dyter said from the entrance with a chuckle, swinging the waterskin as he shifted farther into the large cave.

I glowered at him. "Time for what?"

"That you acknowledge what's between you."

My cheeks flushed. "What are you talking about?"

Dyter lifted a brow. "Come on, Ryn. You're his mate"—he pointed back and forth between the two of us—"and he's yours."

I fell mute, my gaze fixed on Tyrrik. In my peripheral vision, I saw Dyter rest the waterskin beside me, and then he circled around and sat on the other side of the Drae, opposite where I crouched. Dyter was staring at me, I could feel his gaze on my face, but I couldn't meet his eyes. I swallowed hard and stammered, "Y-you don't know that."

"You think Tyrrik would've done the things he has for anything less? He's been enslaved for one hundred years. According to you, he's an expert manipulator, and he'd have to be to save his *own* skin for an entire century. Think of all he's done for you—no one but the two of you know all of it—and tell me if there is any other explanation that makes sense."

Several seconds passed, but I wasn't racking my brain. There was another reason, and it had haunted me ever since I found out what I was. "I was the only other Drae in Verald."

"No, you weren't," Dyter corrected. "He stood by while your mother sacrificed herself to let you get away. If it was a kinship thing, he wouldn't have allowed that."

*Right.* I scowled at the old man, who was now massaging his stump. "You've got it all figured out, haven't you?"

He stopped, the ropey scar on his slack face darkening, and said, "Come now, my girl. You have it figured out, too. That's why you're running so hard."

"I'm crouching," I corrected.

"Don't be immature."

I rolled my eyes, but my heart was pounding. I had known there was something. I wasn't an idiot, but I was scared of what having that connection with another meant. Terrified really.

I snatched up the waterskin and uncorked it. Tipping my head back, I gulped half of the water.

"You see the color of your scales in his," Dyter said.

I choked on the water in my mouth, backwashing a little into the flagon. *Hmm.* Served Tyrrik right for throwing up on me.

Putting my finger in the remaining water, I thought of Tyrrik and how I needed the water to be nectar so I could heal him. Conjuring up that desire was all too easy. Right now, that only made me grit my teeth. I didn't like that in only a couple of weeks, my barriers had fallen so much. My heart knew I wanted Tyrrik alive, and making nectar for him was effortless. It shouldn't be so easy already.

I held the container to his lips, and a mixture of relief and sick satisfaction swept through me when he drank the remainder of the water. I glanced up at Dyter and asked, "You're really going to press the issue?"

"Denial never did anyone any good," he said with a frown.

As if that was enough to convince me. "Seems to be working pretty well, so far."

Dyter shook his head. "You're better than that, Ryn. I'm not saying life has been easy for you the last few months; I know it hasn't. But you chose to come on this journey. You've chosen to join the war against the emperor—"

Picked up on that, did he? "I had to after making such a big deal of Phaetyn sticking their heads in the dirt and ignoring the realm. They were being stupid."

Dyter shifted on the rocky ground, reclining against the wall of the cave. He exhaled slowly, as if bracing himself, and then whispered, "You're doing the same thing with Tyrrik."

*Ouch.* How could he say that?

"It's a little different, Dyter," I said sarcastically. At least, I meant my tone to be sarcastic. What came out seemed more along the lines of bitterness. "No one is dying because of my choice."

"Drae have one mate, Rynnie. Only one. Ever."

I tossed the empty container to the side and exploded to my feet. "What are you saying? I should forget everything that's happened to me? That because he *might* be my mate I just decide, 'oh what the hay, I guess we better get together *for life*?'"

Dyter frowned, but I was just warming up.

"All that abuse? No worries. We're *mates*. It's fine. Oh, and you don't tell me what's happening? That's al'right; we're *mates*, so I don't need to know." My chest heaved as I screamed my frustration at the pathetic reality Dyter was proposing I accept. "And don't worry about telling me *anything*, *ever*, not even about *myself*; I totally trust you because we're *mates*!"

Dyter's eyes were wide, and he stared at me wordlessly.

I took several breaths, forcing myself to calm down. But the emotion hadn't disappeared; I was just barely controlling it when I spoke. "I'm eighteen years old. I'm not meant to make decisions about mates and permanent promises. Not yet." Whirling away, I crossed to the edge of the cave and stood looking out over the hillside before I spoke the truth of my heart. "I don't want to make fake choices that are already chosen for me. I want a *real* choice."

Dyter cleared his throat and said, "You had a choice with Kamoi."

I stiffened, my arms locking where I'd folded them across my chest.

"Why didn't you pick Kamoi?" Dyter asked.

Dyter had never been cruel or malicious, but his words were an arrow that pierced my heart.

*I*ce coiled in my stomach, its freezing tendrils spreading into my chest. I bit my tongue to prevent the painful truth or vitriolic anger from spewing out. I didn't want either to escape. Instead of replying to Dyter, I stared out over the treetops, watching as the overcast sky leaked and drizzled its moisture. Fat drops began to form and drip from the rocky overhang we camped beneath.

"I want you to be happy," Dyter said. "When I'm gone, I want you to be protected."

"I just squished the Phaetyn queen and tore her guards to bits." I sniffed in disdain, but my stomach churned with the acknowledgement of what I'd done. I'd feel terrible later. Their deaths might even give me nightmares. But in this moment, I wasn't the least bit sorry. "Pretty sure I can protect myself."

He chuckled, and my shoulders relaxed as the tension between us dissipated.

"I can't believe you left me dragging Lord Tyrrik away on a blanket while you fought off the Phaetyn army," Dyter said, his laughter swelling. "There you were, stomping around, and I'm hobbling off afraid you were going to breathe fire on the lot of us. *Drak*, I almost wet myself."

I snickered as I turned to Dyter. Seeing his red face and hearing his guffaws made me laugh, and as he chortled on, I laughed harder. Soon, tears were streaming down our faces.

He clutched his stomach, hooting. "Do you know how hard it is to drag a blanket with one arm? A blanket with a Drae on it?"

I doubled up, imagining Dyter dragging Tyrrik through the forest, but after a few seconds, something happened to my laughter, and soon the choking sound coming out of my mouth didn't resemble laughter at all.

Dyter got to his feet and crossed to me. He'd stopped chuckling, like me, but he wasn't crying or gasping for breath. I sniffed as he pulled me into his embrace, inhaling his familiar smell.

"You'll be okay, Rynnie," he said, rocking me.

I wasn't okay, and I wasn't sure I ever would be. I certainly hadn't been *okay* so far. I'd been hurt. So badly. I choked on my words, trying to tell him of my uncertainty.

Dyter didn't acknowledge my incoherent answer, still rocking me as he repeated, "You'll do okay."

An overwhelming pressure rose through my throat, a darkness I'd suppressed for weeks. I struggled to reign it in, but I was too exhausted, too hungry, too emotionally drained to battle it back. The low wail escaped, and the dam burst.

A terrible mourning keen drove up from my injured soul, tearing through my chest, searing my throat as it ravaged me. My abrupt introduction to evil escalated to horror I'd never imagined possible. For three months, I'd been tortured, controlled, intimidated, abused, and manipulated. I'd lost my innocence, almost like the girl who'd been protected so well by her mother never existed.

I'd lost my naivety and ignorance, and I wanted *that* back.

I didn't want to know nightmares existed. I didn't want to know I could die. Before, I'd known both of these things, but *before,* I hadn't understood them. In the dungeons, I'd become not only acquainted with nightmares but intimately familiar with their terror. Death was rapidly becoming my devoted companion, and I seemed impotent to put either of them aside. Why couldn't I put my fear for these things aside?

I grieved, shedding tears for the death of the girl I'd been before entering that foul castle.

I wept, soaking Dyter's aketon, draining myself of the pitiful reserve I had left. I cried, and the darkness released and poured out of me.

I shed every single tear in me as I mourned for what I would never have.

I lamented the losses I knew and the ones I had yet to discover. I cried, letting my heartbreak rule me.

I cried, finally feeling safe to mourn. For tonight, I was in the arms of my father, the only security I knew I could count on.

---

I HADN'T WOKEN up chilled in days, and confusion clouded my mind as awareness greeted me. Where was I? Why was I so cold? The smell of campfire hung in the air, but there was no fire nearby.

Tyrrik. He wasn't close, or I would be warm. Had I rolled away? Seemed unlikely given my subconscious tendencies. I reached out, but my hand froze mid-air as I fully awoke.

I should feel lighter after shedding so much of my emotional pain last night, but my head felt filled with bricks from the toll. My eyes were gritty, and I rubbed the salty crust off and blinked them open.

I was alone in the cave. The filtered light was plenty to illuminate the shallow cavern. Dyter's pack was propped against a rock, but Dyter was absent. I took a deep breath and heard Tyrrik's breath hitch.

He was awake. My heartbeat picked up, and I *felt* him several meters in front of me.

His heartbeat picked up, too.

Tyrrik was watching me.

"*Khosana,*" he said. "I know you're awake."

I wasn't sure I was ready for this. To see him now after things had changed. Nervous energy skittered over my skin and deep in my belly. I wanted to go back to sleep, maybe even forever if it meant I didn't have to deal with the jumble of feelings I had for the Drae.

When we first plummeted from the sky and he'd been awake, caring for him was easy. His near-death experience forced me to realize I didn't want him dead, and in the heat of the moment, that acknowledgement had been easy and simple. But I would've done the same for Arnik, Dyter, and possibly even a stranger.

Over the last few days, I'd been Tyrrik's lifeline. Sure, turns out I did a sucky job of protecting him, but I'd done my best to provide for his every need. I hadn't hesitated for one moment to do everything I could for him: making nectar, washing his immobile body, pouring nectar down his throat. There was something about his unconsciousness that made the effort uncomplicated, and if I was being honest with myself, being close to him felt right at the time. But that level of intimacy, in retrospect, felt different than healing a wound that would've otherwise killed him.

Tyrrik had been asleep and unaware then, but *now* he was awake. He would not continue to be unaware of anything I did. If I didn't block him, he would even know why.

*Denial doesn't get you anywhere,* Dyter had said.

But *denial* had been my lifeline since the castle dungeons. To throw that lifeline away felt akin to pulling off my skin to don another person's: impossible.

"Open your eyes," Tyrrik said in a low voice as he drew closer. "Please show them to me. I've dreamed of them lately, but I know my dreams don't do them justice."

My heart skipped a *stupid* beat, and I could tell by the *stupid* hitch in his breath that he'd heard. *Stupid Drae-mate hormones.*

I opened my eyes.

Tyrrik stood just outside the rocky overhang. He'd lost weight. The nectar had been enough to keep him alive but not enough to satisfy the demands of a man's body. Stubble covered the bottom half of his face. His silky hair was disheveled as though he'd run his hands through the tangle many times. He was wearing one of Dyter's aketons but no trousers or shoes. The Drae's broad shoulders and direct look made his bearing just as threatening as ever.

I doubted he was even aware of that.

Tyrrik's face though—the slight rounding of his eyes, the fleeting way he searched my expression, and the heavy silence with which he watched me . . . Could he be as out of his depth as I felt?

I swallowed and got to my feet. "How do you feel?"

His gaze didn't shift from my face as he stepped into the cave. "As though I've been an inch from death for several days." He gestured to the forest outside. "Dyter has gone to hunt and collect more water."

Dyter's timing was as convenient as the dead queen's illness. Curse him for leaving me alone with Tyrrik. The old bugger probably felt he was doing me a favor.

"How long will it take for you to heal?" I asked, walking around the rocky space. I was at a loss for how to busy myself so looking at him wasn't mandatory.

"A few days," he said. "I should've been well healed by now."

"They were draining you. Dyter and I didn't know," I said, hating that I'd failed him. I stopped my pacing and met his eyes. "I'm sorry, Tyrrik. I let you down."

He shrugged. "You're not to blame for the Phaetyn's actions. I could hear what was going on; I just couldn't respond."

My heart flipped, and I frantically tried to remember what I'd said to Dyter while we were in Zivost. "What did you hear?"

He got to his feet, and I resumed my slow pacing to ensure there was a good distance between us.

"I heard you threaten the guards and their families."

I nodded. *I did that.* That wasn't so bad.

"I heard you and Dyter discussing whether you should wear a dress for the gathering," he said, his eyes turning ink black as his gaze roved my frame.

My heart flipped again. The corset and wispy skirt had seen

better days by this stage. My silver hair was a tangled mess. My feet were dirty, I had grime smeared on my face, and I was splattered with Phaetyn blood.

Tyrrik didn't seem to mind. Where I'd been gratified for Kamoi's attention, Tyrrik's appraisal of the outfit—the way his eyes lingered on my breasts, the way he stared at the skirt as though hoping it would burn away—*that* made me feel something else entirely. A foreign heat coiled deep in my stomach. My breathing quickened as a strange heaviness settled in my chest like a magnet, pulling me toward the Drae. The rocky space felt far too small to contain what was possible between us.

"I heard you asking Dyter why sometimes my scales seemed blue," he whispered, taking a step toward me.

Shivers broke over me, and I felt the eruption of scales on my forearms. I squeezed my eyes shut as the Drae continued to draw closer in the same way, I supposed, he'd always moved, a predatory stalk. "I . . ."

The heaviness of wanting eased as his warm breath brushed the top of my cheekbone. He stood in front of me and said, "I heard you tell Dyter I hurt you, that I broke your heart."

Tyrrik brushed the area over my heart with the back of his hand, and my eyes flew open. I lifted my gaze from the base of his neck, over the sculpted plains of his face, to his midnight eyes.

"You al-already knew that," I said, my voice trembling. My fear was not of him, or rather not that he would hurt me physically. But of the magnitude of what lay between us, past and present; fear of what *could* lay between us . . . if I let it.

He nodded and turned his hand so his palm rested on my skin. "I did," he said. "But I don't know how to fix it. I don't know if it is possible for you to feel for me again. To feel for me what you felt so strongly for *Tyr*."

Yet, wasn't he Tyr? Wasn't Tyr's gentleness and protectiveness somewhere inside this Drae? And Ty, my friend who made me smile, my confidant, wasn't he in there somewhere, too? Or were Tyr and Ty merely personas he'd assumed to manipulate me? My voice wasn't the only thing shaking now, but I couldn't control my trembling as I asked, gaze dropping to the base of his throat again. "Do you *really* want to fix my heart?"

The question was uttered in a voice so low I was surprised he made it out.

"Yes," he said. He swept his hand to the top of my shoulder and then up the side of my neck.

I sighed, leaning into the warmth, and did not resist as the Drae tilted my chin so I was forced to meet his eyes once more. Fire spread through my body at his touch; the burning awareness I'd felt from the first time our skin had touched was rampant and unchecked. My lips parted as I stared up at him, and I sighed. "Why?" I whispered, my words breathy, "Why do you want to heal my heart?"

He searched my eyes for an eternity that was likely only a few seconds, but time lost meaning and measure with him so close.

"Because," Tyrrik said, the pulse in his throat feathering as he stroked my skin. "You are my mate."

Though he still had a finger under my chin, I closed my eyes. I couldn't let him see my reaction, not when I didn't, *couldn't*, understand it. How long had he been waiting to tell me? Had he been afraid to say the words out loud? Was he afraid now? At his utterance of the word *mate*, I'd felt a warm sense of *belonging* I hadn't felt since Mother's death or since I'd had a home. The sensation was stronger than what I'd felt at the elm tree, more personal.

Yet our past stretched between us. Not just the manipulative way he'd broken the Blood Oath. *His* dark, terrible years of enslavement. The barely scarring wounds left inside me. People with battered souls shouldn't make decisions like this. Surely that could only lead to disaster.

He wasn't asking me to sit next to him at a gathering or to make him nectar a few times or dance with him. Tyrrik was asking me . . . I frowned, realizing he hadn't asked me anything.

I freed myself of his grip and looked at him. In the brief moment I'd spent with my eyes shut, he'd smoothed the expression from his face, and he wore the impassive mask I was most familiar with. "What does it mean exactly? That I am your mate?"

"We are each other's mates," he corrected, a hint of a growl in his voice as emotion lit his eyes. "And it means we are made for each other. Drae only ever have one mate. They can only bear children together."

"So, we can just have children together." Why did this stuff always come back to dancing the maypole? My fault for asking about children, I suppose.

"Amongst other things," he said. Tyrrik turned and took several paces toward the front of the cave before sitting on a shelf of rock.

I simultaneously felt relief and a bone-deep cold at the distance. But I wasn't done. "Like?"

27

yrrik settled like a raptor on a branch. Despite his obvious fatigue, everything about him was predatory. His inky gaze remained fixed on me. "You've felt the connection between us. I'm able to hear your thoughts, and you hear mine. *If* we keep that bond open."

I flushed, remembering the time I'd severed the emotional tie with him when flying over the mountains.

"The connection doesn't just allow us to speak," he said, glancing at his hands. "In our culture, the male is the protector. The female—"

"Do not tell me I'm meant to be peaceful again. I have perfectly violent tendencies myself."

"I was not going to say that." He raised a brow, but his expression remained dark. "Drae females are perfectly capable of defending themselves. But their role in a mated couple is to balance the male's violence, to ground him, and when they are threatened, to strengthen him."

Despite myself, I edged closer, not wanting to miss a single word. Leaning toward him, I asked, "Strengthen him how?"

He glanced up, meeting my gaze for only a moment before looking away.

I studied the hang of his shoulders and bit my lip. Even though I was filled with confusion, the prominent feeling racking me was guilt. Tyrrik had divulged the truth to me, and I couldn't find it within myself to give him what he so clearly wanted. Why did that seem like such a grave offense?

"You have felt the push and pull of Drae energy," he finally answered. "You've practiced pulling the tendrils of power that flow between us back into yourself."

Our lesson in the mountains felt like so long ago, but I remembered asking him how to protect my thoughts from the emperor. "Yes."

He shrugged. "Instead of pulling the tendrils into yourself, you push them into me."

I stirred uneasily at the thought. Putting more into the tendrils weaving between us? When I used my Phaetyn powers on Tyrrik, it was almost business-like, the same as I'd do for anybody with an injury. I saw the problem, and I healed it. But the tendrils of Drae power between us . . . they were different. I knew they were specific to us. The idea of expanding the threads of force that connected us, increasing them in size and strength so the attachment was more powerful, made me feel faintly unwell. I didn't want to be chained to Tyrrik; I didn't want to be chained to *anyone*. I changed the subject. "Anything else I should know?"

"Plenty you should know, but not much you'll want to."

I crossed my arms, irritated that he seemed so confident in his assessment. "Try me."

A ghost of a smile lit his face, and his eyes warmed. "Your sudden obsession with shiny objects."

My hand went to the top of my corset, and Tyrrik chuckled. Inside the corset sat my ruby and golden pill box. "What about them?"

"It is a courtship ritual between male and female Drae, just as my scales reflect the color of your scales to show I am the right mate for you."

213

*A courtship ritual.* "Me collecting precious things does something . . . for you?"

Scales appeared on his shoulder and climbed up his neck. "The way you care for precious things does."

My face slackened. "You're right. I don't want to know any more."

His face closed off, and the guilt gnawing in my chest roared in protest.

I sighed and went to sit beside him on the rock. Dyter could come back as soon as he liked in my humble opinion. "Tyrrik," I said. "When did you know we were mates?"

He slowly turned to me, and I saw the scales had a lapis lazuli glow to their onyx shine. His gaze dropped to my lips, and he said, "When I first touched you."

"The nape of my neck," I said. I remembered the moment; it was seared in my memory.

A shiver rippled down him, and the twist of his neck was decidedly Drae. "Yes," he rumbled, his guttural voice filling the rocky shelter. "The nape of your neck, though it could have been anywhere."

I remembered the pain, falling to my knees, knowing something had just happened to me, and chalking up the sensation to the Lord Drae before me. He'd known from the very first moment, our first meeting. He'd kept this to himself the entire time? His actions in the room with my mother took on new meaning, his desperation to get me out of my bedroom and away from the guards to save me from the king. My heart clenched as I thought of Tyrrik as Ty and about all the information he'd disclosed, the effort he'd made to be close to me while in prison. I thought of his tender ministrations as Tyr. He wasn't just trying to clean up my blood to keep me from being discovered by the king. Tyr hadn't needed to be gentle to wash the evidence away. He'd risked a lot to even bring me food. I thought of the emotion in his eyes when he'd come as Irrik to give me a bath. I'd thought I was part of some game, and I was right, just not about who he was playing for. My throat clogged with feeling. I swallowed the lump as the memories washed over me. Was Dyter right?

Tyrrik had been watching my face, and he slowly raised his fingers toward the nape of my neck.

His scent made me dizzy; his eyes stared to the deepest recesses in me. My head and my heart were no longer in agreement of the certainty I'd known a few minutes ago. That's what made me jerk my upper body away.

We were both panting hard with only an arm's length between us. With wide eyes, we stared at each other.

"Tyrrik, I . . ." I started then cut off. How could I put my reaction into words? How did I explain to him my doubts regarding *him* shrank every day, no, *every second*, but my self-doubt only grew?

I felt him seal himself off. He pulled his energy back into himself, his expression smoothed, and his eyes hardened. He slid the mask he'd worn for a century back into place, and still I could not think of a word to say.

"It is no less than I expected," he said, his voice rough.

I reached out a hand, and this time it was Tyrrik who lurched away, going so far as to stand.

"It's not you—" I said, even though there were some reservations against him in my heart. "I need time. Mating seems so . . ." *Final.*

"For Drae, there is no between," Tyrrik said, brusquely. "Mates feel too much to be slowed by petty human traditions of courtship. You either accept me, or you do not." His eyes turned to slits, and he spun away. "I cannot woo you as you would like or expect."

The comment slapped me across the face. "That's too much to ask? To know you better?"

"Yes," he said, striding for the edge of the shelter as blue-black scales covered his exposed skin.

*Yes, it is,* his final words echoed through our bond.

---

A PART of me felt bad Dyter was stuck in the middle of the

awkwardness between Tyrrik and me. Over the next two days, the cave was seriously uncomfortable and not because the only furniture it offered was rocks. More than once, I thought of offering an apology, but then what was I apologizing for? Binding was a serious decision, and I shouldn't be guilted or manipulated into it. As for Dyter, he'd left me alone with the Drae, so maybe I shouldn't feel bad about that either.

Tyrrik needed time to regain his strength, and I'd be lying if I said my body wasn't craving the same.

The two days passed with hunting, drinking, sleeping, and Tyrrik's sulking—or so I'd dubbed it. The Drae was back to his Lord Broody-Pants days, except without pants. He was sullen and withdrawn, only answering if he was asked a direct question, and then only with as few words as possible.

On the other hand, I had every reason to be in a bad mood, which was why I felt no guilt for my grumpiness.

I couldn't understand his last comment. I'd assumed he wanted to mate with me; I still did, but if he wanted to be with me for life, which was a freakin' long time judging by the emperor's lifespan and the fact that Tyrrik had been alive for over a century, why didn't he want to court me? The mate . . . *thing* didn't seem like an option really, although I wasn't fully Drae, so things could be different for me. If being each other's mate *wasn't* an option, why didn't he want us to get to know each other?

I'd spent yesterday certain he only wanted me for my baby-making ovaries. Then, most of today, I was sure I was only an annoyance to him, which reinforced my previous point about making Drae babies. But, a part of me, a little bit of Ryn, kept telling me I had it completely wrong. Though *that bit of Ryn* was the part that felt warm when Tyrrik neared her and dizzy at his scent.

That Ryn seemed a little untrustworthy.

And now, I was talking about myself in third person. Maybe I was going crazy. I nodded as I came to the conclusion.

Everything was on the up and up.

"We need to leave for Gemond today," Tyrrik said, interrupting the internal assessment of my sanity.

Dyter glanced at me, and I replied to him, "*You* need another few days to recover."

Dyter's gaze slid to Tyrrik, who answered, "It's not safe for us to stay here."

Dyter looked back at me.

"We haven't seen the emperor at all in the last two days," I said, my eyes narrowing. "Not since before entering Zivost."

"You think that means he's not here in some capacity? His Druman are a direct extension of the emperor himself," Tyrrik replied, facing me now. "You think he won't have guessed the Zivost was our first stop and Gemond our second?"

What I *thought* was that Tyrrik should still be using Dyter as a conversational middleman.

Crossing my arms, I turned to the Drae with a sniff. "You're not strong enough yet. What if we come across the emperor on the way to Gemond? What then? You probably couldn't fight off a Druman right now."

Tyrrik's eyes flooded with inky black.

"He's right, my girl," Dyter said, clearing his throat. "We've stayed too long in one place, and it makes us sitting prey." Dyter stood and grabbed all of our possessions—his pack and the water-skin. "I believe Kamini and Kamoi will take control of the Phaetyn in time, but we risk too much by lingering. The queen's supporters may decide to come after us."

"Fine, let's go. Who cares if we encounter the freakin' emperor? Or Druman?" I stood abruptly, and fear spiked my gut when I spoke of Jotun's kind. The thought of encountering more like him made my heart race. Cheeks flushing, I strode for the edge of the rocky overhang.

Tyrrik caught my arm as I passed him, halting me. He frowned as he studied me, and his thumb caressed my arm. "You know I'll protect you, Ryn."

*Oh sure.* Now he'd speak to me and act like *I* was the unreasonable one. I yanked my arm free and started down the rocky hill. I resisted the urge to kick at the patches of scrub on the way down, muttering to myself about stupid old men and stupid Drae.

The sun had only peeked over the horizon in the last hour, and its rays were still tentative as they stretched into day. Rain had fallen overnight, and the once-packed dirt between the rocks and shrubs was mud and puddles of clear water. I reached the bottom of the hill, realized I didn't know where I was going, and turned to wait for Dyter and *him*.

Dyter lifted a brow and pointed right.

I rolled my eyes and waited for them, inhaling the strong pine smell with the undercurrent of charred wood from our meager fires that must've settled in the valley of trees. When Dyter took the lead, I asked him, "How long until we get to Gemond?"

"On foot, two weeks. If we were flying, a day."

"Then why aren't we flying?"

I picked after Dyter through the forest. Only the trickle of a stream disturbed the silence, a reminder of what Tyrrik and I were from the absence of animal sound. Of course, the creatures of the forest sensed our presence, and they knew to make themselves scarce.

That's how I felt about the emperor, but I still preferred to risk flying to Gemond. Besides the speed of travel, I wanted to scout the area. Kamini's sister could be right under our noses.

"Tyrrik is not strong enough to carry me," Dyter replied. "And he thought you might not feel comfortable flying with me."

The Drae was right, but I wasn't going to admit it. Instead of answering, I remained mute, which still felt like an admission. *Drak.*

We continued picking our way through the underbrush, and I became painfully aware of Tyrrik walking behind me. What was he looking at? As we began to climb the next mountain, I was convinced he was staring at my butt. As I pushed up and over a large boulder, I glanced back.

*Totally staring at my butt.*

He smirked when he caught my gaze, and I turned up my nose,

facing the front. Didn't our argument two days prior bother him? I couldn't think of anything else. What had he meant with his parting remark? Not knowing was driving me mad.

I panted as we climbed, but it wasn't because I was out of shape. "I hate corsets," I said. "I'm pretty sure I dreamed of aketons last night." An aketon and my usual ankle-length skirt or trousers. I'd even take an aketon without pants at this point. "Dyter, why didn't you pack another aketon?"

Dyter turned and said, "If you remember, we were in a bit of a hurry when we left Zivost. I'm sure we can find you other clothing in Gemond."

I thought of the mountains we'd have to climb between now and then. "I'll die before we get there."

"Then take it off," Dyter snapped without looking back.

A menacing growl rippled over my head before I'd fully processed Dyter's response.

"She's not taking anything off," Tyrrik snarled.

I ignored the big lizard stalking behind me. I already knew his aketon was in a bunch. "What's blocking your pipe, Dyter?"

He threw a scowl over his shoulder, taking a moment to let his disapproval settle first on me and then the Drae behind me. "You two have frayed my last nerve."

My brief flash of good humor disappeared. "It's Tyrrik's fault. He's sulking."

"I'm not sulking," the one-hundred-and-nine-year old said.

"Mmm-hmm, sure."

Dyter exploded. "Enough!" He whirled on us, stomping back to wave a finger in my face. "If you can't say anything nice, don't speak at all."

"That's what we were doing before," I huffed. "You said it made you cranky." By this point, I was needling the old man, but I craved an outlet for my frustration, and he'd offered one.

"Not cranky . . . irritable." He sighed, his anger draining away as he looked at me.

"So you're not cranky, and Tyrrik's not sulking," I said, nodding as I doubled down on my own stupidity.

"Ryn?" Dyter offered me a weary half-smile.

"Yes?"

"I love you. But shut up." He marched ahead to lead the way again.

## 28

*I* pushed aside a branch, smiling as I let it fling back. It probably wasn't high enough to hit Tyrrik's face, but I grinned at his grunt when the branch thwacked against him. A quick peek told me he still found my rear end far too interesting. I wonder how many branches I could catch him with between now and Gemond.

Which reminded me. "Why are we going to Gemond? The king lets his people eat each other."

"Did you listen to nothing I told you about King Zakai?" the old man groaned.

I pushed aside another branch and then let it go. The thin tree limb flicked back, and I smirked as Tyrrik grunted again.

"Yeah, I listened," I answered, jumping a small creek, my wispy skirt bouncing around my thighs. "But I didn't believe you."

"You don't believe a man you've known most of your life?" Tyrrik asked, speaking for the first time in a while.

Dyter laughed derisively. "Rynnie didn't believe plants came from seeds until we put a pot in her room and made her check it every day for three months."

"I thought it was a scheme to give the people of Verald hope."

"You didn't know what a scheme was at five."

I might not have had the words to express how I felt at five, but I did think seeds were a hustle. Most people in Verald *couldn't* get them to grow and bear fruit, so it wasn't really a stretch for my childhood mind.

"Wait," Tyrrik said. "She didn't believe plants came from seeds until five?"

I scowled at the grin in his voice.

"No one was more surprised than I to find out she was Phaetyn," Dyter quipped.

The conversation was feeling like a man alliance, and Dyter was supposed to be firmly team Ryn. The next words passed from my lips without filtering. "I can't believe Mum never told you, Dyter. She told you *everything*."

The old man was silent, and I had time to wonder if I could've phrased my comment better. Definitely could have.

He turned back, his features darkening. "She loved you more than life itself, my girl. When you love someone that much, you don't take risks that could lead to hurt. I was your mother's best friend, and she was mine, truly. There were very few who were in the confidence of Ryhl, and I consider myself honored to have been one of them."

I stared at the blurry ground in front of me, stepping in a puddle. The muddy water splashed up on my calves as I was still bare footed. I didn't want to bawl again, so I focused on the only other thing in my head: I needed shoes.

*It is normal to be sad, Khosana.*

Even now, months later, I missed my mother terribly. For the most part, I seemed to get by without thinking of her, and then in moments like these, the sadness, the *regret*, hit me with the force of a brick wall. Shoes fled my mind as my emotions echoed through Tyrrik.

"Dyter," I said. "Can you tell me about her? About how you met?"

Dyter wouldn't normally hesitate to tell me, but I held my breath, remembering Tyrrik. Despite my easy relationship with the old man, he wasn't one to spill his guts, and he was the king of secrets.

Sure enough, Dyter stiffened. He flung a quick look at the Drae then met my gaze, and his eyes steeled. No one was more surprised than I when he started talking.

Dyter trusted Tyrrik? But my memory niggled at the back of my mind that this wasn't the first time Dyter had made this decision in front of me.

I shook my head and focused on what he was saying.

"My sister, Dyrell met her first," Dyter spoke. "Your mother was searching the bins behind The Raven's Hollow in Harvest Zone Eight."

I grimaced. Amateur. Dumpsters were always picked clean. Not that I'd had occasion to pick through them like many others, but growing up in starving Verald, rubbish bin-dipping had been common among the poor in the Penny Wheel. Still, life had probably been a bit easier back then, or at least more food was available if my mother's stories were true.

"My sister took one look at the baby swaddled on your mother's back and invited her in for a meal, but your mother refused to go inside. Dyrell thought it odd but put it from her mind; even then, people were just scraping by, and Dyrell was busy. A week later, five of the emperor's men came through the zone asking after a young woman and a child. Dyrell denied it, having forgotten all about your mum; there were too many going hungry to remember any one in particular. But, a few days later, Dyrell saw your mum again and put things together after that. Enough to realize your mother was in trouble."

My mother had told me she'd run from my abusive father to start a new life. Talk about the understatement of the century.

"When Dyrell asked if Ryhl was in trouble and offered to help, your mum ran off," Dyter broke off. "But four weeks later, your mother knocked on the back door of my sister's tavern and asked for food. She was starving, and her milk had dried up. She could no longer feed her child.

"Your mum worked for Dyrell for a month, for room and board, and then the king's men stumbled into Dyrell's tavern with several Druman. Your mother hid again, this time returning a few days later. Dyrell wrestled the truth from her. Zone Eight had more money than Seven, so there were more patrols, and your mother insisted she leave. So, my sister and your mother fabricated a story between them, and my sister sent the pair of you to me. We told everyone your mum had recently been widowed and decided to start afresh in a different Harvest Zone. My sister acted like your mother's dear friend, giving plausibility to the story and fooling everyone in our Zone. We got her a house, and she kept quiet for a good long time, and after several months, it was as though she'd always lived in our part of the realm."

"Didn't guards notice someone new?"

Dyter nodded. "They did."

"And they didn't think a new woman and child in a Zone that suddenly had more food a bit suspicious?"

"What would you do if you were hungry and you found a patch of carrots hidden in the middle of nowhere?"

Easy. "I wouldn't tell anyone about them."

"Exactly," Dyter said. "And Ryhl was our patch of carrots. She could grow things. Not only that, she helped a lot of others grow things. I'm not sure you realize how many people revered your mother, Rynnie. In such hard times, many people of Verald would've gone to significant lengths to ensure her safety, not merely myself."

"So no one told the king or the emperor?" I asked. As my mentor shook his head, I felt a swift and fierce pride for the people of Verald.

"Though it took me a long time to understand why, Ryhl's house was always dark at night," Dyter said. "One day, it clicked that your mother wasn't actually sleeping there. Back then, she didn't rely on anyone to keep her secrets. I don't know where she slept those first few years, but she always turned up during the day. I hadn't bought the tavern off the prior owner at that point, and I had to walk past your house to get to my own back then." Dyter tipped his head back to look at the blue sky. "It took three years for me to see a candle lit in your house at night."

*Three years?* "She didn't trust anyone for three years?"

Dyter turned to me. "I told you I was honored to be a confidant of your mother's, and I meant that. I can count the people she trusted on one hand. I never asked where she came from or what she ran from, but it didn't take a genius to see your mother had been taught trust was a weakness."

I breathed through the tightness in my chest. Hadn't I learned that lesson myself? I knew anyone could snap under the right pressure. You couldn't really trust another, not unless they were willing to die for you.

"Her life sounds so isolated and forlorn," I said hoarsely. "I never saw her as a lonely, frightened person." But to live life in the company of such fear, always running, never trusting, constantly expecting to be captured. I'd always believed my mother to be a happy person, firm and unafraid, loving and kind to those around her. From Dyter's description, she was someone who had few friends, and she'd never learned to trust again.

Was that my fate? To be unable to trust? Unable to live a peaceful life?

"She eased up as the years went on, Rynnie. She began sleeping in the house, remember? It took your mother time, but she began to live life in time, and much of that was thanks to you. You brought so much happiness to her life—"

Dyter broke off, and a burning sensation built behind my eyes.

I whispered, "Is that true, Dyter? Was Mum happy?"

Dyter's shoulders shook, and at least a full minute passed before he replied, "She was truly happy, Rynnie. For the time she spent in Verald, in Harvest Zone Seven, I can say that with certainty. She found love and joy again through *you*."

A tear slipped down my cheek, and despite my struggle to keep my emotions in check, I knew my choked breathing wasn't missed by the Drae behind me. There was warmth at my back as he approached, and I stiffened, conflicted. I hoped Tyrrik would touch me, I longed for it, *and* I worried about what it may mean to give into that longing.

He fell back once more and spoke in my mind instead. *There's another branch ahead.*

I wiped my eyes and saw he was right. I pushed the branch out of the way and let it fling back. This time when Tyrrik grunted, I knew he'd let me tree-whip him on purpose, and the thought struck me that he might've been letting me fling branches at him all morning.

*Holy pancakes*, he sure knew how to treat a woman. I couldn't completely stop the smile tugging on my lips or the tickle of warmth spreading through my heart.

We started up a grassy hill, and the trees grew sparse.

I glanced ahead to where Dyter strode through the knee-length grass of a clearing in front of me.

For months, I'd been struggling to understand my mother. In many ways, the person revealed on the night she died had been a stranger to me, and deep down, I'd been left wondering if I'd known her at all. Dyter's story erased my fears. My mother was happy. I was just one of the few people to witness her that way. I might not have known she was Drae and running from the emperor, or I was Phaetyn and Drae, but I understood *why* she'd lied. I didn't just understand; I knew the fierce loyalty and love it took to protect those I loved—after my dungeon time, especially. She'd protected me *because* she loved me, and my heart beat easier for seeing I *had* known my mother.

Dyter didn't look back, and I didn't expect him to. I'd seen him cry once, not too long ago, but he would hide his tears from me if at all possible. I raised my voice so he would hear. "Thank you for telling me about her, Dyter."

"Any time, my girl," he said gruffly.

I looked at the sky, to the hidden stars where my mother now resided. *I miss you, Mum*, I thought, not caring that Tyrrik would hear me. *Thank you for protecting me.*

I pushed into the long grass, feeling more at peace than I had in a long time. My mother had been enslaved and learned to trust again.

That meant Tyrrik could, too.

My mother had been broken, and in time she'd found herself and happiness.

That meant I would be okay.

*I* accepted a charred bit of rabbit from Tyrrik the next morning, sighing when he didn't say a word. Didn't he realize he was supposed to talk first? As the first offender, he should extend the olive branch and all that. I heaved another sigh as I shouldered the responsibility of being Ryn the Peacemaker. "Thanks."

His brow quirked. "You're welcome."

Was that an I-admit-I'm-sulking quirk? Or an I'm-surprised-you're-speaking-to-me-because-*you're*-sulking quirk? Somehow, I doubted the former. Ryn the Peacemaker pursed her lips but said nothing.

Dyter licked the grease from his fingers as I wolfed down my portion.

"Are you strong enough to fly today?" Dyter asked when he finished.

Tyrrik's face was turned upward as he scanned the skies, his eyes narrowed and reptilian. "I am strong enough to fly and carry you for a time, but I doubt the entire way. At least, not without help."

I stiffened. Did he mean help from me? Like pushing my female Drae mojo into him?

"Definitely stay hydrated," I said, deflecting.

I stood and imagined Tyrrik's touch on my wings, and then shivered as scales erupted over my skin. My neck, tail, and fangs lengthened, and I shifted. In a handful of days, turning into my Drae form felt so natural and so right.

I stood on the side of the mountain, a magnificent lapis lazuli Drae. Dyter had only seen my Drae form on the run in Phaetynville, but he now had a chance to openly gape. Which he did in an awed way appropriate for a creature possessing my grace. Did he think all Drae had such vibrant, opulent scales? Such powerful tails? Such a deadly curve to their talons. I preened, reveling in his open admiration.

*You are truly beautiful, Ryn.*

I sniffed, trying to ignore Tyrrik, and stretched my neck to look in the opposite direction.

But when the shimmering of Tyrrik's transformation caught the corner of my eye, I couldn't not look. I turned back and gazed upward at the massive onyx Drae. Even after seeing him in this form many times, the ferocity of his talons, fangs, the lethal edges to his body and tail, took my breath away.

Dyter's, too, apparently, who hastily backed away.

*You're bigger than me,* I grumbled to Tyrrik as I compared our Drae forms.

Tyrrik swung his head toward me, white fangs gleaming. *You are much faster, Princess.*

I huffed. That was probably true, given my streamlined frame. I bet I could beat him in a race.

*You definitely would,* he agreed.

I purred with his praise and then mentally slapped myself.

As Tyrrik held out a claw for Dyter to climb aboard, I crouched close to the ground and leaped into the air, beating my wings down to create the lift I needed to fly. As the air caught under my majestic wings, I could barely contain the need to throw my head back and roar. I climbed above the pine trees and glided down over the rocky mountain.

I was flying, and it felt so incredibly right. I was a Phaetyn, I possessed some of their powers, and I wanted to help and to heal. But in my heart, in my soul, I was Drae.

Relenting, in part, to the joy in my heart at knowing who I was, I let loose a small roar.

*You must stay quiet,* Tyrrik said, already in the air behind me.

I did as he said, but I could totally rip the emperor's head off. Probably. With a little more training.

I circled to let Tyrrik lead the way. He altered our course, and we headed farther north. I glanced ahead and saw Dyter sitting on his butt in Tyrrik's claw, pale-faced and wide-eyed. I chortled my amusement and beat my wings hard to surge upward.

Maybe I would remain in my Drae form for a while. I was sick of being human-Ryn, barefoot in a corset.

*Where is the Gemond Kingdom?* I asked.

Tyrrik answered, *Straight ahead, nestled in the mountains at the northern end of the realm. They are much closer to the emperor's lands there. Not as close as Azule but within his reach. You must be on guard.*

*Okay, what should I be looking for?*

*You watch the ground for Druman; I'll watch the skies for the emperor.*

That suited me just fine. I needed to be searching for signs of Phaetyn anyway. I'd briefly forgotten Kamini's sister during my joy ride.

*Even if she's been very careful, finding her shouldn't be too hard if she's still alive and in these mountains.*

I startled before remembering Tyrrik would've heard the last conversation I'd had with Prince Kamoi. If I couldn't see any signs of Phaetyn-juiced growth between here and the Gemond Kingdom, I'd have to search the mountains farther east the first chance I got.

*To the west,* Tyrrik said.

I peered west and saw a dozen clusters of vibrant green standing out in stark contrast to the barren land below. *I'm looking at the ground.* I gnashed my fangs together.

*I just happened to see it out of the corner of my eye.*

*Sure you did.*

He didn't answer, but I felt his amusement through the weaving bond between us. The bond reminded me of his push and pull hoo-ha, and I blocked out the memory, setting my attention to the ground.

We didn't come across another patch of green for half an hour, and this time, there were several dozen patches in clusters over a dozen or so mountain ranges. I lowered as movement caught my eye. *Tyrrik, what's that?*

His great head swung to look down, and his alarm blared through my mind. *Druman*, he spoke. *We need to get in the cloud line.*

I obeyed, beating my wings and following him higher until we floated through wisps of cloud with a foggier view of the ground.

I scanned the Druman below, spotting five of them milling around the patches of green. My thoughts stirred uneasily. *Why are they around the green patches?* I asked Tyrrik.

*Maybe they're digging for potatoes.*

I rolled my eyes.

*Or maybe they know a Phaetyn has to have caused that growth.*

That was my concern. *Tyrrik, they can't find Kamini's sister before us.*

*I know, but we don't need to worry. It's just one Druman scouting party. Even if they report the sighting to Draedyn, it will take him a while to respond. Once we get to Gemond and heal, we'll go out looking for her.*

We passed over the range and left the Druman behind us. I redoubled my efforts, scanning the ground. Despite Tyrrik's reassurances, I felt his focus on the skies had also increased.

The next grouping of luscious green emerged two hours later.

*Do you think they're just random patches?* I asked. Maybe we were getting way too excited over patches of green.

He hadn't spoken in a while, and by now I could feel him straining to keep going through the bond.

*No. This Phaetyn is careful, just as your mother was when distributing your gift.*

That was a nice way to say she'd sprinkled people's gardens with my bath water.

*Or your chamber pot*, he added. *But there is a Phaetyn down there.*

I had to agree with him. From up here, the contrast of the otherwise barren land to the pockets of water was blatant. *How long did you know there was a Phaetyn in Verald?*

*How old were you when you came to Verald?*

*Just a baby, I think.*

*Then eighteen years,* he said.

*You knew the entire time there was a Phaetyn and never told the king?*

*I didn't have to. The presence of a Phaetyn posed no threat to his life or his rule. I wasn't compelled to tell him through the Blood Oath.*

My mother had eighteen years of peace because Tyrrik wasn't the monster everyone, myself included, had assumed. *Thank you.*

*No one is more grateful than I that I never had to divulge information regarding your presence.*

Things would be a lot different if I'd been Irdelron's prisoner as a baby. I never would've survived. My gaze slid to Tyrrik, and he shivered. I focused on him, eyes narrowed, and caught the words, *had to wait eighteen years.*

*Wait eighteen years for what?* I asked.

He jerked so hard, Dyter almost flew from his grip. In my old life, I'd never imagined seeing a sheepish Drae, but Tyrrik fit that description right now, confirming my suspicions his thoughts had turned back to dancing potential maypoles.

As the next two hours whittled by, the green patches sprung up in clusters more frequently. Not overly, but instead of every thirty to forty minutes of flight time, the lush vegetation appeared every twenty or so. Was that a sign the Phaetyn was in the area below? Or was Kamini's elder sibling purposely misleading us?

Movement below put me on alert. *More Druman,* I said, already pushing up into the cloud line.

Tyrrik followed, much slower.

The scouting party was gathered around a cluster of the green growth again, and there were eight of them this time. *That can't be coincidence.*

The Drae took his time answering. *Two scouting parties around the green patches is suspicious,* he admitted. *But if they are hunting for her, they are spread out over a huge area. They have no more idea where she is than we do.*

*But what if they get to her first?*

He sighed mentally, and I heard his weariness and frustration. *If I was stronger, we could search for her right now. But I can't risk an encounter with Druman. I wouldn't be able to protect you.*

Not being able to protect me bothered him way more than it should. But I could feel his strain. Moreover, he was right; two scouting parties over hundreds of miles wasn't enough to get my skirt in a twist. *Al'right. We have time. Let's go to Gemond, and then we can go out from there and search, once you're better.*

He glanced back. *Thank you, Princess. I'm sorry . . . I'm weakened.*

I'd never heard a stupider apology in my life, and I told him so. His lack of response was real confirmation of his fatigue.

*I'll need to rest soon,* Tyrrik said.

Only thirty minutes or so had passed since our previous conversation. He sounded exhausted in my head, and I blew out through my nostrils. This was taking much longer than I'd anticipated. *Okay, for how long?*

He bared his fangs and grudgingly answered, *I don't think I should take flight again today.*

I scanned the ground for Druman, but I hadn't seen any since the last group. I could take the opportunity of Tyrrik resting to scout the area for Kamini's sister. *You land,* I thought, *I want to continue searching for the Phaetyn.*

*No.*

If I had eyebrows right now, they'd be raised. *Excuse me?*

*You are not remaining in the sky without me. It's not safe.*

My tail twitched. *Care to rephrase that? Really fast.*

Tyrrik twisted to glance back at me. *Princess, I'm tired, very tired, and I require rest. If you're in the sky and I cannot see you, I will not be able to rest.*

*Sure you can. Just close your little ol' eyes and have a kip.*

He chuffed, a frustrated sound coming from his Drae lips. *It's exhausting to act against my protective instincts, and I'm far too tired to fight the mating . . .* He faced the front. *The thought of you in danger without me there to defend you will drive me mad. You have no idea how much effort it took to keep up the pretense while you were in the castle.* When I said nothing he added, *I was only able to do it because the alternative was so much worse. If you wish to continue, I'll stay with you for as long as I can, but I cannot leave you alone and unprotected.*

I took a final glance around.

*Unless you wish to help me?* he asked.

I growled, knowing he'd hear the sound despite the wind snatching the snarl away. *And that won't mean anything to you. To the bond between us?*

Some of my Drae powers were instinctual like my sense of smell or talking with Tyrrik in my head. Shifting had been difficult at first, and I still struggled to control my body when my emotions were high. The energy between Tyrrik and me was something I didn't understand.

My Phaetyn powers felt different. That energy was fluid, and it seemed like the well of power was deep and all mine. Yes, there was a learning curve, but it was still all me.

This mating-bond power felt like tenacious fibers, the threads were thin but incredibly strong. I wasn't sure I wanted to be tied to anyone. At least not now, and maybe not ever. If I pushed power into those bonds . . .

Tyrrik didn't reply.

*Will giving you some of my Drae energy affect the bond between us?* I asked again, so irritated I was about ready to bite his tail off. My frustration might've been why Tyrrik chose that moment to descend.

*Yes*, he finally answered.

I knew it! Freakin' manipulative Drae! *Yes? How?*

He descended faster. Dyter was looking between us, and I struggled to remember that beating Tyrrik to death with my tail would hurt the human I loved.

Tyrrik's voice came to me strained with trepidation as he

replied, *Doing so will tie us closer together. It will also break more of the barriers between our thoughts.*

He'd offered the innocuous information with far too much anxiety. *Tyrrik, tell me everything. I'm serious. If you don't, I will never, ever mate with you.* How could I trust someone with my life, want to protect theirs, yet still have to make sure they weren't keeping me in the dark?

*You will begin to feel more as I do. Anxious to be parted, nearly overwhelmed by my smell, and your body will want mine.*

My body already was pretty interested in his. That wasn't my problem. *You were just going to leave that part out? Am I going to go crazy? Am I going to lose my mind?*

He hesitated, one hundred meters above the mountain tops. *If you strengthen the bond, my hold over you will grow stronger.*

Even in this Drae form, my heart grew cold. *What do you mean?*

*Do you remember when I used to kiss you?*

Why did I get the feeling I wasn't going to like what he said next?

*A male Drae is able to control his mate in life and death situations; it's for survival of the species. The effect of my kiss used to wear off on you quickly, I assume because of your Phaetyn side, but as the mate bond grows, so will my protective power over you.*

*Control me? Like a blood oath?*

Tyrrik didn't have time to answer as we neared the ground. I pulled away to give him space to land safely with Dyter, but fury gnawed in my chest. I landed and immediately shifted back to Phaetyn. My power in Phaetyn form was limited, but I didn't trust my Drae with the explosive emotions racking me while Dyter was close by.

I began to pace the rocky mountain, breathing hard as I waited for Tyrrik to change back. How could he hide *that* from me? Did he really think I was going to give him any more power to manipulate me?

Turns out I couldn't wait for him to change back. I stomped over to the onyx Drae and screamed, "Were you even going to tell me before I pushed energy into you?"

As soon as I was within striking distance, I slapped his scaled hide as hard as I could and then shouted up at him. "Do you want to know why I can't decide if I want to be your mate?" I asked, gulping air, chest heaving. "It's because you treat me like a freakin' sheep! I'm not here to be herded. I'm not here to baa and be ignored." My hand was smarting, but I whacked his haunch again. "I don't want to be controlled! I don't want to be part of a game."

Tyrrik growled and swiped me up in his claw. I fell on my behind and got to my feet in a furious blur. In his clutches, I gripped two of his talons and stared through them to where he'd brought his great Drae face down. His inky eyes regarded me.

"We're not in the castle anymore, Tyrrik," I said. I made to squeeze my eyes shut, to hide the hurt as I'd done with Tyrrik so often. But hiding my pain from him wasn't helping me or him. He needed to know so he could understand. I kept my eyes open and stared into his black gaze. I let my barrier drop, allowing him to see and feel how much I hurt inside from what he'd just done. "We're not in the castle anymore," I repeated in a whisper. "Please stop acting like you're still under the Blood Oath. Hiding things from me won't keep you or me safe. You hated being controlled." I blinked, and the tears spilled over the corners of my eyes. "I hate being controlled, too."

His eyes widened, and in a blink, he set me on the ground. The air shimmered for only a moment before Tyrrik unfolded from a crouch.

"Ryn," he began, reaching out a hand.

I couldn't even look at him. I let the tears drip down my cheeks as I turned and walked away.

## 30

The mountaintop was too small to storm very far from Lord Tyrrik, and I eyed the next peak longingly. Our space had a sparse collection of low trees which would offer minimal veiling from aerial eyes while we slept, but there wasn't anything better nearby.

I kept my back to the Drae and stared out over the mountains. In the distance, the range abruptly stopped and then picked back up, making the start of Gemond's realm clear. We were likely a few days away if we walked, an hour if we flew—which we would be doing. I had wings now, and I planned to use them for every little thing I could. I stared in the direction of Gemond, listening to Dyter and Tyrrik settling down for the night behind me. I stared until my heart rate settled and I wasn't seeing red anymore. I probably shouldn't face Tyrrik yet with my temper simmering just below boiling.

Judging by Tyrrik's slow even breaths, he was asleep already. Kicking him a few times to let him know how I felt was tempting, but Ryn the Peacemaker held me back, curse her. I'd wait until he woke up again and kick him then. Ryn the Peacemaker seemed to be just fine with that.

I closed my eyes and took a deep breath, letting the scent of pine and crisp mountain air ground me though the faint smell of old smoke interrupted the serenity I was trying to achieve.

"Did he lie to you?" Dyter whispered as he approached, unaware his lumbering gait was plenty loud enough to wake the Drae. Though . . . Tyrrik looked pretty out of it after flying all day.

I kept my eyes closed and released a slow breath. "No. Not really. Tyrrik isn't an outright liar. He deceives by omission."

Dyter brushed needles and bits of dried vegetation off a flat rock before taking a seat. He patted the space next to him. "That doesn't make it any easier than a true lie when you're on the receiving end. Not in my experience."

I snorted. "Understatement of the year." I sat down next to him and leaned into the familiar warmth of his thick body. "Is this where you're going to give me sage advice that will solve all my problems?"

I'd meant the words as a joke, but in truth, I *did* want him to tell me what I should do. My mind felt cloudy and thick with the churning in my head. How had I ever craved adventure? Adventure sucked big time. I wanted to go to the girl I'd been and have a serious talking-to with her, maybe smack her around a bit. Dwelling on what-ifs wasn't really in my nature, but right now, I couldn't help thinking that if I could change one decision in my past, I would do it in a heartbeat.

"I've never pretended to have the answers for you. You'll have to live with whatever decisions you make, not me. There are plenty of decisions that still haunt me, most especially when I'm worn out. But, my girl, in the morning, things won't look quite so bad."

"That's all you've got?" I chuckled darkly. "Get a good night's sleep? I feel like my life's being decided for me, but I should just have a kip?" My eyes were heavy as was my heart. I knew it was too much to demand advice, especially on something he couldn't truly understand. But he was Dyter.

He took a breath, and my body was moved by his inhalation and then again as he exhaled.

Dyter cleared his throat, and I peeled my eyelids open to give him my attention.

"I'm not going to tell you how to sort this out with Lord Tyrrik; that's between the two of you. But I want you to have an honest think about this mate business from all angles. I know," he said, holding up his hand to stop my interruption, "I don't understand all of it. I don't even want to. But have a think. You didn't get to choose your mum either, right? You didn't get to choose who she was, but you did choose to love her though you didn't have a choice initially because you knew she was yours and she knew you were hers."

I bristled. "You're over—"

"Oversimplifying, I know," he said with a wave. "I'm not saying you should be okay with deceit. That breeds distrust, and distrust will destroy any partnership or alliance: mated pairs, businesses, or kingdoms."

I frowned as I thought through his words. "So you think I should—"

Dyter shook his head. "I'm not telling you what you should do. I want you to think, Ryn. You need to have realistic expectations of what might happen between the pair of you, and be clear on what you want." He turned and looked at me. "I'm going to oversimplify again, okay?" When I nodded, he continued, "Think of how many times in a single day you told your mum you were sorry."

I grimaced. Not nearly enough.

"Love doesn't mean you're perfect. Loving someone doesn't mean you don't screw up. In fact, I'd say the more you love some- one, the more time you spend with that someone, the more you're going to have to say you're sorry. Love means you say sorry sooner because when you realize you've hurt someone you truly love, you want to do whatever you can to make it right."

I shifted on the rock, tucking a few of the wispy dress panels under my butt and legs while I digested Dyter's wisdom. I felt I wasn't fully understanding his words. They made sense on a surface level. He was saying that when you were in love, you wanted the other person to be happy. "You think I owe Tyrrik an apology?"

*Like that would happen.*

Dyter grinned. "I think you owe *me* an apology."

239

"You're still hanging onto the burned soup incident, aren't you?" I asked. Then seriously, I said, "I'm so grateful you're in my life, Dyter, and I'm sorry for all of the times I might've been a brat."

Dyter wrapped his arm around me and pulled me to him. He planted a loud kiss on top of my head and then rested his cheek on my hair. "Thank you, my girl. And I apologize if I'm grumpy sometimes."

"Just sometimes?" I asked. At his scowl, I mumbled a hasty, "Thank you. Apology accepted."

He patted my knee. "When you're done having a think, you might also consider having a talk with Tyrrik. You don't lose the power to choose whether or not you want to be with him and whether or not to love him if you're just talking."

The sun had dipped below the mountains during our chat, and soon after, the sky darkened. The sister moons were continuing their monthly merging, and I pointed at the double-circle shape while still nestled by Dyter's side. "I'll always remember how I got the best relationship advice ever while sitting underneath a moon that looked like a butt."

Dyter chuckled. "How does that look like a butt to you? It looks like a fat peanut to me."

I tilted my head. "I guess it could be that too."

"You're twisted. Let's go to sleep, my girl. I'm too tired to stay up and share any more wisdom."

He stood and extended his arm, but I waved him off.

"I'll be there in a minute. I'm going to have that think you encouraged."

He leaned over and kissed my hair again. "Don't stay up too late." He looked up at the sky and then smiled his scar-pulling grin. "You know, as kids we used to say if you slept under a butt-moon, you were destined to get crapped on."

I quirked a brow, waiting for the good part.

Dyter's grin widened. "Right then. Good night."

I glared at his retreating back and then peered suspiciously at the butt-moon and stars above. I muttered up at the sky, "Do not crap on me."

In my opinion, I'd been crapped on more than enough already.

---

THE SCENT of searing meat awoke me, but the pleasant low murmur of voices kept me in sleep's embrace. I had no idea how long Tyrrik and Dyter had been awake, but it was long enough for the space next to me, where Tyrrik should have been, to have grown cold. Dyter's cloak was draped over me, but my super-amazing Drae senses failed to alert me then. When I had some spare time, I needed to work on activating each of my senses. Not having them when I wanted was a serious pain. Tyrrik had said I'd be able to control a partial shift; that had to mean my eyes and ears, right?

"She was not raised Drae; you can't expect her to accept your customs and culture without guidance and time," Dyter whispered. "And even then, you need to be open to accepting some of hers. A little patience would go a long way—"

"It is not in my nature to be patient," Tyrrik said. "It's not in the nature of *any* male Drae."

I mentally rolled my eyes. *Male schmale.*

"To be so close without bonding with her is nearly unbearable—,"

I froze.

"—She wants me to court her, I know, and if our mating meant *less*, I could. But my soul knows her, and my Drae craves her. My control is not infinite. I fear harming her or you if I continue to deny my instincts. I'm fighting the very nature of our species."

Dyter said nothing at first, and in my mind, I could see the furrow he would wear while contemplating his answer.

"I'm surprised to hear that," he said slowly. Small pieces of rock scrabbled to the ground as he got to his feet. "I don't know much about Drae instincts or nature, but I would think a century of waiting would've taught you patience."

Ouch. Harsh. I knew Dyter was taking my side, but I couldn't help the smolder of injustice for Tyrrik churning underneath my ribs. I couldn't imagine waiting a hundred years for *anything*. And just how hard was it for Tyrrik to deny these *instincts?* When he'd said he didn't want to know me better, I'd thought he meant I was annoying or something, not that he was in physical pain around me.

"Are you up, Ryn?" Dyter called as he crossed from the clearing into the small thicket of trees. "We should start our descent soon so we can be up the other side before it gets dark."

*Ugh, we're walking again?* I grumbled as I sat up, my gaze going to Tyrrik to let him know he was the source of my bad mood. His back was to me, and he leaned over the fire to turn the spit roast, rabbit by the looks of it.

He stretched his arms up, his borrowed aketon rising to mid-muscly-thigh.

Attraction for the Drae was not part of my current problems. Fire flared low in my belly, and I eyed the bottom of the aketon, willing it to inch up a little more. *Show me some more toned Drae leg.*

Tyrrik froze, and I blushed though he couldn't see me where I peeked over the rocks. Dyter, however, did. He glanced back at Tyrrik and faced me with a chuckle.

"Like the view?" the old man asked.

I narrowed my eyes. "Nah, I've seen better." I stood and folded up his cloak. Handing it back to Dyter, I said, "Thanks for keeping me warm."

He shook his head and pointed at Tyrrik who was now casually cutting the spit roast into edible pieces with his talon. "Thank him; he's the one who covered you."

Of course he did. Great.

Dyter shoved the cloak in his pack. I couldn't explain my nervousness, but it was there, crawling through my body at an unreasonable pace.

I shifted from foot to foot, asking, "What's for breakfast?"

"Tyrrik caught three rabbits. He saved one for you."

Whoever said the way to a man's heart was through his stomach was clearly raised in Verald—*I* thought the saying pertained more accurately to women. Either way, my heart melted just a little as I watched Tyrrik finish slicing the roast. "A whole rabbit? For me?"

Dyter looked up from the pack and nodded. "Hurry up. As soon as you're done, we're leaving."

I took three blissfully unaware steps toward Tyrrik before the conversation with Dyter fully resurfaced, and my conscience reminded me: I owed Tyrrik an apology for slapping him with thirty-seven branches yesterday. My mum had taught me slapping people was rude. Even if it involved trees. Though I wasn't entirely sure Tyrrik's recent *lie of omission* wouldn't bend my mother's etiquette guidelines, I found I wanted to apologize to Tyrrik for the sake of, well, *Tyrrik*. Because his face had to have hurt after the twentieth branch slap, and I should've stopped after thirteen or fourteen.

I trudged forward, distinctly uncomfortable. What should I say? Sorry, I whacked you a bunch with the branches under the premise I wasn't aware they would rebound into your really handsome face? I sounded twelve. Probably because I was acting twelve. *Nice.* As if I didn't already feel bad enough. Holy pancakes, he was watching me.

Tyrrik sat on a rock by the fire. His feet were set wide apart, and his inky eyes searched my face with the focus of a hunter searching for his prey's weakness. Was that aketon normal length? I eyed the hem askance, sure this was a skimpier design. A broody Drae in a skimpy aketon was going to be the death of me. The closer I got to Tyrrik, the more tongue-tied I became. My stomach picked this same time to tie *itself* in knots.

I was Ryn the Peacemaker who was also Fearless, and I could do hard things.

I took a deep breath and stopped in front of the fire, staring at my filthy feet instead of acknowledging Tyrrik. The panels of my skirt were frayed and spotted with mud and other stuff. Tyrrik's feet were clean except for a dusting of recent dirt. How was that even possible?

"Here's your breakfast," he said in a low voice.

RAYE WAGNER & KELLY ST. CLARE

I gulped and raised my chin, but I couldn't quite get my gaze to meet his. I managed to accept the roasted rabbit, noticing how it was evenly browned and glistening with grease. "Thank you." I swallowed again and said in a rush, "I'm-sorry-I'm-twelve-and-I-hit-you-with-the-branches-it-won't-happen- again."

He pursed his lips. "Pardon me?"

Really? He was going to make me say it again? I met his gaze, and everything else fell away. Tyrrik's dark eyes were flooded, wholly focused on me, intently so. His brow was furrowed but not in displeasure, more like I was a puzzle he couldn't solve.

I let my mental defenses slip, and his concern and worry flooded in. All of it for me.

"I'm sorry," I whispered. "I'm sorry I hit you with all those branches yesterday. That was immature and . . . unkind."

He swallowed. "It made you smile, and you know I would do—"

"Sorry, love-birds," Dyter blurted, barreling toward us. "You'll have to kiss and make up later. We need to leave, right now."

*What the hay?* He'd been all 'talk to Tyrrik, Rynnie,' last night. I turned on Dyter to give him a piece of my mind, but the fear on his face stopped the words.

"What is it?" I asked.

Both men spoke at once.

Dyter said, "Movement coming down the mountain."

"Druman," Tyrrik said, his obsidian eyes hardening. "Closing in fast."

He kicked dirt on the fire, extinguishing the flames.

I watched Tyrrik move, but my mind was fixated on the memory of Jotun's cruelty. I blinked but otherwise remained frozen, my breath tripping in my chest. *Flee.* We needed to get out of here. They were going to catch us again. Tyrrik, Dyter, me. They'd use Tyrrik and Dyter against me. I wouldn't be able to get free.

I sucked in a breath and gagged on the stench of unwashed Druman, a mixture of body odor and dust and sunbaked leather hide. They were here. They were here for me. I couldn't go back.

"Ryn," Dyter said, pulling me after him. "We need to go, girl.

They're coming down the mountain, so we should slip away while we still can."

My feet moved, but I couldn't shake the feeling something was off. "Why are we running? Why not go Drae and kill them? We can do that, right?"

"As soon as they die, the emperor will know," Tyrrik said, scanning the clearing. "He'll feel them die. If the Druman have to waste time reporting to the emperor, we'll be inside Gemond before he even knows it. If he feels his Druman die, he'll investigate, and he could intercept us."

I nodded. "We need to get in the air."

No one answered, but Tyrrik jerked his head toward the edge of our campsite. His features hardened, and his lips thinned into a grim line.

"Be careful," he said to Dyter. "The drop is steep."

I peered over the edge of the mountaintop—calling this drop *steep* was like calling night day. "You're not suggesting we walk down the side of the cliff . . . are you?"

Dyter sat down on the ledge and then pushed his body off and disappeared.

I yelped, and my muscles coiled to leap after him.

"Shh." Tyrrik intercepted my spring, covering my mouth, and whispering, "There's a path below. He'll be fine."

I glared, and he removed his hand from my face only to grab my wrist and tug me after him. "I thought you said we weren't going to walk down—"

"We're not."

The tension in my body eased a fraction until Tyrrik stood where Dyter had been a moment before.

"I'd rather avoid detection if at all possible," Tyrrik said, not meeting my eyes.

I heard what he didn't want to say: Tyrrik wasn't sure he could shift and fight them off. He didn't want to admit he was weak.

"We won't walk," he continued. "We'll need to run."

I felt like someone had kicked the backs of my knees. Tyrrik grabbed my waist and lifted me over the side. I dangled for a second until he lowered me from above.

A moment later, I hugged the rocky wall of a narrow ledge. The path curved around the cliff face before reaching the wide expanse of a steep slope covered in a sparse thicket of low trees. I inched my way along, turning back in time to see Tyrrik drop to safety where I'd been standing seconds before.

He tilted his chin again, and I took the hint, side stepping along the ledge until I was able to scurry into the woods.

31

The smell of Druman was growing, and so was the cold sweat on my forehead and palms. We edged down the almost-vertical pass as quickly as Dyter could quietly move. Dyter couldn't contain his labored breathing as the ground began to flatten out, and we sprinted and jumped over rocks and hidden gaps in the rough terrain.

Soon, Tyrrik's breathing was labored, too. This run shouldn't have been tiring me, but my chest was tight, and my breath wouldn't completely fill my lungs. I kept seeing my dungeon cell with its solitary drip of water, the sharp rocky ground, the dank smell.

Believing that the scent of Druman was truly lessening took a long time, at least until the ascent of the next mountain. Eventually, even I had to admit their smell had disappeared.

Tyrrik kept us in the foliage as much as possible. Our pace slowed as the ground sloped upward once more.

Dyter held up his hand for a stop and pulled out the now stone-cold roasted rabbit and the waterskin.

"You guys need to eat, too," I puffed, hands on my knees. I felt absolutely wrung out. Like I'd been sprinting for days.

After some insistence, the two men took a third each of the rabbit.

Tyrrik took the waterskin from Dyter after the old man had a few gulps. The Drae handed it to me a moment later. I guzzled back the nectar Tyrrik offered and then focused for a few seconds before passing the waterskin back.

We continued our climb, our pace slowing further as fatigue settled in. Dyter puffed as he led the way, stopping to consult his compass more frequently as afternoon settled in.

"Are we going to make it?" I asked. My question wasn't to anyone in particular, and the answer didn't even matter, not really. The silence was driving me crazy, and I wanted something to fill it. *The silence.* I hadn't noticed Tyrrik in my head since the moment by the fire.

I whirled around and stared at him.

*Why aren't you in my head?* I pushed my thought at him and couldn't help the tone of accusation that leaked with it. Usually, when the Drae was conscious, I could feel little spikes of his emotion, and *usually,* he spoke to me several times even when I didn't want him in there. What had changed?

He lifted his head and met my gaze. His face was lined with exhaustion that made my heart ache.

"It's an invasion of your privacy for me to be in your head without your permission, and I shouldn't have done it before now. Not without asking you if that was okay," Tyrrik said; his sad smile touched the deep recesses of my heart. "I'm sorry, Ryn," he said in a weary voice. "I want to say I never meant to take advantage of you, but that would be a lie because I wanted to establish a presence inside you. I forced my way in when you were vulnerable in the castle. I gave over to my mating instincts when I should have tapered them. But I . . . don't want that to be how we start, how we might go on. Not anymore. You were right. We're not in the castle. I'm not under a blood oath. I need to stop acting that way." He released a shaking breath.

I blinked. Trying to make sense of why his reasonable statement and thoughtful apology made me so unreasonably angry while simultaneously breaking my heart.

I faced forward and asked Dyter's back, "Did you tell him that's how I felt?"

"No," they chorused.

I turned back to Tyrrik.

He watched me, inky eyes pools of darkness that seemed to mirror his soul's secrets.

I located the source of my anger as I stared into his eyes, and it wasn't what I'd expected. I was oddly thankful Tyrrik had forced his way in, against my better judgment, because how would I have ever opened that door between us? Now I'd experienced that mental connection, I could appreciate all the comfort having Tyrrik in my head had to offer. If the choice had been mine to speak in Tyrrik's head first? I probably would have resisted it with everything I had. Even saying that, I knew on some level I'd clearly accepted our telepathy or I'd be fighting it still. Was that what I was doing with the mating bond? Was I resisting it just for the sake of resisting? Maybe Tyrrik's behavior since being released from the blood oath wasn't meant to be manipulative. Maybe he was just wary of giving his trust, too.

I opened my mouth to say something, but rational thought fled when I smelled *them*. My body flooded with terror, and I whispered, "Druman."

Tyrrik's face blanched and his eyes widened as he inhaled me, my fear. His face hardened, his black eyes gaining a wild edge as he reacted to the terror seeping out of my pores.

I blinked, and in less than a heartbeat Tyrrik was Drae.

He roared, a sound of defiance and challenge. Thrashing his tail, he twisted his neck and stomped as he tried to gain his footing on the mountain side. Talons clutching the boulders, he leapt into the air, whipped in a circle, and exhaled a stream of scalding fire into the trees behind us. Druman's screams filled the air. Tyrrik bellowed his hatred into the sky, neck outstretched. Roaring flames devoured the trees, and Dyter's loud gasp echoed in my ears.

Tyrrik roared again, vibrant fire poured from between his deadly fangs, but there was something off about his roar. Then the world tilted, and as I fell back, already my mind told me the feeling of disorientation wasn't originating from me. The air around his Drae form shimmered, and a full minute later, far too long I knew, Tyrrik's human form lay in the dirt. Agony squeezed my chest, wringing my heart until I saw him lift his head.

*Go*, Tyrrik mouthed, his face white and sweating. *The emperor will come.* The effort of shifting to kill the Druman had completely drained him.

I grabbed Dyter. "Can you point me to Gemond?"

I didn't wait for him to answer. I shifted, the change rippling over me in the time it took me to exhale. I scooped Dyter into one foreclaw and Tyrrik into the other, leaping into the air using my hind legs as soon as I had them secure.

I screamed my rage across the mountain peaks, wishing I could exact revenge on the dead Druman all over again for taking what little energy Tyrrik had. But Tyrrik's and Dyter's safety took precedence over everything right now. I had to get them to safety.

Something pinched me, and I heard Dyter's muffled voice yell, "Too tight."

I loosened my grip on the two males in my claws and pushed higher into the air. As soon as I'd cleared the mountaintops, I realized I didn't need Dyter to tell me the way to Gemond. I could see the kingdom from here.

The minutes as I bolted across the skies felt like hours. Each second, I imagined the emperor's flames licking the back of my neck, but my initial panic about Tyrrik diminished as I studied his state through our touch. He was unconscious but still breathing. There was no gold Phaetyn poison in his pitch-black Drae; he was literally depleted.

My fear had set him off. He hadn't been able to resist shifting after he inhaled and my terror hit him. He'd pushed himself for me, all this time, again and again. He . . . truly couldn't control his reaction to me. I hadn't believed him until now.

Yet Tyrrik was trying to control his reaction, against his very instincts, because I had been unable to understand why he couldn't act as human males would, as Arnik might have done, even as Kamoi would have. What did it say that Tyrrik was doing that, something which I could now see was near impossible for a Drae, all for me?

The setting sun bathed the valley of Gemond in warm golden light as I soared down the final mountainside to the valley below. The realm was surrounded by majestic peaks, and like in Verald, the castle was nestled in the center of the vale. I pushed my emotions into the recesses of my mind, locking them away to deal with later. Later, when we were safe. Later, when we weren't being chased by Druman. Later, when the King of Gemond hopefully didn't eat us. Later, when . . . There would never be a perfect time to discuss what Tyrrik and I needed to, so I settled on the next best thing. *Later*, when Tyrrik was conscious again.

I landed outside the granite gates and bellowed my arrival before setting Tyrrik and Dyter down on the ground. Being afraid of landing with them hadn't occurred to me which showed how stupid a thing fear was.

I would conquer my reaction to the presence of Druman if it was the last thing I did.

The gate cracked open, and two stocky golden-plated soldiers with rounded helmets lurched forward, stutter-stepping as they saw me. They halted well out of reach of my swinging tail. Clever men. I wouldn't hesitate to use it; I hadn't come all this way to have Dyter or Tyrrik killed by guards dressed in gold. How stupid. Gold was soft. Was this just to show their wealth? I ran my gaze over the gold soldiers. I bet their armor was worth a pretty penny. The two men would look great in my collection . . . but I'd have to feed them.

Dyter got to his feet and ran his hand over his head as he gulped several breaths. He looked a little green after the flight. I narrowed my Drae eyes, daring him to insult my aerial ability.

"Thank you, Ryn," he said.

My tail twitched at the blatant lie.

He turned to the guards and announced us. "We seek an audience with King Zakai. Please inform him that Lord Tyrrik the . . .

Free Drae, Dyter of Verald—ambassador to King Caltevyn, and Ryn are here."

I practically gave myself Drae whiplash at that. I lowered my head to Dyter, a low growl rumbling in my chest. Shouldn't I be Ryn the Coolest Drae, or Ryn the Phaetyn-Drae? Or maybe Ryn the Phaetyn-Drae, daughter of Ryhl—

Dyter eyed me nervously and blurted, "I mean to say, Ryn the most powerful Drae."

*Most powerful Drae.* I smiled, showing every one of my fangs to Dyter who rolled his eyes. I could work with most powerful Drae.

The guards disappeared, and minutes later, the heavy gates inched opened with an ominous groan. The shiny soldiers bowed us through, and I picked up Tyrrik in my claw, walking forward awkwardly. I ducked through the high gate and straightened inside the cavernous mountain space. In the distance, I heard another Drae roar, and my heart raced, knowing who it would be. The gates closed behind me, and my Drae jaw dropped as I stared at the royal lands of Gemond.

*Mistress Butt-moon.*

I shook off the shock, and the air shimmered as I shifted back to my Phaetyn form.

I pushed my silver hair behind my ears, one leg on either side of Tyrrik's body, and studied the guards. *Their* shock halted their advance. They really weren't dumb.

I knelt by Tyrrik and rested my head on his chest. His heartbeat was steady. How long would Tyrrik need to rest before regaining his strength now that we would have the comfort and resources he would need—if the king felt like giving those to us? After seeing what I'd seen, I couldn't be sure.

Satisfied Tyrrik wasn't in immediate danger, I took in my surroundings. The castle walls were encrusted with gems at least seven or eight feet up from the floor. I had no idea how one would get rubies, sapphires, emeralds, and diamonds to stick to the stone, but there they were, ripe and ready for the picking . . . if someone was inclined to do so for the sake of her collection.

Dyter cleared his throat, and I realized I'd been staring and missed the welcoming party that now stood before us.

Three men, dressed in ill-fitting uniforms, nodded in unison. The one in front spoke.

"Welcome to Gemond. King Zakai is resting, but he's asked that we take you to your rooms. He will join you for supper tonight."

I resisted the urge to let my attention return to the precious gems and forced myself to look at the men.

These men were likely in their thirties or forties, if Gemond people aged normally, but their sunken cheeks and thin frames made them appear much older. Two were missing one of their arms, and their empty sleeves were tucked into their belts. The third one wore an eye patch, and the left side of his face had large chunks of flesh missing. The only indication of their true age was the smoothness of their skin around their eyes where the skin was visible.

I thought of the women outcasts in the mountains and how they'd resorted to cannibalism to stay alive. These men weren't as emaciated, but they weren't healthy by any stretch. My disgust for King Zakai multiplied as I wondered how a king could have unlimited wealth and still starve his people. And he was resting, taking a late afternoon nap and couldn't be bothered to greet the ambassador of Verald. How could the king rest while such hardship was everywhere around him? Queen Alani had spent her life resting. Was this king the same? Yet another leader who was taking advantage of his people? My face firmed, and I tried to come up with a way to say what I thought in a way that wouldn't get us murdered. However, Dyter beat me to it.

"My Lord Tyrrik has fallen ill and will require a dark room with ample access to water," Dyter said. "If you were to have a suite where we could all reside, we would be most grateful. The Drae will need his . . . he will require significant attention, and if we don't have to break up our traveling party—"

"We'll take you to your rooms where you can wash, rest, and have a light luncheon. Supper is still several hours away."

I slid my gaze to Dyter, but his attention was fixed on our escort.

Something was bothering him, but I didn't dare ask. Worrying about the problems of yet another race would have to wait until Tyrrik was cared for.

I cleared my throat and jerked my head at Tyrrik. "I'd sure appreciate your help, Lord Dyter."

I had no idea what role I was meant to play here, and I didn't want to do anything to screw up Dyter's plans. Not yet.

When I met King Zakai, I might rip his head off, but for right now, I had more pressing concerns.

"What are you doing?" Dyter asked.

I jumped, and the dagger I held clattered to the stone floor of the huge bathroom.

"Nothing," I said, clearing my throat.

Leaning down, I scooped the dagger up and passed it to Dyter who stood in the ornate archway.

He looked past me to the large emerald in the wall. The one that now had scratch marks around it from where I'd tried to pry it out. I wasn't perfect, and I was the first to admit it.

"When did you wake up?" he asked, sheathing the dagger in the scabbard at his belt.

"Not long ago." Long enough for me to use the restroom and get distracted by that emerald. He wasn't going to make it easy for me to get that blade back either. I was going to need to find another tool.

"How long did we sleep?" I asked. Judging by the stiffness I'd felt upon awaking, our nap had been more than a few hours.

I followed Dyter back into the large bedroom, and the sparkling walls captured my attention before I forced it back to the old man. This place was driving me crazy, although I could see why they shoved gems into the dark gray walls. The refracted jewel-toned light in here was deep and rich. If I had a lair, I would want it to be like this.

"A guard came to the door before," Dyter said. "We slept nearly eighteen hours."

I whistled low, but I wasn't truly surprised. We hadn't really rested since setting out from Verald, and even then, there had been the overhanging feeling of danger. Dyter had placed his packs in front of the sole door into our echoing, shared chamber, and after tending to Tyrrik—shoving as much food as possible into the slurring man—we'd slipped into a deep slumber.

"Is the king rested enough to see us now?" I asked, sitting on the narrow bed beside Tyrrik. His beard was filling in, and dirt smudged his cheek. I looked down at my tattered dress. *I* needed a bath and some clean clothes.

Tyrrik jolted at the movement and then blinked up at me.

"Evening," I said, reaching for a platter of fruit. I grabbed a bunch of grapes and popped one in my mouth.

We'd received plenty of food yesterday, and the guards had brought us more. This king was no good. If he could spare all this, he could afford to feed his people.

Tyrrik rolled onto his back, and I stiffened as the blanket fell mid-way down his bare chest. I know I usually slept next to that each night, but at night I could pretend our sleeping arrangements didn't mean anything. In the light of day, noticing his sculpted chest somehow meant more. Tyrrik plucked a grape from my hand and dropped the red globe in his mouth. He leaned back, placing one hand behind his head.

I took him in and swallowed. Holy pancakes. *Look at the sparkling gems, Ryn.* But I just stared at the Drae.

"So . . ." Dyter said, breaking the spell.

"Yes?" I said, facing him eagerly. I needed to get myself under better control. If he laughed, I'd hit him.

He didn't. "We're expected in a couple of hours."

Great. I cracked my knuckles. "Time to heal Tyrrik then."

Tyrrik shook his head. "I'm fine. In a few hours, I'll be able to get through the meeting with the king."

"You're fine? You exhausted yourself and collapsed on the ground . . . unconscious."

"But I slept eighteen hours," he said. "There's no need for you to deplete your energy."

I rested my hands on his chest under the guise of healing him, which I guess I was, but—yeah—there were also ulterior motives. *Classic trick.*

I peeked up at Tyrrik and scowled at the wry smile on his lips.

I ignored him and tuned into my Phaetyn energy. Kamini was right, each time I used my powers, healing became easier, just like making plants grow. There wasn't any gold poison in Tyrrik at all now. In fact, his body was fine, just like he'd said, but the flow of his blood was sluggish, and I could feel his exhaustion.

I studied the pulsing blue power coursing down my arms and gathering in my hands, invisible to all but me. I guess I'd stuff as much in as possible to help him regain his stamina. I exhaled and opened the gates of my Phaetyn powers, the energy immediately flowing into him. I took another breath and threw the force at Tyrrik.

With a yell, he jolted a meter in the air and flopped on the bed.

I echoed his yell, jumping away from the bed, frightened by the strength of his reaction. Holding my hands in the air, I stared at him. "Are you al'right? What just happened?"

Dyter snorted. "I saw a donkey do that once when it was branded."

Tyrrik panted and pushed up to sitting, the blanket puddling at his waist.

"Whoa, Tyrrik, you're practically glowing," I said fidgeting on the spot. There was a bluish aura around his body. Maybe I'd over healed him. Was that a thing?

"Maybe a bit slower next time," he wheezed, slumping back. "And less at once."

That was nice of him. I sat next to him again and cautiously lay a hand on his chest, silently wondering if glowing was healthy. I frowned as I studied his new state. I'd poured plenty of energy into him, but the aura around his body faded, soaking into him like he was a dry sponge.

"You need more," I said. "But I think we better wait a little."

Tyrrik's face was smooth and relaxed now, but he rested a hand over where mine lay against his chest. "Yes, Khosana. That might be a good idea."

I met his eyes, heat creeping into my cheeks. "And you're not coming to dinner," I said, my voice a breathy whisper. I cleared my throat and tried again, but my words came out more like pillow talk. "You'll be resting."

The tone of my voice made it sound like I was asking to rest *with* him, but I couldn't seem to find enough protest within myself to clarify the point. Our bond pulsed, and I felt his desire quicken.

He inhaled sharply, and black scales erupted where our skin touched, climbing up his arm. I stared at the luminescent blue in their depths, and my breath caught at the intimacy of his response.

"I don't know what's happening," Dyter said. "But I know I don't want to watch it."

His voice was distant and worked its way to my awareness slowly. I finally blinked, severing contact with Tyrrik's intense onyx eyes. When had our gazes met?

My hand was shaking as I slid my arm free, but there was something I'd promised to say.

"Tyrrik," I said, still perching on the edge of the bed though I planned to make a quick getaway after this. "I just wanted you to know that you can listen in my head." I winced at the garbled words. "Like put your head in mine." I sighed and stood. That bath-gem-getaway seemed like a good idea right now. "Anyway, you know what I mean. Thank you for being respectful and asking. I really appreciate that, and I'm okay with your thoughts rubbing against mine."

I glanced back and saw Dyter's eyes were squeezed shut.

"That's not exactly what I meant—" I blurted.

"Ryn," Tyrrik said.

I peeked up and saw him studying me with heightened intensity. His lips parted as he took a deep breath.

"Yeah?" Next time I told a mate they could jump in my head, I should think about what I wanted to say beforehand.

The Drae's voice trembled. "Thank you for this gift. It is priceless, and I will treasure our connection."

My chest rose as some kind of warm, joyful sickness spread through me. "You're welcome," I whispered. I made tracks for the bathroom. I had a bath to take and an emerald to pry out of the wall, and both seemed something I should attend to immediately. I paused, though, halfway there. "Tyrrik, did you plan what you were going to say beforehand?"

"No, Khosana." He'd turned on his side to watch me leave.

"Huh," I mused. I guess some people just had a gift with words.

---

"How big is this place?" I whispered to Dyter. The old man knew a lot more about the realm than I did because of his talks with King Cal. Probably a good idea to learn as much as I could.

Dyter tilted his head toward me so our conversation wouldn't be overheard by the gold guards trailing behind us. Thankfully, Tyrrik had been asleep when we snuck out, so a debate on his health wasn't necessary.

"King Caltevyn told me the Gemond kingdom extends throughout this entire mountain range," Dyter answered.

My eyes rounded. I'd seen how huge this range was from the air.

"They mine throughout the Gemond mountains, however," he continued. "Not all of the area is inhabitable. This valley is where most of the population lives."

I heard what he wasn't saying, too. Out there wasn't like in here. Well, we'd see about that.

The guards stopped in front of a set of gold-plated doors and drew them back, gesturing us through. Considering the grandeur of the palace, I'd expected to be led to a ballroom, something similar to Irdelron's throne room with long tables overflowing with food. The room we entered was plain in comparison to our chambers. The walls were plain without the adornment of gems we'd seen everywhere else. A heavy stone table sat in the middle of the room with gilded, high-backed chairs set around it. A diamond chandelier hung above, but only a few of the candles were lit, casting the room in shadows. In the middle of the table was a small arrangement of food. Nothing like Irdelron's groaning food benches.

At the head of the table sat an emaciated man, draped in finery. As we neared, I noticed the robes he wore were threadbare and ill-fitting. If those were his robes, they'd been made for him a long time ago.

Dyter took the lead, and I shuffled behind, trying to reconcile the thin king with the fat, crass man I'd created in my head.

"Greetings, King Zakai," Dyter said. "Thank you for granting us an audience."

The king used the table to stand and paused for a long moment before moving forward to meet Dyter. Zakai extended his hand. "I am pleased to have you here," he said. "I'm eager to hear of Verald's new king and to discuss how we may improve the bonds between our kingdoms."

Straightforward. Polite. Open mannered. I narrowed my eyes, clinging to my expectations of his character. He let his people eat each other, I reminded myself.

He turned to me and, with a slight bow, said, "You must be Ryn the Most Powerful Drae."

"I am," I answered, dipping my head at him, ignoring Dyter's eye roll. I wasn't curtseying to rulers anymore. The sheer fact I'd entered this place was a miracle and one I hadn't even thought about in my desperation to find shelter before the emperor found us.

"It is an honor to meet you, Ryn, one of the last free Drae. Please," the king said, pointing at the chairs behind him. "Take a seat so we may talk further. You must be hungry."

I swept my gaze down his frail frame. Dyter said the king was in his forties, but he looked much older, like the starving people in the Penny Wheel of Verald. There was no way we were as hungry as he was. Unease crawled through me at the disparity of my expectations and the reality before me.

I sat on the king's left, Dyter on his right, and servers rested plates before us and removed the gilded domes covering the platters. The aromas of roasted meat and rosemary, rich gravy, potatoes with thyme, and baked apples with cinnamon assailed me, and all thought fled my mind but one.

"What kind of meat is that?" I asked. There was no way I was going to eat another person, no matter how good it smelled.

The king glanced at one of the servers who answered, "It's roasted pheasant."

The bird was in an arrangement of herb-roasted vegetables. My mouth watered in anticipation as Dyter and I loaded up our plates.

I cut into a potato, popped it in my mouth, and vowed I would never begrudge a potato again. As I chewed, I glanced at the king and found him watching me. His eyes were a rich blue . . . in fact, his eyes were the color of my scales, lapis lazuli.

More confusion twisted my insides, and my gaze fell to his empty plate.

"You're not eating?" I asked.

He gave a small smile and a casual wave of his hand. "I'm not hungry just at the moment."

Uh-huh, and I was the queen of walking potatoes. I shrugged, choosing to take him at face value for now, and placed some of the greasy bird meat in my mouth. I withheld a moan. Just.

"I hear Verald is prospering as never before under Caltevyn's rule," the king said. "It's been what? Just two weeks since his ascension to the throne, yes?"

I heard a rumbling sound and looked to the source . . . the Gemond king's stomach.

Dyter swallowed a huge mouthful of meat and gravy and answered, "You've heard right." He glanced at me. "King Irdelron kept a store of Phaetyn blood to preserve his immortality. With the Phaetyn's permission, this is now being put to use on the land."

The king leaned forward. "The lands are healing?"

"They are." Dyter nodded. "And they will continue to heal and provide a more bountiful harvest with each year. The Veraldian people will grow in strength."

"I am happy for your people," the king said, and I paused mid-chew, hearing the complete honesty of his words.

He sighed, resting his head in his hand. "If I could do the same for my people, I would."

*Yeah, right.* I opened my mouth, but Dyter intercepted me. No doubt on purpose.

Dyter leaned down and picked up a small case, placing it on the table. I'd seen Caltevyn give it to him before we left Verald. He'd guarded the case during our trip as zealously as I guarded my meager collection. He pushed the case toward the Gemond king. "King Caltevyn sends his regards and this gift."

The king glanced at the case. "With what intention?"

"No strings, King Zakai," Dyter said, resting his cutlery on the table.

I cut a baby carrot in half, but for some reason, I wasn't feeling hungry anymore.

"King Caltevyn wanted you to have this gift. He asked me to press upon you that this is yours, no matter what your decisions are regarding other matters."

"The other matters being what?" the king asked drily, his mouth twisting into a sardonic smile. Zakai wasn't a fool, regardless of his frailty.

Dyter wiped at his chin. "Joining our alliance against Emperor Draedyn."

One of the servers gasped, and the king cut the woman a severe look. The servers fell silent.

"Indeed," the king said, his gaze flitting between us, spending a long time on me before he leaned forward and opened the case.

The Gemond king's eyes widened, and his jaw dropped. Several moments passed before he lifted his gaze to Dyter and asked, "This isn't—is this—"

"Two vials of Phaetyn blood," Dyter finished for him. "Enough to heal your lands now and for a long time to come."

The king didn't speak, staring at the vials. Tears gathered in his rich blue eyes, dripping to the stone table, staining the dark gray slate black with moisture.

*A* lump of emotion formed at the back of my throat. King Zakai was nothing like I'd anticipated, and the contradiction of depravity I'd seen in the mountains to the emotion of the ruler of Gemond made no sense.

"Thank you," he whispered, lifting his head. "You cannot know what this means to us, what it will mean to our people."

Dyter dipped his head. "Actually, I do. Most of Verald was on the brink of starving for the last twenty years. I've starved more often than I'd like in my lifetime."

The king swallowed hard, blinking several times. "Yes, of course. Everyone in this realm is hungry."

"Not Verald," I said. "And with this, not your people." Dyter shot me a look I couldn't fail to interpret as *I told you so.* I was prepared to grudgingly admit he'd been partially right about the Gemond king. The guy was crying over Phaetyn blood, so whatever monster he was, he wasn't completely oblivious or calloused to the struggles of his people.

He closed the lid as though the case held his heart, and his expression became reflective. He leaned back in his chair. "You have two Drae."

Well, that made me feel like a possession.

"We do," Dyter said with an amused glance at me.

"I'm actually a bit Phaetyn," I said, resuming eating.

The king started, and I enjoyed his shocked reaction in silence.

"You're a land healer?" he asked. "How?"

I shrugged and swallowed. "Emperor's experiments. Anyway, yes our side has two Drae, and Tyrrik is normally really strong. And he can breathe fire."

"We also have thirty-seven Druman who are sworn to King Caltevyn and the people of Verald. Recently, we passed through the Zivost Forest, and the new leaders have assured us of aid when the time comes to fight."

That was stretching the truth, but more important was the way the king's face had dimmed at the mention of the Zivost Forest.

"New rulers, you say?" he asked.

I nodded. "Things were hectic when we left, but Princess Kamini is expected to rule." I decided to take a risk by adding, "She formed a rebellion against Queen Alani and King Kaelan."

"Good," the king spat, his face turning fierce. They were the first bitter words to leave his mouth since our arrival.

"You've had dealings with Alani?"

"Me, my father, and even my grandfather. We've begged them for aid, and occasionally we'll see evidence of their work in the mountains, but they refused to come to Gemond. Did they let you in because you're Phaetyn? That's why they agreed to an alliance?"

I frowned as his stomach rumbled again. Why wasn't he eating? "Initially, yes. I'd hoped to learn more about my Phaetyn side, but we caught them in the middle of a civil war. I squashed Queen Alani and killed the King."

The king's eyes rounded. "They're dead?"

The word kill had left a sour taste in my mouth, so I just nodded again.

"Good," the king blurted, pounding his bony fist on top of the stone table. "They were cruel and selfish. This Princess Kamini . . . She will do better?"

Dyter sighed. "The Phaetyn are in a weakened position. Their barrier against the emperor depended on ancestral powers, and the barrier was broken at Queen Alani's death. Kamini will not be able to put it up again."

"They are vulnerable?" the king asked, aghast.

Kudos to the guy, he didn't even seem like he wanted to go corral the Phaetyn to keep his people alive.

"They are for now, but —" Dyter started.

"But the Phaetyn will find a way as they have in the past." I cut Dyter off with a warning look. This king wasn't what I'd expected, but I wasn't willing to impart any more information to him, especially not about Kamini's sister, at least not until I knew him better. The Phaetyn girl would be the Phaetyn's last hope.

The king glanced between Dyter and me as his stomach rumbled again.

"Why aren't you eating?" I asked with a huff, throwing manners to the wind. "If you don't hurry, Dyter and I will finish the lot."

The king smiled. "I'll eat whatever is left."

I watched him, listening to his stomach gurgle yet again. "But you're hungry. I can hear it."

"Yes," he admitted, spreading his fingers on the table edge.

"Then eat," I exploded.

Dyter frowned at me. "Ryn."

"No, no," Zakai said. "I'm not offended. My behavior is peculiar, I know."

"You're not eating until we're done eating," I said slowly, digesting his words. "Tell me why."

"Ryn, manners," Dyter said in a low voice.

"She is both Phaetyn and Drae, Ambassador Dyter," the king said. "Only a fool would not answer her questions." He leaned forward and met my gaze. "You seem to be good people, and you've given my people a hope they have long been bereft of," King Zakai rested a hand on the closed case, "I do not eat because my people do not eat. I take what is necessary to survive and to rule. The rest goes to my subjects, that they may live another day until I find a solution."

I looked at the remnants of my meal. "But you just let us eat all of that food." I'd eaten more than I'd *needed*. I'd been so certain the display meant food was ample here. Since we'd arrived, there had been a steady stream of food. "We've been eating since we arrived," I said in horror. "Why did you give us so much food?"

"You are guests," the king said. "You've traveled far, and you've had hardships. Even a fool human, such as myself, could see you were hungry and in need of nourishment."

But we'd been eating on the way. None of us were truly starving. I was upset I'd eaten so much now, and a glance at Dyter's stricken face told me he felt the same. We were on a strict diet for the rest of our visit, and I'd put my powers to use where I could during our stay.

The king paused. "When I saw you fly down the mountainside opposite us, I felt something akin to what I felt upon opening this case." The king studied me and said, "Did you know, your scales are the color of our royal family? My father's name was Lapyz after the stone. Lapis lazuli is known to bring both protection and peace. Seeing a Drae that color felt like a sign."

Considering I'd seen the resemblance between his eyes and my scales, I knew what he meant about a sign, but I'd never known about the properties of the stone.

"My people have suffered for a long time, and times have gotten worse," the king said, his shining blue gaze on the table. "For the last dozen years, the Gemondians over the age of fifty have left the walled kingdom to survive as best they can in the mountains."

A horrible memory resurfaced. "They go willingly?"

The king sighed. "Of course, they would stay if they could, but they go so their children and grandchildren have a chance to survive. My grandfather left at age seventy, and my father did too. In a few more years, I will also leave, and my son, Zardin will ascend the throne. Though, now things may be different. Maybe we can abolish that custom altogether."

"Maybe your exiled elderly will stop eating each other then," I said, watching him.

*Because* I watched him closely, I did not miss any of the horror that rocked him.

"W-what?" he asked, staring at me.

Dyter was shaking his head, but if I was queen of somewhere, I'd want to know how my people were suffering. "Your elderly women form small communities. Tyrrik and I flew over an encampment in the mountains outside of Verald. They ate one of the women."

"They . . ." The king swayed on his seat, his slack face turning green. "They . . ."

"Your elderly are eating each other to stay alive," I said again. Now that I knew Zakai wasn't the monster I'd thought, a part of me sympathized with his shock, but I hardened myself, thinking of the way his people were living outside this kingdom.

For a moment, it seemed he would lose the contents of his stomach, though I wasn't sure if there was anything significant in there.

"I had no idea," he said, brushing a hand across his eyes.

I reached across and took his hand; his thin skin was dry and pale. "I'm glad you had no idea," I said. "Or I would've killed you for letting your people live that way."

He looked up, and his torn soul was evident in his lapis lazuli eyes. "Perhaps I still deserve to die. Ignorance is no excuse. My people do not do such things . . . What kind of sickness or desperation drove them to do such a thing to each other?"

The king bowed his head as he muttered under his breath about his failure.

I closed my eyes, unable to resist a quick search of his body with my powers. Not that you could put on 'emaciated,' but I was interested to know how much he'd suffered on behalf of his people. I nearly gasped aloud as the tally of the damage to his body hit me. Several of his organs were failing, some just barely getting by, and there was permanent damage to all of them, including his heart. I sent through a subtle stream of my healing power, hoping it wasn't too late.

When I let go of his hand, he stared at it with a furrowed brow rubbing his fingertips together.

I grabbed his plate and loaded meat and vegetables onto it, and then I shoved it back at him. "Eat."

"No, I—"

I snarled at him, some of my Drae entering my words. "You'll be dead in a week if you do not. Who will lead your people then?"

He blinked. "Y-you just told me my people are eating each other. I don't have any appetite."

I rolled my eyes. "Yeah, well, you can suffer as you eat if you want, but that won't make anything better."

"*Ryn!*" Dyter gasped.

Scales erupted up my arms, and I snapped my growing fangs at the old man who didn't look scared in the slightest at my display.

The king had more sense, slamming back into his chair. He swallowed hard, but when he noticed Dyter wasn't fazed, Zakai relaxed enough to take a good look at my scales. He looked at the plate of food, and then the case, and eventually back at my vibrant blue scales.

"I knew you were our salvation as soon as I saw you," he said with a curious smile. His gaze slid to Dyter. "Gemond is with Verald and the Phaetyn. We will fight Emperor Draedyn alongside you."

The King of Gemond picked up his knife and fork and began to eat.

---

"YOU HANDLED THAT QUITE WELL, my girl," Dyter said as we walked back through the sapphire-encrusted halls to our rooms. "The king's eyes brightened when you touched him. Did you heal him?"

"I tried," I said, my eyes drifting to the gems glinting behind Dyter. "I'm not sure how well my Phaetyn juice works on humans; it seems to work better on Tyrrik."

I had a difficult time keeping my attention fixed on the old man. The sconces' light made the valuable stones twinkle, teasing me with their preciousness. I really needed a few minutes alone with one of these walls.

My hand went to the billowy folds of the dress I wore and the knife concealed therein. I'd managed to borrow one of the golden utensils from supper and was counting down the minutes until I could pry one of the cut stones out. The sapphires were especially nice, and I liked their deep-blue coloration. Too bad there was no such thing as a black diamond; it might be nice to have a stone that looked like Tyrrik's scales.

As my thoughts went to the Drae, I quickened my pace. I told myself I was just excited to share with him the information I'd learned. That, and I held a small basket with the meager leftovers for him from our meal. Guilt prodded me as I reflected on how much food I'd consumed compared to how much Tyrrik would get. He needed a few . . .

"I'll be back in a few minutes," I said, shoving the basket toward Dyter. "Tell Tyrrik this is a snack and I'll bring him more in a little bit."

Dyter furrowed his brow, and then a slow smile spread across his face. "Of course. And, while you're in their gardens, if they have strawberries, will you help them along, too?"

I waved my hand at him as I scurried down the hall, and then I came across a guard on the level below.

"Excuse me," I asked the guard. "Could you direct me to the nearest garden?"

The gold-plated Gemondian bowed. "Certainly, Mistress. I will take you to them. Please, follow me."

I trailed after the guard up level after level, increasingly grateful for his guidance as I became lost in the mountain labyrinth.

He stopped at the top of a set of stairs several minutes later and gestured down the hall. "You will find the royal gardens down the end of this passage, Mistress."

I bent over, panting hard, not failing to notice the guard hadn't even broken a sweat. "Thank you," I gasped. "For your help."

"It is my pleasure, Mistress. Do you require anything else?"

A new set of lungs? "No, that will be all."

The guard bowed and then disappeared down the stairs as, clutching my side, I walked down the passage.

The royal gardens were like a sad memory. I could see once the stone columns and ancient trees had been grand. Now, the light pouring through large circular holes in the mountainside only illuminated the gnarled trunks, yellowed leaves, and crumbling rocky ground.

King Zakai crouched next to an empty garden bed, explaining to the gardener how to diffuse the blood in the water.

"You won't need that here," I said, cracking my knuckles. I let a sheepish smile escape. I thought for a moment about asking for something in return, but my mum's words echoed in my mind, "A good deed isn't a good deed if they pay you for it." I wanted this to be a good deed.

I knelt on the ground beside the king and rested my hands on the rocky soil of the dark garden. I could feel the struggle of the vegetation through the barren dirt. I took a deep breath and thought of the vibrancy of Zivost. My awareness spread throughout the entire royal garden, and I greeted the various plants with a mental caress, recognizing them without effort. I wanted this garden to be as luscious and full of life as the Zivost. Pushing my Phaetyn mojo into the ground, I told the pumpkins, potatoes, carrots, beans, berries, parsnips, and fruit trees to grow. Like a ripple in the water, a wave of power swelled beneath my hands for a while before it undulated outward. I sent another surge directed at the potatoes.

People could always use more potatoes in my experience.

I opened my eyes and pointed where the scraggly potato plants had been a few minutes ago. The foliage was now thick and green. "If you dig those up now, they won't be too big," I said to King Zakai and the gardener. "In the morning, they'll be the size of pumpkins. Will you have your cook roast one or two now and bring them up to Lord Tyrrik, please? He missed supper, and—"

"It would be my pleasure," King Zakai said, his voice breaking. He reached for a hand trowel and then shuffled over to the patch and hacked at the dirt.

In his rush to dig up a potato, he was going to gouge them. I scooted after him. "Here. When you dig them up, the trick is to go at it softly so you don't tear the skin."

I unearthed a potato, and when I followed the tuber to its edges, I found the little spuds were the size of a watermelon already. Yeah, those were definitely mine. Apparently, my mojo was a little stronger now.

I deposited the potato into the gardener's outstretched hand and brushed off my own. Ignoring the king's gaping mouth, I said, "I'm off. Please be sure to round up something hearty for Tyrrik to eat. Drae get very cranky when they're hungry."

The king recovered enough to chuckle weakly, but the soldier's mouth remained open.

"I'll be sure to send up some of the potato to him when it's roasted. Please give my best to him and Lord Dyter. And *thank you*, Ryn."

I brushed off his apology and stooped to pluck a carrot and a couple strawberries the size of apples from the ground, and then I left the walled-off garden.

I strode down several empty halls before I realized I was alone. *Alone.* With my knife. And a bajillion precious jewels. Conditions were *perfect*.

## 34

*I* glanced up and down the hall. The coast was clear. I studied the wall, twirling my golden knife absently.

The stone masons had used a dark cement to adhere the gems to the walls, and I wiggled the tip of the blade into the mortar, gritting my teeth at the grating sound it created. *Mistress Moons*, that sounded worse than Dyter's singing. But I was Ryn the Persistent, and within a few minutes, I'd freed not one but *three* stunning uncut stones the size of my palm. Saliva filled my mouth, and my fingers itched to get a few more out to add to my hoard, but I suppressed the urge. I wasn't greedy. What I was taking was reasonable. Besides, the gaps I'd left weren't *that* noticeable, but if I took too many, someone would inevitably notice the holes. I wanted my collection to be balanced, not just full of one type of shiny.

I placed the three sapphires in my pockets, along with the golden knife, its tip now bent, and returned to our rooms.

"Here's your strawberries, Dyter," I said as I opened the door, dropping my voice as his soft snores registered.

My gaze went from his supine form to the other two beds in our room, and my heart dropped. Both of them were empty. I sucked in a ragged breath, a scream balanced on the edge of my lips. I managed to swallow it back and scanned the room for evidence of a struggle, anything that would give me an indication if Tyrrik left on his own accord or—

"Ryn?" Tyrrik whispered from the open door of the bathroom.

He stood bare-chested, and water ran in rivulets down his skin. A towel was wrapped around his tapered waist.

A new sense of angst replaced my previous panic as heat flooded my cheeks.

"Sorry," I mumbled. He must've felt my fear through the bond. "I thought they'd taken you." I was probably irrationally apprehensive, but my ability to be calm over things like that was shattered.

He took a deep breath, and I stared at his chest muscles. Had he already healed? Because it looked like he was filling back out. I crossed the room, choosing not to ignore the low pull in my abdomen to be near him.

"How are you feeling?" I forced my gaze upward, my heart flipping when I saw the same intensity reflected in his eyes. "You look good."

I did not just say that out loud. Trying to salvage my blunder, I blurted, "Like, not dead."

A low chuckle rumbled from his lips. "You look good, too. Although I liked the way your other dress bounced when you jumped from rock to rock."

I might've hit him if I wasn't still holding the produce. I decided the wall to one side of him was a good place to look. "I knew you were looking at my butt."

Tyrrik reached forward and grabbed my wrist. He reeled me in and tugged me into the bathroom. "There was only one side for me to look at," he said with a lop-sided smile. Tyrrik pointed at the strawberries and carrot. "Did you bring those for me?"

"You can have the carrot and one strawberry. The other strawberry is for Dyter," I said.

I put some space between us, trying to steady my breathing. I went to the wash-basin to clean the dirt off my produce. I set one berry on the countertop, my gaze crossing over the gold-flecked granite, and thought of my new treasures. I smiled. I couldn't wait to set up some kind of dark warm cave with all my objects.

"They're bringing up some potatoes for you," I said then snickered. "I know how much you love potatoes."

I turned to offer him the berry, but he'd dropped the towel and was slipping back into the large tub. My mouth dried up, and I averted my gaze.

*Holy Drae Babies.*

"What are you doing?" I whisper-screamed. I stole another peek, unsure whether to be relieved or disappointed he was submerged in the water. Tyrrik watched me with dark, magnetic eyes.

"Do you want to join me?" he asked, a hint of Drae in his voice.

*Yes.* "No," I blurted. "I—" Was it just me, or was the room getting smaller? "I should probably leave."

No probably about it. I *should* leave, but I didn't want to go out into our room and listen to Dyter snore. *Because that's a really solid reason not to leave a bathroom containing a naked Drae? Totally solid.*

"Then stay," Tyrrik said, slipping down deeper in the water. "I won't pull you in; I promise. Not unless you ask me to."

I rolled my eyes, but part of me wanted to ask. Jerking my thumb at the strawberries and carrot, I asked, "Do you want either of these?"

"Yes, please," he said, his gaze still fixed on me.

I stared at him, and he stared back. The temperature rose a million degrees. Were we both thinking about the moment I'd have to pass him the fruit?

"Which one?" I ground out.

"Either." His gaze dropped to my hands. "Both." He frowned. "What do you have in your pockets?"

My hands went to my skirt, and then I forced them behind me, acting as natural as I could when the gems clinked together. "Nothing."

I grabbed the carrot and one of the berries and threw them at him. In a blur of movement, he caught one right after the other, thankfully while keeping his lower half submerged. Obviously, I hadn't thought that through.

He ate the massive strawberry in a few bites and started in on the carrot.

"So, King Zakai isn't as bad as I thought," I said, trying to alleviate some of the extreme awkwardness—not that Tyrrik would care. "Did Dyter tell you Gemond will fight with us?"

"Yes," he answered between bites. "Do you think his people will be strong enough to be a force when the time comes?"

He made a good point. If all of Gemond looked like their king, there was no way they could fight soon.

"So what's our other option?"

"We have no other option." He took another crunching bite of the carrot, his dark gaze resting on me once more. He heaved a long breath and closed his eyes as he reclined in the tub, resting his head on the edge.

The water steamed, and I was reminded of a time not that long ago when he'd warmed my bath water in his tower. I fanned myself quickly while he wasn't looking.

"May I ask you something?" I asked, glancing around the space for a chair. I settled for a towel on the stone floor. The only other space was on the edge of the bath, and that was asking for trouble.

"Will you tell me about the Drae?" I asked.

Tyrrik's face smoothed. He volleyed, "What do you want to know?"

"About our powers. Like you can breathe fire; somehow you warm up the bathwater. You can read my mind. You're stronger than me—"

"You're faster, remember?" he said with a smile.

"Yes, which is probably the most important skill," I grumbled. "But what else? You can pull the shadows to you and become invisible. Can I do that?"

He shook his head. "Probably not. The male acquires all of the skills necessary to protect. In our culture"—he paused at my outraged growl—"that has always been the way."

276

"What if the male dies and the female is alone?"

"That never used to happen. Most mates die when their other half passes on, so that is a moot point."

I shrugged. "The emperor has female Drae who were mated, doesn't he?"

Tyrrik shook his head, his expression darkening. "Only the ones who were single survived the trip to Azule."

"Well, I think everyone needs the ability to protect themselves," I said.

"You will not need for protection with me here."

"You won't need my foot up your butt, but it could still happen." Somehow, I knew pointing out to Tyrrik that I'd literally been protecting him for most of a week was a bad idea. "I'm only good for giving you an energy boost? That's it? My magical Drae power?"

"Everything you do is magical," he murmured in a rough voice. "Drae were the protectors of the realm. We only fought to preserve the peace for the humans. Drae are naturally a peaceful species. You do not possess the weapons I have because you are pure . . . you are beauty . . . you are worth dying for. The females of our kind are revered; they are more precious than any treasure, which is why the males spend years collecting a stash to give to their mates. We do not give it to her because this will make her rich. We collect and give her these things because this fulfills a need she has and makes her happy—because we know doing so will settle an instinct within her." He pinned me with his heated gaze. "You are my reason for being, my purpose, my world. I would do anything for you. Anything."

I couldn't look away. I couldn't believe he'd said all of those raw, honest things. My breath hitched as my stomach erupted into butterflies. I laughed nervously and tore my gaze from his. I couldn't handle so much emotion when I'd only just decided to let him in my head. I hadn't said I'd mate with him yet. These were courting words, words he wanted me to return. "Where do you come up with these lines?"

He frowned. "You don't like what I say to you?"

"No. I mean, yes, kinda. Also, no." I was being stupid, and it didn't help that Tyrrik was sitting up, distracting me with his naked chest again. "Here," I said, standing up. I grabbed the towel and shoved it at him. "I can't think straight with you in the tub."

"If you joined me, you wouldn't need to worry about whether to join me or not."

I gave him a withering glare and shook the towel. "Not going to happen today. Tyrrik, I know I said you can be in my head, but this might be too fast. I haven't decided . . ." I trailed off helplessly.

He tossed the carrot top to the ground and grabbed the towel. *I know, Khosana. But you did ask.*

*You could've told me a story about how the first Drae was created from mortar and horse dung under the twin moons.* I spun my back to him, the water splashing and moving as he stood. A moment later, I felt him behind me.

"You really don't like my compliments?" he asked, his breath warm on my neck.

"It's like you're trying . . ." To pressure me. But that wasn't really it. Everything he said sounded perfect, effortless, but . . . "I don't know what to say back to things like that."

He trailed his hand down my arm, and his heat licked my skin. I froze. My breath hitched. The gates between our minds were wide open, and his yearning pulsed through me until I couldn't tell if the emotion was his or mine.

"I love when you blush," he said, brushing his fingertips up my neck. "It drives me near madness."

I arched to give him better access.

"I love when your skin touches mine," he continued, his thumb stroking the skin above my collarbone. "It is a sensual gift." He stepped closer, his body fitting to mine.

"I love when your desire pulls me to you," he said, brushing his lips to my neck. "Your smell changes, deepens; like flowers and sunshine."

I said silently what I was too scared to say aloud. *Is that just the mate bond doing that to me?* He pulled me closer, and I shut my eyes as

I fought to gain control of the desire. I didn't want to be with him because of some stupid bond. I wanted our emotions to be real, but how could I even know what was real when *this* was all I felt when I was near him?

"What we share is real, Khosana," he murmured. "There is nothing that makes more sense than what lies between us. If I could choose anyone, I would choose you. I would pick you out of a crowd of thousands. Your Drae calls to me. Please, my love, please . . ." He reached a hand around and rested it at the base of my throat, spanning his fingers above my breasts.

"Tyrrik," I gasped.

He turned me, and I had no thought to resist as his arms circled my waist and pulled me flush to him. I pressed my hands to his chest. His heart was racing, beating in the same erratic rhythm as mine. I slid my arms up until my hands were around his neck and guided him to my mouth.

"I love when you whisper my name. My real name," he said, and he crushed his lips to mine.

Whatever this mate bond forced upon us, there was no doubt in my mind of Tyrrik's desire for me or his joy when we touched.

Heat pulsed between us. Our lips and bodies tangled with a frantic edge I'd never felt before. His lips were soft and warm, and he tasted of nectar. The nectar I'd made for him. He coaxed my lips open and brushed his tongue against mine, pulling me closer. I threaded my hands through his dark hair and stood on my tiptoes to meet his hunger with my own. He pulled away suddenly and I made a sound of protest until his lips pressed to my neck. I arched again as he trailed kisses from my ear to my chest.

"Uvijek sam te voljela," he growled. *I have always loved you.*

His hands tangled in my skirt, and I grabbed either side of his torso, my mind clouded with a thick haze. Tyrrik backed me to the wall, only breaking our kiss to whisper in my ear. My entire body shivered with want for *him.*

"*Mistress moons!*" Dyter sputtered.

I screamed, jumping a meter off the ground.

"Oh my stars," Dyter hollered as he stepped back out the open door. "My eyes. Oh stars. I can't . . . I can't unsee that."

Tyrrik pulled away as I dropped my skirt which had apparently migrated during recent events. As I did so, I heard a series of clinks.

*Drak!*

## 35

*D*yter and I froze and Tyrrik raised his eyebrows, a slow smile spreading as he looked at the three beautiful sapphires on the stone floor.

Dyter's lips dipped into disapproving lines. "Please tell me you're not stealing from our host, who is also a king."

"I wouldn't do that," I protested weakly.

We all stared at the glinting gems again.

Tyrrik wrapped his hand around my waist, and my blush intensified due to Dyter's presence as the Drae spoke. "Ryn is indulging in her instincts."

I had a feeling I didn't want to know anything about this, but I felt braver after our kiss. "What does it mean? This shiny obsession. *Really* mean. I want the full scoop this time." Why had I already assumed I wouldn't be able to crush them in my teeth and spit shiny daggers into my foe's eyes?

"Your hoard is for our family. By collecting precious objects and keeping them safe, you are showing me you would make a good mother to our children."

My attention caught on *good mother* and *children,* and my mind blanked. I edged out of Tyrrik's grip in a subtle movement no one probably noticed.

Dyter chuckled and mumbled something about family jewels. He straightened, grinning at my slack face, and said, "If you're done using the facilities, may I?"

Tyrrik exited the restroom. I blinked, mouth open, and swooped to pick up my pretties and Tyrrik's discarded carrot top. Collecting sapphires and rubies and gold stuff didn't mean a thing. They were an investment. Carrying them was a smart business choice.

I trailed out of the bathroom, unresponsive to Dyter's light pat on the shoulder.

"How many have you taken?" Tyrrik asked, plucking one of the jewels from my hand.

"That's mine!" A fierce protective instinct gripped me. I whirled on him, throwing the carrot top at him.

"Ryn," he said, his voice muffled with laughter. He held the gem out to me. "Please, forgive me."

I grabbed my sapphire from his hand and sauntered past him. "Don't take my jewels."

Dyter came out of the bathroom, and his gaze went from Tyrrik to me. "Enough tomfoolery. We all need our rest. Tomorrow we need to search for the other Phaetyn girl. The emperor likely knows we are here, so we cannot linger before traveling to Azule."

---

"I ALWAYS KNEW you'd be powerful, my Khosana," Tyrrik whispered to me, tracing his fingertip over my face.

Now I was *his* princess, was I? The Drae had boundary issues. I smiled as the last bit of sleepiness rolled away. I stretched and opened my eyes to see Tyrrik sitting beside me, his dark gaze fixed on my face.

"What do you mean?" I asked. "Me tackling you with the carrot greens?"

"Maybe, or perhaps I'm telling you that no one in this Realm can do what you do," he said. "Let's go have some breakfast and go to the garden."

"I thought we were going to find Kamini's twin. What time is it? How long did I sleep?"

"It's late afternoon. But you needed your sleep. You've pushed yourself too hard for several . . . months. You needed the extra rest."

"That's true. Even after the castle, I had to build the tavern business up." I yawned, stretching again.

Tyrrik stood, giving me space to get off the narrow bed. Maybe I should suggest pushing the beds together before we next slept; these beds were barely wide enough for one person, and falling asleep took several hours last night without Tyrrik next to me. Even knowing he was on the other side of the room wasn't enough for my Drae to be comfortable though. Clearly, I was too exhausted to sleepwalk over there.

"Our bond feels stronger," I blurted as realization hit me. "When we kissed in the bathroom yesterday, that intensified the bond, didn't it?"

I wasn't sure how I felt about that. Tyrrik certainly hadn't forced the kiss to happen; I'd practically jumped him. No, I wasn't mad. I felt like I should be mad, but I . . . wasn't. I was just, *still*, scared.

I gazed up at Tyrrik and saw worry cross his face before he smoothed his features. But he couldn't hide what he felt through our bond. Not now that the gates were open, and everything seemed to have focused since last night. I could feel his panic, though the panic didn't seem in response to my reaction but over the intensity itself.

He took a deep breath, and after his measured exhale, he said, "It will intensify every time we are intimate."

I tilted my head, studying the Drae. Something about that felt right, even if part of my rational mind screamed I couldn't handle much more intensity. I knew he wanted me to be his mate, but something was off. I puzzled for a moment before asking, "Does that scare you? Our bond growing stronger?"

His fear pulsed through our bond, and I waited for him to explain though I could already guess at what bothered him. Considering his past with a blood oath, and what he'd confessed so far, it seemed reasonable for him to be afraid.

Tyrrik stiffened, his gaze dipping to the floor. Several moments of silence passed before he sat on the edge of the bed again. He scooped my hands in his, bringing them to his lap. With his other hand, he traced the back of mine as he spoke, "I am not afraid of our bond."

Well, there went my guess. I thought he'd been scared of our bond feeling like a binding promise he had no control over.

He met my gaze, his features open, *vulnerable*. "My fear is you will see I am not worthy of you and that you will refuse to be my mate."

"Why would you . . ." I already knew why. I'd screamed my hatred of him not so long ago, right in his face; and perhaps it hadn't been anything he hadn't deserved for manipulating me, but I'd been too hurt at the time to admit he couldn't have acted any other way. He'd hurt me, yes, however he'd also risked *everything* to save me. I knew now that manipulating my feelings, knowing he would hurt me eventually and if the plan succeeded I may never speak to him again, all of that hurt him just as much as it hurt me. If there had been another way, he would have taken it.

He'd made mistakes, horrible, gruesome, terrible ones. And so had I.

I leaned over and kissed his cheek.

"I know you don't want to take it slowly; that you want my acceptance today, right now," I whispered.

He pursed his lips and his eyes widened, but he said nothing to deny what I'd accused. He'd been sincere and direct with me, and he deserved the same.

"I'm afraid, too," I admitted.

I couldn't tell him that I wanted to cling to the remnants of the person I'd been when my mother was alive. Perhaps he didn't need me to verbalize my fear with our strengthened bond because he didn't push. He just nodded and raised my hand to his lips, placing a gentle kiss there before releasing his hold.

"If you want to take it slow, we'll take it slow," he said, mostly ungrudgingly "When . . ." He stopped and ground out, "*If* you decide you want me . . . I will honor whatever decision you make."

The tightness coiled in my chest, loosened, and then flitted away. I stared at Tyrrik, a fluttering, slightly bewildered sensation making me give him a shy smile.

Tyrrik squeezed my hand and then released it before standing. "Come now, my Princess. Let's go see what you can do with your powers. Then, we'll find the Phaetyn queen."

I stood and, after a moment of hesitation, slipped my hand into his. Together we started toward the door.

A moment later, Dyter burst into the room.

I screeched and dropped Tyrrik's hand like it was a hot potato.

"There's smoke coming from the eastern range," Dyter said, his eyes bright. "King Zakai's scouts just came in with the report."

Tyrrik reached over and threaded his fingers back with mine. "And?"

"Smoke?" I asked at the same time.

"Druman," Dyter replied. "The scouting parties we saw on the way here. They're lighting fires out there on the mountains."

"How do you know it's Druman?" Tyrrik asked.

Dyter gave him a pointed look. "Who else would it be?"

My mind caught up to Dyter's. The Druman had been gathered around the areas of growth, likely searching for someone, especially after Tyrrik torched the search party a couple days ago.

Tyrrik squeezed my hand and followed my train of thought. "They're looking for us, even if they don't know it's us."

I began pacing. "But they weren't burning stuff when we saw them before. Why—"

Horror dawned on me, and I spun to look at Dyter.

He nodded. "I think they've found her. Or, at least, suspect she's close. I can't think of any other reason why they're burning the areas of growth."

Tyrrik's face hardened. "They're trying to flush her out of

hiding." He glanced over at me. "The Phaetyn need her, and we need the Phaetyn. I've got to risk going out there to find her."

"*We*," I corrected, rounding on the Drae. "We risk it."

"*We* don't have time to argue."

"No, *we* don't, so stop. This *thing* goes two ways. I'll either go with you now, or I follow you later." I gritted my teeth and waited. If he said no, I was going to be so pissed.

His eyes glinted.

"We don't know that they've found her," Dyter interjected. "But at the very least, you need to go out and make sure. *We* need to scout it out."

Both Tyrrik and I ignored the older man, locked in our own battle of wills.

"If you go out there, I do too," I pressed, taking a predatory step toward him.

Several tense moments of silence passed, but I wasn't about to give in on this. Whatever protection ignorance provided wasn't worth it. Not anymore. Never again.

Tyrrik finally said, "I don't like it, but I understand."

I opened my mouth to protest, and then his words registered. I tried to play my gaping mouth off as a smile, but he wasn't the least bit fooled. Still, he was kind enough not to say anything.

Ryn: 1 Tyrrik: 1

I liked that kind of score.

---

THE DARK GRAY smoke billowed into the sky, making everything smell like singed wood. The blackened expanse stretched past where the Phaetyn's flourishing foliage had once been and into the scraggly trees and brush. Twisted and charred trunks jutted into the air from the scorched earth, their appearance far too similar to the rocks outside Zivost.

*Anything?*

Tyrrik asked his question casually, but I could feel his worry seeping through our tentative bond. Worry was only slightly better than anger, but baby steps were good. But we'd seen no Druman on the ground since leaving Gemond. Not that I'd expected to see lots of them, but we'd been flying for almost an hour, and there were none.

*Let's get closer to the fire.* The crackling and chomping of the roaring flames lay just ahead, and the heat and smoke spread into the sky.

*Druman,* Tyrrik said.

*I can't smell them.* I couldn't smell anything besides the acrid smoke. It burned my eyes and singed my nose. But as we lifted over the final range between us and the fire, I saw them.

Dozens of the emperor's spawn crawling over the rocks and through the low-lying trees. Their unwashed stench wafted into the air, wet leather and body odor, making my stomach churn. In their wake, another fire raged just below, the orange-and-red flames devouring the small copse of plant life. The men shouted and waved at one another in a cut up version of the Drae language I could only understand a few words of. The Druman must have created their own dialect.

*They're headed toward the next mountain range.*

*You can understand that?* Obviously. *Is the emperor here?* I asked nervously, looking back over my shoulder.

*Draedyn's not here. At least, not anywhere close, or I'd feel him. You probably would, too, now. Besides, personally coming doesn't seem to be his style. He's been using his Druman first.*

We flew over the Druman, my insides going cold as we passed. *That's way more than just a Phaetyn search party. You don't think they're here for us . . . do you?*

*They probably all came together when they picked up on her scent. But we shouldn't discount that this force was likely meant for us too. He's testing the strength of his enemies.*

Yes, I remembered. A solid tactical plan: Test the enemy's strength to know how much force will be required to crush them. Even this high up, being near the Druman made my heart race and my chest tighten in panic. I pushed back the fear, but I couldn't make it go away.

*They won't be looking up, Princess. And the smoke will keep us hidden.*

I pressed forward, determined not to let my fear dictate my actions.

The narrow valley was rocky with little visible vegetation. We flew through the mountains, scanning for evidence of habitation.

*There are enough down there to take out a small army. Mistress moons, Tyrrik! They're focused on that next range. Look, the ones at the front are running.* A shiver ran down the long length of my spine. *They've found her.*

Both of us pumped our wings and flattened our necks, streamlining our bodies to gain speed. I narrowed my eyes to try and see through the smoke. Failing that, I tuned in my ears. The thump-thump of heavy boots on the packed ground and crackling of the blaze below overrode everything else.

*She's over the other side,* Tyrrik said. *All the way through the pass.*

*How can you tell?*

*I've had longer to practice my fine tuning. She just gasped, and even though she's running, her step is light. I can't see her though.*

We swept over the next range, and I furiously scanned the area. The smoke was slowly funneling through the pass, but the air was still fairly clear on this side.

A small scraggly thicket of trees with a narrow stream on one side took up most of the valley; the gray cedars butted up against the rocky slope. A golden web was visible in the trees, and a wisp of movement was all that gave away the Phaetyn's location.

Even with her hiding and using her ancestral powers, the Druman were nearly upon her. The Phaetyn was so small in comparison to the muscled frames of the emperor's mules. They surged through the pass and spilled into the valley. The distance separating the two enemy species shrunk, and trepidation crawled through my Drae.

Tyrrik swore, already descending. *We'll not get her out without a fight, Ryn. I'm going down—*

*Tyrrik, no! There's too many of them.*

*I'll hold them off. You can do this. Get in, pick up the Phaetyn, and get out. It's the only way, Princess. If you want to save her, we'll need to do it this way.*

He was right. We had only seconds before the Druman caught up with her, a minute at most. He was right, but . . . *Can you fight that many? I could come down with you. I—*

*Not yet,* he said, continuing his descent. *Promise me you won't come down until it's possible to get away with her safely.*

For a moment all I could process was Tyrrik's panic. I stared at the ground, revulsion's sour taste on the back of my tongue and burning the back of my throat. There had to be close to one hundred Druman down there, and Tyrrik was going to fight them.

He flattened himself, angling his body almost vertically above the front line of Druman.

*Promise me,* he pressed, still thinking more of me than the foe he was about to fight. *I won't be able to concentrate if you're down there.*

I could feel the truth of his words through our bond, but I hesitated, realizing what that promise might mean.

Could I really stay up here if the tide turned against Tyrrik?

# 36

*H*e was nearly upon them. *Please, stay up there, Princess. Be my eyes. Promise me.*

I beat my wings, neck twisting frantically. He'd asked, no begged, for my word three times, and I was desperate to calm him before he started fighting. *I promise,* I threw at him, the words registering only after I'd said them. I hurried to add, *but please, promise me you'll stay alive.*

He didn't answer as he let out an almighty roar. He pulled his front half up as he landed in the valley with a deep boom that echoed through the range. Without pause, he ripped through the front line of Druman with his talons, severing several bodies in half and fatally wounding many more. Blood spilled over the rocky terrain, and Tyrrik advanced.

One Druman flung himself at Tyrrik, at my *mate,* and I instinctively screamed in fury. The ease with which Tyrrik batted the Druman away did nothing to settle my panic. There was the better part of a hundred Druman down there, and they had swarmed into the valley.

My mind went crazy as I watched. Tyrrik may be a near invincible Drae, but he could be overrun, he could be hurt badly enough to weaken him. He could be taken, imprisoned, tortured, and killed.

My thoughts made me sick. The emperor surely had access to Phaetyn blood.

Tyrrik still had weaknesses.

He stamped below me and inhaled. Molten red appeared between the scales in his chest a scant moment before he extended his neck and spewed jets of flame through the small valley toward the pass. The fire licked the trees, and the crackle of its frenzied appetite sizzled in the air. Warmth billowed up, caressing my underbelly. Only the Druman nearest Tyrrik were caught by the flames, and while their screams of agony were short lived, the emperor's Druman had clearly expected the fire. Many of them scaled the rock walls, dodging the flames altogether. These cross-breeds were fast like Jotun had been, *faster* for having the emperor's lineage.

Tyrrik kept up the fire for at least a minute but only caught another dozen or so Druman. Flames devoured the dry grass, and the fire jumped from tree to tree. I studied the tendrils between us, relieved when the strength of black in the strands of our bond still appeared as strong as ever.

*Tyrrik.*

*I'm okay, Ryn. Where's the Phaetyn?*

I'd been so caught up with what was happening with Tyrrik I'd completely forgotten about her. I drifted lower and found her at the far end of the valley, about to begin climbing the next range. Four Druman had slipped passed Tyrrik and were bearing down on her again. *She's got four Druman on her tail.*

*Please, stay up there.*

Why was he saying please? The word added desperation to his request that made my skin crawl, and I couldn't help glancing back. Tyrrik raked his talons clean through another cluster of the monsters. My tail twitched as two launched onto his back and turned to catch ropes.

*Mistress Moons.* They intended to capture him.

Tyrrik bucked and twisted free. He caught one of the Druman in his mouth, biting him in half and spitting the severed body at another one. He stomped on several more before unleashing another stream of liquid flame.

I drifted lower, tearing my eyes away to line up the Phaetyn below.

*Do not land yet.*

His request came too late; I'd already made up my mind. *There are only four going after her. I'll just go low enough to swipe her up.*

*Ryn, let me clear them away. Don't come down yet.*

I closed my ears to the apprehension in his voice, making no effort to change my descent. Would the seventy Druman on his other side wait patiently while he dealt with these four? He was being irrational. *Tyrrik, there's no time.*

I angled farther down, shooting like a lightning bolt toward the small party of Druman.

*Ryn—*

I glanced once more at my mate. He was still battling though his head was turned toward me. His anxiety ripped through me, but I'd committed myself. I was determined to see this through. We needed the Phaetyn girl . . . no the *Phaetyn* needed the Phaetyn girl, and we needed the Phaetyn. More than that, my kinship to her and her mother demanded I do all I could to save her. I wrenched upward, pulling my upper half back into the air as I'd seen Tyrrik do, and I landed on my hind quarters, between the Druman and the Phaetyn girl, poised and ready.

My silent approach must have stunned them, and I seized the advantage. I whipped my tail one way and then the other, lashing out with my spikes. The lead Druman dodged, but I connected with the torso of the second, and he launched into the air, flying far off to the right.

The leader advanced on me, and I snarled at him, baring my fangs. He dodged, advanced, and landed a punch to my left foreleg. Startled by the Druman's strength, I halted my advance long enough for him to dart past me.

I roared my frustration and twisted to catch him. Snapping a wing out, I caught him on the back of his head. He dropped to the ground, and before he could stand, I stomped my back foot. His bones crunched under the weight, and he thrashed for a moment before his body stilled.

I hoped the Phaetyn girl was running.

*Talons,* Tyrrik said, reminding me of my other weapons.

*You're supposed to be focused on your problems,* I shot back. He still had plenty of Druman to deal with, far too many. I focused on the two remaining Druman before me.

These looked nothing like the Druman in Irdelron's castle. Those Druman looked human, clean, kempt, civilized. These cross-breeds looked like animals. Their hair was matted and filthy. Their aketons were torn, rumpled, and stained. And the feral look in their eyes made me feel like *they* were the predators and I was prey. No freakin' way. *I* was Drae. A fierce hatred for their kind pulsed through me. I didn't care if these creatures were slaves to their alpha; I didn't care if their violent tendencies were enhanced or encouraged. I *hated* them.

With an earsplitting roar, I reared up. The Druman inched forward, and when I hesitated, they took the bait and rushed me. Just before they attacked, I dropped down, slashing my talons side-ways in front of me. Like deadly blades, my claws cut through their flesh and bone as if their bodies were softened butter. Their dark blood gushed, pooling on the rocky ground, and their bodies heaved and then fell still. The Druman stood no chance against Drae. I bellowed my triumph.

*Well done.*

The strain in Tyrrik's voice startled me, and I couldn't help glancing in his direction. He released more flame, but the fire did not extend as far as it had, nor did it burn with the same intensity as it had before. The flames were red and dull, no longer bright and vibrant, and the deeper reds, oranges, and whites were gone. I turned inward, studying the bond between us.

Terror doused me, and I stood ramrod straight. How was that possible? In only a few minutes, the inky black had waned and faded to a hazy gray.

*Are you okay?* I asked, my alarm holding me captive.

*Don't get distracted.*

Too late.

A Druman landed on my shoulder, startling me back to the fight. A heavy pressure pounded on my left and then my right side. The pressure and movement made it impossible to determine if there was one or two of the creatures on me. I mimicked Tyrrik's earlier movements, bucking and twisting, but the Druman clung tenaciously, and I couldn't dislodge him.

Tyrrik's roar rent the air, but he was surrounded by an unrelenting horde and unable to help me.

The Druman crawled up my back; I could feel him pulling himself higher, using the bumps on my spine to aid him. I shook my body, arching and whipping my tail, but he continued to climb. Another Druman appeared and ducked under me to get to the softer side of my underbelly. I shuffled to find him, but he rained blow after blow upon my body. Blistering pain made me see stars, and I screamed.

I fell to the ground, hoping to crush him, but I saw him dart from underneath even before I landed. As I heaved my body up to whirl on him, a root shot from the ground and skewered him through the heart. The Phaetyn girl raced in, hand bleeding, and swiped her hand across his grizzly wound. In the fraction of an instant, black cracks appeared on his chest, climbing up his neck as her toxic blood entered his system. He opened his mouth and vomited black blood before slumping to the ground. When I'd poisoned Jotun, his Drae side had died in seconds, and it was the same for this Druman except, with a wound to his heart, his human side had no chance of surviving.

The Druman on my back reached the base of my neck and wrapped his legs around me. With his feet locked, he punched over and over on both sides. I snarled and boomed in pain. The persistent hammering blows had me seeing red, but I couldn't find a way to dislodge my opponent and retaliate.

Tyrrik roared in tandem, but he could not reach me. I bent my head to try and escape the Druman, and my vision snagged and halted as I caught my mate's gaze through the chaos between us. He faced me, frozen at attention, his eyes glowing black. The Druman swarmed him, but he stood still, so distracted by my pain he was unable to fight back. Several of the Druman surrounding him managed to get a rope over his back and then another.

*Tyrrik,* I snarled. *You will not be captured because of me. Fight!*

I needed this to be over. One Druman was not going to be my undoing. Out of ideas and unable to dislodge my attacker, I rolled onto my back. My instincts screamed in protest, and I couldn't hold back the bellow of pain as the fine bones of my wings bore the heavy weight of my reptilian body. I wriggled, still on my back with the Druman pinned, and then repeatedly banged my neck backward until I felt his grip release. I rolled back to my feet and jumped, leaping as high as I could without taking flight. I landed, coming down on the Druman's head with the full weight of my body, and felt his skull pop beneath me.

"There are no more here," the Phaetyn girl yelled to me.

I nodded once at her, relieved she recognized me as a friend, while panting to catch my breath. Despite all I'd been told about instincts, I was exhausted by this activity I was so unfamiliar with. How was Tyrrik doing this?

The Druman tossed another rope over Tyrrik, and I took three bounding steps in his direction before pulling up sharp at his menacing words.

*If you come over here, I will never forgive you.*

I'd never heard him use that tone, and the certainty of his statement rang through me. I whined low in my throat, a sound of worry and care, pleading with Tyrrik to let me help him. There were so many of them, and they were winning. I studied the tendrils of our bond, whining again as I saw the vibrant blue nearly overwhelming all traces of black. No, not black, a dull, flat gray. My mate was weakening fast, and I rose up to count; there were still dozens of Druman alive—dozens of Druman still assaulting him.

They threw another rope over Tyrrik, and several Druman on either side pulled him flat.

*No! Tyrrik, no, please.*

*Shh, Princess. You must take the Phaetyn and get out of here. I'll join you back at Gemond.*

I wasn't a fool. My mind raced as I tried to think of how I could help him. I could hear the doubt in his voice and feel it through our bond, and while he begged me not to go to him, I wasn't leaving.

*Please, can I come over there?* I knew I could help. I could do something. I had to. *Tyrrik, please. Please?*

The Phaetyn girl gasped beside me as Druman crawled over Tyrrik.

My heart pounded, and a roar filled my mind. There was no more time to think. Every fraction of every second lessened the possibility of success, and I would *not* fail. I would not lose my mate. I would not let him sacrifice himself, not when I could save him.

And I could. I could save him.

Even knowing this would change my life—knowing in my mind, my soul, and my body that I would be bound to Tyrrik forever, that we would never be separated, that I would never be just Ryn— I *happily* said goodbye to the girl I'd been because somewhere along the line, I'd already accepted this moment. And I wasn't worried. I was relieved.

Closing my eyes, the threads of our bond drifted into focus. So little black, the plainness of my blue threads was heartbreaking. I wanted the contrast of his onyx black wrapped with the blue of my Drae energy. The beauty of our bond was in the contrast and complement of colors, and I wanted his strength, chivalry, and support in my life. I wanted his wisdom to balance my naivety, his humor to lift me from sadness, his soberness to ground me, and his strength to protect me.

The blue tendrils still held us together, and I understood then they also served as channels. He'd shown me how to pull my energy away from him when we were flying to Zivost, how to lock it deep within my core and block him with mental barricades. I imagined the fortifications I'd constructed, the tall and thick walls of stone meant to keep us separate—and I dropped them, crumbling them to dust to forever disappear in the darkness. I instantly felt the change. Nothing remained between Tyrrik and me.

*Princess.*

His pain tore at me, and I wanted to tear the world apart for his suffering. *I'm coming.*

I could *not* do otherwise; it would be against everything I was, betraying my very existence, to not aid him. But, more than that, I did not *want* to do otherwise.

Tyrrik was *mine*. Mine alone. He was mine forever.

With a roar, I pushed my energy through the blue channels, willing them to thicken, to expand, to burn brighter as I fed him with the strength of my Drae. My Phaetyn powers had prepared me in part for this, but I didn't merely wish to increase his energy or heal him. I thought of the risks Tyrrik had taken as Ty and Tyr to make sure I was fed, his generosity and patience. I imagined his hands scooping nectar over my body in the cave after turning Drae, and I gathered the power of those moments inside the center of my body where the most vibrant blue resided just underneath my ribs. I pulled and scraped armfuls of that force and heaved it out through the now thick bonds, and I did it over and over again.

I shoved my very essence into my mate, panting as the lapis-blue glowed between us. *Stronger, thicker, more, more, more.* I saw the flicker of blue deep within him surge and brighten.

*I feel you.* Tyrrik's awe pulsed through me.

*Mistress butt-Moons!* He wasn't allowed to feel awe. *Fight! You need to win!* I shouted at him through our bond. *Fight and survive. Fight for me, Tyrrik. Please. I . . . I need you.*

My vision tunneled until all I could see was our bond. I staggered to the side and collapsed to the ground, but even then, I didn't stop. I wouldn't stop. Not until I knew he was safe. I shoved everything I could into those tendrils, triumph swelling in my breast as thin gray strands darkened and widened. Our colors danced and intertwined, and my heart soared.

Even in the darkness of my mind, I could hear his roar. I could feel him moving through our bond, the coil of his muscles as he tore through the ropes, the searing heat as he hurled white-hot liquid death on our enemies. I felt his power ricochet back to me, and still I pushed. I could see everything he did now though my eyes were closed. I watched with pride as Tyrrik *demolished* the Druman.

And still, I didn't stop sharing my power to him.

I couldn't stop.

I wouldn't stop.

I would *never* stop.

# 37

"*R*yn."
　　　　I knew that voice; it made warm embers spark in my chest, washing away all residual doubt. I moaned and rolled onto my back so my face met the sky.

A hand touched my shoulder. *His* hand.

I opened my eyes and looked up into Tyrrik's face.

I'd shifted back to my human form, and so had Tyrrik.

"You can stop now," he said hoarsely.

I blinked. Now that I'd started shoving energy into him, I found it difficult to reign in the flow. "Do I have to?"

Tyrrik chuckled and gathered me in his arms, pulling me close. "My *Khosana.*"

With arms like lead, I reached up around his neck and hugged him close so our hearts beat against each other.

"You're okay," I said, my voice trembling. My entire body quaked with exhaustion.

He nodded, burying his face in my hair. "The Druman are dead." He kissed me and whispered, "You'll get your energy back faster if you stop feeding it all to me."

*All of them?* I asked, not willing to pull back until I knew.

"All of them," he promised, inhaling deeply.

I relaxed, letting the focus I'd held on our bonds go so I was no longer shoving my power at him. Vitality recoiled and pulsed through me. I inhaled, and my chest expanded so easily it almost hurt. I lifted my head from his shoulder and gasped. "Tyrrik!"

A blaze of blue-and-black fire danced around us. The flame touched our bodies, dancing and twisting, tying us together. I lifted my gaze and saw the brilliant light shone across the bloodied valley. I stared in awe at the capering fire. I'd never been able to see the tendrils between us like this. As a Phaetyn, I could see my power working inside him during healing, but I'd never seen our Drae energy outside us with my eyes open.

"Isn't it beautiful?" he whispered.

Overwhelming emotion choked me, stealing my voice. My head and my heart felt light. Words were not enough to describe the sight or the feeling of the deep hues of blue-and-black flames encasing us in their midst. *Are the flames real?*

"No one can see them but us," he said. *They're ours alone.*

I knew what this was. *It's our mate bond.*

He pulled his head back, his onyx eyes as wild as I'd ever seen them. They glowed so much that I lost myself in the depths of those inky pools. This Drae was my mate. More than a friend or a lover. More than a companion or partner. He was made to complement me. He was *created* for me.

In a voice rough with emotion, he said, "You accept me?"

I lifted both hands to cup his face and stared at him in awe. "How could you be in doubt?" I kissed him, just brushing my lips to his. "After what just happened, how could you not know?" I kissed him again as I spoke through our bond. *I accept you as my mate, Tyrrik.*

He pulled back and studied me, his gaze penetrating me to my core. He brought his hands up to mimic my position. *I didn't doubt; I just did not wish to hope.*

I felt his love pulse through the bond, warm honey and the soft caress of night. He brushed his thumbs over my cheeks and repeated, "You are my mate."

*I am your mate,* I agreed.

He touched his lips to my forehead. *One hundred and nine years, and I have found you. You are mine.*

Our mouths met with a clash of teeth. His hands dropped to my shoulders while I placed one on the nape of his neck and threaded the other through his black hair. I moaned loudly into his mouth as his lips coaxed mine apart. His tongue stroked mine, and I pressed tighter to him, not wanting to ever stop the thrill of his touch.

A growl rumbled in his chest, a menacing threat to all but me, as he declared me his. One of his hands trailed down my back, settling around my waist.

And then, Tyrrik reached up and untangled my arms from around his head and neck. He brought both hands in front of his mouth and kissed the back of each, his gaze not moving from mine.

"Ryn, I love you more than life itself."

I shouldn't have been embarrassed. I'd just accepted him as my mate, but my cheeks warmed at the strength of his declaration of love because I'd just witnessed the truth of his words. I ducked and mumbled, "I was so scared, Tyrrik."

My admission broke his heart. I felt it and gained a better understanding of my mate. He didn't want me to be scared. He'd eagerly take *any* pain to rid me of that fear. As I studied his sentiment, I grasped a better understanding of the balance of female and male Drae.

Tyrrik's instinct was to protect what he loved. He would destroy, maim, kill, or do whatever he needed to get rid of bad things. He also wanted to provide, food, clothing, a bath . . . I closed my eyes as I thought of all he'd done to take care of me. Almost all of it, protecting and providing, through physical means. *That* was his strength.

But sometimes solutions required feelings, intuition, caring. Nurturing was necessary for growth, to cultivate relationships and alliances. Nurturing was fostering growth, developing bonds and strengthening them. And that power was just as important as physical might and prowess. And in the instances when violence *was* the only way, I literally strengthened him. I gave him the power to do what needed to be done. We weren't the same, but we were equals. And that's why we were stronger together.

I smiled at him, and he kissed my hands again.

*You are exactly right,* he said.

*Maybe I should've sent you a top up sooner,* I joked.

His gaze darkened, and his features grew troubled. "I hope you won't have cause to do that frequently."

I glanced back over my shoulder.

Druman remains littered the valley. Black ash and smoke floated high in the sky from the Druman unlucky enough to meet Tyrrik's fire. Some of the rock across the valley had melted under the heat of his flame and was reforming in warped patches. A few scraggly trees still burned, but the fire was waning as it ran out of fuel.

Every single one of them was dead. And it so easily should've been us instead.

With a start, I remembered the Phaetyn.

*Sitting on a rock to your left,* Tyrrik supplied.

*You knew she was there watching us?*

I scowled at his mental shrug. Bloody Drae. I untangled myself from him enough to glance that way. The Phaetyn girl sat cross-legged on a flattened stone a small distance from where we'd been kissing. No, we'd been making out like it was going to be outlawed tomorrow. Nice first impression.

One glance was enough to tell me the trees hadn't been lying. The Phaetyn girl looked a lot like Kamini, only older and fiercer. If the trees hadn't told me this Phaetyn existed, I still would've known her to be the princess's sister.

"I guess we need to go say hello," I whispered to Tyrrik.

"If we want to win this war, then yes, we best go and greet her," Tyrrik said, a smile in his voice.

I sighed, shouldering the responsibility I needed to take.

Tyrrik gently held my jaw and turned me back to face him. "You're sure you want this, Ryn? To join this fight? We could go anywhere. Leave Draedyn's Realm, go to another land."

Another land but not one that contained people I cared about. Because even if it was just Tyrrik and Dyter, I'd stay and fight. But there were so many more. "I'm sure," I said, glancing at the Phaetyn and then back at Tyrrik, who looked unaccountably sad. I brushed my hands through his liquid-black hair. "This is my fight, too, now. Which means we'll see it through to the end."

*Together.*

***Black Crown***
The Darkest Drae: Book Three

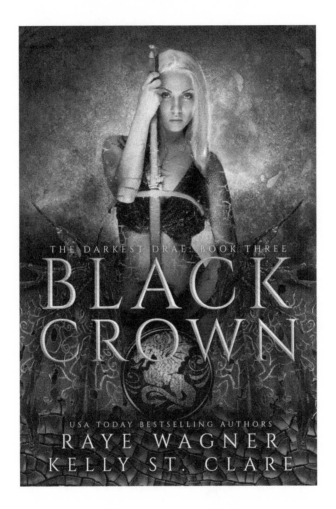

*Coming May, 2018*

# KELLY'S ACKNOWLEDGEMENTS

The last few months while writing this book were an amazing blur of potatoes, soap, shiny gems, onyx scales, and pointy ears.

Thank you to the following people:

- Our betas, Jennifer and Kate, for providing amazing feedback.
- Our manuscript team for their hard work; Krystal Wade, Dawn Yacovetta and Michelle Lynn.
- Our cover designer, Daqri at Covers by Combs, for another incredible cover.
- Our ARC team – I love watching your excitement in the lead up to each release day.

Thank you to my readers—yet again—for coming along for the ride.

To my husband, who never fails to ask what I'm laughing at, and who never fails to accept my explanation of, 'Just talking to Raye' or 'Just talking to the people in my head', without batting an eyelid.

To my family and friends, spending time with you over Christmas and New Years in New Zealand was the highlight of my year. If we don't do it again soon, I'll get saltier than those fries we had in Whitianga.

Last but not least, thank you to Raye Wagner for her dedication to this series and for being so much fun to work with.

Here is a glimpse of our average conversation:

Raye: *Want to talk about business stuff?*

Kelly: *Sure, just let me change out of my pajamas.*

Raye: *\*rings fifteen minutes later\* So. I did a chapter of Black Crown... When are you coming over to visit again?*

Kelly and Raye: *\*Proceed to talk for three hours about everything except the series they are writing\**

I'm not sure how we manage to get work done, Drae-bae (magic mojo, probably), but I enjoy our really important business chats.

Lurv you, Pretzel Dealer,

Kelly

# RAYE'S ACKNOWLEDGEMENTS

Most of the time, real life is not as fun as fantasy. However, I'm not fighting for my life, slaying wicked kings, or responsible for learning how to do magic under duress, either. At least not usually. But if I was, it's awesome to know I have an amazing team of support to help me slay the bad guys, give me the tools I need, and cheer me on . . . in both the real world as well as my imaginary ones.

Thank you to my family and my besties. Words are inadequate to express how much I love each one of you. You get my crazy and still hang out with me. I love every moment we get to spend together and appreciate your friendship (even if our relationship started because of our genetics).

Thank you to the Drae-team: Jennifer and Kate for the early feedback, Dawn and Krystal for all the polish, Daqri for a gorgeous cover (gah! so pretty!) and Michelle for putting it all together so we can load it up! To my PA and admins: Lela, Courtney, and Joy, if I had to go to Phaetynville, I would totes want you guys to come with me! Also, we have the best launch team – I love your enthusiasm for Ryn and Tyrrik!

To my readers: Journeys are always better with friends. Thanks for taking this one with me! I appreciate your continued support of my imagination.

And to Kelly, my #draebae... I've gained better skills, increased perspective, a love of preztels, and about five pounds writing Shadow Wings (bags of pretzels, I tell you!!). I can't wait to see what comes with Black Crown. Mostly, I love how much fun you make "work". Btw, I'm still waiting for that call about our neighboring islands...

XOXO,

Raye

# ABOUT KELLY ST. CLARE

When Kelly is not reading or writing, she is lost in her latest reverie. Books have always been magical and mysterious to her. One day she decided to start unravelling this mystery and began writing.

The Tainted Accords was her debut series. The After Trilogy and The Darkest Drae are her latest series.

A New Zealander in origin and in heart, Kelly currently resides in Australia with her ginger-haired husband, a great group of friends, and some huntsman spiders who love to come inside when it rains. Their love is not returned.

# ABOUT RAYE WAGNER

Raye Wagner grew up in Seattle, the second of eight children, and learned to escape chaos through the pages of fiction. As a youth, she read the likes of David Eddings, Leon Uris, and Jane Austen. As an adult she fell in love with Percy Jackson Olympian series (shocker!) and Twilight (really!) and was inspired to pursue her dream of writing young adult fiction. Raye enjoys baking, puzzles, Tae Kwon Do, and the sound of waves lapping at the sand. She lives with her husband and three children in Middle Tennessee.

**Fantasy of Frost**
(The Tainted Accords, #1)

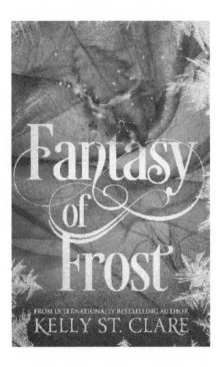

I know many things. What I am capable of, what I will change, what
I will become. But there is one thing I will never know.
The veil I've worn from birth carries with it a terrible loneliness; a
suppression I cannot imagine ever being free of.
*Some things never change...*
My mother will always hate me. Her court will always shun me.
*...Until they do.*
When the peace delegation arrives from the savage world of
Glacium, my life is shoved wildly out of control by the handsome
Prince Kedrick, who for unfathomable reasons shows me kindness.
*And the harshest lessons are learned.*

Sometimes it takes the world bringing you to your knees to find
that spark you thought forever lost.
Sometimes it takes death to show you how to live.

COMPLETE SERIES NOW AVAILABLE

## Cursed by the Gods
(The Sphinx, Book 1)

### Hope has a deadly secret...

Hope has spent her entire life on the run, but no one is chasing her. In fact, no one even knows she exists. And she'll have to keep it that way.

Even though mortals think the gods have disappeared, Olympus still rules. Demigods are elite hunters, who track and kill monsters. And shadow-demons from the Underworld prey on immortals, stealing their souls for Hades.

When tragedy destroys the only security she's ever known, Hope's life shatters. Forced to hide, alone this time, Hope pretends to be mortal. She'll do whatever it takes to keep her secret safe— and her heart protected. But when Athan arrives, her world is turned upside down.

With gods, demigods, and demons closing in, how long can a monster stay hidden in plain sight?
Join Hope on her unforgettable journey to discover what it means to live and her daring fight to break Apollo's curse.

COMPLETE SERIES NOW AVAILABLE

CPSIA information can be obtained
at www.ICGtesting.com
Printed in the USA
LVHW09*2257200918
590876LV00002B/21/P